The Lavender Ladies
Detective Agency:

DEATH IN
SUNSET GROVE

The Lavender Ladies
Detective Agency:

DEATH IN
SUNSET GROVE

Translated by Lola Rogers

Minna Lindgren

PAN BOOKS

First published 2016 by Pan Books
an imprint of Pan Macmillan
20 New Wharf Road, London N1 9RR
Associated companies throughout the world
www.panmacmillan.com

ISBN 978-1-4472-8932-6

Originally published 2013 as *Kuolema Ehtoolehdossa* by Teos Publishing, Finland

5 7 9 8 6 4

A CIP catalogue record for this book is available from the British Library.

Typeset by Ellipsis Digital Limited, Glasgow
Printed and bound by CPI Group (UK) Ltd, Croydon, CR0 4YY

Visit **www.panmacmillan.com** to read more about all our books
and to buy them. You will also find features, author interviews and
news of any author events, and you can sign up for e-newsletters
so that you're always first to hear about our new releases.

Prologue

'Is that a new blouse?' Irma asked, fiddling with the fabric of Siiri's old shirt. 'It's a pretty lavender. I once had a sofa this colour.'

'Is it lavender? I thought it was violet,' Siiri said, and only then did she notice the lovely shawl that Anna-Liisa was wearing. 'Your throw is violet too, isn't it?'

'Well,' Anna-Liisa said, straightening the scarf and looking as if she were about to begin a long lecture on colour definitions. But all she said was that she felt her wrap was more of a pale shade of purple. 'Irma's dress, on the other hand, might be called lavender, if there even is such a colour.'

'You are such a ninny, Anna-Liisa. This dress is blue. Or is it? Maybe it does tend more towards purple. Did you notice how all of us happen to be wearing something this colour today?'

They laughed at the coincidence, and soon none of them could remember whose turn it was to start the next hand of cards. It hardly mattered, though, since they had been playing the same game for much too long already. Irma let out a deep sigh and Siiri took her lace handkerchief out of her handbag and wiped her eyes. For a moment it was terribly quiet, until Anna-Liisa started to drum her fingers on the cloth-covered card table. But that didn't do much to lighten the mood. Life at Sunset Grove was certainly dull, if their only bright moment was when they noticed that they were all wearing the same colour, and they all called it by a different name.

'I've finessed it!' Irma suddenly crowed, her voice so high and loud that Siiri jumped. 'Listen, you know how there are all sorts of things happening here at Sunset Grove? We could start snooping around, do some meddling.'

'What exactly do you feel is happening?' Anna-Liisa asked, but Irma was undaunted.

'We'll start a detective agency. I think that's what I'm thinking.'

'So you reckon you're Miss Marple? Lord above, you are childish,' Anna-Liisa said, and fumbled for her Zimmer frame to indicate that she'd had quite enough nonsense for one day.

'It might be fun,' Siiri said helpfully. 'We certainly could use a little play in our lives.'

'Exactly! There's no harm in having some fun. And I already know what the name should be: The Lavender Ladies Detective Agency.'

Irma pronounced this ceremoniously, her voice trembling as if it were a stroke of genius. Siiri laughed approvingly, but Anna-Liisa didn't say anything. She headed towards the cafeteria, shoving her Zimmer frame so forcefully that her purple shawl swung from side to side.

Chapter 1

Every morning Siiri Kettunen woke up and realized that she wasn't dead yet. Then she got out of bed, washed, dressed and ate something for breakfast. It took her a while, but she had the time. She read the newspaper diligently and listened to the morning radio shows. It made her feel like she belonged in this world. She often went for a ride on the tram around eleven o'clock, but she didn't feel like it today.

The bright institutional lighting gave the common room of Sunset Grove retirement home the atmosphere of a dentist's waiting room. Several residents dozed on the sofas, waiting for lunch. In the corner Anna-Liisa, Irma and the Ambassador were playing rummy at the cloth-covered card table. The Ambassador was absorbed in his own cards, Anna-Liisa was keeping up a running commentary on the other players' hands, and Irma was looking impatient at the slow progress of the game. Then she saw Siiri and her eyes brightened.

'Cock-a-doodle-doo!' she crowed in a high falsetto, waving with a broad sweep of her arm like a train conductor. Irma Lännenleimu had taken singing lessons in her youth and

3

had once sung the Cherubino aria to piano accompaniment at the conservatory matinee, and since student performances were reviewed back then, a newspaper music critic had praised her voice as supple and resonant. This crowing call was Irma and Siiri's customary greeting. It always worked, even in the middle of a noisy conversation or on a busy street.

'Guess what?' Irma said, before Siiri had even sat down at the table. 'The Hat Lady in C wing isn't dead after all. And we'd practically finished grieving for her!' She laughed until her plump body jiggled and her voice rang even higher. Irma always wore a dress, preferably dark in colour, and even on ordinary days wore earrings with many-faceted stones, a string of pearls around her neck and two gold bracelets on her left wrist. When she spoke, her exuberant gestures made the bracelets jangle pleasantly.

Last week the flag at Sunset Grove had been flown at half mast, and since they hadn't seen the Hat Lady for several days, they'd thought she had died. But yesterday she had re-appeared, wearing her broad-brimmed turquoise hat and playing bingo like she always did. She'd just been out getting a spare part for her heart, and in the process had nearly died of a cardiac infarction.

'She says she may live for ten more years, poor thing,' Irma said.

Siiri laughed, her grey eyes twinkling. Irma made the woman's medical recovery sound like an extended sentence, which, of course, it was.

'It wasn't a spare part for her heart, strictly speaking,'

Anna-Liisa said in that no-nonsense way she had of correct-
ing any errors or discrepancies of meaning. It was an
obsession with her. Siiri and Irma thought it was due to the
fact that Anna-Liisa had once been a Finnish language and
literature teacher.

'I got a red three!' the Ambassador shouted but that didn't
stop Anna-Liisa.

'Angioplasty is the vernacular, the most commonly used
term for it. They use a thing called a stent, a sort of mesh
tube, to hold the artery open.'

Anna-Liisa was a tall woman with a deep, full-throated
voice. She knew everything you could possibly know about
angioplasty, replacement parts, local anaesthetic and arthro-
scopic surgery, but they never paid any attention to her
explanations. Having worked as a teacher, however, Anna-
Liisa was used to not being listened to.

'It's sheer lunacy to get spare parts at the age of ninety,'
Siiri said. Everyone else agreed.

'Do you think you'll live to be a hundred, girls?' the
Ambassador asked, laying his cards down on the table and
straightening his tie. He always dressed correctly, as befitted
a former diplomat, in a smart shirt, tie, brown smoking
jacket and straight-legged trousers, which was nice, since
many of the men at Sunset Grove shambled around in ugly
tracksuits. On important days and Sundays the Ambassador
wore a tidy suit with an oak-leaf veteran's insignia on the
lapel.

'It's not as if it matters what we think,' Siiri said, because that's what she thought. 'I wouldn't want to be that old, though.'

'If it wasn't the Hat Lady who died last week, I wonder who it was,' Irma said. She was very curious and always on the lookout for gossip at Sunset Grove. Her information on this event had been proved wrong, and so, understandably, she was a little upset about it.

'It was that boy, the cook. Tero, I think his name was,' Anna-Liisa said, laying down three sevens.

Siiri's head buzzed and her throat felt dry. She stared at Anna-Liisa. She couldn't believe that Tero could be dead. Irma, on the other hand, looked delighted at the news because she remembered that she had heard about it before, and then promptly forgotten about it.

'That's right! You really liked Tero, didn't you, Siiri? Was his name Tero? Have you noticed how young men nowadays all have two-syllable names: Tero, Pasi, Vesa, Tomi? Imagine my not telling you about it right away. I heard about it yesterday from the masseuse, but after all her pummelling I was so worn out that I just had a whisky and went to bed. My doctor has prescribed whisky for my . . . my everything. Look, I've got two sevens for you, Anna-Liisa!'

Suddenly Siiri felt sad. She missed Tero so much that her stomach hurt. How was it possible that such a healthy young man could die while ninety-four-year-olds never seemed to? Siiri had read in the paper that once you lived to be ninety you stopped ageing. How horrible. That meant that over-aged people like her were late for their death. First everybody died – friends, spouses – then nobody did. Two of Siiri's children were already dead: her eldest son from too much alcohol and her youngest from too much food. He'd been the baby of the family – a handsome, athletic boy when he was young. But then he ate himself to such a girth, doing nothing outside work, driving everywhere he went, eating pizza and crisps and smoking cigarettes. It was called affluenza – when a person reaches such a high standard of living that they die from it at the age of sixty-five.

But Tero, the cook at Sunset Grove, was thirty-five if he was a day, and he hadn't looked sick at all. On the contrary, he'd been glowing with good health, the way only a healthy young man can. Broad shoulders, strong hands, good colour in his face – that was the kind of person he was. And when he smiled he had dimples in both cheeks.

Their friendship had begun over the mashed potatoes. The Sunset Grove cafeteria served mashed potatoes altogether too often. They never offered rice. They thought that old people didn't have any teeth and mashed potatoes would go down easily, like baby food. None of the food was ever salted, and unminced meat was something they could only dream of. Siiri didn't like mashed potatoes, so Tero kindly arranged to have some other side dish for her under the counter, some carrots or beetroot or something. After lunch he would come over to her table for a cup of coffee and when Siiri asked if he had a girlfriend he said that he didn't need one because he had her. They had a way of flirting like that – and it was fun. A kind of harmless, happy chatter, which there wasn't much of at Sunset Grove.

The card game seemed to be over. The Ambassador asked

Irma how old she was. No one except Siiri really seemed to care about the young cook's death.

'Ninety-two?' the Ambassador marvelled. 'So you don't have a driver's licence any more? You're welcome to my taxis, Irma, dear. I have so many taxi coupons that I would have to ride around in a taxi all day long to use them up.'

'Of course I have a driver's licence!' Irma puffed, resenting the suggestion. 'I have an old classmate who's a gynaecologist and she writes out driver's-licence certificates at every alumni meeting. But then my children took my car away, just like that, and me a grown woman, with the right to go where I please! I'm sure you remember my little red car?'

Siiri was the only one who remembered it; she had been friends with Irma for a long time. She had been in it when Irma drove the wrong way down Mannerheimintie, the busiest thoroughfare in Helsinki, and the police pulled her over in front of the Swedish Theatre. That was enough for her children to take the little red car back to the dealer's. The Ambassador thought taking the car away was too severe a punishment. It was no great sin to drive a bit crazily past the Swedish Theatre; they were always doing roadworks on that corner, and even a tenth-generation Helsinki resident like Irma couldn't be sure which way you were supposed to go on any given day.

'But that's the way it is,' Irma said. 'Old people have every little thing decided for them.'

Irma's children and grandchildren, of which there were many, whom she referred to as her darlings, had sold her apartment in Töölö and put her in a one-bedroom flat at

Sunset Grove without further discussion. They'd said it was for her own good, and it was safer, and this way they would know that she was getting up and taking her medicine every morning and wasn't running around the city in her nightgown.

'And then they installed a surveillance camera in my apartment so that they can get on the computer whenever they like and watch what I'm doing. As if I were a three-toed sloth at the zoo! I moon the camera every night before I go to bed.'

The Ambassador sat with his shoulders slumped and stared glumly at the worn tabletop.

'At least you have someone who bothers to look after you,' he said. 'Someone to moon.'

'Don't worry, we loners have people watching us, too, I can assure you,' Anna-Liisa said. 'The nurses have their own keys and go snooping around in our homes all the time.'

'Yeah! The other day a man came into my apartment at seven a.m., when I was still lying in bed!' Irma shouted.

'Really?' the Ambassador said with delight, picking up the deck of cards to start a new game.

'He was looking for my will, of course. *Döden, döden, döden.*'

Siiri smiled when Irma said that. It was Swedish for 'death', and she said it with a sound of doom in her voice. Irma had a lot of words of her own and tired refrains that she repeated constantly, but Siiri liked this one, especially when Irma said it at just the right moment.

Then Anna-Liisa started to talk about her missing silver

9

hand mirror again. She was sure it had been stolen, just like the Ambassador's beautiful *ryijy* wall rug, while they had been out attending a memory group, a session of chair aerobics and an accordion concert. Siiri didn't go to those sorts of scheduled events, especially not the accordion concert, although there was one every week. Why did it always have to be the accordion? Didn't anyone know how to play a real instrument any more? There were three pianos sitting unused at Sunset Grove.

There were other useless items scattered around the halls, too, left when residents died and no one came to get their belongings. Pianos, books and dining tables and chairs that nobody wanted were scattered here and there to create a cosy atmosphere, although they didn't fit the decor since Sunset Grove was a modern building, the rooms low-ceilinged and the walls made of thin plasterboard. Somebody had probably even left the mahogany table they were sitting at.

'They do it on purpose,' Anna-Liisa said. 'They leave an old art nouveau table, a couple of pianos, and six metres of encyclopaedias in the hallways so nobody will think they're stealing from the residents. Though that, of course, is by no means certain.'

'It's thievery enough the way they charge us for every little thing without us even seeing the money zipping from one account to the other,' Irma said. 'But my darlings take care of my money matters, because the banks have all been moved to computers. Direct deposit! I finessed it!'

'What do you mean you "finessed" it? Isn't that a bridge term?' Anna-Liisa said indignantly.

'Do you know how to play bridge?' the Ambassador asked enthusiastically.

'I mean I remembered the word. Isn't that what they call that kind of stealing – direct deposit?'

Irma didn't trust her memory. If she surprised herself by remembering something she thought she'd forgotten, she said she'd finessed it, or said that 'some odd instinct' had told her that her beret was on top of the television. Anna-Liisa found it extremely annoying.

But Irma was right. At Sunset Grove the money went straight from the residents' bank accounts into the accounts of various providers of treatments and services, and no one noticed a thing. Just the rent for a small one-bedroom apartment was a thousand euros a month, and on top of that were assorted service fees and other costs. The prices were constantly changing, based on the assumption that the residents didn't understand the value of money. Many of them still calculated their purchases in the old marks that hadn't been used since 1963. The residents' relatives felt too guilty to quibble about the prices and convinced themselves that the more the place cost, the better it must be.

'Pants down, fourteen euros. Pants up, sixteen euros,' Anna-Liisa said, reading from the Sunset Grove price list. 'That's a high price for a single service.'

'Thirty euros. Holy smoke, that's a hundred and eighty marks!' Irma calculated.

'Incontinence pads are cheaper,' Siiri said, although she

didn't know how much incontinence pads cost or where to buy them. In Spain you could get them at the regular supermarket. There were a few returnees at Sunset Grove, people who had retired to Spain and the sunshine and, now that they had incontinence, cataracts and a hip condition, had hurried back to the safety of a retirement home in Finland. Like the new couple in A wing, who had such noisy sex every afternoon that their neighbours complained. They were thrifty, too. They'd brought cheap incontinence pads from Spain home with them.

Irma happened to know that they had a balcony stuffed with boxes of them. 'It looks terrible,' she said. 'There's not even room for a geranium. Can you imagine?'

Irma's daughter had ordered government-issue incontinence pads for her through the geriatric workers' union, but Irma had returned them, because she had no place to store them. She preferred to keep flowers on her balcony.

'I think the woman's name is Margit. Is that possible? And I have a feeling her husband's name is Eino. Eino and Margit? What does your intuition tell you?'

They couldn't decide what the new couple's names were.

'Why does it cost more to pull pants up than to pull them down?' asked Anna-Liisa, trying to get the conversation back on track.

'Would a skirt be cheaper?' the Ambassador wondered.

'It's always easier to take your trousers off than it is to put them on again!' Reino the Printer shouted, coming over from the drinks machine. He was a greedy-eyed man who always called Siiri 'the most beautiful girl at Sunset Grove'.

Irma claimed that he'd tried to kiss her once in the lift, but Irma said all sorts of nonsense. Reino, pushing his Zimmer frame, rushed upon them with surprising speed. He was wearing hospital slippers and a loose tracksuit. He had a bib around his neck, although it wasn't a mealtime.

'Isn't it because of the belt?' Siiri said, smoothing down her trousers and getting up to leave. 'It's harder to do up a belt and buttons than it is to undo them. I mean if the person's properly dressed.'

She gathered up her things and put them in her handbag – glasses, handkerchief and mints – and Irma started to do the same. They thought it was a bit revolting that Reino was so dirty; he was always poorly shaven, with gunk between his teeth, hairs poking out of his ears and eyebrows like briar bushes.

'I think a woman's shirt buttons and bra hooks are easier to open than to close,' Reino said. 'It's the gravitational pull.'

'Rubbish, Reino,' Anna-Liisa said frostily. 'You've never fastened a woman's hooks in your life.'

'It has been quite a while. Want to come up to my place? Take a little ride in the lift?'

That was enough for Anna-Liisa. She snorted glumly and said she was going to the auditorium for a presentation on 'A Varied Diet for Increasing the Performance of the Aged'. The Ambassador liked the idea, and offered to escort her. He stood up, came gallantly over to her chair with his Zimmer frame, and offered his arm like a cavalier at a ball. Irma winked at Siiri and they headed to the lift together, Irma keen to get away, Siiri still sad and mystified at the news of Tero's death.

Reino was left alone at the card table, wondering where everyone was going, and why he had a bib around his neck.

'Nurse! Nurse! Miss! Hello? Help me!'

But it was no use shouting for the nurses because they didn't have time to come running to see what was troubling a perfectly healthy person. He tried to take the bib off himself. It was difficult. The string was tightly knotted in the back. The harder he pulled on it, the tighter the knot became. He rose to a standing position and tore the bib free, cursing bitterly, and threw it on the floor. Then he slumped onto the common room sofa, hoping that Siiri Kettunen or one of the other queens of Sunset Grove would appear and entertain him, and fell asleep.

Chapter 2

Siiri went down to the ground floor to look for Pasi, the social worker, who was usually in his office. She wanted to talk to him about Tero's death. Pasi and Tero got along well; she'd often seen them chatting in the kitchen. But now Pasi's office door was locked and there was a sign taped to it that read: 'The social worker's duties will be temporarily performed by the head nurse, Virpi Hiukkanen.'

Virpi Hiukkanen was a confidante of the managing director, Sinikka Sundström, her right and left hand, a dedicated member of staff who was responsible not just for the residents' care but also for employee welfare and recruitment. Virpi was a lifesaver, because although the director was a sweet, friendly woman, she was very disorganized.

A situation like this required cunning. If Siiri asked Sinikka Sundström directly about the cook's death and the social worker's absence, Sinikka might think she was accusing her of something. Straightforward communication with the director was sometimes difficult because she carried all the troubles of the world on her shoulders and blamed herself first in every situation. Siiri would have to think up some other excuse for speaking to her.

She went back to her apartment, watched an episode of *Poirot* on television, and lay down on her bed for a rest. She imagined that she lived in a 1930s house as beautiful as Poirot's house in London, surrounded by sleek modern furniture, and was about to fall asleep with Poirot stroking his whiskers, smiling at her with his friendly brown eyes, and lifting a hand to the brim of his hat, when the telephone rang.

Siiri had to get up because the phone was on a small table near the front door. Many people keep the telephone next to the bed, but Siiri was accustomed to having a telephone table and a chair next to the front door. It was a better place to talk than sitting on the edge of the bed swinging her feet. Plus it was good exercise getting out of bed. But she couldn't get up very quickly because once she was upright she had to wait a few moments to let the dizziness and the buzzing in her head pass. The phone rang for a long time.

'Hi, it's Tuukka. You got a cleaning bill that's a bit peculiar.'

Siiri had long ago asked if one of her grandchildren could handle her banking on the computer, since she didn't know how, and her great granddaughter's boyfriend had kindly agreed to do it. Tuukka was a very pleasant boy who was studying something weird at university.

'Microbial and environmental technology,' he always said, which didn't mean a thing to anyone.

Now he was saying that he'd seen on his computer that

seventy-six euros had been taken out of Siiri's bank account for cleaning. Just for a girl in a black dress to come by and give the middle of the floor a once-over the week before last. Even her lips were painted black, and her hair was dyed blacker than the night sky.

'She didn't say a word to me, standing there leaning on her mop.'

'The bill says it's for two hours,' Tuukka said. Being a businesslike man, he didn't comment on the cleaner's appearance or behaviour.

'That creature was only here for half an hour, if that. I was here the whole time, looking at the clock.'

Siiri felt pleased after the call. The unreasonable cleaning bill was a stroke of luck, just the excuse she needed to go and talk to the director. She decided to file a written complaint, too, so that she had some sort of official documentation. She had to write it by hand, though, in ballpoint pen on notebook paper, and it didn't look very persuasive. This from a former typist who'd worked for decades at the National Public Health Institute, touch-typing other people's scribbles. She knew how to make clean documents with the proper margins, line spacing, and layout, never making an error. She could still remember how upset she used to be when she'd got a letter on paper perfectly only to have the office manager decide to change his greeting, so she'd have to do the whole thing all over again. But typing was a skill that was no longer needed or appreciated.

When she finished writing her complaint she thought about the title for a moment, then wrote: 'Doesn't anybody know how to clean any more?' and left to take the paper to Sinikka Sundström's office. On the way there she started regretting the title, since the point was to complain about the bill, not about poor cleaning, although she certainly had reason to discuss that as well. She and the other residents had wondered many times why somebody didn't take the housekeepers by the hand and teach them how to sweep the dust from behind a radiator and wipe a door frame with a damp cloth.

The director's office was on the ground floor at the front of the hallway, right next to the waiting room. Many people thought she had her office there so that she could monitor and spy on the residents. Anna-Liisa insisted that the staff at Sunset Grove had an obsessive need to control everything. From what Siiri had heard, Virpi Hiukkanen's husband was the worst snoop of them all.

Erkki Hiukkanen was noticeably older than his wife, a somewhat stupid, lazy man who was referred to as the caretaker, although his official title was probably something like Unit Operations Manager. Erkki had grey hair and would sometimes come in uninvited to change a lightbulb, even though there was nothing wrong with the old one. Or he might come to check the pipes or the ventilator ducts, which seemed to be continually acting up. Everyone had learned that if someone surprised you with a knock on the door it was probably Erkki Hiukkanen in his blue overalls – the only service at Sunset Grove that didn't cost anything.

But regardless of what the residents said, Siiri liked

Sinikka Sundström. She thought Sinikka sincerely cared about the residents and wanted to do everything she could to keep the place running smoothly. Director Sundström was a typical career-oriented woman who enjoyed making other people feel good.

Siiri made her way to the director's office. She found Sundström sitting at her desk, absorbed in something on her computer screen. The room was dimly lit, the dark curtains drawn over the window, an unpleasant-smelling candle burning on the desk. Siiri saw what looked like playing cards on the director's computer screen, but that couldn't be right – playing cards on a computer? When she saw Siiri, the director smiled warmly and hurried to give her a hug. Siiri felt swallowed up in the too-deep embrace, lost in folds of clothing and strong perfume. She worried that she might have a sneezing attack. But Sinikka Sundström had studied the science of caregiving and she knew that old people needed physical contact.

'Siiri, dear! How are you?' she asked, once she had let go. Siiri could once again breathe freely.

She got straight to the point and handed Sinikka the complaint. She apologized that it was written on notebook paper.

'Oh, that's all right. You have lovely handwriting. Just like my grandmother's. Of course, she died years ago, when I was just a little girl.'

Sundström read the complaint, raised her plucked eyebrows, and looked worried. She was terribly sorry that such a thing had happened to Siiri and promised to look into the matter immediately, although housekeeping wasn't actually the responsibility of her office, since it was contracted out. She asked Siiri to sit down and explained briefly that they used a private cleaning company, that Sunset Grove had taken bids from several companies and Muhuv Su Putz and Planck had been far and away the most reasonable and reliable, and that all matters regarding subcontractors were the responsibility of Pertti Sundström in Quality Control.

'Pertti Sundström? Is he a relative of yours?' Siiri asked, not having ever heard of Quality Control, despite having lived at Sunset Grove for twelve years.

Pertti Sundström was Sinikka's husband, and Sinikka said she would be happy to introduce Siiri to him but, unfortunately, he was on a business trip so Siiri would just have to drop her complaint in the suggestion box there in the hallway by the big picture of the rose. That was the wisest course of action, since Pertti took care of all the quality-control issues through his limited partnership.

'His office is in the new development at Fish Harbour, but I can certainly bring this to his attention,' Sinikka said with a smile, and thanked Siiri for her active interest, because the facility could only improve itself if the residents provided feedback. 'Even if we do have a five-star quality rating, there's always room for improvement!' she added.

Siiri used the desk for support as she stood up, and then she noticed a folder on the director's desk with Tero the cook's name on it. What a lucky coincidence! If she hadn't seen it, she would have forgotten why she had really come here in the first place.

'Tero Lehtinen. He was a nice man, and a good cook. I

wonder, can you tell me what he died of, so suddenly, a young man like him?'

Sinikka was already on her way out of the room, waving Siiri's slip of notebook paper, but when she heard Tero's name she stopped, turned quickly around, closed the door behind her, and hurried over to give Siiri another hug. Her large, wooden necklace pressed unpleasantly against Siiri's cheek.

'We're all grieving for Tero,' Sinikka sputtered. 'What a tragedy. He was very dear to us.' She patted Siiri like a beloved pet. When she was finished consoling her, she escorted her out of the door and excused herself, explaining that she had a meeting to attend in town. She continued her lament about Tero's tragic end as she put on her coat, and Siiri started to wonder if she ought to do something to help the poor woman. But she didn't know what.

'We're organizing a therapy group for anyone who feels they need help in dealing with Tero's death. Would you like to participate, dear Siiri?' She tossed her colourful scarf over her shoulder with such flair that the fringe brushed Siiri's face.

'No, thank you. We old people don't need anything like that, but I'm sure it will be helpful to the staff,' Siiri said, trying to give the director a reassuring smile.

'Don't call yourself old! It's such an ugly word. Well, I'm off. Bye-bye!'

But Siiri wasn't satisfied with Sinikka's response. She was determined to get to the bottom of what had happened to Tero. She must speak to Irma about it.

Chapter 3

Irma and Siiri lived in neighbouring one-bedrooms on the second floor of the A wing of Sunset Grove. Their apartments were identical and yet completely different. Siiri had furnished hers very sparsely, while Irma had wanted to bring all the beloved things from her former large apartment into her much smaller one. She had rugs all over the floor, pictures, shelves, *ryijy* tapestries on the walls, bookcases full of books, a sofa in the living room and a low porcelain-topped table with flowers painted on it that she had done herself in a community education course. There was also a rocking chair, a piano bench in memory of her piano, two zany-looking stools, a dining table and chairs, a television and, of course, rose-printed Sanderson fabric on everything – the curtains, cushions, wallpaper and chair covers.

The two friends enjoyed a cup of instant coffee and some bundt cake together almost every day at Irma's place. Irma sat in the armchair in the light of the floor lamp and Siiri sat on the sofa, where none of the lamps from Irma's childhood home cast any light. Sometimes they popped over to each other's places in their nightgowns, on a whim. That was the best part of old age – being able to walk around in your nightie, eating whatever you wanted, doing whatever you felt like doing. They'd never eaten so much cake when they were younger.

'Caaake,' Irma corrected Siiri. 'It should have a lot of As, so it sounds as good as it tastes. Have some more caaake while I get my pillies.'

Irma believed that if she took her diabetes pills at the same time she ate her cake, she wouldn't have to worry about her blood sugar. She could eat three ice-cream cones, one after the other, so long as she popped a pill and drank a little whisky. Siiri took diabetes pills, but she didn't worry about what a little cake would do to her blood sugar and she'd never stopped to think about whether Irma's method made any sense.

Siiri decided that now was the time to voice her concerns to Irma.

'Irma, do you think there's more to Tero's death than meets the eye?'

Irma finished a mouthful of cake and licked her lips before replying. 'I know you're upset about it, but we have to get used to people dying at our age.'

'Yes, at our age. But not at Tero's age. He was far too young.'

Irma nodded thoughtfully, and Siiri took this as her cue to continue.

'There's something suspicious going on and I want to find out what happened to Tero. Someone has to.' Siiri was slightly red in the face; she was getting herself worked up.

'Now dear, there's no need to get in a state,' Irma said kindly. 'What are you planning to do about it?'

'I'm going to investigate!' Siiri said decisively. 'And you're going to help me,' she said with a twinkle in her eyes.

Irma laughed. 'Help you? How? Do you want me to turn into Miss Marple, at my age?'

'Yes, that's exactly it! Why not? It would give us something to put our minds to. And the police don't seem to be acting very fast. We owe it to Tero.'

Irma beamed; Siiri's enthusiasm was catching. 'Count me in!' she cried.

'We'll solve the mystery. Just leave it to us: The Lavender Ladies Detective Agency.'

Irma crowed with joy. The name seemed appropriate as Siiri sat there in her mauve jumper. 'OK, so where shall we start?' she asked.

'Do you think Pasi's been on sick leave, since Tero died like that?' Siiri said.

But Irma didn't think Sunset Grove would give anyone sick leave just because a member of staff had died. She said that Virpi Hiukkanen, the head nurse, ran a tight ship, drove the staff to work long shifts back to back, paid poorly and never acknowledged anyone for their work. That was why the young people who worked there were worn out with entertaining and taking care of old people. In a place where nobody else was in any hurry to do anything and nothing ever happened, the staff were always in a dreadful rush. So the nurses got burned out and ended up quitting to find a job that was more fun. Or they went on state sabbatical. Siiri had no idea what state sabbatical was.

'That's when an employer pays a worker to do nothing for a year,' Irma explained, but Siiri didn't believe her. You couldn't always trust Irma's stories. She was a bit batty sometimes.

'Sure they do. The employer fills the position with a refugee or somebody who's unemployed and they get money from the state,' Irma said. Siiri decided to look it up later.

Irma had been diligent and found out that there was a funeral service for Tero in two weeks at the old chapel at Hietaniemi cemetery. They both decided to go to the funeral – to pay their respects, and also because they might learn something about Tero's unexpected death there.

'We can do some of our Lavender Ladies Detecting!' Irma said. Siiri didn't like funerals, but Irma always looked forward to social events.

'Let's invite everyone to Tero's funeral!' she said excitedly. 'We can make it a real autumn outing. We can take the *scram*, so even you'll enjoy it.' By scram, she meant the tram. 'Where have you been lately on your travel card?'

Siiri told her she'd taken the number 3 and number 7 trams yesterday, and of course the 4, to get to and from Sunset Grove. At the stop by the Aurora Hospital a nutcase had got on again, yelling to herself, and as the buildings in that neighbourhood were so ugly, it had made for a very oppressive mood. But when the tram had reached the greener, narrower streets of Vallila, the mood had brightened up. Siiri had noticed a restaurant on the corner of Mäkelänkatu and

Sturenkatu where they served breakfast in the middle of the day for three euros, which amused them both.

'We should go there sometime, instead of always having our coffee here,' Irma said.

'There isn't really a corner at the corner of Mäkelänkatu and Sturenkatu, just one of those round things like they have in Central Europe. But you probably don't know that because you've never been there.'

Irma was one of those women who'd never been to the wrong side of Pitkäsilta, the bridge that separated the southern half of Helsinki from the working-class northern half. But she had been to Vallila at some point, of course, and she remembered that it had a lovely aroma of coffee.

'Veikko told me that there are whole blocks of 1920s buildings in Vallila with courtyards that you ought to see because you look in and it's like you're suddenly in a lovely park.'

Veikko was Irma's husband. He had died long ago of lung cancer after smoking two packs a day for years. Irma talked about her husband occasionally, but didn't seem to miss him the way Siiri missed her husband, yearning for him every day.

'It would be terrible if Veikko was still alive. I'm sure he would be very sick and I would have to take care of him. Or he'd be batty and get put in the closed unit.'

The official name of the unit for patients with severe dementia was the Group Home. It was in a low building off the common area, and its door was always locked, so they often called it 'the closed unit'. None of the residents were allowed to go there and a mystique of secrecy hovered over the place, a combination of fear and fascination. The nurses ran in and out of the door with their keys jangling, always in a hurry, with worry lines on their foreheads.

Every so often the Hat Lady reported that someone from the apartments had been moved to the closed unit. When the fat woman from the ground floor of A wing was sent there, Irma had suggested that they go and sing to her and read her stories, but Nurse Hiukkanen had absolutely forbidden it. She said caregiving required professional skills and training. They couldn't let just anyone drop in to play. So Siiri and Irma had never seen inside the closed unit.

'It's an awful bustle in there,' Irma said. 'They wake you up at eight every evening and give you a sleeping pill. Then they wake you up at eight in the morning and give you a pep pill. That's no way to live. Veikko was smart to smoke cigarettes and die on time. What do you think – should we start smoking? Otherwise we're never going to die. *Döden, döden, döden.*'

The doctor at the health clinic had told Siiri that she should take a sleeping pill every night at eight thirty because that was a good time for an old person to be asleep. That amused them both tremendously.

'Eight thirty? In the middle of the news?' Irma said, and crowed so hard that her cake went down the wrong way and she started coughing.

'Don't choke! I'll get you something to drink!'

Siiri went to the kitchen and found the bottle of red wine

that always stood by the sink next to the bottle of washing-up liquid. Irma had a rule that she never drank anything but red wine. She said water was for washing and milk was for growing children. She often had a couple of glasses of wine with lunch, plus the whisky her doctor prescribed in the evening. Sometimes she couldn't remember if it was evening, or morning, or afternoon, and the wine and the whisky got mixed up.

The wine worked wonders. Irma was able to speak again after a couple of swallows.

'It's just that I was thinking you don't really need a sleeping pill to fall asleep while the news is on.'

Chapter 4

A few days later, Siiri and Irma were enjoying a very peaceful, ordinary afternoon at Sunset Grove. Everyone had had their lunch and their midday rest, and around 3 p.m. they came down to the common room to play cards. The afternoon card game wasn't one of Sunset Grove's services; it had sprung up spontaneously when they realized how many of them liked to play.

Irma shuffled the deck and dealt everyone eleven cards. It was something she enjoyed immensely; she was a skilful shuffler and a nimble dealer. They didn't play in teams because it only caused arguments and there wouldn't have been a partner for everyone. The ritual they performed after the cards were dealt was always the same: Irma would show her hand and crow over the twos and jokers, which made Anna-Liisa tense, while Siiri, Reino and the Ambassador calmly and quietly arranged their hands. The Ambassador sat to Irma's left, so that he could start the play.

'I'm on the table,' he said, laying down three jacks. Irma praised this achievement and Anna-Liisa coughed nervously – she had probably been hoping to collect jacks herself. Siiri drew a joker on her turn, tried not to smile, and discarded a four of diamonds.

'Did you get something nice?' Irma asked. 'It's your turn, Reino.'

But Reino didn't draw a card. He looked like he wasn't following the game. He was just staring straight ahead, muttering to himself and holding the cards unsorted in his hand. Everyone looked at him expectantly.

'Olavi Raudanheimo . . . a war veteran! In a wheelchair! If he hadn't told me himself, I wouldn't . . . ! My God! How the hell could this happen?'

He shook his head and shouted so that the spit flew out of his mouth and his cards flew onto the floor. He waved his arms and wailed, then slumped in a lifeless heap and started to cry. He was a big man, and usually so happy, but he was crying like a child, sobbing and whimpering, his whole body shaking. It was frightening. Irma offered him her hand-kerchief. Siiri took his hand, leaned towards him, and asked him what the matter was. Anna-Liisa pushed her chair half a metre further from the table and watched him sniffle and sputter with a severe look on her face.

'Speak up,' she said. 'Articulate. We can't understand you.' She was right, of course. His weeping had grown to a howl, and no one could make out a word he was saying.

Olavi Raudanheimo was Reino's neighbour in C wing. He lived in a studio apartment and got around in a wheel-chair, but they rarely saw him. Sometimes Reino took him out to the nearest park, but he didn't participate in the Sunset Grove activities. Olavi was more of a bookish man who kept himself to himself. He enjoyed solving crossword puzzles and listening to the news on the radio. He had lost both legs in the war and lived in Sunset Grove on a state pension.

'Is Olavi dead?' Irma asked excitedly.

'No, no. If only . . .' Reino said, blowing his nose loudly into her lace handkerchief. 'That's something an old man could take, damn it.'

'That's my mother's old handkerchief,' Irma said, looking worriedly at the wet wad in his hand. 'But it doesn't matter,' she said, smiling. 'Just an old rag.' She always tried to keep her spirits up, whatever the situation. 'It seems we'll never die! *Döden, döden, döden.* Now what was that card . . . drat, it's a king! Did Olavi have a fall in his apartment? Did he have a heart attack? Or is it that his children have started dying? Is it my turn? To play a card, I mean.'

'Assaulted! Olavi was assaulted, yesterday evening, in his own home!' Reino shouted, and everyone went quiet. Then he sniffed and started to bawl again. Irma dropped her cards into her lap and Siiri looked helplessly at Anna-Liisa and continued clutching Reino's hand. The Ambassador stared at his cards as if nothing had happened.

Reino stood up to his full height, knocking his chair over with a clatter.

'Olavi Raudanheimo was assaulted yesterday in the shower!' he shouted, even louder than before. He looked dreadful bellowing like that, his face covered in tears and anger, his chin half unshaven. A large man in tracksuit bottoms with his dirty shirt hem flapping.

'We heard you the first time,' Anna-Liisa said calmly.

'What exactly do you mean by assaulted? You must remember that assault is a way of wielding power. It doesn't necessarily have anything to do with pleasure or desire, if you get my meaning. It's an act of subjugation and humiliation.'

'Whose turn is it?' the Ambassador asked restlessly. He wanted the game to continue because he had a good hand.

Reino tried to pick up his chair but grew flustered when he couldn't get it upright, and started to wail again.

'That damned male nurse . . . that fag! He was supposed to be giving him a shower . . . Olavi told me himself, damn it all!'

'Sit down, Reino,' Anna-Liisa said. 'And please watch your language. Was this in the morning or the evening? Could somebody help him with his chair?'

As a language and literature teacher, Anna-Liisa was clearly used to handling the unruly and shepherding the restless. Irma was first to obey, picking up Reino's chair and trying to get him to sit down. It wasn't easy; Reino resisted, trembling and rubbing his face compulsively with his sleeve.

'*An, auf, hinter, in* – I just drew a nice red ten,' the Ambassador trilled, continuing the game by himself. He had a habit of reciting the German prepositions he'd learned in grammar school while he sorted his cards. Irma and Reino's cards were on the floor but Siiri gripped hers in one hand until her fingers hurt.

'I don't know when it happened. I don't remember. It doesn't matter,' Reino said, finally sitting back down, slightly calmer. He tried to take a deep breath and blew his nose again into Irma's handkerchief, which looked smaller than before. 'But Good God! A war veteran . . . can't even wash himself.'

'What are you all worked up about, Mr Reino?'

Head nurse Virpi Hiukkanen had appeared. None of them had ever seen her run before, but now she was moving so fast that her nurse's shoes were flapping. She took hold of Reino's shoulder with a firm grip, which only made him angrier. Now he started to really throw a fit. His walker took off on its own, the deck of cards flew into the air, and the chair fell over again, and even Virpi was frightened. A flock of startled members of staff gathered around them, all of them strangers except for Virpi, whose thin, sharp voice pierced through the general hubbub.

'Get this patient to the dementia ward and sedate him!'

Four Russian women grabbed hold of Reino, who had suddenly changed from a resident to a patient, and gave him an injection. Reino yelled some choice obscenities and thrashed around. His voice echoed down the hall all the way to the locked ward. Irma started picking the cards up off the floor although it was hard to bend over because she was somewhat plump and very busty. The Ambassador hurried to help her, peeping down her blouse all the while.

'I don't think damn is such a terrible word,' Irma puffed, putting the red stack of cards down on the table.

Then she told the story of the time her husband Veikko was screwing a bookshelf to the wall and the shelf fell with all the books on it onto the back of his neck and he shouted 'damn it', and Irma's mother heard it and was horrified, because she thought a son-in-law of hers should have just said 'hell'.

'But I don't think so. Hell is just as strong a word as damn,' she said, which was how she always ended the story.

They started a new game, at the Ambassador's request. Irma shuffled and dealt the cards. The Ambassador was upset because Reino's outburst had cost him a good hand.

Chapter 5

After she heard about Tero's death, Siiri stopped going to the cafeteria to eat. At her age she didn't need much food as long as she remembered to drink something other than red wine. The supermarket was selling liver casseroles that were nearing their sell-by date for 30 per cent off. Siiri always paid for her purchases in cash because she didn't trust the machines at the supermarket. She preferred getting cash 'from the wall'. It was easier. She had a trick for remembering her PIN: the second number was the first number cubed, the third number was the first and second numbers multiplied and then divided by three, and the fourth number was the sum of the first two minus three.

Irma could never remember her number. 'Should I punch in zero six six eight?' she asked as she and Siiri brought a liver casserole up to the counter at Low Price Market on the high street and the cashier put her card into the little machine.

'It's asking for your PIN,' the cashier said, but that didn't help.

'Is my PIN zero six six eight? Or is that my state identity number?'

'You don't need your state ID number,' the young woman said, glancing at the queue forming behind them.

'I don't even know what my state ID number is,' Irma said nervously. 'Maybe I should just put in zero six six eight. I think my state identity number ends in one three two H, but this machine doesn't have any letters on the keys, or maybe I'm just not seeing it because I—'

'You don't need any letters,' the cashier interrupted.

The machine didn't accept 0668. The people in the queue shook their heads and craned their necks, trying to see how long this was going to take. Siiri took Irma's wallet and found a piece of paper in it with '7245' written in large numbers.

'There it is!' Irma said, as if it were a friend she hadn't seen in years. She remembered why it was written so large, too. 'So I can see it without my glasses, you know. But what the heck is zero six six eight, then?'

They would never know, unless some day they did, as Irma always said. They took the liver casserole and went back to Irma's apartment to eat lunch and get ready for Tero's funeral.

Irma's plan for a large autumn outing was coming true; even the new couple in A wing had announced that they would be attending the funeral. Irma and Anna-Liisa were so nervous that they'd ordered a bag of tranquillizers from the health clinic. The newest on their ever-changing roster of 'personal physicians' had been a foreigner this time, with an African name that didn't tell them whether he was a man or a woman.

'Do you play basketball?' Anna-Liisa asked the physician in her resonant, crisply articulated voice, but he didn't know what she meant. Irma silenced her and hastened to explain why they had come, and Anna-Liisa continued to interrupt whenever she felt a need to correct her.

'. . . and this boy, Pasi, has been our cook for at least ten years, so I'm sure you understand what the loss means to us—'

'The cook's name was Tero. And he can't have been at Sunset Grove for ten years, Irma. Even we haven't been there that long.'

'You see how upset we all are?' Irma exclaimed. The doctor, clearly keen to get rid of them, wrote out two prescriptions and asked them to come separately on their next visit.

Siiri didn't intend to touch Irma's and Anna-Liisa's pills, not even at the funeral, although she was mourning Tero's death even more than she had that of her cat, who'd died two years before. She regretted now that she hadn't got a new cat. She had been sure at the time that she was going to die within a week, which would have been hard on a cat, although Irma had suggested that she could provide for it in her will.

There had been an article in the newspaper about a Japanese robot cat used to take care of the elderly. It saved a lot of money because they didn't need to pay an overworked carer to do the caring. The grey, robotic-looking Japanese old people in the newspaper were sitting with the artificial cats in their laps. Siiri wondered why the cats had to be robots.

'Surely real cats aren't that expensive?'

But then Irma started to count up how expensive taking care of a cat could be, probably much more expensive than an old person. Finland was full of defenders of animals and other activists, so animal care was a carefully monitored activity. You had to give them a certain amount of space, sunlight, regular outings, species-appropriate stimuli, a varied diet, and other things that old people could only dream of.

'Even chickens are free and happy nowadays, thanks to the activists!'

'I saw a dog-food store from the tram the other day, on Snellmaninkatu,' Siiri said, and they laughed at the thought that there was a shop selling dog sausages in a spot where, when they were young, there had been a butcher's that sold only bones.

'What are you going to wear for the funeral?' Irma asked suddenly, as if you could wear anything at all to a funeral. Siiri had worn the same black wool dress to every funeral for the past twelve years, but Irma had several to choose from and she wanted Siiri's opinion on them.

'I'll give you a real fashion show!' she said, disappearing into her bedroom, after first pouring Siiri a glass of red wine so that she wouldn't get bored waiting. There was a jangling sound from the wardrobe and Irma appeared in a loose black dress and a pillbox hat and twirled around.

'It's too big. You've shrunk,' Siiri said.

Irma stopped, put one foot in front of the other, and looked in the mirror over her shoulder dramatically.

'You're right.'

It was strange how so many old people didn't enjoy buying new clothes, because as they got older their bodies shrank and their clothes started to hang on them. Some people didn't pay any attention to their appearance at all once they got old. But Siiri thought it ought to be just the opposite – the older she got, the more well-groomed she wanted to be. She went to the hairdresser's every Wednesday and got a perm twice a year. It was hard to wash and set her hair herself, and besides, going to the hairdresser's was just the kind of little self-indulgence she loved most.

'Yes, you even remember to pluck your chin hairs every morning,' Irma agreed, looking at herself in the mirror.

In the retirement home you saw far too many pitiful-looking old people. People who once were senior inspectors, police officers, nurses, contractors, teachers, and here they were dragging themselves to singalongs in dirty tracksuits with bibs around their necks. Sometimes it felt like they'd lost all self-respect.

You had to surrender eventually, but not necessarily give up altogether. Siiri and Irma had talked about this a lot. The world revolved too much around work, and once you didn't have a job any more it didn't make you free, it just made you a slave to your age, stuck in an endless string of empty days. It was no wonder people their children's age fought against growing old with everything they had. There were pieces in the paper practically every day written by some person at retirement age declaring that they weren't yet ready for the rocking chair.

'What's wrong with rocking chairs?' Irma said. 'I rock in my rocking chair every day, and it's awfully pleasant. I heard on the radio that it's good for your brain. For children's brains, anyway. I think that's what they said.'

'If it's good for children, it's good for us,' Siiri said, going back to the subject of ageing. If only working-age people understood what a small part of life a career was. If her own children had worked less, they wouldn't have been worn out by the time they retired. 'And the way everybody is a former something,' she said. 'Former printer, former telegraph operator, former copy-editor. I'm not a former anything; my profession doesn't even exist any more!'

Irma had always been able to focus on the essential things in life. She had studied to be a nurse, but since she had so many children, she'd mostly stayed home. She also always remembered to say that of her six children, only her last was planned. Siiri doubted that Irma's accidental children enjoyed hearing that story, but Irma disagreed.

'The accidental children are the ones you love best!' Irma shouted shrilly from the bedroom. 'And anyway, no one had birth control back then. You would have had to go to the wrong side of the bridge to get it. You just had children. It was the same for everyone. Other people don't talk about it like I do, because I had one that was on purpose. How did your children come into the world?'

Siiri had always wanted a large family. She had been happy to have three healthy children. But Irma was right.

Children just came; you didn't plan those things. People used to be afraid of getting pregnant, and now they needed expensive fertility drugs because they couldn't have children, no matter how hard they tried.

Irma appeared again and twirled in front of the dining table. She had on a stylish black suit which had a beautiful pleated skirt.

'That's a good one. When did you get that?'

'I bought this for my son-in-law's funeral. Wait, that was almost five years ago. I must have bought this just last year, but I don't remember whose funeral it was. Maybe my brother-in-law's.' When you were over ninety, funerals were practically a profession.

On Friday evening, Siiri and Irma were right on time and everything was ready. The flowers were ordered from the nice girl at the flower shop on Katajanokka, their clothes were well pressed and Irma's medicine laid out in the pill counter that she kept next to her bottle of wine. Siiri had put her green cushion on the chair in her hallway that morning so that she wouldn't forget to bring it with her, because the chairs at the chapel were so hard. They decided to go to sleep early, or at least go to bed and read, and wished each other goodnight.

'Don't die tonight. I can't go to Tero's funeral without you.'

'*Döden, döden, döden!*' Irma's voice boomed down the corridor.

Chapter 6

On Saturday the liveliest of Sunset Grove's old folk set out
on the tram for Tero Lehtinen's funeral. The Ambassador
took a taxi, and the Hat Lady rode with him, which no one
opposed. There was nothing wrong with the Ambassador's
legs, but he was accustomed to travelling at others' expense
and drinking free wine and he wasn't going to change his
habits at the age of ninety – everyone understood that. Irma
also happened to know that he was a Freemason.

'They have their own doctors; not like us, with our "personal physicians" who are never the same person from one
week to the next,' Irma said as they waited for the tram.
'They get their pills and taxi coupons without even having to
ask.'

They ended up having to walk a few roads to change from
the number 4 to the number 8. The new couple from Spain
didn't like that at all. They both complained loudly when the
traffic lights wasted their valuable time. The woman, whose
name was indeed Margit – Margit Partanen – was particularly peevish and vociferous. She was a straight-backed,

sizeable woman who still dyed her hair black, although it didn't make her look any younger.

'Tickets, please, everyone,' said a young tram inspector the moment they boarded. The Partanens didn't have any tickets and there was no getting out of a fine, although Margit tried pretending that she only spoke German. Their funeral outing turned out to be more expensive than they had planned, and Margit thought it was Siiri's fault because she had insisted on taking public transport.

'You'll get a free ride to your own funeral,' Irma said to lighten the mood.

'Oh, but you won't,' Anna-Liisa corrected her. 'The deceased should leave some money for the funeral to their heirs. It isn't right to let others pay for it. I have life insurance to pay for mine.'

'So do I,' Siiri said, with a sudden look of alarm. Life insurance ought to have been a safe subject, but just then, as they turned onto Mechelininkatu, Siiri had a horrifying thought. She remembered that her insurance would run out when she turned ninety-five. 'That means that if I don't die soon all my payments will be down the drain.'

'You'll just have to die, then,' Irma said, and started to reminisce about watching the brick buildings being built in Töölö when she and the other little girls in the neighbourhood hadn't thought twice about women carrying heavy loads of bricks on their backs over dangerous-looking scaffolding. '*Döden, döden, döden.*'

'I, for one, refuse to save up for my funeral, when I'm not even going to be there,' Margit said, continuing the already forgotten thread of conversation. 'You can just lay me in a cardboard box,' she said to her husband, who was looking out of the window at the strange new apartment blocks. Half of them looked like their roofs and balconies were falling off.

'Of course you're going to be there,' Irma said. 'In the cardboard box.'

'You want to get laid in a cardboard box?' Margit's husband muttered. This unconventional suggestion didn't particularly surprise anyone, since all of A wing had heard Margit's whoops every afternoon. Margit was hard of hearing and no doubt didn't know she was making so much noise. She didn't hear her husband's muttering on the tram, either, although she was wearing her hearing aid. Those things never worked. The only reason they gave old people a hearing aid in one ear was so that other people would know they couldn't hear. If hearing aids were meant to be of some use, they would put them in both ears, like they do for children.

They got to the chapel on time and took off their coats in the narrow foyer, which was always crowded with people elbowing each other and opening up packages of flowers and trying to find someplace to put the wrappers. A friendly verger with a beard recognized Irma and led the group to good seats in the sanctuary, like an old-fashioned usher. The chapel was pretty on the inside, bright and open and just the right size. The best seats for a funeral were to the left of the coffin, near the centre, not too close and not too far away. From there you could see the dear departed and the pastor and hear everything, although the words of remembrance that people said as they left their flowers in front were always vague and mumbled. Siiri and Irma couldn't understand why Finland had this custom of baring one's soul about the deceased in front of everyone, when people otherwise never expressed their feelings, but Anna-Liisa thought it was an important part of the grieving process. There were all kinds of silly, strange messages written on the flower-arrangement ribbons brought for Tero.

'For a man who the angels wish to thank,' a large, handsome young man read from his bouquet.

'Whom,' Anna-Liisa said, tapping her hymnal on the back of the seat in front of her.

The large man had come to the funeral in a leather jacket. Actually there were a lot of leather jackets, all the same. Siiri looked on, mesmerized, at the man who dared to stand next to a coffin and talk about angels. If ever there was an angel, it was Tero Lehtinen, with his long hair and dimples.

'Do you think he shaves his head?' Irma asked in a too-loud voice. 'He doesn't look naturally bald.'

'Nowadays even very young men want to be bald,' Siiri whispered, and Irma shot back, 'Yes, when they're not wearing a topknot.'

This made them start to laugh and then feel immediately ashamed of themselves because it was very inappropriate to whisper and giggle at a young man's funeral.

When it was their turn to go up to the coffin, a considerable operation commenced. Canes clattered against the floor, Siiri dropped her cushion, Zimmer frames got stuck between the pews and Margit Partanen's hearing aid started to beep, but she couldn't hear it, of course. The handsome man who talked about angels helped them, pulling Anna-Liisa's Zimmer frame loose from the flower ribbon and picking Siiri's cushion up off the floor.

'A thousand thanks,' Siiri said, taking her green cushion from him with some embarrassment.

'Don't mention it,' the angel man said and looked at her with soft blue eyes. 'Nice pillow.'

'The residents of Sunset Grove want to thank our cook, Tero, for the moments of pleasure he gave us,' the Ambassador read in his quavering men's-chorus tenor, making the moments of pleasure sound so indecent that some of the funeral guests had to hold back laughter instead of tears. Irma nudged Margit Partanen with her elbow and told her to do something about her beeping hearing aid. Margit took the gadget out and stuffed it hurriedly in her handbag. It stayed there beeping throughout the service, competing with the snores of the Hat Lady.

Director Sundström and Nurse Hiukkanen weren't at the funeral and so they weren't able to witness the Sunset Grove residents' condolences for Tero's loved ones. It was also a great disappointment that Pasi, the social worker, wasn't there either. As soon as the coffin was in the hearse, Irma walked briskly up to Tero's mother, introduced herself, and talked about all sorts of things. Unfortunately, it was difficult to get any useful information out of the woman because she was so deranged by grief and strong medication.

'Why did he do it? Why?' she sputtered.

Chapter 7

On Wednesday Irma had a book-club meeting at her daughter-in-law's house in some godforsaken place, probably East Helsinki or Espoo. She was supposed to have read George Perec's *Life: A User's Manual* for the meeting but she'd found it so tiresomely long-winded and convoluted that she had stopped reading. It was definitely intended for someone younger than ninety.

'You didn't finish it? How are you going to participate in the discussion, then?' Siiri asked nervously, but Irma just waved her hand with her jangling golden bracelets and laughed.

'I'm sort of their mascot. They invite me because they're afraid I'll be lonely. They think I'm senile and they don't expect me to understand what they're talking about anyway. The fun thing about being my age is that I can act however I like and no one's surprised. My daughter-in-law always serves the most wonderful goodies. That's why I go. Of course, I have to remember to bring my pillies.'

Irma hopped into a taxi in front of the Japanese restaurant at Laajalahti Square and Siiri went to catch the tram, taking a few running steps to make the nearest one. First the number 4, then one and a half times around the loop on the number 3. When the number 3 got to the last stop, at the Zoological Gardens, she had to sit in the tram and wait for several minutes. It felt awkward to just sit and watch the driver smoke his cigarette. A proper last stop has a little turn-around, like the number 4 has at Munkkiniemi. She particularly liked the little loop on Arabianranta, where the number 6 and the number 8 had their last stops. When the tram was going at a good clip it made her stomach do a lovely flip.

The driver had left the radio on, tuned to a programme about the unusually large number of people in Finland who mixed alcohol and drugs, much more than in other European countries. In other places people knew to use just one or the other. Mixing the two was most common among the young and the old. This surprised her. There was no denying that everyone at Sunset Grove drank large quantities of alcohol and popped large quantities of pills, but they were doctor's prescriptions for various maladies. However, Siiri never took anything but a little red wine with Irma now and then, and a blood sugar pill every morning, like everybody else. She needed it because she was too fat, or too thin. Was she a mixed user? What about Irma, who drank nothing but red wine and took all kinds of pills? The Serbian doctor who prescribed Siiri's diabetes medicine didn't say anything about the dangers of mixing them with alcohol, he just tried to convince her to change her eating habits and drink her coffee without sugar, but Siiri told him that a ninety-four-year-old can eat what she likes and she still won't die.

Finally the driver finished his smoke and the trip continued to Alppila. There, behind the amusement park, was one of Siiri's favourite buildings, the Alppila parish hall. Its white beauty always had a strangely calming effect on her. Or was it the actual church? Churches were all just boxes nowadays. The one in Munkkiniemi was such a grey-brick monstrosity that people would stand in front of it and ask passers-by how to get to the church. Eventually, they built a tower on one corner of the building and put a cross on top so people would understand what it was. Siiri had wondered why there were no church bells in the tower, not one, and the vicar had explained that the bells were played on a CD player.

'Isn't it just as much trouble to climb the tower to turn on a stereo as it would be to play real bells?' Siiri had asked, trying to be amusing, but the vicar was a serious woman.

'The stereo is not in the tower; just the speakers.'

The number 3 tram was getting lively. A confused but smartly dressed woman started to give a speech in such a smooth, resonant voice that even Anna-Liisa would have approved.

'There are tremendous numbers of laboratory rats in Helsinki. They bring bacteria and diseases with them and this organ-transplant business is important, particularly in Spain, with which Finland has significant ties. They use old people's organs, too, kidneys and livers, anything at all. In our laboratory there were hallways full of large boxes of kidneys and livers, styrofoam boxes that were taken away and hidden in the basement, but I saw everything.'

The woman sitting next to Siiri got out her phone and started shouting into it to drown out the story of rats and organ transplants.

'Are you going to start the potatoes?' she said, without announcing herself or asking who she was speaking to, as was the custom now. She apparently meant put the potatoes on to cook. Her husband – or maybe it was her child – had started the potatoes. The food would be on the table when she got home. Siiri's husband had never cooked. He hadn't known how. He was lucky if he could get the skin off his own potato once it was cooked.

The woman from the laboratory hallway had moved on to a new subject. 'Once, when I was talking on the tram, a man got on who looked like Prime Minister Paavo Lipponen. He lived in Töölö. I had been to the door of his building and the trams don't go there because people in Töölö are so fancy that they live in a closed society and nobody's allowed to see their lives from the window of a tram. I also know which building Kai Korte lives in. Nobody remembers who Kai Korte is any more, but he was the Finnish Chancellor of Justice until 1986, and there are now almost a million people who have this device inside them, which I have, too. They install them in people and they cause inflammation of the soles of your feet.'

The other passengers exchanged glances, some moved further away from the lunatic, some spoke louder into their phones, and a schoolgirl with multiple piercings sitting across from Siiri started to giggle nervously. Siiri wished she could relax and enjoy the beautiful buildings and the sounds of the children. In fact, the incident at the card table the previous week was still playing on her mind. No one had seen Reino or Olavi Raudanheimo since Reino had been sent to the Group Home to calm down.

'He's probably been drugged into dementia and sent to the closed unit permanently,' Irma had said that morning when she'd come to Siiri's apartment for coffee before the book-club meeting.

They had both heard horror stories about old people being drugged into unconsciousness. People who had seemed deeply senile might be completely in their right minds once their medication was stopped. Old people who'd forgotten their own names would suddenly recognize everyone in their family, and even their neighbour's relatives. They couldn't comprehend how such a thing could happen. What good would it do anyone to drug an old person senseless? It certainly was no way to save money. It would be cheaper for them just to die and get it over with.

The confused woman on the tram was shouting even louder now, working herself into a kind of frenzy. The driver glanced at her nervously in the rear-view mirror, but he couldn't do anything because he had to keep driving.

'I can tell you that Kai Korte was a good man, but even he, among all those piggy banks and brokerages, couldn't do anything about the bacteria from the laboratories and the infected feet. It may be that the doctors were eating the rats. They eat rats in China and they have better medicine than we do! They used styrofoam boxes to transfer the rats – and I saw everything!'

Siiri escaped from the tram at the railway station, along with many other passengers. She pitied the driver, who had to continue his route with the woman on board. She looked at the railway station and the City Centre building with its sausage-shaped concrete awnings, two of Helsinki's ugliest structures, and wondered why Eliel Saarinen and Viljo Revell had designed both ugly and beautiful buildings – Revell, the Sausage Building and the Glass Palace; Saarinen, the railway station and the Marble Palace at Kaivopuisto. And why did Helsinki call such little buildings palaces?

Chapter 8

It had been a long time since Siiri and Irma had been in C
wing, so they got lost for a while before they found Olavi
Raudanheimo's door on the second floor. It wasn't customary at Sunset Grove to go ringing somebody's doorbell
unannounced. You weren't supposed to disturb people. You
don't do it in a real apartment block and this wasn't a com-
mune. You could meet the people you knew, and those you
didn't, downstairs in the common rooms. In addition to the
card players, there was a magazine-reading group and a
gigantic television in the lobby. It was constantly on, showing singing competitions and cooking shows, and a couple of
deaf old grannies were always shoved in front of it to be
entertained.

Olavi Raudanheimo didn't answer his doorbell. But they
thought they could hear noises in his apartment. There was
definitely someone in there. Irma tried to shout through the
keyhole, although there was no keyhole, just a big, chunky
lock. They doubted Olavi could hear her. Reino had once
told them that a grenade exploded right next to Olavi during
the war and he could never hear properly after that.

'Mr Raudanheimo! Mr Raudanheimo!' Irma shouted in a high-pitched voice like a ninety-two-year-old who had taken singing lessons in her youth. 'It's Mrs Kettunen and Mrs Lännenleimu from A wing! From the one-bedroom apartments!'

'Why shout that?' Siiri grumbled. 'It hardly matters which wing we're in or what our tenancy arrangements are.'

'He has to have some way to figure out who we are. Otherwise he'll be afraid to open the door,' Irma explained, then continued to yell. 'Siiri Kettunen and Irma Lännenleimu want to see you, Mr Raudanheimo! I have short hair in a perm and I've become a bit plump as I've got older, but I was very slender when I was young, and I have a blue dress, a real pearl necklace, and lovely earrings with real diamonds in them, and Siiri always wears long trousers and one of those . . . is that thing a cardigan?'

Siiri was starting to get nervous about the ruckus Irma was making. She glanced around crossly and noticed Virpi Hiukkanen at the end of the long hallway. Virpi gave her an icy stare and walked calmly towards them. Irma didn't notice her ominous form approaching and continued shouting. Virpi was just a few metres away and Siiri couldn't get any words out; she tugged on Irma's sleeve in a panic.

'We're not Erkki Hiukkanen!' Irma shouted into the lock, just as Virpi reached them. Siiri shrank like a schoolgirl in the head teacher's office.

'That's enough of this nonsense. Here at Sunset Grove it's important to leave the residents in peace and to create an atmosphere of tranquillity,' Virpi said, forcing her face into a calm smile. Then she suddenly broke into a yell. 'What is wrong with you two? Why are you shouting at the door of a total stranger? Who gave you permission to be here? You seem to have no concept of the principles of Sunset Grove! We are committed to the privacy of every resident and this behaviour is ridiculous. You're endangering the safety of the entire institution with your silly whims. Do I have to call the police, or an ambulance, to keep you two in check?'

Virpi looked at them threateningly and adjusted her large, plastic-rimmed glasses, as if to add to her air of authority. Siiri started to feel dizzy and had to grab Irma's arm.

'I think I'm going to faint,' she said, but she managed to stay upright with Irma's support. Her vision grew foggy and she had to focus what little strength she had on breathing.

'This place doesn't ensure privacy, it ensures privation!' Irma yelled, helping Siiri into a Biedermeier chair. 'Siiri's having a heart attack because of you! There are all kinds of shady things going on in this institution and all you do is spy on healthy people in the hallways! You ought to be ashamed of yourself. Where is Olavi Raudanheimo? Where have you put Reino Luukkanen? What's going on around here?'

Siiri wasn't having a heart attack. It was probably just the arrhythmia that she suffered now and then. But that was no joking matter, either, and she really did feel like she might black out at any moment. It was a lucky thing that there were chairs left by dead people in the hallways at Sunset Grove for situations such as these. When she opened her eyes Irma was holding her hand and Virpi Hiukkanen was standing a couple of metres away looking frightened. Virpi didn't try to help her, she just gnawed nervously on her chewing gum, took a phone out of her pocket, as though she had something important to do, and moved off without another word.

'And they say caregiving is a calling,' Irma puffed, pulling a flask of whisky out of her handbag. She made Siiri take a gulp and wiped her brow with her lace handkerchief. 'It's not the one Reino mangled,' she reassured her.

They thought that Virpi had gone to fetch a blood pressure cuff, since nurses always thought that anything troubling an old person could be made better by taking their blood pressure, but when she didn't return after a quarter of an hour, Irma led Siiri back to her apartment. She helped her lie down on the bed, took off her shoes, and laid her nap blanket over her. Then she went to the front door and tried to call for help because Siiri was very pale and still wasn't breathing normally.

The basic fee at Sunset Grove included a safety system – if a resident needed help, all they had to do was leave their phone receiver on the table and a member of staff would quickly appear. Of course anything they did when they arrived would be added to your bill, as would the call, but the system itself was part of the basic service. Irma picked up the receiver, laid it on the table, and listened for a while. Then she swore to herself, slammed down the receiver and went downstairs to find some help.

Siiri fell asleep. When she woke up, the room was full of people. Irma was talking with three or four strangers, young people, only one of whom seemed to understand Finnish. Irma tried Swedish, French and a little Russian, with no results. Luckily, the boy who spoke Finnish was calm and pleasant.

'Siiri Kettunen,' Siiri said by way of introduction, offering him her hand.

'Seems alert,' the medic said, wrapping a cuff around her outstretched arm and reading her blood pressure. 'Readings are fine. No need for an ambulance. If another attack occurs, call a taxi to take her to the hospital. No need to call us again.'

He packed up his first-aid kit and the foreign women followed him out of the door. Irma sank exhausted into the old armchair and told her that Virpi had called an ambulance because she didn't know what else to do.

The pleasant man was from the ambulance, as was the girl in the white uniform. The other two girls were Sunset Grove's new Indonesian interns. Irma didn't remember where Indonesia was, and Siiri couldn't understand why the interns had come to peer at her in her bed.

'They were sent to spy on you,' Irma said. She thought that everything that happened at Sunset Grove was connected. 'Tero's death, too. *Döden, döden, döden,*' she whispered before she left.

Three days later Siiri Kettunen received a bill for nineteen euros from a firm called Emergencion, for 'Non-urgent ambulance visit, no immediate care. Code X5.'

Chapter 9

On her way back from a visit to the hairdresser Siiri Kettunen met a man at the lift who looked like someone she knew, though he wasn't. Because it was so embarrassing to not be able to place someone who looked familiar, Siiri did as she always did in these situations and greeted the man, introducing herself, just to be on the safe side.

'Antti Raudanheimo,' the slightly greying, upright man said by way of introduction. He must be Olavi Raudanheimo's son. He had the same narrow face and straight nose.

He was an intelligent fellow and told her he'd rescued Olavi from Sunset Grove and taken him to the hospital, where he still was at the moment. He spoke of the 'terrible incident', and Siiri knew he meant the assault in the shower, although he didn't use those words. But something very distressing had happened and Olavi's son intended to file a criminal report. He had tried to discuss the matter with Sinikka Sundström, but the director wouldn't believe that anything so awful could happen in her retirement home.

'She's very sweet, but perhaps not informed about everything that goes on here,' he said.

They stood for such a long time in the foyer talking about Olavi that Siiri started to feel uneasy. She couldn't concentrate on what the man was saying, but instead kept glancing towards the office and looking behind her, although there didn't seem to be anyone about. Then she remembered that even the walls had ears at Sunset Grove, and she grabbed Olavi's son by the arm and pulled him closer.

'I don't think it's a good idea to talk about these matters here,' she whispered.

The man looked at her in bewilderment. 'Has anything else happened here besides my father's terrible incident?'

Siiri asked him to come to her apartment, although she didn't really know him and couldn't remember ever inviting a strange man into her home before. But he seemed trustworthy and direct; he looked her in the eye and spoke in a strong baritone. He came into her apartment but didn't take off his coat, just sat down at the table and talked for a long time about everything. He was almost more thorough than Anna-Liisa in his attention to detail, and at times Siiri felt like she might fall asleep, but luckily she wasn't sitting in the comfortable armchair. She was sitting on a hard kitchen chair that squeaked whenever she moved. What with her fatigue and the squeaking, she couldn't quite commit everything he said to memory, and she knew that Irma would be mad at her for this later. But one thing was quite clear in her mind: he had arranged to get his father out of the Group Home, where he had indeed been relegated, just as Irma had said.

'Do you happen to know if your father's friend, Reino

Luukkanen, is in the Group Home too? A large man in tracksuit bottoms, poorly shaved?'

'That I don't know,' the man said apologetically. 'I couldn't really work out who all those poor souls were. One man was sleeping in the same room as my father, but I have no idea how long he'd been lying there or what kind of trousers he was wearing. He hadn't been shaved in a long while, but then no one there had.'

Siiri got up and pulled a bottle of red wine out of the flour bin, but Olavi's son declined to have any alcohol in the middle of the day.

'I usually don't either, but I've heard that red wine is good for you. It has some sort of particle in it that halts the ageing process. Are you sure you won't have just a little?' she asked, but he said that he had to get back to work.

Siiri escorted Antti Raudanheimo down in the lift. He intended to work for three more years before retiring, had two adult sons and a very nice wife. He laughed happily as he said goodbye, and his handshake was manly and soothing. Nevertheless, Siiri was quite worked up after he left. Some red wine really could have done her good. She stood dumbly in the lobby and regretted that the Sunset Grove cafeteria wasn't a real restaurant where you could buy yourself a little sip, in the evening at least. The residents had to sit alone in their own little boxes to drink their nightcaps.

'Cock-a-doodle-doo!'

Irma and Anna-Liisa were coming down the hallway of C wing, on their way back from the activity session. Irma showed Siiri a cardboard tube peculiarly decorated with glued-on curls of wool. 'It's a lamb. I can give it to you as a Christmas present.'

'I didn't make anything. I just watched the others having fun,' Anna-Liisa hurriedly explained, so Siiri wouldn't think she was silly.

'I'm so glad you two are here! Do you have a moment? Sit down on the sofa and rest a bit.'

'You're agitated,' Anna-Liisa said as she installed her red Zimmer frame between two chairs.

'She must have met some charming man!' Irma laughed and automatically started to search her handbag for a deck of cards. Her glasses, lipstick and coin purse were soon on the table.

'Yes, I have, and I invited him to my apartment.'

Irma screeched with delight, stopped emptying her bag, and started picking her things up off the table and putting them back into it. Anna-Liisa turned her good ear towards Siiri, and Siiri quickly told them what Antti Raudanheimo had said, or as much of it as she remembered, and especially how she felt about it all.

'It's really horrible. Nightmarish. The whole thing makes me feel sick. My ears are ringing and my head is aching. But Olavi Raudanheimo is at the Hilton now, and quite clear-headed. Not a sign of any dementia.'

'You mean the Meilahti Hospital,' Anna-Liisa said. Siiri nodded in agreement. The fifteen-storey Meilahti Hospital tower looked so much like a large hotel that people called it the Hilton. 'If there's going to be a criminal report, they'll need witnesses. Were there any eyewitnesses to this terrible incident?'

'Just Olavi's word,' Siiri said, looking sad. 'Do you think the police will believe him?'

'Of course they'll believe him!' Anna-Liisa shouted, rapping on the table as if the whole episode invigorated her. 'It would be a strange state of affairs if they didn't listen to the word of a war veteran!'

They knew Anna-Liisa was right again. They were all reassured by the fact that Olavi's son had taken care of the matter in such an upright manner. Luckily there were still some people with decent relatives. The fact that Sinikka Sundström didn't want to believe what she'd been told about what had happened to Olavi didn't surprise any of them. Sinikka was so well-intentioned and so stressed. Lately she had been even more nervous and absent-minded than usual. A lot of staff had left. There were always a lot of staff changes among the nurses, but this autumn the turnover rate had sped up so much that Director Sundström herself didn't seem able to keep up.

'Oh my, I don't know. Ask Virpi. Or somebody else,' Director Sundström would answer desperately whenever anyone made the mistake of asking her why there was no nurse available, why the physical therapist had cancelled all her appointments, or why the activity director hadn't shown up for the joke group. The young girls who made up things for the residents to do were called activity directors. They believed that old people could be cheered up with songs from the war years, black-and-white movies and crafts.

Sunset Grove also offered rehabilitation and memory exercises. There were pictures and activities glued to the walls for the Memory Game. They looked almost like they might have been donated from a preschool centre – hand-drawn flowers, boats, houses and animals. Siiri was particularly bothered by the one that someone had glued right next to her door, a picture of a family of bunnies on a summer outing. But Irma was a curious person and had played the Memory Game more times than she could remember. Anna-Liisa came at regular intervals for a 'memory check' at the afternoon activity session, because she knew that the more you use your brain, the slower your memory breaks down. She started every day with a crossword puzzle and every night in bed she went through all the case endings for the Finnish interrogative articles, to keep her mind in working order.

'Self-care. It saves the state money,' she always said proudly.

Rehabilitation was a very broad concept at Sunset Grove; it might include anything from massage to toe wiggling. It was compulsory and free for the men because they were veterans, but the women had to pay for their own rehabilitation, even though many of them had been in the Lotta women's auxiliary, and some of them, like Siiri, were even stationed at the front. Of course all she'd done was wash bodies and put them in their coffins. It hadn't really felt like front-line work, but still, it was a tough job for a young girl. During the Winter War the bodies were frozen so you had to thaw them out. In the Continuation War they were full of maggots and had a sickening smell.

Siiri and Irma occasionally went to exercise class or to the pedicurist out of sheer pity for the nurses. They didn't really know what they were being rehabilitated for.

'For death,' Irma said. '*Döden, döden, döden.*'

'Why in heaven's name do you keep repeating that?' Anna-Liisa said, almost angrily.

The Swedish author Astrid Lindgren had said in a TV interview, when she was quite old, that she often talked on the phone with her sister about who would be the last to die, and when they realized that all they talked about was death and dying, they got into the habit of starting their phone conversations by saying, '*Döden, döden, döden.*' That's where Irma had got it. She still liked to read Astrid Lindgren's books, and often had a copy of *Pippi Longstocking* on her bedside table.

'*Emil of Lönneberga* is my favourite, though. He's just like my third son – the one who ran away to China. He was a real Emil when he was little, just as sweet, and quite impossible.'

'I heard that the boy who was the cook here hung himself,' Anna-Liisa said.

'Who?' Siiri said, but Irma was still talking.

'I like the Moomin books, too,' Irma continued. 'They're such clever stories!' She thought that the older a person got, the more like a Moomin they became. 'Until eventually it's hard to tell whether someone's a man or a woman – or maybe it's not, but anyway. Just think how fun it would be if we could all grow tails. We could hold them out at right angles and the nurses would urge us to cheer up like Moominpappa did at the Hemulens' kindergarten.'

'What are you girls lazing about for?' Exercise Annie said, interrupting their wandering conversation. She smiled brightly, patted Siiri and Anna-Liisa, and waved her exercise stick invitingly. They called all the young rehabilitation directors Exercise Annie.

'You're not too late for the stick exercises! And today we get to play with balls, too!'

Anna-Liisa and Irma promised they would come to the exercise class and left to get their exercise clothes from their apartments. Siiri didn't feel like it. There was something degrading about messing around with sticks and balls, especially when you had to do it in front of a wall of mirrors with everyone looking so old and wrinkled that it was difficult to recognize yourself. They did, in fact, look like Moomins in their grey exercise outfits, just as Irma had said.

Siiri went out and caught the number 4 tram, accidentally ending up at the stop in front of Stockmann department store although she had intended to get off earlier and transfer to the number 10. She walked through the store, past the perfume counter and the magazine racks, to the stop on Mannerheimintie. The number 10 came quickly and she took it past the old Surgery Hospital, which wasn't a hospital any more. She'd read in the paper that they were building new hospitals in Meilahti for hundreds of millions of euros so that they could move out of the beautiful old buildings. The more medicine progressed, the more expensive it became because people were healthier and didn't die when they were supposed to any more.

When the tram came back around to the Mannerheim statue, Siiri got on the number 6 and rode it to Hietalahti market square. That was where the old brick and stucco market hall designed by Selim A. Lindqvist was, the most beautiful market hall in Helsinki. On her way home she got off on Bulevardi and glanced in the window at Cafe Ekberg. She'd never been in, and she didn't go in this time, either, although Irma always talked about how nice it was. Irma liked to go to the Ekberg with her old schoolmates.

Siiri walked through the Plague Park to Yrjönkatu and stopped to look at Wäinö Aaltonen's relief sculpture on the Suomi building, with its heavy horses and strange, ungainly angels. She continued to the Swimming Hall and couldn't think of the architect's name and wondered when she had last been swimming. But she couldn't remember. Then she went around the back of the ugly Forum building and looked into the courtyard of the Amos Anderson Museum, and missed her husband, and turned onto Simonkatu, and finally arrived at the tram stop for her own number 4, in front of the Glass Palace.

She almost fell asleep on the tram and was so tired when she got off that she stopped to catch her breath at the tram stop. She leaned on her cane and looked at Sunset Grove through the trees. It was a repulsive, 1970s concrete building with a flat roof and little windows. It was probably impossible to build anything beautiful out of concrete. Then suddenly, seemingly out of nowhere, an image of Tero, beautiful, long-haired Tero, hanged, came into her mind: his face swollen and distorted, his feet swinging loose in the air.

She'd seen hanged people like that on television. But why did this horrible vision come to her so powerfully, so realistically? Even his familiar red checked shirt was vivid in her mind. She closed her eyes to get rid of the sight, but the image didn't go away, the buzz in her head only grew louder. She started to feel dizzy, her cane fell out of her hand, and she had to hold on to the tram stop railing for support. She hoped her feeling of nausea wouldn't make her vomit, and she realized she was crying.

Chapter 10

'Cock-a-doodle-doo!' rang brightly across the lobby of Meilahti Hospital. 'Where have you been?'

Irma had begun to get nervous waiting for Siiri and Anna-Liisa. She had arrived on time, contrary to habit, and ended up having to wait at the reception desk for nearly four minutes. The neighbourhood around the hospital had changed completely since the last time Siiri had been there, to see her husband, around the turn of the millennium. Without Anna-Liisa she never would have found the place, now called Meilahti Hospital, its entrance painted a ghastly orange.

'It's like walking into a metro station,' Irma said.

Irma found some art photographs of Helsinki on the wall and looked at them more closely to see if a tenth-generation Helsinkian would recognize anything in them. Anna-Liisa and Siiri weren't interested in this game and went to find out what ward Olavi Raudanheimo was in. Siiri asked the attendant to write down the floor and room number on a slip of paper and with this they wandered down the hallway, following a white line painted on the floor, as they had been instructed.

They walked along the line single file and felt like children holding a rope on a preschool outing to the zoo or the museum. Siiri had the idea that it might be a sobriety test, to see if they could walk in a straight line, like the tests police give to drivers. Maybe the hospital had painted the line on the floor so they could tell exactly how drunk their visitors were. Irma thought it was like walking a tightrope in the circus, but she had a hard time staying on the line and started to get so dizzy that she had to step off it.

They continued onwards in this manner and didn't notice where the line was taking them. When eventually they stopped to clear Irma's head, they realized they were in the basement, although Olavi's room was on the twelfth floor. They had to ask directions several times before they found him. Anna-Liisa found it hard to believe that they really needed to go down two floors before they could go up, and Irma wanted to ask a real doctor, preferably a medical professor, whether it mattered if they didn't get there via the white line.

'The staff are very friendly,' Irma said, pleased. 'Much nicer than at Sunset Grove. They stop and talk to you and look you in the eye.'

Anna-Liisa was impressed, too. 'They even speak Finnish. Did you notice that the last person we talked to used the formal *you* correctly? That's unusual. I would have been impressed at the attempt even if he'd got it wrong.'

When finally they reached Olavi, they found he had been given a good room with only four beds and a private toilet. It was quiet, too – no television blaring trivial chatter in a corner. And you could see a long way from the window, at least as far as Lauttasaari, if not all the way to Espoo. Siiri, Irma and Anna-Liisa admired the view and soon got into a quarrel over where the proper boundary of Töölö began, but then Olavi's room-mate, who said he was a townie, intervened.

'Stenbäckinkatu,' he said, coughing loudly. 'That's the boundary of Töölö.'

Anna-Liisa was obviously of a different opinion, and Irma was curious to know if the man was a drunk, since it seemed that the only people who called themselves townies were chronic alcoholics. But neither woman said anything because they remembered that they had come to see Olavi Raudanheimo, who was sitting in his bed looking very thin but perfectly alert.

'You certainly have it good here,' Irma began cheerfully, but Anna-Liisa got straight to the point, like a good interrogator.

'What happened to you?' she said. 'Do you remember what happened afterwards? Were there any witnesses?'

Siiri would have liked to ask about Reino as well, whether Olavi knew where he'd ended up. But it was hard for Olavi to answer any of their questions. He said he had been sent to the dementia section of the Group Home and that he was glad that he was at the hospital now. He didn't remember anything about the Group Home and wouldn't even know he'd been there if his son hadn't told him.

'The hospital examined me thoroughly and found out all kinds of things,' he said almost proudly, as if he were talking about his accomplishments. He started boasting about his numerous cysts, hernias and blockages, and Anna-Liisa got impatient and demanded that he tell them how the criminal investigation was progressing.

'We didn't come here to listen to your medical history,' she explained. Olavi looked frightened.

Then he started to cry. He had a different way of crying to Reino. He didn't bark or curse. He wept silently, holding it in and letting it out. Like something had grabbed him deep at the pit of his stomach. The alcoholic townie thought it best to go out on the balcony for a cigarette. It was hard to tell if the room's other occupants were alive or not. So Olavi was able to tell them what had happened.

'I had asked for a male nurse to help with my bathing and showering,' he began. 'Because it bothered me having a young woman assisting an ugly old man like me. I thought it was more natural to have a man do it. It never occurred to me that a male nurse would . . . somehow . . . think that he could . . .'

He started to cry again. Irma patted his shoulder, Siiri held his hand, and Anna-Liisa straightened out his blanket.

'We understand, Olavi,' she said, as if she were an expert in such things. 'And there's such a serious shortage of male nurses, too.'

Olavi said it was a new nurse named Jere, whose last name he couldn't remember, but his son had promised to find out. Since Jere was new, the social worker had to come with him.

'There's your witness!' Siiri exclaimed.

'No. He was the one who was . . . I was crying, asking them to let me out of the shower, and he just laughed . . . It was . . . terribly unpleasant . . . Do you believe me?' He spoke quietly and looked at them and they could see the tremendous shame and embarrassment in his eyes. Irma dug her lace handkerchief out of her handbag and handed it to him.

'Perhaps they are homosexuals,' Anna-Liisa said.

'Not necessarily,' Irma said. 'Certainly not normal homosexuals, anyway.' She blew her nose loudly.

'I'm never going back to Sunset Grove,' Olavi sighed. 'But my son can't take me in and I'm not sick enough to stay here in the hospital. Friends, where am I going to go?'

His voice nearly faded away completely and he was left staring out of the window. They didn't know what to say, they just stood in shock for what felt like an eternity while the silence grew heavier.

'Don't worry, we'll think of something,' Siiri said, not quite knowing what she meant, and fluffed his pillow.

'Pasi was fired at the same time that Tero died. Or was it after he died? Does anybody know Pasi's last name?' Anna-Liisa said, making an effort to change the subject. Before anyone could respond, a heavy-set nurse wheeled a food trolley in with a terrible racket.

'Maybe this isn't such a high-quality place,' Irma said when she saw the limp porridge.

The nurse was sweaty and cross-looking. They felt like they ought to leave quickly, and were in such a hurry that they didn't give Olavi a proper goodbye.

On the tram Siiri realized she'd left her cane at the hospital and decided to go there first thing in the morning to get it. She always took care of unpleasant tasks sooner rather than later. It was easier than letting things pile up. Her son who died of alcoholism had always suffered less for what he'd done than for what he'd left undone. It was hard to understand how she could have raised him so badly. All her children, really, because it wasn't quite healthy the way her daughter had taken up teaching yoga and then become a nun.

Siiri didn't really need her cane, but it was an expensive model and a gallant companion, as Irma put it.

'My Carl the Cane always finds his way home,' Irma said the next morning at coffee, as Siiri was getting ready to go and pick hers up.

Siiri asked about her cane at the hospital reception desk but the girl there didn't know how to help her. Siiri thought she'd left the cane in Olavi's room with a view, so she decided to check there, if she could remember the way. She had some memory of it, but it was a vague kind of memory that she couldn't swear to as fact. That must be what Irma was talking about when she said she'd 'finessed' something.

Olavi Raudanheimo was happy when Siiri surprised him at his lunch. They served lunch very early in hospitals, which was probably good, since they woke the patients up so early in the morning. They had, in fact, poked Olavi awake an hour before breakfast that morning at half past five to take his temperature. He didn't know why they did it since he couldn't remember the last time he'd had a fever. But it was a compulsory procedure and there was no getting out of it. There was a white plate on his tray and on the plate was one potato and something grey.

'Pork gravy, I think,' he said. 'I'm not sure. I don't see any meat in it.'

'Maybe it's to give you something to hope for,' Siiri said, and Olavi laughed in his normal voice, but didn't touch his food.

They had such a pleasant time sitting and chatting that Siiri forgot why she had come and thought that she must have come to ask about Reino, since she'd forgotten to ask the day before. Olavi said that Reino had been sent to the closed unit's severe dementia ward – Olavi's son had found that out, too.

'A healthy man, not even that old,' Olavi said soberly. 'Reino's only eighty-seven, isn't he?'

Olavi was well-informed about everything. Siiri couldn't understand how such a person could be mistaken for a half-wit. Even Alzheimer's wouldn't strike someone like a bolt of lightning. But Olavi said that anyone would seem demented if they were given enough medication.

'That's what my son said. There Reino sat tied to a wheel-chair, unable to even remember his own name, a Russian nurse changing his nappy once a day and feeding him gruel with a spoon. What a fate for a veteran of the war.'

Olavi's son had rescued him from the closed unit by tell-ing them that his father needed to go to the hospital for some tests, and once Olavi was out he'd recovered from his 'dementia' immediately.

'It was a truly miraculous recovery! They won't do anything here until they've peeled you off your medication. But Reino doesn't have any children to help him. His only son died a couple of years ago from a heart attack while jogging. He'd suddenly taken up exercise, the lunatic.'

When Olavi's gravy had cooled and solidified, he moved it aside and picked up the newspaper. It was fun reading the news together. There was an article about an integrated retirement home built in combination with a children's nursery. It sounded like a good idea to Siiri and Olavi. The children would brighten up the retirement home and the old people could help the overworked nursery staff with the babysitting. They could eat together, draw, sing, read, and they wouldn't need to make up any activity busywork. But the paper said that they'd had to give up the experiment because there had been so many complaints from the children's parents that the old people were a danger to the children because they were confused and unpredictable and taking strong medication.

Siiri and Olavi laughed at that until the tears flowed. Then Siiri went away, without her cane. Although they couldn't say 'went away' any more because it meant 'died'. At Sunset Grove there'd been a nice woman who had moved into her own apartment on Solnantie because, as she put it, all the people at Sunset Grove were old and toothless. For a long time everyone thought she had died, until one day she appeared on the same tram as Siiri.

'Oh, you aren't dead, then,' Siiri had said, thoughtlessly, and then she had hastened to explain, 'They said you went away.'

Chapter 11

Irma had marked on her calendar that it was her turn to reserve a restaurant table for her next class reunion. She asked Siiri to come with her to reserve it because she'd decided that this time they would have the meeting in a real restaurant instead of Cafe Ekberg.

'Come with you? Can't you just call and reserve a table?' Siiri said. She didn't know Helsinki restaurants and wasn't sure how she could help.

'I'm not calling somewhere. I'm going in person. It's more fun that way. And I have to try out the restaurant so I won't embarrass myself by choosing a place with bad food. We can take a taxi.' She was enthused at the idea.

'Don't you think a taxi's too expensive?' Siiri said, since Irma didn't have any of the Ambassador's taxi coupons. But Irma's daughter had told her that now that she didn't have a car she could afford to take a taxi every day. Siiri wasn't used to calling a cab just like that. It made her feel a little guilty. But Irma was more carefree than Siiri was in many ways. She liked all kinds of little vices, like whisky and cigarettes.

They went to the Sunset Grove information desk to ask

them to call a taxi and were happy to see that for once there was someone at the counter.

'Two euros,' the woman said before picking up the phone.

'I see. So it costs the same as one emptying of the rubbish,' Irma said, and cheerfully handed her a fifty-euro note.

'Don't you have anything smaller?' Siiri said in horror, and Irma said that when you get money out of the wall it only dispenses large bills. There was nothing she could do about it.

They got a taxi, but a problem arrived with it. There was a large-breasted, naked woman painted on the side of the car with a phone number for sex services. Siiri felt that they couldn't take such a porn-mobile, but Irma told her to stop being silly; no one was going to mistake them for sex workers.

'Or customers!' Irma said with a hearty laugh and sat down on a large stain in the back seat of the taxi.

The next problem was where to go. Irma asked the driver if he could recommend a nice restaurant for students from the class of 1940, but the man clearly wasn't from Helsinki. Then Irma remembered the Lehtovaara.

'What's the address?' the driver asked. He gripped the steering wheel with both hands and stared straight ahead.

'Well, it's on Mechelininkatu. On the corner of Mechelin and something, right near the Töölö library,' Irma said as she put on her lipstick. With that information you would have thought that the taxi would get moving, but the driver demanded the address again. He had a little gadget on the dashboard where apparently he had to type in the exact address before he could start driving.

'Goodness,' Irma said, snapping her compact mirror shut. 'Type in "Mechelininkatu eight". That's with a C H.'

'Is it eight C or eight H?'

'Not the address, the spelling. Try eight A.'

And so the taxi started off, but the address she'd given him was wrong, of course. She gave a shout when they passed the furniture store on Mechelininkatu and told the driver to stop. But the man said that he couldn't turn left until he got to Mechelininkatu 8, and stubbornly continued driving.

'So this is what it's like to go by taxi,' Siiri said triumphantly. If she'd had her way, they would have taken the tram.

'It's not usually like this. This fellow isn't quite qualified for the job,' Irma said in a low voice. She glanced out of the window and waved her arm with its rattling bracelets in front of Siiri's face. 'Look! Quick! See how the Sibelius monument is gleaming in the sunshine? What a marvellous sculpture! You'd never see this riding the scram. And it won't take you anywhere near Restaurant Lehtovaara.'

The scram was one of Irma's joke words, something one of her darlings had made up when they were little, along with calling a housefly a flouse-lie. But she was right. It was something Siiri had thought about ever since the mentally ill lab assistant had mentioned it in her sermon on rats and Prime Minister Lipponen. Why didn't the trams go to Töölö? All the trams took the same route straight down

Mannerheimintie. Why didn't some of them go down Mech-elininkatu or Topeliuksenkatu?

'You're not from Helsinki, are you?' Irma asked the driver while she searched her handbag for her wallet. Her pill counter, lace handkerchief, wristwatch, spare tights, two pairs of glasses and a small bottle of whisky were already lying on the back seat.

'No.'

'Where are you from? Vaasa?'

Now Irma's blood-sugar meter, wallet and the sticky note with 7245 written on it in large numbers were also on the seat.

'I'm from Azerbaijan,' the man answered.

Irma paid with a fifty-euro note, but the driver refused to take it because he had no change and no way to check that the bill was genuine. He tried to get her to pay with a credit card but then her strange intuition reminded her that she'd been given change at the Sunset Grove info desk when they'd called the taxi. She handed the driver a bill and told him to bite it to make sure it wasn't counterfeit. Siiri was starting to feel weak from the bad air and the peculiar mood in the car.

'Why did you think he was from Vaasa?' Siiri asked when they'd got out of the cab and were standing in front of the Lehtovaara breathing the fresh air.

'His Finnish was as bad as it is in Vaasa. But where on God's green earth is Azerbaijan? And how can some-one from there pass a Helsinki taxi driver's test?' Irma

wondered, just as the two of them noticed that the Lehtovaara was closed.

Now they were really in a pickle. There were no taxi
stands nearby, and no tram stops. How were they going to
get off Mechelininkatu? Siiri was afraid they might have to
resort to using Irma's mobile phone.

'Wait! I've just finessed it! We'll go to the library!'

It was a wonderful idea. They both loved the Töölö
library, Aarne Ervi's most beautiful building, which made
the modernist utopia of Tapiola look like a concrete suburb
by comparison. The Töölö library was one of those rare
buildings that were beautiful both inside and out. Some
buildings are only beautiful on the inside, like the Opera
House – which was an awful pile of tiles until you took the
time to go inside. Siiri and Irma walked through the library
and admired the railings, the stairs, the windows, the light
and the view. Finally a friendly librarian came up to them
and asked if she could help them.

'ARE YOU LOOKING FOR A SPECIFIC BOOK?
HAVE YOU LOST SOMETHING?' she enquired in a loud
voice, speaking slowly and moving the muscles of her face
so vigorously that Irma and Siiri started to laugh.

'No, thank you. We need a taxi. Could you call one for
us?' Irma said sweetly. The librarian was taken aback, but
just for a moment, and then she called them a cab. She
wouldn't take any payment for this service, though calling a
cab had to cost her just as much trouble and expense as it did
at Sunset Grove.

The new taxi was driven by a young Finnish man who

might even have been from Helsinki. He had a leather jacket and friendly blue eyes. As he opened the door for Siiri, he flashed a sweet smile at her and she felt as if she'd seen him before.

He recommended Restaurant Kämp. They were very happy because they hadn't known it had opened again.

'Sibelius used to go there regularly,' Irma told the driver.

'I don't know about him, but it's a good restaurant,' he replied.

Suddenly he slammed on the brakes and cursed. Siiri rocked forward and hit her head on the front-seat headrest, then Irma fell on top of her and they flopped against the door.

'Pardon me,' Irma said as she lifted her head off Siiri's lap, although it wasn't her fault. They looked at each other, flabbergasted, saw that they were both still alive, and started to laugh. The driver didn't even glance at them and seemed entirely unconcerned with what was happening in the back seat.

'God damned tram! Is there any more stupid invention?'

It was clear the man didn't like trams. Siiri felt uncomfortable and Irma grinned gleefully. The driver thought trams should be outlawed. They killed people, clogged traffic, derailed, and were expensive to maintain.

'The trams are so heavy they break their own tracks. And so few people will fit in one! When was the last time you saw the metro collide with an automobile? When?'

The man looked at them in the rear-view mirror with his bright blue eyes. Where could they have met him? Siiri racked her brains, but no thoughts seemed to be coming to her; she couldn't finesse it.

'Never, because the metro is underground. They ought to send the trams straight to hell and replace them with metro trains. No shivering at the stop, no accidents, nobody run over. You two wouldn't be sitting in a taxi if Helsinki had a decent metro. There wouldn't be any need for taxis.'

'But then you wouldn't have a job,' Irma said worriedly.

'Well, no, but cooking is my actual profession.'

'Cooking? Then you could come to work at Sunset Grove, since our cook died. Perhaps you know him. His name was Tero.'

Irma talked as if there were only one cook in the world and his name was Tero. Sometimes Irma was so silly that Siiri was ashamed of her.

'Tero Lehtinen?' the driver asked, turning to look at them. 'At the Sunset Grove retirement home?'

Then Siiri remembered where she had seen him before. At Tero's funeral! He had made a beautiful speech about angels and helped them up to the front, even picked up Siiri's cushion, and he had given her that searching look, like he was doing now.

'I think we've met before,' Siiri said, and the driver nodded. He had recognized them but he'd thought they didn't remember him.

'We are old, but we do remember some things. Like pretty blue eyes,' Siiri said, and immediately regretted flirting in such a manner when they should be talking about Tero. Irma was digging in her handbag for her mirror and comb. She found them and started to fix her mussed hairdo, now that she knew the driver wasn't just a driver but someone they knew.

'What do you know about Tero's death? Anna-Liisa has all kinds of theories about it but I don't quite believe her. You hear such wild rumours in a retirement home and Anna-Liisa is a bit of a grim sort of person. She lives at Sunset Grove, too, in A wing with us, although she just has a studio and we have nice, spacious one-bedroom complexes. Of course they stupidly combined the living room and kitchen, which I don't like at all, being able to see the dishes from the sofa, but . . . of course that's not important right now. You must not really be bald. You must just want to be bald, so you've shaved your hair off, right? Do you have to shave it every day like a beard? Tero's hair was very long, and a lovely colour. Are you a good friend of his? He sometimes even wore his hair in a ponytail.'

They had come to Restaurant Kämp, on the pedestrian street side. The driver switched off the meter and the engine, turned to face them, and didn't look at all like he wanted them to pay. He was talking about angels and for some reason he cursed every time he mentioned them, referring to them as 'hell's angels', although he didn't seem to particularly dislike them. In fact, he said that he was one himself. In any case, these angels had learned something about Sunset Grove and they hadn't been at all happy about what they'd found out. And it all had something to do with Tero's death. Siiri and Irma's heads were spinning trying to understand the man's story.

'Tero couldn't take it,' he said at the end.

'Was Tero an angel, too?' Siiri asked.

'No. He was too sensitive for that sort of thing. He'd rather mess around with bicycles. But he was a friend.'

'So are these bad angels some sort of hardened police special forces?' Irma asked earnestly, but the man said, almost angrily, that the angels were anything but cops.

'So they're criminals, then?' Irma asked, rather boldly, considering that the man had just said that he himself was one of these angels. He didn't answer her question, just muttered an obscenity. They thought the conversation was over, and Irma got out her wallet to pay.

'There are all sorts of things happening at Sunset Grove and the police couldn't care less.'

They didn't know what the police had to do with Sunset Grove and they weren't sure if this seemingly kind man was, in fact, a criminal. But he definitely wanted to tell them something, so Irma suggested that he leave off driving for today and go with them to the Kämp for lunch. He looked surprised at first, but then thought it was a good idea.

'I'm Irma Lännenleimu, and this is my friend Siiri Kettunen,' Irma said as they stood on the street in front of the Kämp. The man said his name was Mika, which had that same, short sound as Pasi and Tero, like the stroke of an axe blade.

'I'm sorry. I didn't hear your last name, Mika,' Irma said, squeezing his hand and not letting go until he'd introduced himself properly.

'Korhonen. Mika Korhonen. But you can just call me Mika.'

'Lunch will be my treat,' Irma said, and they went into the Kämp, which was rather different to what Irma and Siiri had expected. Too much plastic and very no-frills. You could see that everything was new, not the genuine old stuff. But they were diplomatically silent about this so as not to offend their new friend, Mika Korhonen.

Irma and Siiri didn't know what to eat because the menu was crammed with strange words they didn't understand. Every dish had a tremendous quantity of fine print. That's what food had come to. It wasn't a means of sustenance any more, it was a hobby. It was different during the war, and afterwards. Back then you didn't play with your food.

'Do you cook these kinds of . . . unusual foods?' Siiri asked Mika, who said he was more of a fan of basic food, but knew how to make stuffed cabbage, which was somewhat unusual. He had worked at the university cafeteria – the real one in the main building – until they'd outsourced the food service.

'You can't cook outside in Finland!' Irma said with a bright laugh.

'They changed to a restaurant company and I got fired. So I started driving a cab,' Mika explained, and Siiri and Irma felt so sorry for him that they ordered some red wine. But Mika wouldn't drink since he had the taxi waiting outside.

'Illegally parked,' he said, and flashed a beautiful smile.

'Yes, you don't like the police,' Irma said, and they clinked their glasses – Mika with water and Irma and Siiri with wine, and Irma was already explaining that she never drank anything but red wine, and what a stroke of luck it was that they hadn't taken the tram like Siiri had wanted and had taken a taxi instead.

'You've got a homo mafia there at Sunset Grove,' Mika said.

After that Irma and Siiri just listened.

They didn't understand everything he said and they knew they would forget half of it, but they struggled valiantly to keep up. Mika was talking about their prescriptions but he seemed to have them mixed up with drugs. Siiri didn't quite grasp how something a doctor prescribed to old people could be dangerous for young people or addle their heads.

'Oh, that dope is rattling your brains, too. It's just legal.'

'I don't take anything but my diabetes medication,' Siiri hastened to say, so he wouldn't get the wrong idea about her. Irma rummaged in her handbag for her pill counter and started to wonder what all her different-coloured tablets were.

'This is my glucose tablet and this one helps you fall asleep – it's very gentle, not a sleeping pill, but it does make you go to sleep in a snap. This is my Amaryl and that's my blood-pressure lozenge, but I don't know what these two are. Do you?'

Mika didn't know. It seemed to Siiri that some new medications had appeared in Irma's pill counter. Mika took one of each and said he would find out what they were. That felt good. It meant he wanted to help them. Either that or he was going to start selling Irma's pills to some criminal acquaintance. But that wasn't likely – he was such a pleasant young man, so peaceful, and charismatic in his own way. A large man who knew how to make stuffed cabbage. Siiri's and Irma's husbands had never cooked; they hadn't even known how to make coffee in an automatic coffeemaker. Once, when Irma had a high fever, Veikko had tried to boil an egg, and they'd learned that you can, in fact, burn a boiled egg, by boiling it until it's black on the outside and green on the inside. Irma's vivid description of how poor Veikko couldn't so much as boil an egg to keep body and soul together without nearly burning the house down even made Mika laugh.

'You seem like a man with courage and a sense of humour,' Siiri said. 'Do you have enough courage and sense of humour to come and see us at Sunset Grove?'

Mika smiled kindly, thanked them for the invitation, and promised to visit. Irma and Siiri were exceedingly pleased and Irma paid the restaurant bill with two fifty-euro notes. She asked Siiri to calculate what it came to in marks but Siiri refused to tell her because Irma had said it was her treat, and it was poor form to quibble about the price afterwards.

'That's right! My class reunion!' Irma shouted, and it was only then that Siiri remembered why they had started this adventure. The waiter was standing next to the table counting out their change and Irma explained that she needed to make a table reservation for two weeks from Wednesday at twelve o'clock.

'We have our class get-together the first Wednesday of every month. None of the other class reunions have them as often. I was kept back four times in school and now that there are so few of us left I'm invited to all the reunions. But my graduating class is the most fun. The first Wednesday of the month is two weeks from now, isn't it? Time goes by so quickly, don't you agree?'

'Yes,' the waiter said, stupefied. 'How many people are you reserving for?'

'Well, I don't really quite know!' Irma said, grabbing him by the arm and laughing as if she'd said something amusing.

'You don't know how many people there will be?'

'I don't. Somebody dies every week. *Döden, döden, döden.* I'm ninety-two years old, but even I'm not wise enough to predict how many of my classmates will be alive two weeks from Wednesday. I'm sure you understand.'

'Certainly,' the waiter answered, and went to get the head waiter. In the end, Mika manfully handled this problem, too. He reserved a table for ten for Irma's classmates on the first Wednesday of November, which was, in fact, only a week away.

'Put it down as a partially posthumous reservation. That way the staff won't be surprised if the group is a bit smaller,' he told the head waiter with a wink, and when a large man says such a thing in a deep voice, head waiters listen.

Mika drove them back to Sunset Grove and on the way Irma and Siiri told him about Akseli Gallen-Kallela's group portrait of the Symposium, and how Gallen-Kallela had used a turnip as a stand-in for Oskar Merikanto. Mika didn't want any fare for the journey but Irma thought he should have some money and made him take a fifty-euro note.

'How many of those fifty-euro notes do you have?' Siiri asked when they got to their apartments and started digging through their handbags for their keys.

'That was my last one,' Irma said, unconcerned. 'But I can get more of them from the hole in the wall if I haven't lost my PIN. And when they run out, I can just have a little slightly spoiled liver casserole for dinner. What a fun day!'

Chapter 12

Siiri Kettunen, wearing nothing but her polka-dot night-gown, was on her way to Irma's apartment for some crumb cake when she noticed a package on top of her postbox. Instead of letter boxes in their doors, like in a real apartment block, everyone at Sunset Grove had a large postbox in the hallway outside their apartment for receiving packages. Head Nurse Virpi Hiukkanen had explained that this, too, was done to promote safety and respect for privacy. Siiri was surprised by the package. She never got letters, or even post-cards. Just junk mail. Besides, it was only 9 a.m., and the post wasn't delivered this early. She picked up the package and went to Irma's place.

'Don't open it,' Irma said. She hadn't got dressed yet, either. She was sitting in her rose-printed armchair in her dressing gown, reading the newspaper. She looked at the package suspiciously. 'It doesn't even have the sender's name on it.'

She was right. In fact, even Siiri's name wasn't on it, so it was impossible to know if it was meant for her. What if someone had just set it down on her postbox and forgotten it? Or maybe it was from someone at Sunset Grove?

'Aha! What if you have an admirer?' Irma said excitedly, throwing the newspaper on the floor. 'Who could it be, now that Reino is in the closed unit? He always did try to flatter you, "The prettiest girl at Sunset Grove".'

'Don't talk nonsense!'

'Maybe your admirer is Margit Partanen's husband,' Irma continued. She thought it was fun to think about these silly sorts of things. 'Margit is so gruff all the time, and her husband is clearly very virile; we can hear that every afternoon in the hallway. He was looking at you an awful lot at Tero's funeral.'

Then she got up to boil some water and put some pea soup in the microwave and took a slightly eaten chocolate cake, left over from the day before when one of her darlings had come to visit, out of the refrigerator. Siiri thought it was odd that her darlings never invited her to their houses, or out to a restaurant, but instead always came to eat at Irma's table as if they were still little children. The cake and soup went exceptionally well with the instant coffee.

'Caaake,' Irma corrected her. 'Caaake and pea soup is what it is. Will you have some red wine?'

Siiri reminded her that it was only nine o'clock in the morning, but Irma didn't believe her, and poured herself a full glass.

'How could you get post if it's only nine in the morning?'

Siiri had to explain the whole thing again: the package

didn't even have any stamps on it. It hadn't come through the post.

'Right,' Irma said, taking a great gulp of wine. 'Wine and caaake, sure is good. Trust me, that package is from Margit's husband. What's in it? Why don't you open it? Maybe there's underwear in it.'

'Are you crazy?' Siiri puffed, and pointed out that Irma had just told her not to open it. Irma wasn't having a very good morning. Siiri decided to take the box down to the main office, because it was without doubt a suspicious package.

'I just finessed it!' Irma said in the middle of a slurp of her pea soup. Then she grimaced – red wine and pea soup from a silver spoon didn't really go well together. 'It's from Erkki Hiukkanen. He's apologizing for surprising me without my clothes on the other morning. I don't dare to sleep in the nude any more, even though I think it's wonderful. Do you know I wear a pair of silk pyjamas to bed now because of him?'

'But Irma, the package was on my postbox,' Siiri said, beginning to feel the conversation was hopeless.

Irma started to wonder whether Erkki could have got their postboxes mixed up, and whether it was late enough in the day for her to have the whisky her doctor had prescribed, because the wine tasted terrible. Maybe it had gone off. She must not be drinking enough red wine, since her large box of wine was spoiling before she could finish drinking it.

'I should tell the off-licence that they ought to make smaller boxes, for one person. The boxes are lighter to carry

Minna Lindgren

than bottles – even I can carry one all the way home from the store quite easily.'

Siiri left, taking the mysterious package with her to show the people in the office downstairs, and in the lift noticed that she was still wearing her nightgown. Irma had muddled her head. Or the package had. All of it. She went back up to her apartment, got dressed, and got ready to leave again. It all went very slowly, but she had plenty of time, always nothing but time. That was something you could buy nowadays. Her grandson's daughter's boyfriend had bought time for her on her tram card, so she never had to pay a fare. She looked for her cane but couldn't find it. Oh well, she could manage all right without it. She did remember to bring the package with her, just as she was about to close the door.

It was already lively downstairs. The Ambassador was playing cards with the Partanens, and even though Siiri didn't believe a word Irma had said, she did feel a bit uncomfortable in the Partanens' presence.

'What's the package?' the Ambassador asked.

'I don't know,' Siiri said, and looked at Margit Partanen's husband to see how he reacted. He didn't. He looked like he'd never seen Siiri before.

'Eino Partanen, agronomist,' he said, standing and extending his hand.

Actually, they'd never been officially introduced. New residents at Sunset Grove just gradually slipped in among the rest, and there were a lot of people there whom she knew nothing about. So maybe Margit's husband wasn't as confused as he seemed. Siiri introduced herself, without

94

mentioning her former profession, but before they could shake hands Margit tugged her husband back into his chair and told him to be quiet.

'Why don't you open it?' the Ambassador asked, and Siiri explained that she was returning it. The Ambassador started to talk about all the packages he'd had to open in his exciting diplomatic career during the Cold-War years in the communist countries, but no one was listening. Margit was scolding her husband, who was trembling. Siiri wished them a good day and went to Director Sundström's office, where the candle was flickering again, apparently to give the place some atmosphere.

'Well, isn't this a surprise,' Sinikka Sundström said happily, and asked Siiri to sit down. 'How are you?'

'I got a package,' Siiri said. She thought it best to get straight to the point. There was no sense in burdening the director any more than was necessary. She already looked like she'd cried all night; her hair was mussed, her eyes were red. Siiri felt sorry for her. 'I think it was left by mistake. There's no name on it, not mine or the sender's. I thought you might find out what it is and who it belongs to.'

Sinikka Sundström looked at the package in horror. She didn't dare even touch it. She probably thought it was a bomb. Siiri turned the package over in her hands and smiled so the director would understand that there was no assassination attempt going on. She hoped it would help.

'Should I take it to someone else? Perhaps to Pertti Sundström in Quality Control? Or is this Erkki Hiukkanen's job?'

A look of relief spread over Director Sundström's face. She grabbed the phone and asked Virpi Hiukkanen to come to her office. A moment later the head nurse was standing in front of the file shelf with gum in her mouth, not saying a word. Siiri suspected she was a former smoker. There was no other reason for a grown person to be constantly chewing gum the way she did.

'Could you help our dear Siiri? She has a package that there's some confusion about,' Sundström said, shooing Siiri and Virpi out of the room and patting them both on the shoulder to calm herself down.

'Have a good day! Bye-bye now!'

Virpi Hiukkanen didn't even look at Siiri, she just strode swiftly to her own office. Siiri ran after her. When she'd got inside, Virpi slammed the door, put her gum in a cup on the desk, and snatched the package from her.

'Where did you get this? Why did you bring this to Director Sundström? Just what are you insinuating?'

Then she took a breath, flipped her thin hair, and tried to begin again, more calmly. 'One of the founding principles of Sunset Grove is safety, and respect for privacy,' she said, as if listing these principles was a mantra for tranquillity. But the mantra didn't work. In a moment she was worked up again, unable even to sit down. She stalked back and forth, shouting so loudly that the deafest and most demented residents couldn't fail to hear her.

'Who brought you this package? Who was it, and when? Did you open it? It's no use trying to look like you don't know anything. Don't think I don't know you. You're going to tell me everything you know about this package. Everything! Tell me who you got it from! Or did you put it there yourself? Where did you put it?'

It would have been good to have Irma there. Only Irma could have stood up to Virpi Hiukkanen's blind fury. Siiri started to ponder how Irma would have said that they provided more privation than privacy, but then she felt weak and her eyes grew dim.

'Can you help me?' she said, leaning against the desk, but Virpi didn't stop.

'Don't play invalid. Who gave you this package? Tell me the truth!'

'I feel dizzy,' Siiri managed to say, before falling to the floor. There was a loud thud. Siiri was a smallish woman, but on her way down she pulled a chair and part of a pile of papers with her.

When Siiri came to there was no one else in the head nurse's office. She had no idea how long she'd been lying on the floor with her sweater up around her ears. She was embarrassed and tried to get up, but she couldn't manage it the way she usually could. She had to wait a moment. She moved her eyes around. They seemed to be working normally. It was completely silent except that she could hear a hiss and hum in her head, but that was normal at her age. She wiggled her feet warily. They both moved, and felt like they were in one piece. She lifted her arms. Her right arm hurt a little, and so did her side. She was just about to sit up when Virpi Hiukkanen's phone rang. Virpi rushed in to answer it.

'Are you still here?' Virpi said, stepping over her. The

phone call was brief. Virpi just said, 'I have it. I'll call you back.'

Then she hung up and stepped over Siiri again, so that Siiri could see her black slip under her skirt. She marvelled that anyone still wore slips nowadays. They were so impractical.

'Can someone come and help me?' Siiri called to the hallway, and a young resident nurse came in and seemed not to wonder at all why Siiri Kettunen was lying on the floor in the head nurse's office. She helped Siiri up without a word, fumbling awkwardly, and took her by the elbow to the lift. Siiri couldn't believe that a nurse wouldn't know how to lead someone gently, without hurting them. What were they teaching them in nursing school?

'I'm sorry. I'm a little scared,' the girl said. 'I've never met any old people before. We practised on dolls.'

'Don't you have a grandmother?' Siiri asked in astonishment, pulling herself out of the girl's vice grip.

'My grandma's sixty-seven. Not terribly old.'

'Unlike me! You could be my great-grandchild. Shall I adopt you?'

Now the girl laughed. Siiri suggested that she always offer her arm to someone she was helping somewhere, and not grab them. Then they walked side by side to the lift and Siiri said she would be all right the rest of the way on her own, because she did feel quite strong compared to the timid girl.

'What happened to you?' the girl asked nervously.

'I think I had an attack of arrhythmia,' Siiri said, but the girl didn't believe her because she thought arrhythmia was a life-threatening condition, and Siiri was fine.

'You just had a fainting spell. These things happen at your age. That's what they told us. It's quite normal. Remember to drink plenty of water every day.'

The lift had arrived. The frail child-nurse gave her a sprightly wave and walked away with such speed that her ponytail bounced perkily from side to side. Siiri liked her. She would be a good nurse one day.

Siiri stood alone in the lift and thought about all the things in her life that had been normal: growing pains when she was young, menstrual cramps, the fear of pregnancy and giving birth, the tiredness of middle age, the listlessness, sleeplessness, headaches, the aches and pains of old age, the twinges, the stiffness, the hum in her head and buzzing in her ears, and now this arrhythmia. But not death. She started to feel weak again. Her head throbbed. She leaned against the lift wall and held on to the rail with both hands. She looked in the mirror at a shockingly pale old woman – herself.

'*Döden, döden, döden*,' she said to the monster in the mirror, and walked slowly to her apartment. At the door she realized she'd left the mysterious package in the head nurse's office, and decided that was where it really belonged.

'How lovely to have no responsibilities and to be able to take a catnap whenever you like,' she said out loud to herself as she settled on the bed, sighed, and closed her eyes. This is how she would look when she died, hopefully. Happy are they who die in their sleep.

Chapter 13

'What package?' Irma said, sitting at dinner in Siiri's apartment. Siiri had warmed up some blood pancakes – another item that was often on sale at Low Price Market. A pack of blood pancakes was a lot of food for two people, and they were delicious with lingonberry jam.

Irma had also had a nap, which was good because as she had been drinking whisky and red wine since her morning coffee there was no telling what state she'd be in otherwise. As it was she didn't remember what had happened that very morning. Siiri explained it all again. When she got to the part about Virpi Hiukkanen and the attack of arrhythmia, Irma got very angry. She thought that it was downright shameful that there were people working in a retirement home who didn't have the least bit of interest in the well-being of others.

'It's against the law to leave an old woman who's fainted lying on the floor!' she said, her voice so high that it sounded like she was singing. 'Telling you there's nothing to worry about!'

'I doubt there's a law about it,' Siiri said, trying to calm her, but she wouldn't be calmed.

'There must be some law to promote the safety of the elderly. After all, there are laws about letting your pigs out. I read in the paper that you have to let your pigs go outside every day now, and if they're not used to it their feet get messed up from the constant outings. I thought it was quite funny.' She laughed happily, then blew her nose in her lace handkerchief and thought for a moment. 'If they could train old people to find truffles, it would kill two birds with one stone. Two houseflies with one swat. By which I mean flouse-lies. The old people and the pigs could go out in the woods together – and they would find truffles, too. That's three flouse-lies! I've heard that nowadays people can't tell a chanterelle from an agaric. Is a truffle a mushroom?'

Siiri didn't know, so Irma continued mumbling. She and her husband had once bought truffles in Prague. They were sold by weight, and the vendor shaved off tiny slices onto a postal scale. She sighed, missing her husband for a moment, then roused herself when she remembered what they'd been talking about.

'We have to file a complaint against Virpi Hiukkanen. I'm going to do it right now. Do you have a pen and paper?'

Before Siiri could answer, Irma was rummaging through Siiri's kitchen drawers. She found some old photographs.

'Who's this beautiful woman?' Irma asked, looking at a picture of Siiri in her Women's Auxiliary uniform.

Siiri got her a pen and paper and wondered where a person could possibly send such a complaint.

'There has to be some place,' Irma said decisively, and announced that she was going to write to the retirement home's board of directors. 'There must be a board of directors. I can't imagine that Director Sundström's husband is in charge of the whole thing.'

She sat down at the table to write, now and then asking Siiri a question she couldn't answer.

'How long were you unconscious? Did Virpi blame the package on you? Did you ask for help before you passed out? Has your arrhythmia been diagnosed?'

In the end the complaint was very no-nonsense. Siiri was proud of Irma, and grateful, because Irma was right, after all, that they shouldn't treat a sick person that way in a retirement home. Or anywhere, really.

'If a woman was lying unconscious on the pavement, would you just step over her?' Irma asked, looking Siiri in the eye with the heat of righteous indignation.

They were certain that the governing body of Sunset Grove would intervene in matters such as this. They found the Sunset Grove information pack in its blue folder on Siiri's bookshelf, the one that was sent to everyone in the facility. It said that Sunset Grove was owned by the Loving Care Foundation, which was governed by a board made up of four people they'd never heard of, and Virpi Hiukkanen.

'How can she be her own boss?' Irma said with puzzlement.

They decided to write four letters of complaint and send them to each of the other members of the board individually. Siiri still had stamps and envelopes from last year's Christmas cards.

'Christmas stamps? Are you sure these will work?' Irma said, but the stamps were marked first class, so they must be acceptable, even if they did have elves on them. It was quite a lot of work writing the same letter three more times, but Siiri made some instant coffee and got the red wine out of the cleaning cupboard, and Irma was able to carry on.

'Elderly person left unaided,' was the title of the complaint. It told what had happened, and when and where, and finished by demanding prompt resolution of the matter and an apology at the very least. Siiri wasn't sure about the apology, because the idea of Virpi Hiukkanen coming to her and asking forgiveness was repellent to her. Virpi wouldn't be sincerely sorry, and besides, she might hug her to show her regret. That would be even more horrible than Sinikka Sundström's constant hugging, because Virpi was a hard, bony woman. It seemed strange to hug all the time instead of shaking hands. Even Siiri's son, the one who died from obesity, was always hugging everybody, even though he could hardly get his arms around his own belly. And he had been such a sweet baby! Siiri could never forget how he sat up in his white pram, smiling, always smiling. Even when he did cry occasionally, he never yelled. The big tears would just roll down his cheeks, but he would be quiet, and look like an angel.

'I believe in forgiving. The new testament is much better than the old one,' Irma said, but she dropped the subject because she knew that Siiri wasn't interested in that sort of thing. Then they went straight out to post the letters. Irma suggested, to Siiri's great surprise, that they should take a tram into the city.

'You can't leave letters like this in the retirement home postbox. Virpi might take them and read them. I don't trust that woman at all, or her husband.'

In the post office by the railway station they couldn't find the box to put the letters in, although they found all kinds of other useless things, like elf dolls, coffee cups, aprons and key rings.

'Can you drop a letter off here, like you could at the post office in the old days?' Irma asked a cashier sitting behind a display of chocolate bars and reflector tags.

'Certainly, you can drop them off right here,' was the answer.

They left the four letters with the young cashier, looked around a little, and argued over whether or not this was still the main post office. Was it possible that the same architect built the post office and the Olympic Swimming Stadium? Was the main post office any faster than the other branches, and was a main post office even necessary at all? Why in the world didn't they move the main post office to Pasila, since the main library was there now? Then they noticed that there was a library in the post office, and went in to read the newspapers. But there was nothing interesting in the newspapers, just politicians so young they seemed like mere children throwing tantrums, interviews with celebrities they'd never heard of. There were also several letters to the editor about poor care for the elderly. So Siiri talked Irma into taking another tram journey, on the number 6. But of course first they had to travel for one stop on the number 10, which Irma didn't like the smell of.

'This smell must be the myrrh that they sing about at the Christmas concerts,' she said, and sang a bit of the star boys' song in falsetto. 'And they hastened to offer him precious gifts, gold, frankincense, and myyyyrrh. And myyyyrrh.'

Siiri was happy that Irma was in a good mood, and sang along without embarrassment. There were so many bizarre people on the tram that two singing grannies fitted right in. She knew that on a sunny day like today, Irma loved going down Bulevardi, the turnaround at the Hietalahti flea market and then the route around the block along the seashore.

Irma spoke of her admiration of the old buildings on Bulevardi, which were a bit too imposing for Siiri's tastes. Simple structures pleased her more, and there were only a few of those on Bulevardi. One of them had such wonderful broad balconies.

'You mean that dirty green functionalist thing? But it's so dreary!' Irma exclaimed, then sighed when she saw the old red opera house. She hummed the Cherubino aria until they got to the market square. She thought the Helsinki College of Technology was finer than the presidential palace, and wondered why the president's official residence was called a palace, when it was just an ordinary building.

'Oh, no!' Irma cried. 'Have they turned the Hietalahti market square into a car park, too?'

'Yes. And they don't sell food in the market hall any more, just antiques.'

'Have you noticed how silly antiques have got? Perfectly ordinary dishes and stools sold as antiques. But I love Wenzel Hagelstam's antique show. I hope they never take that off the air. I'd call up and complain. But they probably have a different host now. Such a pity.'

Irma talked the whole way there and back. They switched from the number 6 to the 10 again, and then to the number 4, at the stop by the old tram halls. Irma admired the tram halls so much that there was almost no end to her praise. Earlier she had criticized – unnecessarily loudly – the dirty walls of the old conference centre and the trashy black make-up that two girls were wearing. Luckily the girls had earphones in and were listening to loud rock so they didn't hear Irma's criticism.

As they passed the school of nursing, Irma was quiet for a moment. She looked at Siiri and said: 'I'm sorry – who are you?'

Siiri didn't understand what she meant, and said she was a home-care nurse and a close relative of Napoleon, but Irma didn't laugh at all, she just looked distressed and asked where they were taking her.

'Home, Irma,' Siiri said, and felt with a painful clarity her heart beating out a poor rhythm. She started to sweat. In her panic she took hold of Irma's hand and tried to sound calm. 'I'm your good friend Siiri Kettunen, and I'm taking you back to our home at Sunset Grove.'

'"Grove of Tuoni, grove of night",' Irma answered, from the Sibelius dirge, and a smile returned to her eyes. '*Döden, döden, döden.*'

She was herself again, and resumed blurting out whatever came into her head. Siiri wasn't listening any more, she was wondering with horror if Irma's unexpected moment of confusion was a normal part of ageing, the kind of thing that happens to everyone, or if it was something that she should be worried about. And how would she know if that sort of thing started happening to her?

Chapter 14

Irma and Anna-Liisa made Siiri go to the doctor. They thought her dizzy spells were far from harmless and ought to be looked at. Siiri thought it was unnecessary. Even if the doctor did find a heart defect, she would just feel relieved. She'd rather die of a heart defect than cancer or Alzheimer's disease. And under no circumstances would she agree to any sort of procedure in the hopes of spending her one hundredth birthday at Sunset Grove and getting a rose and a hug from Sinikka Sundström. That's what they did there when some poor soul reached that advanced age. Last week one utterly muddle-headed hundred-year-old was caked and flowered even though nobody there even knew her name; neither the residents nor the nurses – nor even the woman herself.

But Irma had become very suspicious about everything and she thought that Virpi Hiukkanen was meddling in some way in all the residents' affairs, including their health.

'You should get an advocate,' she told Siiri. 'Senile old ladies whose relatives aren't up on the situation are fair game at Sunset Grove. If Virpi says that you have dementia, your

daughter will believe her. After all, she lives in a convent on
the other side of the world. Do they even have telephones
there? An elder-care advocate can look out for your in-
terests. It said in the paper that every old person should have
one.'

'Do you mean you think I should be put under guardianship?'

Siiri was a little offended, although she tried not to take
Irma's talk too seriously, since Irma herself was often confused. She also remembered reading that paranoia was a
part of Alzheimer's, and was distressed at Irma's increasing
symptoms of dementia. But Irma was hard-headed and
wouldn't back down about the doctor. She thought their
complaint about the neglect of the elderly needed a doctor's
report on Siiri's arrhythmia, otherwise no one would believe
their story. She made her case quite persuasively and Siiri
found herself wondering how she'd become so well-versed
in filing complaints.

'Oh, I've filed them before,' Irma said. 'Two complaints
to the Uudenmaan County Administrative Board. But they
have a new name nowadays, since they're probably going
to abolish the counties. How can you abolish something like
that? Imagine if one day they announced that the county of
Savo no longer existed. That would be pretty funny.'

Siiri was surprised about the complaints to the county
board because Irma had never mentioned them before. Irma
said she had complained about an unnecessary billing and
about the constant changes in the nursing staff too.

'They've got new girls every week in this place. The

newest ones can't even speak Finnish. And besides, the place is completely understaffed so they're overworked, with one girl having to be in ten places at once,' Irma said, then a sudden odd instinct told her the new name of the Uudenmaa County Administrative Board. 'The ETE Centre, that's what it's called! Now there's a meaningless name. What genius thought that up?'

Complaining to various 'centres' seemed to be mostly a waste of time. Irma wasn't the only one who had complained about Sunset Grove. The fat woman in A wing had complained that they were giving her insulin shots in a completely random fashion, but she died before she received a reply. And blind Mrs Kukkonen had complained because she didn't get food every day, and when she did, it was always cold.

'This boy would just come in and slam a box on the table and leave a blind woman sitting there alone. And now Mrs Kukkonen has dementia and is shut up in the closed unit,' Irma said. She said that if a complaint reached its destination before the sender died or was rendered senile, the ETE centre or some other centre sent a friendly-looking lady inspector to have a cup of coffee with Sinikka Sundström.

'Always the same woman – Ritva Niemistö! Look at that, I even remember her name. Then she writes a report that says the procedures at Sunset Grove are exemplary. They have her reports pasted up on the wall of the lift, have you noticed?'

Siiri had, in fact, sometimes seen the sticker there, never guessing that it was a report generated by a complaint from

Irma. Her friend was a lot sharper than she appeared to be. Maybe these occasional spells of confusion were pure theatre – you never knew with Irma. And so Siiri promised to go to the doctor. She got an appointment surprisingly quickly, just two weeks away, when she told the appointment girl that it was a case of a ninety-four-year-old woman with a heart defect.

'As if it were an urgent matter!' she told Irma with a laugh.

Chapter 15

At the Health Clinic, Siiri Kettunen once more found a new 'personal physician' waiting for her. The doctor was so young that Siiri was moved to ask whether a little girl like her could be a real doctor at all, but that was a mistake. By the time she remembered that there had been a series of articles in the paper about fake doctors, the girl doctor had already taken offence.

'Shall we get straight to business?' the unknown personal physician said, after a brief lecture. She ordered Siiri to take off her blouse, then listened to her lungs with an ice-cold stethoscope that almost stopped her heart, and wrote a referral to Meilahti Hospital for urgent tests. Apparently, the stethoscope was an instrument that gave the doctor a sense of certainty, the way a blood-pressure cuff does a nurse.

'I can order an ambulance,' the doctor said, but that was a bit much, in Siiri's opinion, so she thanked her politely for listening to her lungs and promised to catch the very next tram to the hospital.

*

When Siiri got to Meilahti, she waited for two and a half hours. She read some Donald Duck comics, solved seven sudokus, and learned two long articles from last year's Health News by heart – one about sea buckthorn oil and another about dry mucous membranes – before she went in for her urgent tests. The handsome specialist figured out what Siiri already knew: she had a heart arrhythmia. He spoke in a strained voice and wanted Siiri to have more tests and have a pacemaker installed to reset her rhythm.

'What rhythm will I be set for? I hope it's not a waltz, although there is a song about a waltzing heart. It would be hard to use two feet to walk in threes.' She was trying to lighten the mood, but this doctor was very serious.

'Generator node and electrical impulse pathways, at which point the sinoatrial node and frequency limit, respectively . . . in which case, an elective surgery or micro-process, perhaps also a telemetry device – all in all a nearly risk-free procedure.'

Siiri listened for a while and then said that she was ninety-four years old and they weren't going to make her live any longer by installing some gadget inside her.

'This is a very small operation that's done under local anaesthetic. The pacemaker is placed under the skin and the electrodes are threaded through a vein to the heart. It will remove the unpleasant symptoms and increase your quality of life,' the doctor said.

'Are you sure about that?' Siiri asked. 'What kinds of things do you think would give an old person's life quality?'

'Well . . . studies show that, for the aged . . . after all, good health is the first step to a quality life. An untreated heart arrhythmia can be life threatening.'

'You mean that, in the worst-case scenario, I could die?' Siiri said, feeling very brisk and strong. 'You're still a young person, so maybe you don't know that getting old is mostly unpleasant. Days pass slowly and nothing happens. Your friends and relatives are dead and gone, and your food has no flavour. There's nothing worth watching on television and your eyes get tired when you read. You feel sleepy, but sleep doesn't come, so you end up lying awake all night and dozing off all day. You feel all kinds of aches and pains, constantly – small pains, but still. Even the most ordinary tasks become slow and difficult. Like cutting your toenails. You can hardly imagine. It's a huge, all-day operation that you do almost anything to put off.'

The doctor glanced nervously at his watch and promised to write Siiri a referral for a pedicure, for which she could request state health compensation. He turned his back to her and became absorbed in his computer screen.

'As far as the pacemaker is concerned, studies show that these small matters affecting health can be crucially important in increasing well-being, not to mention the fact that a pacemaker would go a long way to increasing the length of your life. According to Current Care Guidelines—'

'In that case, the answer is clear,' Siiri interrupted with relief. 'Install the pacemaker in someone younger, some fat person who makes the mistake of thinking he's fit enough to go for a run and gives himself a coronary. Even my sons have died. And Reino's son. And a lot of other people too.

We old people can't seem to die from anything, even if we want to. Sometimes at the nursing home we talk about how you doctors don't seem to understand that death is a natural thing. Life ends in death, and there's no sense in offering longer life to someone my age and denying me sugar for my coffee. It isn't a failure of medicine when people eventually die of old age.'

The doctor turned around and looked at her in surprise. 'But you're a lively person in good health. Why in the world should you die? Current Care Guidelines—'

'Because everybody has to die,' Siiri said. She squeezed the doctor's muscular hands, holding them in her own wrinkled ones, so that he would understand that guidelines and studies and pacemakers can't change this fact about the world.

'One day you'll die, too. And I hope that you'll be old enough then to know what dying is, and not fight it. Maybe you'll even be waiting for it, like me and my friends at Sunset Grove. Even if you put pacemakers in all of us, you won't change our everyday lives one bit. So I thank you, from the bottom of my heart. I need your report and I'm grateful that you're writing it. May I have two copies of that paper? That's all I need from you, and I hope that you'll take care of young people who are too tired to work any more. The nurses at Sunset Grove are so overworked that we're practically left alone there.'

The doctor looked distressed. He tugged his hands forcefully out of Siiri's well-intentioned grip, rushed to the sink, disinfected them, tightened his tie, straightened his doctor's coat, and sat back down in his chair to stare at the computer screen as if the machine actually knew something and would give him the solution to this dilemma. Then he straightened up, picked up his Dictaphone, and started to murmur into it, glancing now and then at Siiri.

'. . . otherwise healthy for her age comma memory functional and the patient is alert full stop refuses pacemaker however full stop in respect for patient's wishes taking into account her advanced age full stop.' The doctor turned off the Dictaphone and asked her if she wanted some anti-depression medication in addition to the heart medicine.

'What for?' Siiri asked, sincerely surprised.

'They can help your . . . condition. You might regain your zest for life.'

Siiri got up. She had a mind to put the silly man straight about the hard facts of life and death, but she remembered her heart and its raggedy impulse pathways and took a deep breath before replying that she didn't need any of his peppity-pills. She didn't need them now and she hadn't needed them back when her husband died either. The doctor was persistent.

'Some sleep medication might be helpful. You said that you weren't sleeping at night, and there's no reason for that.' Siiri started to have the desperate feeling that she would never get out of there without a stack of prescriptions. There had been something in the papers about responsibility for outcomes, how it was becoming a problem for public-sector employees. Outcomes were measured in numbers, so child-protection services were considered more effective when more children were reported to state custody officials, and doctors apparently were only earning their salaries if they sent patients for surgery and wrote them a certain number of prescriptions. 'I'm just trying to help you and do my job as well as I possibly can,' the doctor said wearily.

Siiri realized she'd behaved badly. The doctor surely had enough work to do without her making more work for him. He had studied hard to be able to prescribe sleeping pills to old people, and what would happen if all his patients refused his pills and pacemakers? He had no need, at his age, to know what a ninety-year-old's life was like. It wasn't his fault that Siiri had lived to be too old. She thanked him for a job well done, left the hospital, and headed for the tram stop. It was such a beautiful early winter day that she decided to walk one stop further towards town just so that she could look at the imposing Aura Building, designed by Erkko Virkkunen. It was still handsome even though they had ruined the window frames a long time ago when they renovated it.

Chapter 16

Irma and Siiri decided to tell Anna-Liisa about Mika Korhonen, the taxi driver. They thought it was peculiar that Mika had been so friendly, even promised to visit, and then they hadn't heard anything from him. Anna-Liisa's logical way of thinking was bound to be a help in such a situation. But when they went to the card table in the common room Anna-Liisa was playing double solitaire with the Ambassador and it was a long time before the Ambassador got the hint that he should leave. The poor man was terribly starved for company now that Reino was shut up in the closed unit. Only one of the Ambassador's children was still alive, and he lived in another country. Irma thought it was as clear as day that because he had dragged his family all over the world his children hadn't put down any roots in Finland and that was why they had ended up living abroad. The three women promised to play cards with the Ambassador another time if he went to the auditorium to listen to a presentation on 'Loneliness in the Everyday Life of the Aged'.

'He has homophobia,' Anna-Liisa said when Siiri and Irma had told her about Mika Korhonen.

'He looked healthy enough,' Irma said.

'I think the word he used was mafia, not phobia,' Siiri said. She was trying to keep the conversation focused. They'd got so excited that they'd been talking and stumbling over each other's words and forgetting the essentials, making the whole story even more confused.

Anna-Liisa used this opportunity to exercise her lecturer's skills with a brief overview of changes in the meanings of foreign words borrowed into Finnish, of which mafia was, in her opinion, an excellent example, since Mika Korhonen hardly meant to claim that there was actual organized crime at Sunset Grove.

'I think that's exactly what he was saying,' Siiri said emphatically, having got her thoughts back on track. But Irma was muddle-headed.

'My daughter's son is gay and he's a terribly pleasant chap, and so is his boyfriend. They always bring me cake when they come to visit, and they actually come quite often. And they have a little brown dog they've adopted.'

'You don't adopt dogs,' Anna-Liisa said, shooting down Irma's flight of fancy.

'It was one of those orphan dogs. They went by plane to Spain, and my grandson and his boyfriend had to fill out a lot of forms and applications to get to be the dog's "parents". They bring the dog with them everywhere they go. It's been to my place several times and I always give it liver casserole, but they don't like that because they feed it fresh pork liver from the market hall. A stray dog!'

Irma laughed happily and Siiri started to feel nervous

because Anna-Liisa seemed more interested in Irma's grand-son's dog than she was in Mika Korhonen. Then Siiri remembered what Mika had told them about Pasi, the social worker. Mika had said that Pasi was well known to the police.

'Is that what he said?' Anna-Liisa said. 'Did he mean that Pasi is a criminal, like this Mika of yours, or that he co-operates with the police?'

'Hmm. That I don't know. Pasi is somehow connected to the fact that Tero was held for questioning. And that's where Tero died – in his jail cell. Does that make sense?' Siiri felt unpleasantly shaky, and Anna-Liisa's sharp interrogational style wasn't helping. 'As I recall, he said that Sinikka Sund-ström tried to appease the police by giving Pasi the sack. At least, I think that's what he said.'

'I'm sorry, who's Sinikka Sundström?' Irma asked.

Siiri's head spun like someone had struck her. She looked frantically at Anna-Liisa, who didn't flinch in the slightest, just calmly explained who they were talking about, without teasing or taunting Irma, which was unusual for Anna-Liisa. She had obviously noticed the same thing as Siiri: Irma was having more and more frequent moments of confusion. Once she'd calmed Irma down, Anna-Liisa turned firmly back to Siiri and urged her to get in touch with Mika Kor-honen soon, because surely he was a man who could help them.

'But we don't have his telephone number!' Siiri shouted, horrified. How could they have been so stupid? And how could Mika have been so absent-minded? Or was it that he really was a criminal and was only trying to get useful information out of them? What if he'd made the whole thing up?

'Calm down,' Anna-Liisa said, in the stern tone she had perfected through years of addressing rambunctious pre-adolescents. 'He couldn't have made the whole thing up, because he knew a lot of things that are true. And if he is a criminal, we'll have to intervene in his activities.'

She was right, of course. Siiri admired her courage. Anna-Liisa seemed positively thrilled at the possibility of investigating organized crime at Sunset Grove. But there had to be at least ten Mika Korhonens in Helsinki alone, and they didn't even know where he lived. Should they just go through the phone book and call every Mika Korhonen?

All this guesswork was making Siiri feel like she should have had a career as a detective. But it was exhausting just investigating the mysteries at Sunset Grove. Thank goodness she hadn't had to do it for her whole life. She might not have lived so long otherwise.

'People don't put their phone numbers in the phone book any more. You have to look up addresses and phone numbers on the Internet. Or you could look for him on Facebook,' Anna-Liisa said, pronouncing the exotic word with a lilt, as if it were Italian.

'What if we just started taking taxis?' Siiri suggested. 'Maybe one day we would get Mika for a driver.'

She hoped this suggestion would bring Irma back to earth, but Irma was fast asleep in the uncomfortable institutional chair, her head hanging awkwardly, her purple handbag fallen to the floor. She was so quiet that for a moment they thought she had died. Then she breathed, thank heavens, but she wouldn't wake up, even when Anna-Liisa gave her a sharp flick on the back of the hand.

Chapter 17

A couple of weeks after her doctor's visit, Siiri received a report about her heart arrhythmia, two prescriptions, and a complete explanation of why this ninety-four-year-old, alert patient was not having a pacemaker installed. She particularly liked the phrase: 'seems rational for her age'. The doctor had sent two copies of the report, which was very kind of him. Siiri went to find Irma to show her – not exactly a bill of health, but at least she was rational. The weight of an expert's opinion would surely speed up the handling of their complaint to the Loving Care Foundation.

But Irma didn't answer her door. Siiri knew that Irma was in her apartment because she could hear Mozart's piano concerto blaring much too loudly. Luckily, they had given each other spare keys. You never knew what might happen if you left your handbag somewhere or accidentally closed the door when you went out to get the post in your nightgown. Erkki Hiukkanen charged twenty-five euros to open a locked door, and they refused to pay that lazy caretaker such exorbitant fees. Virpi and Erkki Hiukkanen lived on the top floor of Sunset Grove in a large apartment, so it couldn't have been any great inconvenience to come and open an old woman's door. Many of the residents walked around with their keys around their necks like 1970s schoolchildren, including Anna-Liisa, but Siiri thought that a grown woman should keep her keys in her handbag, which she now remembered she had left at home on her kitchen table. So she didn't have her own keys with her, let alone Irma's. There was nothing for it but to pound on Irma's door with her fist and crow loudly. She had to pound for a long time, and kick, too, before there was a pause in the music and Irma came to the door.

'What in the world is all that racket? Have you gone out of your mind?'

Siiri explained the situation with some embarrassment, and Irma offered to make them some instant coffee and dug some ice creams out of the freezer. Siiri sat in Irma's old flowered armchair and told her about the doctor's report and her hope that it would help with their complaint.

'What complaint do you mean?' Irma asked, and Siiri had an uncomfortable feeling. Her hands started to shake and she tried to shove the papers back in the envelope. They got all crumpled and she didn't know where to put them. Irma's table was a jumble of objects, including all sorts of folders, which was odd because her home was usually very tidy. Irma contentedly ate her cloudberry jam ice cream and looked at Siiri in wonder, but didn't say anything.

'Do you ever worry about your memory?' Siiri said, finally finding the courage to bring up the subject after having rehearsed several times. She had to know whether Irma herself realized that she was sometimes very confused. They had always been honest with each other about everything, so she ought to be able to talk about this, too.

'Oh, don't be silly,' Irma said, waving her hand as if a swarm of flouse-lies were buzzing around her. 'Anyone can forget her handbag – even young people do it. What I'm starting to worry about is what Virpi Hiukkanen's up to. Because I think she's spying on me. Also, you're sitting in my spot.'

Siiri got up out of the armchair and moved obediently to the sofa. She remembered how they had often laughed at Irma's husband, who'd had a sacred armchair and a place at the dining table and didn't scruple to show his annoyance if some unwitting soul accidentally sat there. The yellow light of the lamp cast a strange glow on Irma's face and she spoke in a quiet voice, glancing around uncertainly. She said she'd pulled the plugs on the surveillance cameras and even taken her telephone off the wall, because the people downstairs were listening in on her phone calls. She also claimed that some of her important papers had been stolen. That was why she had a pile of folders on the table.

'All of my health-related records were in a green folder, neatly arranged. And somebody's pinched them.'

Siiri started going through the files on the table. None of them were green, and she switched to thumbing through the ones on the bookshelf. Irma had almost a metre of books by Eeva Joenpelto, twice as many Moomin books, Isaac Singer, Astrid Lindgren, Selma Lagerlöf, and a few random newer books, all in alphabetical order by author, as well as two shelves of photo albums. When Siiri had finished going through the bookshelf, she looked through the pile of folders on the telephone table, but she didn't find any medical records or any green folders.

Irma ate another ice cream, then got up, opened the wardrobe door and rummaged for a time. After a moment she stuck her head out and said, 'Hey! What was it we were looking for?'

'What were we looking for!' Siiri snapped. 'We've spent half the day searching because you've got some silly idea in your head. As if anyone would want to steal your papers! What in the world was it that you needed this green folder for? Do you remember? Was it full of old recipes and doctors' notes?'

'Oh right, that. Boy, there's something strange going on. Several months ago I asked Virpi Hiukkanen if I could look at my own medical files and any other files concerning me, but she refused to give them to me. Don't you think that's odd? After all, I have a right to read what they write about me – doctors' reports and that sort of thing. Such strange things have been going on here lately that I'm starting to feel scared of the whole place.'

Perhaps the green folder had been stolen. Maybe there was something shady happening with Irma's files, probably false information about her, faked diagnoses. Irma was very agitated, and she stood there, blank-faced, holding two pairs of silk long johns in her hand. Siiri led her over to sit in her armchair, poured her a glass of red wine, put the long johns back in the wardrobe, and noticed that Irma had at least twenty identical pairs in boxes on the shelves.

Irma drank a large glass of red wine, almost in one gulp, and began to droop. Her speech was laboured, and Siiri couldn't make out what she said except that she wanted to go to sleep, although it was only three in the afternoon. She helped her to lie down on the bed and checked to make sure that she had taken her medicine. There was a pill box full of tablets on the bedside table. There seemed to be more pills than there had been on the day when Mika helped them count out the tablets at Restaurant Kämp. Irma had taken that day's first doses – one of each pill in the morning and one at noon. But why in the world did a ninety-five-year-old woman who was as healthy as a horse need so many pills?

Chapter 18

Siiri sat in her usual seat on the tram and tried to see behind Eira Hospital. That was where Villa Johanna was, a whimsical work by her favourite architect, Selim A. Lindqvist, which you could see from the number 3 as it turned onto Tehtaankatu. She had a habit of concentrating on one building and trying to think of as many other works in Helsinki by the same architect as she could. Selim A. Lindqvist was easy: there were two buildings of his, side by side, on Aleksanterinkatu – numbers 11 and 13.

The number 3B tram changed to the number 3T at Olympia Terminal, and Siiri decided to take it as far as the new opera house. Then she could get on the number 4 to get back to Sunset Grove. She had already ridden around for more than two hours, using any favourite tram route or building she could think of as an excuse to put off going back home, because the mere thought of Sunset Grove gave her a very unpleasant feeling. She didn't want to see Virpi Hiukkanen, she didn't want to think about Irma's confusion and growing suspiciousness, and she didn't know how to bring up all these worries with Anna-Liisa, who was always

128

so logical and business-like that she sometimes made Siiri feel stupid. And she still hadn't heard anything from Mika Korhonen.

A talkative little girl was sitting with her mother next to the ticket dispenser, wearing a funny-looking hat with bear ears on it.

'And that's why I think the boys are stupid, except for Oiva. But guess what, I want one of those Monster High dolls, but I want it now, and not as a Christmas present because it's boring to play with just one and I only have one. I want Draculaura. Can you remember that?'

The mother had her arms full of shopping bags. She looked worn out and wasn't paying any attention to the little girl. But the child didn't give up.

'Mama, why doesn't everybody have kids? Why doesn't Grandma have kids? Why, Mama?'

'Your grandma does have kids. Otherwise she couldn't be your grandma,' said a wino across the aisle. The little girl took an interest in this new acquaintance and got up to stand in the aisle, but her mother continued to stare at the rain hitting the window.

'My grandma is Grandpa's girlfriend and she's much younger than my mother, so she could have kids any time she wanted, but Mama wouldn't want her to. What are your children's names? Do you have a job? Why not? What do you do, then?'

'I sit in the park and ride on the tram.'

'Fun! I want to do that when I'm big!'

The tram made Siiri's beloved curve at Kamppi and the

passengers pricked up their ears to hear the wino's reaction to the little girl's future plans.

'What park do you go to?' the girl asked. 'I usually go to the one on Lapinlahdenkatu, but it's pretty small.'

'Me too. It's a nice park.'

'And Väiski, but only in the winter.'

'I sometimes go and sit on the rocks at Temppeliaukio. There's a nice view from there.'

'I've never been there. Does it have swings? Do you like to swing?'

At that point the girl's mother came to life, gathered her bags, stood up, and tugged the child behind her off the tram. The wino waved at the little girl and the reflectors on the child's dungarees glowed brightly. Siiri felt like waving, too, but she contented herself with watching the bear-eared child, to whom she was grateful, for the little creature had unwittingly brightened her day.

The rest of the trip to Mannerheimintie was reverently silent. Then the number 4 didn't come, although the sign-post said that she had only two minutes to wait. Siiri, tired of standing in the cold, got on the number 10, and almost fell asleep, the carriage was so still and quiet. At the old customs gate she started awake and was confused when the tram turned onto Tukholmankatu instead of going straight like the number 10 should have. To her relief the other passengers were as startled as she was.

'Isn't this the number ten?' a sensible-looking woman asked her.

'That's what I thought,' Siiri answered with a smile. 'Although this route suits me, since I live in Munkkiniemi.'

'I have to get to Tilkka,' the woman said worriedly. 'My shift is starting.'

'Are you a nurse? Isn't Tilkka a retirement home now?' Siiri asked with interest, but the tram stopped at the Aura building and the woman departed in a hurry.

The driver smiled in surprise. Siiri recognized him as the young man who listened to classical music while he drove, as he was doing now. She had talked with him several times before. She went up to him and asked whether something was amiss.

'Well, yeah, I accidentally went the wrong way. I was listening to Bruckner's seventh and forgot I was driving the number ten.'

'You shouldn't listen to the seventh when you're driving the number ten.'

'True, but Bruckner doesn't have a number ten, although he has ten symphonies. The first is symphony zero. Don't ask me why.'

'But what about Mahler? Doesn't he have a tenth symphony?'

'It's unfinished. Just like today's route.'

The driver contacted headquarters. Siiri always found it exciting when instructions and announcements came to the drivers somewhere out of the ether. They only happened occasionally, but sometimes the police were summoned to some designated tram stop to pick up an old person who had escaped from the hospital, at other times an accident necessitated an alternate route. When he'd received his instructions, the driver bent over his microphone.

'OK, passengers. There's been a mistake. I'm sorry,' he began. 'I'm going to have to drive to Munkkiniemi. Anyone who wants the number ten can get off here. There'll be one along there soon.'

Siiri was proud of the driver for openly admitting his mistake, which wasn't easy to do. He did make Munkkiniemi sound like some horrible place, though, where you would only go if you had no other alternative.

'Well, I don't, do I?' he said with a smile. Siiri stood next to him. The trip continued and Bruckner played. Luckily, the seventh symphony was so long that the music wouldn't end before they came to the end of the route.

'Yeah. Bruckner was quite a guy,' the driver said with a sigh.

Siiri thought at first that she would ride along with the driver all the way around the Munkkiniemi shore, just for moral support, but then she started to feel tired from standing there next to the door, and so she got off at her own stop.

'Enjoy the rest of the trip, and thanks for the refreshing company,' she said. 'I'm headed for the terminal.' She thought it was funny to call Sunset Grove the terminal. The driver laughed happily.

'Right! I just missed mine!'

Chapter 19

'What's the matter?' Siiri asked worriedly when Irma didn't want to read the paper, not even the obituaries. 'Are you sick?'

Every Sunday, after they'd drunk their instant coffee, Siiri and Irma would open the paper and Irma would say 'Any fun dead people?' Unfortunately, there were fewer and fewer fun dead people every day, since all the best ones had already died. If they didn't find anyone they knew in the obituaries, they would read the memorial columns aloud and try to decide what kind of people the week's dead had been. On a good Sunday they could spend a pleasant hour and a half at this, but today Irma didn't feel like even looking at the page.

'Irma, you're depressed. Have you stopped taking your peppity-pills?'

Irma didn't answer. She had fallen asleep in her chair. Siiri couldn't get her to wake up, or into a more comfortable position, no matter how she tried. She felt helpless and frustrated, and a sadness tinged with terror made her fidgety. She walked in a circle, moved objects around, and babbled to

Irma about all sorts of harmless things that she thought would perk her friend up, because she'd read in the paper that the last sense a person loses is their hearing.

'*Döden, döden, döden*,' she whispered at last into Irma's ear, before going back to her own apartment to finish reading the paper there.

But Irma wasn't dead. Siiri had hardly had time to look at the christening announcements when she heard a frenzied knocking on the other side of the wall. It was Irma, banging with Carl the Cane, calling for help. Siiri left the paper open on the table and hurried out. Her keys were in her handbag, but her handbag wasn't in its usual place by the door. She looked around for it randomly, starting to feel very nervous, until she spotted the handbag in the bathroom. What idiot had left it there?

Irma was still sitting in the chair, holding a rose-patterned pillow in her arms and rocking silently back and forth, humming to herself. The cane was tossed on the floor. Her eyes were glazed and something was dripping out of her mouth.

'What's wrong?' Siiri shouted, frightened.

'Thanks for coming. Are you new here? Why is everyone new here?'

Siiri didn't know what to say. It felt wrong to lie, and somehow unpleasant to tell Irma to her face how confused she was. But this was no time for reflection. The telephone was torn off the wall and she had to get Irma a nurse right away, whether Irma knew who she was or not.

'Can you get up?' Siiri asked, and started to tug Irma out of the chair. It wasn't easy. She didn't have a nurse's strength, or technique. After a bit of grunting and wrestling she got Irma moving and, little by little, they made their way to the lift and down towards the nurse's station. Throughout the whole operation they didn't say a word. Siiri didn't dare to and Irma didn't know how to, she just stared vacantly at her reflection in the lift mirror.

'Ah. Irma's confused again, is she?' Virpi said when they arrived at the nurse's station, as if they ran down there every day to report these little brain flukes. Virpi took Irma's blood pressure, flipped through some papers, then wrote something down, without looking at them.

'Can I have my medical records now?' Irma said suddenly. 'And while you're at it, you can give me back the green folder, the one you pinched from me. I know you have it.'

Virpi turned to look at Irma with a peculiar expression, almost as if she were savouring some victory. She adjusted her glasses, put her chewing gum in the cup on her desk, and made a call to someone, without giving them her name.

'Same symptoms,' she said into the phone, her eye on Irma. 'No, not aggressive this time, but confused and paranoid.'

'That is enough!' Siiri shouted before she had time to think about her ragged impulse pathways or anything else. 'Who are you telling lies to about Mrs Lännenleimu, saying that Irma's paranoid?'

Siiri directed all of her anger towards the head nurse – all her anxieties and growing outrage about Irma's gradual weakening, the increased number of pills, and the suspicious disappearance of the medical records. Virpi looked at her calmly, took out a syringe, and shoved her into the hallway. Irma had sunk back into her own world and was sitting limp in the chair, unaware of what was happening around her.

'We don't need any unauthorized persons causing a disturbance at the nursing station,' Virpi shrieked at Siiri as she shut the door in her face. Siiri staggered to the sofa in the common room to sit down. She felt weak and frightened. Her heart was beating too quickly, though in an even rhythm, and when she lifted her eyes from the top of the table she saw Virpi pushing Irma away in a wheelchair in a great hurry. Irma was slumped lifelessly, as if in a deep sleep. With tears in her eyes, Siiri tried to call after her, but she couldn't get any sound to come out of her mouth.

'Shall I deal the cards?' the Ambassador asked.

Siiri looked exhaustedly at the perpetually tie-wearing and smoking-jacketed old man, who peered back at her pleadingly, like a puppy. She couldn't bring herself to deny him a game of rummy. In fact, a game of cards seemed like the best idea she'd heard in a long time.

'. . . *neben, über, unter, vor, zwischen*. It looks it'll be a bleak Christmas this year. Hey, I got a pair!'

Siiri took her handkerchief out of her handbag, wiped away her tears, and wondered why she'd started crying so easily again these past few days.

Chapter 20

There wasn't much attention paid to Christmas at the retirement home. Unit Operations Manager Erkki Hiukkanen brought a sparse-limbed spruce tree into the common room, a preschool group came to sing Christmas carols, and they tried their best to make traditional straw ornaments in the craft club. Many of the residents went to visit relatives, but there were even more who spent the holiday at Sunset Grove.

Siiri often spent Christmas with her daughter's children, but this year they informed her well in advance that they were all going on safari in South Africa. Siiri was a bit hurt that they were all going somewhere together and she was no longer a part of the group. But even her daughter was no longer part of her own children's Christmas, since she'd moved into a French convent. And you couldn't have convinced Siiri to spend Christmas on the other side of the world, surrounded by who knew what kind of famine and disease, even if you'd shaken a stick at her.

So under the circumstances, and partly out of choice, Siiri had Christmas at Sunset Grove all to herself. She didn't give or receive any gifts. She honestly didn't need anything any more. The Hat Lady had tried to begin one of those horrible things where everyone gives a present to someone and they pass them all out in the common room with some man dressed up as Santa Claus.

What would have been the point? The gifts the Ambassador bought would have been too expensive and the ones from the Hat Lady too cheap. Director Sundström was the only one who tried to keep up the gift tradition at Sunset Grove, but this year even she had decided to let this lovely idea slip and passed out a memo well beforehand announcing that in lieu of flowers or sweets, the director would prefer a donation to her travel fund.

On Christmas Eve, Siiri slept late, brewed herself some real coffee, and read the newspaper from beginning to end. That easily took an hour. She listened to Christmas music on the radio and was glad to still have Yule Radio 1, which broadcast a proper Christmas programme, until the science programme began talking about stem-cell therapy and space satellites in honour of Christmas. She turned off the radio and looked at the clock: there were still two hours to wait until Christmas Eve dinner, celebrated on Christmas Eve in Finland, in the cafeteria downstairs. Right now they were holding a moment of devotion. After that it would be cake bingo, and she didn't want to participate in that either.

Most of the staff were on holiday, even Virpi and Erkki Hiukkanen, and, of course, the poor director, who'd had two weeks of sick leave before her official holiday, and was getting ready for a trip to India to rest her nerves, which were overtaxed by taking care of old people. There were more temporary staff than usual during the holiday season, mostly Muslim girls, who didn't mind working on Christmas, watching over this crowd of Christians as they sang hymns, ate ham and baked gingerbread.

Siiri had bought a little pre-cooked ham at Low Price Market and planned to carve bits of it for sandwiches when needed, and she wouldn't need anything more than that. She was halfway through Selma Lagerlöf's *Jerusalem* again, for the umpteenth time. It was what she felt like reading. She had put the red Christmas tablecloth from her childhood home on the table. It was much too big for the table the retirement home provided, but she folded it double and smoothed it carefully, and it looked pretty. She put two brass candlesticks over the red wine stains and lit the candles to create a mood. What kind of mood? What did Christmas really mean to her except the passage of time and another full year about to end? Were the last few Christmases she'd had among her last?

She remembered how her little brother Toivo had designed a mathematical equation for subjective time. He had drawn several parabolas to illustrate the fact that the very same year can be significantly longer in the life of a three-year-old than in the life of a ninety-year-old. And yet a child's life passed more quickly than an old person's. Or was it the other way around? Maybe an old person's time passed more quickly but was more tiresome, which sounded like a mercy, of course. Toivo had explained his calculations but she no longer remembered the details.

Toivo was dead now, as were her other siblings. And her husband and her two sons. And her cat. She had an unpleasant, powerful feeling of missing her husband, and all the people who had died. Her little boy, playing in the garden in his ragged clothes. Having Christmas all to herself no longer felt like a good idea. But what would help? She had to think of something to do. She tried doing the crossword, but she didn't recognize the people or things the clues were referring to: 'rap artist and TV presenter', 'minister's manfriend'. The sudoku was easier. After solving a couple of sudokus she felt a bit weak and so sliced some ham and made herself a sandwich and filled a milk tumbler with red wine.

'*Döden, döden, döden,*' she toasted to herself, and had an enjoyable cold Christmas dinner.

After all, it was lovely not to have to slave over a stove to make Christmas dinner for a large family, with no help at all. The herring, the casseroles and beetroot salad – phew! – the pies and gingerbread cakes. Even the ham had to be salted back then, and after that baked, and now she could just slice some nice ham, cooked by somebody else, onto a piece of bread.

She almost missed Irma even more than she did her own family. Siiri could no longer imagine her life without Irma's company. But she didn't know where Irma was. Virpi Hiukkanen had taken her somewhere in a wheelchair and she hadn't been heard from since.

Siiri had asked Virpi about Irma, but the head nurse had just snapped that the medical condition of residents was a private matter and could not be disclosed to anyone but next of kin. Which was true, of course. Siiri had tried several times to call Irma's daughter Tuula, but she hadn't been able to get hold of her and Siiri didn't know Irma's grandchildren well enough to be able to call them.

Irma had customarily spent Christmas with her family, and she always enjoyed having everyone together, and didn't seem to get upset if Christmas dinner ended up being Vietnamese dumplings and Moroccan stew. She didn't even complain about the fact that her darlings gave her goats, sheep and trees as Christmas gifts. They were cooperative-development donations, philanthropy. Irma never saw the gifts, but every Christmas she would laugh and tell Siiri how her herd of cows and grove of trees had grown.

'Who would have thought that a tenth-generation city girl could become a cowherd and forest ranger in her old age?'

Siiri hoped, tried to believe, that Irma was spending Christmas somewhere with her family right now. They must be at the summer house, the one on the lake shore at Lohjanjärvi; there was room for the whole family there. Irma would be happy and she would get another Brazilian goat or African cow, and there would be nothing said about Alzheimer's.

Chapter 21

The sparse-limbed Christmas tree in the common room had already shed its needles on the floor when Siiri finally left her apartment. The tree was where the card table usually stood, and the Ambassador was very cross about it.

'Where am I supposed to play solitaire?' he shouted melodramatically, but no one reacted except for Margit Partanen, who hurriedly pushed her husband out of the room before he could say something lewd.

Eino Partanen had advanced Parkinson's, and probably also Alzheimer's and serious dementia, but since Margit knew how horrible the Group Home was, she had appointed herself his personal caregiver. Caring for one's husband around the clock, week after week, while also living in a retirement home seemed like a strange solution but Margit was glad to get the 150 euros a month. She was actually being paid for not wasting the Sunset Grove staff's time in caring for her Eino. Eino sat in his wheelchair mostly confused and if he spoke he usually said something inappropriate, which embarrassed his wife tremendously. But the disease hadn't taken away all of

Eino's powers, because the residents of A wing could still hear the couple's regular recreational activities.

Anna-Liisa was sitting at the coffee table. For once Siiri was happy that Anna-Liisa was there because she had to talk to somebody. Anna-Liisa listened without the smallest change in expression, her hands resting on her Zimmer frame.

'Don't waste your sorrow,' she said. 'Irma's not dead. At least not yet. Everything happens in its time.'

'But listen, I think that Irma has been taken to the closed unit,' Siiri said finally. She had turned the idea over in her mind for such a long time without being able to think of how to proceed. Sometimes she thought she herself was going soft in the head, or paranoid or whatever, but she was more frightened that she might be right.

Anna-Liisa was silent for a moment. She didn't say anything, which Siiri thought was a good sign. If Anna-Liisa had immediately started a lecture, she wouldn't have been thinking about the matter, she would have just been talking for the sake of it.

'Yes, I'm sure she has,' Anna-Liisa said finally, folding her napkin into ever smaller triangles where it lay on the table. She started folding the plastic bags into smaller and smaller triangles, too – she had these peculiar habits, which she was rather proud of. 'Reino was locked in the dementia ward when he made a fuss about Olavi Raudanheimo's terrible treatment. And Olavi would have remained in the closed unit if his son hadn't rescued him and taken him to Meilahti Hospital. And Irma has written numerous complaints, and very well-founded ones, which is even worse. Her last complaint was about head nurse Virpi Hiukkanen, when she left you lying on the floor unconscious. This measure is probably Irma's punishment.'

Anna-Liisa weighed every word, wrestling for precision and articulating very distinctly. Everything she said was horrifying. But Siiri was relieved to have someone say so lucidly what she had feared. Maybe she wasn't going crazy after all.

'I just don't know what to think,' she explained. 'Virpi Hiukkanen claimed that Irma was paranoid. It's one of the symptoms of dementia, so you could use it to label anyone who suspects you.'

'Dementia is the symptom, not paranoia,' Anna-Liisa corrected her, and then thought again for a moment. 'Irma did ask to see her medical files, didn't she? And she didn't get them. Virpi didn't want to give them back to her.'

This was something Siiri had worried about too. Maybe someone had falsified Irma's records so that transferring her to the closed unit would seem like a justifiable decision.

'I'm afraid that soon they'll shut me up in there, because I suspect all kinds of things. What can a person do?'

Anna-Liisa didn't speak, but this time her thoughtful pause was so long that Siiri began to lose hope. Anna-Liisa must be as helpless, as much at a loss, as she was. They sank into a deep, gloomy silence and stared into empty space. A paper angel on a stick lay on the table, they could hear the grunt and slap of the Ambassador playing solitaire in the corner behind the tree, and somewhere further off the thump of Exercise Annie's aerobics cassette. On the television some children were having a crabwalk race.

And then an amazing thing happened. Siiri Kettunen lifted her eyes from the paper angel and saw something that she had almost forgotten about, and at that moment she knew that it was the solution to everything.

Chapter 22

A large man stood in front of Siiri and Anna-Liisa, looking at them with tender blue eyes. He held out a red poinsettia.

'Merry Christmas,' he said. 'Or should I say Happy New Year's, since Christmas is more or less over now?'

'Mika Korhonen!' Siiri shouted as if the Angel Gabriel himself had appeared out of the heavens. And that's exactly how she felt, because no one but Mika could help them out of the mess they were in, a mess that had only grown more befuddling as the weeks went by.

'Have you ever thought about what a fun word be-fuddling is? Almost as good as flummoxed,' Siiri said to Mika, giving him a hug – which was totally unlike her – because at that moment a big hug from her new friend with his squeaky leather jacket and his wonderful smell was just what she needed. It made her feel safer than any childhood memory.

'You don't need the plural, or the possessive, in this case. It's "Happy New Year", not "Happy New Year's",' Anna-Liisa informed him, and Siiri realized she hadn't introduced them.

'This is my friend, Anna-Liisa Petäjä,' Siiri said to Mika, who extended his strong hand.

'Master of Philosophy, language and literature teacher. Very nice to meet you, Mr Korhonen.' Anna-Liisa squeezed Mika's hand, obviously satisfied by his grip.

'Right, yeah. Just Mika. And where's the other happy lady? I have a flower for her, too.'

'Poinsettias are poisonous,' Anna-Liisa began, but Siiri interrupted and invited both of them to her apartment, feeling that it would be a safer place to talk. You never knew which of the people dozing around you were actually in full possession of their faculties and ready to pass on everything you said. Good gracious, she was getting paranoid!

Mika glanced around with curiosity as they went to the lift and took it to Siiri's second-floor apartment. He sniffed the air and grimaced now and then – no doubt the retirement home had a strange smell to outsiders, a mixture of disinfectant and excretions that the residents had reluctantly grown used to. Siiri opened her apartment door and regretted that she hadn't cleared the remains of her breakfast. She hurried to put things away and wiped the table. Anna-Liisa had never been to her apartment and so was making an eager inspection of it. She stopped her Zimmer frame in front of the bookshelf and scanned it with apparent approbation, though it only contained Siiri's most beloved, and newest, books. She had given most of her books to the antiquarian bookstore when she moved into the retirement home. The bookstore owner had wanted to give her a few hundred for them, but she wasn't worried about the money because she felt that second-hand book dealers were performing a public good by rescuing books and spreading the word about them.

Mika looked at the framed photos of Siiri's husband and children on the windowsill, peeked into the bedroom, and sat down on the sofa, which looked smaller with him filling half of it. It was a rather silly sofa, low and curved, from Stockmann department store, and had followed Siiri in every move she'd made since the 1930s. Siiri put the poinsettias on the table and asked if her guests would like some coffee and nookies. She didn't give it a thought – it was what she and Irma always said. Mika laughed in astonishment and Anna-Liisa saw it as an opportunity to launch into an explanation of why an old person from Helsinki might call cookies nookies.

'. . . a similar transposition of the initial consonant happens with other expressions, such as spoving louse,' she said.

'Yep. Plenty of louses and nookie these days,' Mika said, and drummed his fingers on the table. Anna-Liisa furrowed her brow doubtfully.

'Are such expressions still in use among young people today?' Anna-Liisa asked.

Siiri had to raise her voice to focus the conversation. She gently reminded her guests that it would be best to forget about the nookies and concentrate on talking about Irma. And then she told them everything, just as if she'd been uncorked. She told them in no particular order about the medical records, the forgetfulness, the sudden sleepiness, the additional drugs, the apathy, the missing green folder, the strange package, the complaints, Virpi Hiukkanen's fits of rage, and how she'd been left lying unconscious on the floor. Anna-Liisa corrected, supplemented, and elucidated whenever an opportunity presented itself.

'It's a bit unusual these days to wear a slip under a dress, you see,' she interjected.

Mika listened, not interrupting or asking any questions. Siiri felt tremendously relieved, and positively giddy, from finally putting all the oppressive thoughts she'd been carrying inside her all these months into words. Anna-Liisa was full of energy. She remembered the dreadful incident with Olavi Raudanheimo and described what had happened as far as she understood it. 'And Reino has been in the closed unit ever since. But I don't remember where Olavi Raudanheimo is, do you, Siiri?'

Siiri had completely forgotten Olavi's room with a view at the Hilton! So much had happened that she couldn't keep up with it all. Tero and Pasi seemed like far-off creatures on this rainy Christmas, although, just a short time ago, all of Sunset Grove had been abuzz about their fate and Siiri had thought that she would never get over the young cook's death.

'Didn't Irma say in a lucid moment that Olavi had been moved from Meilahti to the chronic ward at Laakso Hospital?' Anna-Liisa said, digging the fact out of her memory.

Yes, that might be right. But no one had even thought to miss Reino. Even the Ambassador hadn't said anything about him. Siiri was worried that Mika might be getting a very confused picture of everything and he might think they were a couple of scatter-brained old ladies. But Mika didn't say anything unpleasant, he just wanted to know Olavi's son's name and phone number.

'Oh, we don't have any of that kind of information,' Siiri said hopelessly. 'We don't have your telephone number either.'

Mika gave her a quick glance, but made no comment on this remark. An uncomfortable moment ensued, which Anna-Liisa defused by pondering whether Irma might have Olavi's son's contact information, since she had been so curious about him and was always figuring such things out when she'd been in her right mind.

'She had a habit of writing down any important name and number on a yellow sticky note and sticking it to the wall or the cupboard door, which was ridiculous, but that information might be among the rest.'

'Let's go and look,' Mika suggested. 'You probably have a key?'

Siiri and Anna-Liisa were frightened. They didn't think it was appropriate to go into someone else's home uninvited. Mika assured them that they were doing it to help Irma, so eventually Siiri gave in.

They were shocked when they saw the state of Irma's apartment. Although Irma had a lot of things, she always kept them well organized, in stacks and piles that had some kind of logic. But now her place was a terrible mess, as if someone had been there before them and rummaged through her possessions. Even the cupboard doors were open, and the dry goods and bags of flour that Irma had collected for emergencies were scattered over the worktop. There were jumbles of medicine bottles on the sofa and tables and the only things that seemed to be in their usual places were Irma's sticky notes. They were on the walls, mirrors and doors, and they all said, 'Remember to buy ice cream and wine.'

'As if she was going to forget,' Anna-Liisa muttered, venting her perplexity in anger.

'Someone's been searching for something here,' Mika said. He examined Irma's medicine bottles, and Siiri thought she saw him put some of them in the pocket of his leather jacket.

'And returning something,' Anna-Liisa said, picking up a green folder from the floor with remarkable dexterity.

Mika grabbed the folder, flipped quickly through it, and stuffed it into his backpack. He said he had to leave, but would be back on Sunday to clean Irma's apartment. Which was, of course, very kind of him.

Chapter 23

Siiri was sitting on the number 6, watching the January rain and admiring the buildings along Hämeentie, when a group from a children's nursery got on the tram. She was too shy to chat with them and just watched as the children explained to the other passengers that they were on their way to the Trunk. It sounded ridiculous. One woman asked if the children were planning to get in the trunk, and said she didn't think such big girls and boys could possibly all fit in even the largest suitcase.

'The Trunk is a theatre, silly,' one little girl with her head covered in plaits explained, and they all laughed at the woman's stupidity.

The children got off at Lautatarhankatu, but when the doors closed the little girl with the plaits was left behind. She was in a panic, the poor thing, in her fluorescent jacket, and when no one did anything, Siiri went over to her, took her by the hand, and promised to help, although she wasn't sure how. The girl stopped yelling at that point and looked completely certain that this unknown old woman would rescue her, no matter the circumstances. Siiri introduced herself and asked the little girl's name.

'Julia. Julia Jumpity-Jump. I'm four years old.'

She held up three fingers. Siiri asked her what her mother's name was, just in case. If the field trip wasn't actually going to the theatre, she would have to contact the girl's mother. She wondered where she could find a phone box or some other place to call the girl's mother, and she couldn't think of any. There probably weren't any public telephones any more, even in the restaurants.

'Her name is Mama Jumpity-Jump, of course.'

The little girl said that there were two Siiris at the children's nursery. She wanted to know Siiri's mother's name and how old Siiri was. Once she'd incorporated this new friend into her map of the world, Julia Jumpity-Jump started to babble on about every aspect of a four-year-old's life.

'Today is Thursday and Thursday is field-trip day. Monday is toy day and that was yesterday. Tomorrow we went with Mama to Thailand, we were there for two weeks and that's why I have these wonderful plaits. We have pet stick insects at my house because Mama's allergic to animals, cats and dogs and guinea pigs and gerbils and bunnies, but not snakes. I don't want a snake in the house.'

They got off at the next stop and walked to the Trunk, which was, in fact, a theatre, just like Julia Jumpity-Jump had told her. Maybe she really had stick insects at home, too, whatever they were. One of the nursery teachers was standing in front of the theatre looking worried, with a telephone to her ear. When she saw them she ran to meet them and wrenched Julia Jumpity-Jump away from Siiri's hand.

'Where have you been? This is no way to have an adventure! We nearly called the police! You are impossible. You give us nothing but worry and trouble. Everyone else is inside, in their seats.'

The teacher lectured just like a retirement-home worker, and didn't even acknowledge Siiri, who suddenly found herself standing alone on the street with no idea where she should go. Where had she been dropped off? In Vallila? Or was this Sörnäinen? Did something just happen, or had she imagined it?

With her head spinning, she crossed the street to the tram stop and got on the first tram that came along. It was a number 6. She missed Irma's laugh and could hear her bubbling voice and the clink of her bracelets in her imagination. For a moment she even thought she could smell Irma's slightly sugary perfume. Tears came to her eyes and it was hard to breathe. How could she have ever thought that Irma was tiresome? Now she would have been glad to listen seven times over to the story of how Irma's husband said 'damn it' when he was installing the bookshelves. Or did he say 'hell'? She was beginning to be confused about everything, too.

Siiri gave a start when she passed the Sörnäinen metro station and saw that crazy Jugendstijl Ebeneser building, designed by Wivi Lönn. Had she changed trams? The number 6 didn't go down Helsinginkatu. She was sure she'd got on the number 6 at the Trunk Theatre, but that had been a long time ago. Or had it? Her throat tightened as she thought how confused she might be and not even notice it. Had she been babbling out loud? She had her handbag with her, at least, and her coin purse was there in the zip pocket, but she didn't see her cane anywhere. Maybe she hadn't brought it with her. She felt like shouting for help like a four-year-old, hoping someone would take her by the hand and lead her home, but instead she got up and asked the driver what was going on. But the driver had his compartment door closed and refused to answer her. Siiri knocked and knocked, until he yelled, 'You can buy a ticket with your phone!'

Siiri stumbled back down the aisle and sank into one of the disabled seats. She didn't normally use them because there was usually someone on the tram who was in worse shape than she was. She felt weak, her ears were buzzing and her head was pounding. She was unspeakably tired. It was probably just hunger. She hadn't eaten anything since break-fast, although she couldn't be sure of that. It was dark out, but that didn't tell her what time it was, since it was always dark at this time of year. She looked at her watch, but she couldn't see the hands without her glasses and she didn't feel like fishing them out of her handbag.

A friendly-looking woman came over to her and bent her face close to speak to her. Was it someone she knew?

'This is the number 8. It goes from Arabianranta to Jätkäsaari. Do you have a ticket?'

Jätkäsaari – Bloke Island – was a truly ugly name for a neighbourhood. It sounded like it got its name from a prison. A townie's neighbourhood, that's what Irma would have said. Siiri wouldn't even have known how to find such a neighbourhood. And here she was on her way to Jätkäsaari, for heaven's sake, a respectable woman like herself.

The woman gave her a worried look and started speaking more loudly, stretching her face out comically.

'DO YOU REMEMBER YOUR NAME? DO YOU KNOW WHAT DAY OF THE WEEK IT IS?'

Siiri remembered her friend Julia Jumpity-Jump, who she'd thought a little silly, and started to laugh. The little girl hadn't known her own name, or the difference between yesterday and tomorrow. This kindly woman was testing her just like she herself had tested the plaited-haired four-year-old.

'Maybe I should wear a fluorescent jacket, too. Today is Thursday, field-trip day, and my name is Great-great-ancient-grandma Jumpity-Jump. If you'll permit me, I'll get off here at the new Opera House. Thanks for your kindness.'

She left the worried woman behind and went home to lie down. Not that Sunset Grove was her home. It was just a logical solution for those who weren't dead yet. 'Waiting for the crematorium,' as Reino put it. And he had, in fact, died. Reino, that dirty talker and kiss stealer, the man who thought that Siiri was the prettiest girl at Sunset Grove. The Ambassador had told them at the card table about Reino's death. He said rather offhandedly that his friend was dead, *neben*, *über*, *unter*, *vor*, *zwischen*, and Anna-Liisa had added that there was, after all, no other way out of the Group Home.

Chapter 24

Siiri finally got hold of Tuula, the only one of Irma's children who wasn't an accident. Tuula had been around the world a couple of times, first to spend Christmas on an island somewhere in the Pacific, then to conferences in Mexico and South Korea, and that's why she hadn't answered when Siiri had tried to call her. Tuula was a doctor, a real scientist, and always in a great hurry, a specialist in prosthetic coatings and the outer ear canals of children, although Irma and Siiri had never understood how the two things were connected.

'Mother's situation is sad, of course,' Tuula said on the phone. 'But there's not much we can do about it, she's so old. Luckily, she receives good care at Sunset Grove. She's safe in the Group Home. I used some of my connections and got her a quick diagnosis of rapidly advancing dementia. Sometimes you have to wait for months if you don't know the right people. But they responded quickly at Sunset Grove, thank goodness. We can't take care of her. You might not know, but I have two horses, which is an incredible amount of work, although it's fun, too, of course. But as I'm sure you can understand, they take up all my spare time.'

So it was true. Irma was in the closed unit and had been for weeks, while her daughter was flying around researching outer ear canals and her darlings were celebrating Christmas in the Tonga islands. All these weeks, while Siiri had done nothing but fret, not knowing what else to do but break into Irma's apartment with a total stranger, an angel boy, to steal a green folder that had already been stolen from her once before.

Irma's daughter didn't understand at all when Siiri said that the entire dementia story was an invention of the head nurse and things like that happened all the time at Sunset Grove. Siiri tried to explain the whole thing thoroughly, the reasons, and the results.

'What complaints?' Tuula asked, clearly beginning to feel nervous when Siiri told her how Irma had been a thorn in the side of the staff. She told Tuula about the county administration, the ETE Centre, and the Loving Care Foundation. And, of course, the green folder and the constantly increasing number of pills.

'What are you going on about? Finnish doctors don't just prescribe things willy-nilly. Besides, complaints about treatment aren't filed through the ETE Centre. Don't you mean the regional centre? Are you feeling tired, Siiri, dear?'

Tuula hadn't yet had time to come and visit Irma in the closed unit and didn't know what it was like there. She told Siiri to trust the experts in the medical profession and she was glad when Siiri asked if she could obtain permission for her to visit Irma.

'Yes, you have plenty of time for such things. I'll let the

office know that they should give you a visitor's pass. I won't be able to make it until maybe the end of next month; I've got such an awful lot to do at work after all these conference trips. And then there are the horses. But I don't feel guilty about it, since Mother won't even know to miss me there in the dementia ward. She doesn't even remember her own name.'

The telephone call had brought no one any joy. Luckily there were still angels in the world, like Mika Korhonen, a true gift from heaven. He had cleaned Irma's apartment assiduously, like he'd promised, thrown out nine years' worth of old flour and rye crisps, and put everything back in its place. Although he didn't seem to like it when Siiri called him an angel, because he wasn't just any angel, he was a specific kind of angel. He belonged to an international club that combined motorcycling and philanthropy. But Siiri couldn't take any interest in Mika's hobbies. Motorcycling sounded dangerous to her. The main thing was that for some reason Mika wanted to help them, unlike every last one of Irma's darlings, whose only offer of help was to hustle Irma off to the dementia ward.

'It's for Tero,' Mika said. 'He died for no reason.'

He had been in a hurry, couldn't even stay for a cup of instant coffee. As he was leaving he said he was going to meet Tero's good friend Pasi, who Mika called a snitch. Pasi ought to be taught a lesson, but Mika was going to have to take care of that himself. Siiri certainly didn't intend to teach anyone any lessons. She didn't really even know this Pasi, because he'd spent most of his time at Sunset Grove in his office handling something to do with funding and billing matters.

'And I'm not teaching anybody any more, that's for certain!' Anna-Liisa said as they played a game of double solitaire. 'You have no idea what it's like teaching the forty-two grammatical case constructions of Finnish to a classroom of pre-teens. At that stage of life a person doesn't yet understand the usefulness of learning grammar. And yet it's so extremely important. Do you know what the ablative case is?'

'No, and I don't want to. It said in the paper that you shouldn't tax your brain with unnecessary information. You should concentrate on essentials as your mental capacities start to deteriorate.'

They almost had a fight about this, and in the end Siiri had to apologize, realizing that she had offended Anna-Liisa. As a token of her forgiveness Anna-Liisa gave her a comprehensive lecture on the fascinating grammatical case constructions of the Finnish language.

'... and then there's the comitative case, which, of course, means with, as in *kissoineen* – 'with their cats'. Is that clear?'

Siiri had no use for the comitative case at the moment. She wasn't with Irma, and being without Irma was no way to live, and there didn't seem to be anyone who could help her solve this problem. Mika Korhonen was concentrating on Pasi, Irma's daughter didn't understand the problem, and even Siiri's granddaughter's boyfriend Tuukka hadn't called in ages. It felt like the whole world had shifted onto the

Internet somewhere, a place where Siiri couldn't go. The only point of light in the darkness was shut up in that closed unit. And soon she was going to get in there, and see Irma.

Chapter 25

Reino's funeral was held on a weekday, the same week that the temperature finally fell below freezing and the continuous rain changed to snow. The snow had been falling around the clock for three days and traffic was a mess. City workers were in a hurry to clear a route for the cars, so they were dumping the snow on the pavements and courtyards. With Zimmer frames and wheelchairs it was impossible to travel even a couple of metres.

So the residents of Sunset Grove hired two vans, designed especially for elderly passengers, with the Ambassador's taxi coupons. Anna-Liisa, Siiri and the Ambassador took one and in the other were the Partanens and the Hat Lady, who had recovered from her cardiac infarction and started going from door to door in the retirement home. Siiri and Anna-Liisa assumed she was going begging, hoping for some coffee and sweet rolls, but she claimed she was on Jesus's business. And when she came to visit, it didn't take her long, in fact, to fish out a Bible and start grilling her host on personal matters.

'I haven't yet come to a decision,' Siiri had told her, trying to be tactful, but that was a mistake. The Hat Lady had been giving her the full treatment ever since, thinking she was easy pickings. She'd got to be quite a nuisance, and Siiri took care to make sure they didn't travel in the same van.

There was no car access to the front door of the crematorium. The vans had to drop them off along the street and the drivers offered no help with the slog to the entrance; they just dumped the chairs and Zimmer frames in the wet snow and sped off. The old people took so long getting to the door, nudging each other along through the snowdrifts, that they were late for the ceremony. Clumps of snow stuck to the wheels of their chairs and Zimmer frames and made them nearly impossible to push. The Ambassador's cane got stuck in the handle of Anna-Liisa's Zimmer frame, the Hat Lady fell into a mound of snow, hat and all, and Margit Partanen looked like she was going to have a heart attack.

'It's all right, we'll all end up at the crematorium eventually!' the Ambassador shouted gamely.

Finally, the chapel verger, a frail-looking woman with no coat on, hurried over to help them. By the time she'd hoisted all the wheelchairs, Zimmer frames and old people inside she was soaked with sweat. They crammed themselves into the small foyer to take off their coats and hats and unwrap the flowers they'd brought. There was no bin for the wrappers – there never seemed to be, in any church or chapel. Anna-Liisa left her Zimmer frame by the coat rack, thinking it would only be in the way and that since it was red it wasn't suitable for the occasion.

The old crematorium was a gloomy place, small but

echoey and unadorned. The door at the other end of the hall was particularly ghastly, because it led to the oven. Siiri had never liked the way they slid the coffin on rails into the oven and left the pall bearers standing there watching it go. She always imagined the rising flames and pain of purgatory, although Anna-Liisa said that the body was burnt with heat alone, without any flames, and it all happened automatically at the press of a button, like making coffee. Siiri thought the funerals at the Hietaniemi chapel were better. The building there was designed by Theodor Höijer, and was unusually beautiful. She didn't know who was responsible for the dismal design of this crematorium.

There was hardly anyone else at Reino's funeral besides them. The residents of Sunset Grove sat on the left in the fourth and fifth rows, not wanting to be too close to the coffin as it rolled along its final track. On the other side of the aisle there were just two men, relatives of the deceased, whom they had never seen before.

'We're his nephews,' one of the men said, nodding politely.

'Ah. Here to get your inheritance,' the Ambassador said, somewhat inappropriately, but the two men smiled.

'Uncle Jaakko didn't really leave anything. Everything he owned was spent on the retirement home.'

'Are we at Jaakko's funeral?' asked Eino Partanen, who wasn't even wearing a dark suit, just tracksuit bottoms and a pullover.

'But it was good that he was there at the retirement home. We didn't have to worry about him.'

'This is Reino's funeral. Would you be quiet?' Margit Partanen hissed at her husband, wishing there was a mute button on his wheelchair.

The funeral was an unusually bad one. They almost felt sorry for Reino. The pastor kept his speech short, however, and the nephews didn't start reciting poetry next to the coffin, but the Hat Lady fell asleep in the middle of the ceremony, and it took them quite a long time to get the wheelchairs to the coffin. Since Reino had always been the one to say a few words about the deceased, there was a little moment of uncertainty over what to do once they were all next to the coffin.

'To the memory of a card partner and a good fellow,' the Ambassador said finally, or rather mumbled, which annoyed Anna-Liisa.

'Whose bedfellow? Jaakko's?' Eino Partanen shouted to his wife as they went back to their seats, but just then the organ started up a hymn, so they were spared from explaining it to him. No one sang, since Irma wasn't with them, and, once again, Siiri felt unsettled. Irma would have so enjoyed this outing if she weren't lying in the closed unit, tied to her bed, with no idea that anything fun was happening.

A deadly dull memorial reception was held in Restaurant Perho on Mechelininkatu. The service was always slow there because it was staffed by students from the restaurant school. On one visit, Siiri hadn't got the salt she'd asked for until the bill came, and this time they waited twenty minutes for their coffee.

The nephews were snow dumpers by trade, making their living by shovelling snow off rooftops and dropping it on people's heads. They were very quiet men, but Irma would have managed to show enthusiasm even for them. She might have asked them something funny about what snow dumpers do in the summer. Now Anna-Liisa was assiduously taking the reins.

'When there's this much snow, you can't get anywhere with a Zimmer frame. We've had quite enough snow in our lives, we don't need any more.'

A snow discussion of sorts ensued, but Siiri didn't participate. She looked out of the window and tried to wash away the gloom with weak coffee. They didn't even serve cake, these stingy nephews of his. The elderly group took the tram home, since no one had a mobile phone and their attempts to have the restaurant staff order a van for the disabled didn't quite work out.

When she got back to Sunset Grove, it dawned on Siiri that their friend had been known as Reino and yet the nephews had kept talking about their Uncle Jaakko. It was quite possible that they'd gone to the wrong funeral!

'*Döden, döden, döden,*' she said to herself and laughed out loud until she gave herself a stomach cramp.

Chapter 26

The doorbell rang so loudly and insistently that Siiri nearly jumped out of bed, dropping her newspaper on the floor. She pulled on her dressing gown but forgot her slippers as she hurried to open the door, a little nervous, since she didn't usually have unexpected visitors, at least not any who rang the doorbell. She had to stop for a moment and hold on to the dining table because the buzzing in her head had turned unpleasantly loud from her sudden movement. She shouted 'Cock-a-doodle-doo!' to keep the visitor from leaving, then was instantly ashamed of herself because it would have been more sensible to shout something else.

But she was happy to see Mika Korhonen standing at her door in his leather jacket. She threw herself around his neck, then pulled herself away just as quickly, because he seemed tense and in a hurry.

Mika declined her offer of a cup of instant coffee and strode into the middle of the living room. 'There's something I want to talk to you about. Can you turn off the symphony?'

'It's a concerto, a solo work for orchestra and piano.

Beethoven's third concerto,' Siiri said, and turned off the record player. She felt as if Mika had something very important he wanted to discuss, and it would be best to call Anna-Liisa to come and act as a witness. Mika didn't say anything; he just sat down on the little sofa and rummaged through his backpack. Siiri asked him to take off his muddy boots and he politely obeyed. He had holes in his socks, and they weren't even wool, and Siiri knew what she was going to give him as a present someday, if she remembered. She didn't enjoy knitting herself, but Margit Partanen knitted every day; she could make a pair of wool socks in no time.

Anna-Liisa arrived with her Zimmer frame amazingly quickly. Now that the two of them were more accustomed to each other's company, Siiri had noticed that Anna-Liisa didn't really need the Zimmer frame to get around. She was very nimble and could, in fact, walk very briskly. But Anna-Liisa said she kept the Zimmer frame because it was good for balance problems; it was a precautionary measure, to prevent falls. It cost society great sums of money when old people walked around in their stockinged feet without any assistive devices and then broke their bones.

Mika took a large stack of papers out of his backpack and put them on the table.

'These are Irma Lännenleimu's medical records and a few other files – everything Sunset Grove had listed under her name.'

Siiri and Anna-Liisa looked at the stack of papers in horror. So much information about Irma! Did Sunset Grove have huge files like that on them, too? Anna-Liisa was the first to pull herself together, and started questioning Mika as if he were a fifteen-year-old who'd forgotten his adverbials.

'Where did you get those papers? Who gave you permission to take them? Are they originals or copies?'

'I stole them,' Mika said. He dropped the words calmly and pointedly into the silence and gave Siiri and Anna-Liisa a moment to catch their breath before continuing. 'I got the Sunset Grove keys from Pasi, the whole key ring. Pasi is in cahoots with your head nurse, the one who runs the nursing agency.'

'Virpi Hiukkanen? Hardly. She's the one who fired him,' Siiri informed him.

'Yep. The business continues, thanks to Tero. There's no better scapegoat than a dead scapegoat. And Pasi doesn't have to be an employee of Sunset Grove to work for Hiukkanen. Do you know what the name of her nursing agency is?'

'Well, no, we've never had a reason to ask.'

'Piri Care Suppliers. They're suppliers all right!'

Sometimes Mika was confusing and a bit peculiar. Now he laughed with a strangely loud guffaw at the name of Virpi Hiukkanen's company and kept repeating something that they couldn't understand. He thought that both Pasi and the police were in cahoots with Virpi Hiukkanen, which couldn't be true. But Siiri didn't dare to contradict him, because there was something frightening about him now that he'd taken to stealing on their behalf.

'Are we your accomplices?' Anna-Liisa asked formally, straightening her spine like a former gymnast. Secretly, she was thrilled at the new turn in events. Mika handed Irma's papers to her, copies of the originals, he said, so that they could study them at their leisure.

'It's ugly reading,' he warned.

Then he left as quickly as he had come. He had already pulled on his boots when Siiri asked when they would see him again and what was to come of all this. Mika couldn't promise anything.

'Look out for your own affairs, and I'll take care of Pasi,' he said, and closed the door behind him.

They were left sitting at the table in bewilderment. Siiri didn't understand how it had become so important to take care of Pasi, or what Mika was actually up to. The case was taking a new turn. Anna-Liisa didn't say anything; finally, she picked up the papers fearfully and started to read them as if they were just another stack of exams to be marked. She was quiet for a long time, until she paused, leaned back, and said:

'Mika was right. This is ugly reading.'

Anna-Liisa asked for a glass of whisky, something Siiri had never seen her do before. Siiri got herself a little red wine, in honour of Irma. Irma had been much braver than they'd realized, writing vehement complaints to everyone from the Ombudsman of Parliament to the Social Services Minister, and every complaint had ended up on the desk in the offices of Sunset Grove.

'Your complaint has been received and will be processed according to standard procedures,' said the paper from Parliament, which was dated three years ago. Nothing more was heard from the Ombudsman of Parliament – no doubt the wheels of the standard procedures were still turning.

'These aren't medical records,' Anna-Liisa said solemnly.

And yet someone had added this documentation of Irma's complaints to her medical records. There were also two letters from the Uudenmaa County Administrative Board, the oldest one from five years ago, plus a few more recent letters, including the one they'd written together to the members of the board of the Loving Care Foundation, which was on the top of the stack.

The worst documents, however, were the ones concerning Irma's health. The staff had sent Irma's ever-changing personal physicians incorrect information about her over a year ago. They'd said that she had shown signs of suspiciousness, serious paranoia, intermittent aggressiveness, and increasingly serious memory loss. The doctors' consultations had been conducted entirely by email and telephone, and various prescriptions had been written without them ever seeing the patient. The last correspondence read: 'The only solution to these worsening problems is immediate removal to the Group Home dementia unit. The patient's daughter will provide a statement.'

'They could at least have arranged a doctor's visit for her. Then someone could have seen that she wasn't sick,' Anna-Liisa said, her voice even more sombre than usual.

'Sharp as a tack, that's what she always said. Although she was very confused and tired in December, and even before that, actually, like it says here. And her suspicions only got worse. Is it possible . . . do you think that they might have been . . . ?'

'It's as clear as day. Multiple drugs acting on the central nervous system will make an old person sick. It was somebody's long-term plan to give Irma dementia.'

Irma had been prescribed pills for irritability, restlessness, insomnia, muscle stiffness, extreme pain, depression and who knows what else, in ever larger doses and increasing numbers over the course of a year. It was as if, when one pill caused one symptom, they prescribed another pill for that, in an endless chain.

Siiri started to feel weak. There was nothing in her head but emptiness. This really would be a good time to go to sleep for good. She couldn't comprehend why anyone would go to the trouble of doing such a thing. Surely one old woman in a dementia ward couldn't generate so much money from the city that the Loving Care Foundation would institute such a complicated course of action. There must be easier ways to silence an old lady's complaints.

'I guess there's no one looking out for us, to make sure everything is legitimate,' Siiri said numbly. 'And they write about it so much in the papers.'

'The only good old person is a dead old person,' Anna-Liisa said grimly, then drank down the rest of her whisky and hastened to add, 'And don't say "*döden, döden, döden*". Have you heard anything from Olavi Raudanheimo?'

'I forgot about Olavi. There's been so much going on. Are you leaving?'

Anna-Liisa hadn't lost her ability to function just because

of Irma's files. She had a chair aerobics session starting at eleven and after lunch she planned to go with the Ambassador to play bingo in the auditorium. She tried to coax Siiri to come along, but in vain.

'I'm not so senile that I'm going to start playing bingo. Are these your keys? Don't tell me they're mine, because I'm sure I've never seen them before.'

There was a ring of keys lying on the table. It wasn't Anna-Liisa's or Siiri's.

'Do you think Mika left them here ... on purpose?' Anna-Liisa asked.

Siiri looked at the key ring more closely. There were three keys, and one of them was labelled 'Group Home'.

Chapter 27

'Hello Siiri, dear. It's the director calling. Good news! Your cane was found at Laakso Hospital.'

All through the winter Siiri had wondered where her cane had disappeared to, but she hadn't yet bought a new one. It certainly would have been useful to have one in the slippery weather; the freezing temperatures had made the streets treacherous. Director Sundström's voice on the phone was even more energetic than usual as she shared the exciting news. She commended Siiri for being so clever as to put a label on the cane with its owner's name and address, as if she were a small child. Siiri asked politely how the director's winter holiday had been, but that was a mistake.

'Absolutely fantastic! You can't imagine what a country India is – it's amazing, absolutely amazing. A lot of tourists just go there to enjoy the hotels and beaches and never see the poverty of the country, which is so heart-rending. Pertti and I were there for three weeks and we really threw our hearts into India's problems, especially the children. Just think, Siiri, there are tens of thousands of orphans there, illiterate and unhealthy, sweet little children, and seeing them touched me so deeply that I've decided to help the orphans of India. We've started up a collection for Indian orphans here at Sunset Grove. You will, of course, contribute, won't you, Siiri?'

'Well, I put quite a lot of money into the collection for the Brotherhood of War Invalids over Christmas.'

'Yes, I understand if the Indian issue seems distant to you. But these orphans don't even have shoes on their feet; they absolutely need help from people like us, who have piles of everything. After all, there are hardly more than a couple of Finnish war invalids still alive.'

'I suppose that's true.'

'Well, we can chat about it some other time. I have lots of photos of Indian orphans, and when you see their pictures I'm sure your heart will melt for this important cause. But listen, unfortunately, you're going to have to go and get the cane from Laakso Hospital yourself. There's no one here who has the time to help. We haven't a single spare hand at the moment, and there's so much work to do that I fear for the health of my employees. Elderly work is difficult, and rather uninteresting, to be honest. And not terribly rewarding. And who ever even thanks us? And the pay is so low, because society doesn't understand the significance of our work. In short, it's very hard nowadays to find workers for retirement homes, and thus we are shorthanded this week.'

As soon as she managed to get off the phone, Siiri started getting ready to leave. She searched for her comb and mirror. When she found them, she noticed Mika's key ring on the table and was going to put it in her handbag, until she realized that her handbag wasn't on the chair by the door. She forgot about combing her hair because she couldn't find her glasses, and then she noticed that they were on top of her head. Next, she wondered where her cane was, before remembering that she was on her way to get it. Finally, she put the keys in her bag. Just as she was ready to leave, and was standing in the hallway with her coat on, she heard someone opening her front door with a key. She froze where she stood and watched as the door slowly opened. The corridor was dark, and the first thing that came through the door was a toolbox.

Siiri wasn't exactly surprised when the man carrying the toolbox, Erkki Hiukkanen, followed, wearing blue overalls and his ever-present billed cap. He tiptoed through the door, looking over his shoulder into the hallway, and fumbled for the light switch. He had a considerable fright when he saw Siiri standing in her winter coat in her own apartment. Closing the door in a panic, he dropped the toolbox loudly on the floor, and pushed his cap to the back of his head. He stood there for a moment, then said with a stutter that he'd come to check the bathroom drain. Siiri said the bathroom drain had worked flawlessly for all the years she'd lived in the apartment.

'Yeah. Well, we're checking all the drains because we've had some complaints,' Hiukkanen lied, so Siiri let him into the bathroom, although she had to leave. She really didn't want to sit there in her coat watching him grub around in the drain.

*

As she sat on the tram, Siiri tried to remember when she had gone to Laakso Hospital. How in the world had her cane ended up there? She didn't dare trust her memory. Just yesterday Virpi Hiukkanen had come to fetch her from the common room in the middle of a game of cards for her blood-pressure check. She could have sworn that she'd never agreed to such a thing. It cost an additional fee, after all.

'Don't you remember, Siiri? We all agreed to it just a short while ago,' Virpi had said, as if she herself were one of the old people, and then she'd dragged Siiri to her office and started asking about arrhythmias and zest for life. Siiri didn't know what she was talking about.

'Well, you did go to Meilahti Hospital in December to chat with a cardiologist. Don't you remember?'

Virpi's questioning had been unpleasant, and Siiri felt a bit nervous, too, because her blood pressure was normal, not low, like it usually was.

'Now, don't be aggressive,' Virpi had scolded her, and that had made Siiri so angry that she had firmly said 'thank you' and 'goodbye' and gone to her apartment. The Ambassador and Anna-Liisa could play cards by themselves, although Siiri was ever so slightly upset about the interruption of the game, because she'd been dealt two jokers. Or was that yesterday? Or the day before? It was best not to think about it, she decided now, and got off at the stop at Tullinpuomi. It was a puzzle that would never be solved, unless it was, as Irma would say. Siiri looked for a moment at the sun shining against the wall of the Aura building and set off on foot to climb the hill to Laakso Hospital.

The hospital was a confusing place and it took Siiri a little while to find someone who had time to hear her reason for coming.

'Ah. I don't have any information for you about where to look for your cane. Have you looked on the web?' said a girl in a booth with a sign that read: 'Information'.

'You mean I should go on the web to get my cane? Where on the web would it be?' Siiri asked in a friendly tone, and then the girl seemed to realize that there was no way for her to get her cane from a computer. The girl said she would find out for Siiri and asked her to sit down in the waiting room. As she sat there Siiri remembered that Olavi Raudanheimo had been moved to the Laakso chronic-care unit before Christmas, but she didn't think she had come to visit him here; she'd only been to see him in his room with a view at the Hilton. They had served him thin pork gravy and they'd had fun reading the newspaper together.

The friendly girl came back with the cane in her hand.

'My trusty cane always comes back to me!' Siiri said, as Irma would have, and the girl smiled such a happy smile that Siiri ventured to ask her how the cane had ended up at Laakso Hospital.

'Because I don't remember ever coming here. But perhaps I don't remember everything any more, since I'm so old.'

'Actually, it was found among one of the patient's belongings,' the girl said, and Siiri instantly realized what had happened.

'Olavi Raudanheimo! Of course. I left my cane in his room at the Hilton and now he's been transferred here with all his things. I could go and see him now, since I'm already here. What ward is he in, can you tell me?'

The Information Girl looked troubled and said that a visit wasn't possible, because Mr Raudanheimo was no longer in the hospital.

'Oh, what a shame. Where's he been transferred to?'

'He's . . . he, um . . . passed, is resting . . . I mean he died.'

The girl said that Olavi had died of old age. But Siiri knew that such a cause of death had been expunged from the Finnish medical establishment long before the girl had even been born, probably because it was the only human function over which they had no control. Eventually, the girl fetched an older nurse, a friendly woman who'd seen something of life, and she explained that they didn't have the authority to tell outsiders about the exact cause of a patient's death.

'But I can tell you that Mr Raudanheimo refused to eat for the last few weeks of his life, and his personal health-care directive prohibited tube feeding. It caused quite a bit of trouble and a lot of meetings among the staff, but what can you do?'

The nurse gave Siiri a meaningful look, and Siiri understood what had happened. She had heard of such things before. Irma had told her about a cousin named Sylvi whose children had put her in such a horrible institution that she eventually stopped eating just to get out of it.

'If you know what I mean,' Irma had said. 'Like that fat woman in A wing.'

'They gave her too much insulin, didn't they?'

'Don't be silly! My cousin didn't have diabetes, not even a touch of high blood sugar. She killed herself by going on a hunger strike, like Gandhi, but in her case nobody came to stop her before it was too late, because it's a good thing when an old person dies, just like it was a good thing Gandhi didn't, although, of course, he did in the end, but not from his hunger strike. Sylvi stopped eating and since she'd always been a skinny thing, she died two weeks later in the hospital. For a thin person it's quite easy. If you remember to stop drinking, too, you'll be in a bad shape in no time.'

Chapter 28

It was time for another funeral at the Hietaniemi chapel. This time they made very sure that they were in the right place at the right time. Siiri, Anna-Liisa and the Hat Lady took the number 4 and the number 8, although Siiri tried her best to talk the Hat Lady into taking a taxi instead. But the Ambassador's taxi was full once Eino and Margit Partanen got in with their wheelchair, and the Hat Lady was afraid to go alone.

Siiri remembered to bring her green cushion, which was a good thing because the chapel pews were terribly hard and since she was so skinny she had to sit on nothing but her tailbone, which was painful after a while.

They hadn't known it, but Olavi Raudanheimo had a large family and many friends. He had always been so solitary at Sunset Grove. The old Hietaniemi chapel was full of people, even his old classmates and numerous co-workers from his years working as the building attendant at the university pathology department. The Ambassador recognized some of the mourners as fellow Freemasons. Olavi's relatives came in all sorts; there was even a girl with a face full of metal rings.

'Those are piercings. It's a kind of jewellery. They put them everywhere, even in their nipples and genitals,' Anna-Liisa explained, and the Ambassador laughed loudly.

Siiri helped Anna-Liisa with her Zimmer frame, but she forgot her cane at her seat when it was their turn to approach the coffin. Margit Partanen had become quite nimble with her husband's wheelchair. She also must have given Eino some strong medication, because he was quiet throughout the whole ceremony. Margit relayed everything to him in a loud voice. The Hat Lady was fast asleep and remained in her seat.

'Rest in peace, Olavi,' Anna-Liisa said very dramatically as she laid the bouquet of flowers on the coffin.

She had told them all beforehand that she wanted to say something, and Siiri, who had expected at least a quote from Uuno Kailas or a snippet of a Runeberg poem, was disappointed that Anna-Liisa was so succinct, and sounded like a gravedigger. As they stood by the coffin Siiri noticed she'd brought her cushion with her, which was embarrassing. There was nothing for it but to stand undaunted with the cushion under her arm and everyone looking at her and think, as Irma would have done, that at her age you can do whatever you like.

The Raudanheimo family sang the hymns handsomely, and Siiri enjoyed other aspects of the funeral, too. The pastor was a wise and kind woman who didn't talk about a journey or any of the other usual things, but about Olavi, as if she'd always known him. She even spoke beautifully about how Olavi had died when he wanted to, and about a world grown impossible for a good man, or something like that.

They didn't feel like going to Restaurant Laulu-Miehet for the reception, although one of the Raudanheimo boys warmly invited them.

'You'll have so many guests there that you'll hardly need us to fill the place,' the Ambassador said politely.

Siiri was able to ask Olavi's son about the police report, regarding the crime against his father. Although she'd thought beforehand that it wouldn't be an appropriate thing to talk about at a funeral. But the son was so down-to-earth that it didn't seem wrong to bring up the subject. He had received a letter eight days after his father's death from the Helsinki criminal police that said that the prosecutor had filed for a motion to dismiss the case, but it didn't say what the reasons were for the decision.

'It may be that the police were relieved that my father had already died so the case could be buried. Not that they were purposely waiting for the old man to kick the bucket, but it was such an awkward thing to investigate. Director Sundström at Sunset Grove sounded on the phone as if she'd been acquitted of a life sentence. She almost burst into tears, the poor woman.'

Chapter 29

'Siiri? Siiri who?' the nurse asked at the door of the Group Home. The name on her lapel read: Yuing Pauk Pulkkinen. Siiri explained that she had come to visit Irma Lännenleimu, and repeated that she had a visitor's pass expressly requested for her by Irma's daughter and approved, finally, by Director Sundström.

'Irma? Irma who?' the nurse asked, and Siiri started to wonder if the company the woman was keeping was starting to rub off on her. Nurse Pulkkinen explained that she was just visiting and thus wasn't acquainted with the patients.

'We're all just visiting, it seems,' Siiri said, but Nurse Pulkkinen didn't understand her.

She let Siiri into a kind of common room, talking the whole time about temp work, bad pay, and Mr Pulkkinen's serious alcohol problem. They went to a glass cubicle that served as the nurses' office and break room, and the nurse started flipping through the papers on the desk. Finally, she found Irma's information and showed Siiri where her room was.

The lighting in the Group Home was glaringly bright and

the place was filled with institutional furniture, as if it were a government auditor's office. The smell of chemicals, urine and floor wax was powerful and Siiri found it hard to breathe.

'What does "expressly requested" mean?' Nurse Pulkkinen asked as they walked down the hall.

All the doors were closed and shouting could be heard from two of the rooms. The hallway ended in an unused sauna and next to it was Irma's room. The nurse went on her way and Siiri stepped fearfully into the little room, which had a picture of Mount Vesuvius on the wall and a window that looked out on the concrete wall of the building next door. There was a woman lying in a bed on the right, and another was tied to a wheelchair, dozing. Siiri warily approached the woman in the wheelchair, who showed no reaction at all, even when Siiri touched her hand. The woman snorted, a glassy look in her eyes, food stains down her front, looking strangely fat – swollen, in fact. Her hair stuck out in every direction, dirty and untrimmed, and long hairs grew from her chin. It was a mighty sad sight. Then Siiri saw a familiar string of pearls around the old lady's neck, and knew that this unfortunate creature was her dear friend Irma Lännenleimu. A cold feeling went right through her, paralysing her limbs and her thoughts, and made the whole room feel like a cellar. She couldn't move her hands; she just stood and stared at the stranger before her. Irma, who was always so particular about cleanliness, who wore a stylish dress even on an ordinary weekday! And now she was in completely unrecognizable clothes, loose green tracksuit bottoms and a shirt that said 'I'm sexy' in sparkly letters.

'*Döden, döden, döden,*' Siiri said in a choked voice into Irma's ear, trying to perk her up, but Irma didn't respond in any way, she just stared at the wall without blinking. Siiri felt like she was going to cry, felt like screaming and throwing herself on the floor, but she had to remain calm. She slumped onto the bed next to the wheelchair, took hold of Irma's hand, gave it a hopeless squeeze, and stroked Irma's cheek. It was incredibly soft, like a little child's.

'Are you taking me to Karelia?' asked the other old woman, who was dressed in pads and overalls and tied to the bed with some kind of harness. She looked intently at Siiri with her small, dark eyes. 'Shall we sing?'

Siiri was startled to find someone watching her, but singing actually seemed like a good idea. She smiled gratefully at the old lady, sighed deeply, and began to sing 'I Remember Karelia', a bit timidly at first. Then, singing more briskly, she switched to 'Cuckoo, Cuckoo, that Faraway Cuckoo'. This clearly made the old woman, who must have been evacuated from Karelia during the war, very happy. Then Siiri sang 'Oh, My Darling Augustine' for Irma. It was a song Irma had once sung in a school song contest. She had been disqualified because, although she sang it well, the teacher had thought the song was indecent because of the lines: 'With pants off and shirt off and socks off and shoes off, oh, my darling Augustine, everything's off!' Irma had tried to explain to the teacher that the song was about a drunk who passes out and gets mistaken for dead and tossed into a mass grave and then wakes up naked and foolish. Granted, it was a strange choice of song for a little girl to sing in a contest, but everybody sang 'Oh, My Darling Augustine' back then without thinking about what it meant.

When Siiri got to the naked part, Irma came to life.

'With pants off and shirt off,' she tried to sing along, but just then the nurse appeared in the doorway.

'Keep your pants on. We're not going to the toilet. You've got your pads,' she yelled in Irma's ear, so loudly that Siiri could see that it hurt. So much so that Irma got angry. She yelled and screamed and when the nurse took hold of both of her hands, Irma bit her. Nurse Pulkkinen yanked her hand away and let out a screech, in that order. Siiri looked on in shock. She didn't recognize this madwoman as the Irma she knew; she couldn't understand what had happened, or why.

Irma kept singing the Augustin song as if it were a political manifesto, so loudly that her voice changed to a strange sort of growl. The old woman in the bed started to pray aloud and the nurse ran away to dress her wound. Irma calmed down immediately once the nurse was gone and started the song over from the beginning very quietly and pleasantly, in her own high soprano. She smiled to herself, not looking at anything, and seemed happy.

'. . . with pants off and shirt off and socks off and shoes off, oh, my darling Augustine . . .'

Siiri was so engrossed in watching Irma, this unpredictable stranger with thoughts she couldn't fathom, that she didn't notice when Nurse Pulkkinen came back into the room. Suddenly the nurse was standing next to Irma, bending over behind her to pull down the back of her tracksuit bottoms and give her a very professional-looking poke with a syringe in the behind. It all happened incredibly quickly and efficiently. Irma wailed as if her heart would break. Siiri realized that she was wailing, too. She got up in a rage, but froze where she stood, unsure of what to do. She sputtered Irma's name, embraced her desperately, and felt Irma gradually go limp, her head lolling backwards, her eyes closing. Nurse Pulkkinen didn't stay to watch the scene, she just took hold of Siiri with both hands and told her that unfortunately she would have to leave and not cause any more disturbances in the Group Home.

Irma's room-mate could be heard all the way down the hallway, praying ecstatically as the nurse tugged Siiri by the hand, scolding her like a four-year-old who'd got lost on a field trip. The ward door locked with a clack behind Siiri's back and the sound of it echoed in her ringing ears until everything around her gradually became a dark grey roar. She couldn't understand where she was. She stood alone, swaying in a hallway somewhere outside the ward, winded and confused, and then felt herself slowly waken from this horrible nightmare that wasn't a dream.

Chapter 30

Anna-Liisa and Siiri sat on the number 3 tram heading towards the handsome apartment blocks of Eira. Siiri tried to tell Anna-Liisa about her experiences in the Group Home, but her explanations were rather confused. After the shock of her longed-for first visit she had been back to see Irma at least twice a week, sometimes three times.

'Irma still hasn't recognized me once. I can't take her outside and she can't be taken for walks.'

'Is she always in a wheelchair? She isn't paralysed.'

All the patients were kept tied to a bed or a wheelchair, because it made it easier to take care of them. At mealtimes the patients were brought one at a time to the table to eat. They were offered a couple of spoonfuls of watery mashed potatoes with one nurse feeding twelve patients. And if one of them wasn't lucid enough to eat them, the nurse concluded that the person wasn't hungry and wheeled them back to their room to stare at the wall. When Siiri had tried to feed Irma, they quickly intervened. Feeding was a task for a trained nurse; they couldn't let just anyone do it. If Siiri fed Irma, they told her, it would interfere with her rehabilitation process.

'Rehabilitation process? How dare they!' Anna-Liisa snapped. 'Nobody in that dementia ward is trying to rehabilitate anyone. They're just storing them there until it's time to send them to the crematorium.'

Every day there was a different nurse on duty, and always only one, often a refugee who spoke little Finnish. Usually, the nurse just sat in the break room drinking coffee and reading the paper. Not once had Siiri seen anyone in the Group Home spend any time with the patients.

She'd often read in the paper about retirement homes where they rubbed the old people's shoulders, manicured their nails, curled their hair, and drank coffee with them out of pretty cups. The closed unit at Sunset Grove was something quite different. Siiri was the only visitor – but who would want to visit old ladies like these? It just made a person feel guilty. Even Irma's daughter Tuula thought that her mother was too out of it to miss her. But could that possibly be true? There was always someone shouting 'help' or 'I need you', but the nurses didn't seem to pay any attention. And they talked about the patients as if they were numbers.

'Bed seven? She always yells, don't let it bother you. Her incontinence pad will be changed in the morning.'

Anna-Liisa and Siiri rode through Eira without speaking. Siiri wondered whether they should switch to the number 1A at some point and take it to Käpylä. It was the world's northernmost tram route, after all, and she hadn't ridden it in years. They could admire the old wooden houses. It would almost be like going out to the country. A trip to Käpylä was all the communing with nature that Siiri needed. She had never been a country girl like Irma, who just last summer had wanted to go to the countryside the way she'd always done and sit on the porch at the family cabin.

Siiri's great-granddaughter's boyfriend Tuukka had called a couple of days earlier. The conversation had been a bit tense because Tuukka claimed that Siiri had had someone in for expensive repairs. Siiri was completely at a loss. She feared that she had forgotten something important again and didn't dare to contradict him. She had come to realize that it was better to keep quiet than to admit to forgetfulness.

'The Loving Care Foundation billed you for a drain replacement, which cost several hundred euros. Plus you still have the cleaning bill every other week, plus a new service increase since last October. Do you know what that is?'

Siiri didn't know. Or didn't remember. Tuukka was awfully nice and promised to put a little money in her account so that she wouldn't be in a pickle. Irma once said that whenever her mother-in-law was low on money she used to say that said she'd 'run into a pickle'. And when they got into real trouble she would send Irma to the neighbouring farm to get some potatoes.

Anna-Liisa didn't seem interested in Tuukka's phone call and Siiri's repair bills. She'd been silent for almost the whole trip. But when the tram arrived at the market square, she grabbed Siiri by the arm and pulled her close. Siiri was surprised at how powerful her grip was; it was just like Siiri's husband on his death bed, long after Siiri had thought he had no strength left in him. Anna-Liisa spoke with firm emphasis, as if she were revealing a state secret: 'We have to go there together. At night.'

Chapter 31

Thus commenced their Plan, in honour of which Anna-Liisa invited Siiri to her apartment for the first time. Her rooms had poor light and books everywhere, even on the floor and windowsills, tall stacks of them all over the place, and a pervasive scent of dust. Siiri hadn't known that Anna-Liisa still read every day, too. They talked about how much fun it is when you're old to reread all the books you liked when you were young.

'I'm reading Galsworthy's *Forsyte Saga* for the fourth time now,' Siiri said excitedly, and sneezed.

'Yes, I like *Buddenbrooks* better, although I wouldn't want to read even that four times.'

'At least I'm getting some use out of the fact that I forget everything!'

Siiri had the key ring that Mika had left with her. She'd kept it carefully in her handbag at all times for the past few weeks so that she wouldn't leave it somewhere where Erkki Hiukkanen could find it. She was sure that Mika meant them to spring into action and use it. And now they had realized what it was they ought to do.

First they planned to see what the corridors of Sunset Grove were like at night and map a route from their wing to the door of the Group Home. They would also use their key to get into the Group Home and investigate what went on there at night. Once they had all the information, they would carry out their Plan. Mika would certainly be proud of them, if he only knew!

'What if I run into Virpi Hiukkanen at night?' Siiri said, a bit frightened at the thought.

'Don't worry! She thinks you're senile anyway. If you wonder aloud who you are and where you are, she'll just order you back to your room. But you won't give her the keys, of course, no matter how confused you are.'

'Do you think I'm senile?' Siiri asked, but Anna-Liisa ignored the question and asked Siiri if she would like her to read aloud from some old books. Anna-Liisa thought it sounded fun, and since Siiri's eyes tired easily, it was an excellent idea. They decided to start this new pastime immediately. Anna-Liisa rummaged through the stacks of books for a moment, found one on top of the refrigerator, petted it as if it were a cat, put it back where she'd found it, then bent with some difficulty to look under the telephone table and found what she was looking for. It was Maria Jotuni's novel *The Tottering House*, which Siiri hadn't read in decades. Anna-Liisa wandered around for a moment more until she spotted her reading glasses on the bedside table, settled into an armchair, and turned on the floor lamp. She looked at the lamp angrily.

'These environmentally friendly light bulbs are so slow to light up!'

Anna-Liisa waited a moment, then opened up *The Tottering House* with a flourish, sniffed the inside of the book, coughed a couple of times, and began to read. Siiri sat quite comfortably in a corner of the hard sofa next to a pile of books, leaning her head on a musty-smelling cushion. The room was dim, Anna-Liisa's deep voice flowed out evenly, and the atmosphere was peculiarly homely, though Lea and Toini's story began with a tough childhood full of alcohol and death.

'Siiri, are you asleep?' Anna-Liisa asked irritably, when she noticed her beginning to doze on the sofa.

Siiri napped much more often these days than she used to – uncontrollably, in fact. Last week she had even fallen asleep on the tram. The familiar driver who listened to Bruckner came to wake her at the last stop and said she'd already gone around the whole route one and a half times.

'Have you been listening at all to what happens in this second chapter?' Anna-Liisa asked, and Siiri had to apologize because she had no idea how far Anna-Liisa had read. Anna-Liisa's reading style was quite monotonous and it positively lulled her to sleep.

'Right. Pearls before swine. We'll continue reading Jotuni some other time,' Anna-Liisa said dourly and slammed the book shut, sending a cloud of dust flying into the air. She put the book and her reading glasses down on the stack nearest her. 'In other words, enough amusement. Let's get down to business. What do you think, should we start our nocturnal exploration this week? I could go first.'

'That suits me. You're much braver than I am. If you have your adventure this week, I'll go at the beginning of next week. Won't that be a good plan for starting the Plan?'

'That's a more leisurely timetable than I would wish, but let's just see what I find out. First, I'll have to acquire the necessary equipment.'

Siiri was beginning to like Anna-Liisa. It wasn't such a bad stroke of luck that they'd been thrown together to concoct their secret Plan. When you'd lived to be as old as they were, it was a roll of the dice as to who you would have to get along with in your final years. The people you had in one way or another chosen as friends in the past were dead. In the end, all that remained were a few people your own age, and you couldn't be picky about who they were; you just had to get along with them. The group at Sunset Grove – Anna-Liisa, the Hat Lady, the Ambassador and the Partanens – were a good example of this. They were all very different.

'Pish,' Anna-Liisa said. 'The place is full of new people. We just haven't met them.'

She was right, of course. Many of the residents had only been there a short time, and they hadn't had a chance to get to know them. People arrived at Sunset Grove in worse condition these days than they used to, even though the new residents were much younger than they were. Anna-Liisa thought it was due to politics.

'Home care is in style now because it's cheaper than lying in a retirement home. If an old person agrees to stay at home alone, the state will order all kinds of services for them. Even hairdressers and handymen, and someone to walk you around the block, which is something we don't have here. People only come to the retirement home when there's no other option.'

Anna-Liisa got worked up into a lecture about the care ratio, which was a new expression and, in her opinion, the worst possible kind. Before she could move on to the problems of language development and the ethics of neologisms, Siiri went back to the subject of the care ratio, because she knew that it didn't mean what it sounded like. A good care ratio didn't mean good care; it meant that there were fewer old people to be a drain on society. She and Irma had read in the paper that the worst possible care ratio was in Japan, because the population was ageing even faster than in Finland. Irma hadn't been able to understand how they could age any faster than anyone else.

That made Anna-Liisa laugh.

'My Lord, we really must get Irma back. We might soon forget how to laugh without her.'

And that was exactly what they planned to do. Once each of them had performed her reconnaissance mission and they had a sufficient grasp of Sunset Grove at night, they were going to steal Irma back. They were going to rescue her!

Chapter 32

'It's quieter than a graveyard here at night,' Anna-Liisa said as they drank their midday coffee at Siiri's apartment.

Siiri hadn't slept at all; she'd been so frightened for Anna-Liisa. But the expedition had gone well, and neither of them felt tired, because now the Plan was really in motion.

'There's no one in the office. The only light is in the closed unit, but it looked to me like the nurse was asleep.'

Anna-Liisa had made a careful drawing, noting all the surveillance cameras between A wing and the Group Home, and there were a lot of them. She told Siiri to take the proper equipment with her on her own expedition; at the very least she must have a torch and a knife, and preferably a backpack as well.

'I always carry a knife in my handbag,' Anna-Liisa said, but Siiri couldn't understand why she would need a knife in the middle of the night. And Siiri didn't have one.

'Will a kitchen knife do? Of course, it's not terribly sharp any more. And I don't have a backpack; I'm not a Girl Scout.'

'You can take my knife.'

'But then you won't have it in your handbag. Will you be able to sleep without it?' Siiri asked, ribbing her a little, and Anna-Liisa smiled.

Then Anna-Liisa immediately pulled a knife with a knotted birch handle out of her handbag and laid it ceremoniously on the table, as if it were Marshall Mannerheim's personal weapon. The knife was old and worn, but dangerously sharp, and it didn't have a sheath. No doubt it had a long and interesting history, but Siiri didn't dare ask about it. It seemed a very serious matter to Anna-Liisa, who at that moment was absorbed in the Plan and the notes she'd taken, bent over the pages with her glasses perched on her nose.

'The last hallway from the lobby to the door of the Group Home isn't as long as I'd thought. I did it in seventy-three steps. And it's just thirty-one steps from Sundström's office to the card table – I measured that, too, while I was at it. Thirty-one steps isn't much. It's a little worrying, because it is within earshot.' Anna-Liisa lifted her gaze from the papers, put her glasses down on top of them, and straightened her back until she looked majestically tall. 'What do you think, how quickly can Irma wake up if we don't give her any medication? Have you checked whether everything's in order in her apartment?'

Siiri hadn't been to Irma's apartment since Mika Korhonen had cleaned it. She thought it better to proceed one step at a time. Besides, something about the whole thing troubled her. She couldn't understand why Irma's apartment had been ransacked like that. It was a nasty thought that she'd tried to get out of her mind. Who had been there, and why?

'It could have been any one of the staff,' said Anna-Liisa, as if the matter had been settled by a police investigation. 'They were looking for evidence to keep Irma in the dementia ward.'

Siiri was still thinking about the green folder, which at first they hadn't been able to find anywhere, and then there it had been, underfoot with the rest of the mess in the apartment.

'It's plain as day,' Anna-Liisa snorted. 'First they took it, and then they returned it to cover their tracks.'

'Cover their tracks? It seems to me that Irma's apartment was full of tracks!'

'But not any more, because Mika Korhonen cleaned it all up. Have you thought about that? Why was your angel Mika in such a hurry to clean away other people's tracks? Or had he been there himself? After all, it was his idea to break into Irma's flat, but if you look at the details, he actually already had the keys in his backpack. Did you happen to notice how many pill bottles he put in his pocket? I don't trust that man. For an ordinary taxi driver he is strangely up to date on everything going on here.'

Anna-Liisa was very worked up at this point, her cheeks glowing and her voice trembling, though she was usually so controlled. Siiri was completely speechless. She wasn't prepared for this kind of outburst, and everything Anna-Liisa was saying seemed frighteningly logical. Siiri had thought that Anna-Liisa believed Mika Korhonen to be a good person at heart, someone who wanted to help them.

'What reason does he have to help us? A bunch of penniless old women?' Anna-Liisa continued. Siiri looked nervously at her hands, which were squeezed into fists.

'I . . . I imagined that he'd made friends with us and . . . and that we . . . had a sort of mutual enemy here, because the cook who hanged himself was a friend of his and somehow . . . somehow it was all connected to Tero. Isn't that what you thought?'

Anna-Liisa didn't say anything. Perhaps she was thinking. Siiri wasn't very persuasive in her defence of Mika. It was all so flimsy and vague. How had she and Irma trusted a stranger, a cab driver, and gone to lunch with him, just like that? And Siiri had invited him into her own home, a strange man who wore a coat with a skull on it. They certainly needed Irma now!

'No; Irma needs us. We have to do it all by ourselves, Siiri Kettunen.'

Chapter 33

Siiri padded very nervously in her slippers towards the dementia ward. Anna-Liisa had advised her to wear her slippers so that she wouldn't make any unnecessary noise as she made her way down the corridor. When she went down to the ground floor, she felt as if the noise of the lift would wake the whole city. With her heart pounding she wandered down the office hallway to the common areas and wondered at how different the rooms she knew so well looked at night. There were no old people who had fallen asleep, no one reading the paper, even the television was dark. Someone had forgotten their Zimmer frame in the middle of the lobby and the Ambassador's deck of cards was waiting on the table for its players.

She continued like an automaton along the B wing corridor, at the end of which was the locked door of the Group Home. Seventy-three steps, Anna-Liisa had counted. Siiri got confused in her count after fifty. Anna-Liisa's steps were clearly longer than hers. The lights in the hallway turned on by themselves, which gave the place a ghostly atmosphere. She had a torch in her hand, which was unnecessary – she didn't know why Anna-Liisa had needed one. Or was the idea to rummage through cupboards and peek into corners? In her excitement Siiri couldn't remember whether that was a part of their Plan.

She tried to find the surveillance cameras Anna-Liisa had talked about and imagined the poor soul whose job it was to watch her on a screen somewhere. She stopped as she came to one of the cameras and examined it. It was round and had a glass dome over it; it looked more like a lamp, and she wouldn't have understood that it was a camera if Anna-Liisa hadn't given her a brief presentation on surveillance equipment and told her that they have them everywhere nowadays, even in taxi cabs.

'*Döden, döden, döden,*' Siiri whispered, and aimed the torch at the device as she passed, just in case. If it was a camera, it wasn't going to get a picture of her. She felt incredibly clever and counted three camera-like protrusions altogether in the corridor and one gadget that might be a fire alarm or an air freshener. A night-time expedition was actually rather fun.

As she approached the Group Home she heard a muffled shout. Some unfortunate dementia sufferer was yelling in vain for help again, not knowing if it was day or night. It didn't sound like Irma's voice, although Siiri couldn't be sure because when Irma had that attack of rage at the nurse in the middle of the Augustin song, her voice had become completely unrecognizable. This was a very feeble moan.

Siiri turned off the torch and stood for a moment in front of the door to the closed unit. She looked through the glass at the slender girl nurse sleeping in a rocking chair with a pale-blue teddy bear in her lap. There were children's teddy bears like that scattered all over the dementia ward; Siiri didn't know why. Maybe they were for the nurses. She glanced out of the hall window and for a moment it seemed as if someone was running across the courtyard in the snow. She looked through the door at the clock on the wall. It was past two. At the same moment, she heard more sounds from inside the closed unit. It sounded like several people were shouting. Why didn't the nurse wake up?

Siiri didn't know how long she stood looking through the closed door, but she started when she saw smoke inside. She became aware of a strong smell and saw that the smoke was coming from the patients' feeding area, where the nurse with the teddy bear was sleeping. There was already smoke in the hallway, too, and slowly Siiri's apprehension changed to confused horror.

'Fire! Fire! Help!' she shouted high and loud, without thinking that she shouldn't have been sniffing around at the door to the closed unit in the middle of the night. The nurse didn't wake up, although Siiri pounded on the door with both fists. Siiri was in a panic and she felt like a helpless crackpot, not knowing what to do. Smoke was billowing around the nurse, and suddenly Siiri remembered that she had a key in her handbag.

'It's a good thing I finessed that,' she muttered to herself, and started searching her bag for the key. Her hands were trembling and the zip on her handbag pocket was stuck. She tore the zip open, pulled out the key, and pushed it into the lock with both hands. She was afraid that the burglar alarm would start to ring, but the thought of Irma among the flames made her open the door. The acrid stench of smoke whirled through the hallway, stinging her eyes and making her cough. She strode swiftly inside, and although she felt like running straight to Irma's room, she first tried to shake the nurse awake. She could hear numerous patients calling for help from their rooms. It looked like the smoke was coming from the end of the hallway. The girl snapped awake and took such fright that she started to scream in terror.

'All right, now. Try to stay focused,' Siiri told the child soothingly. 'There's a fire here and we have to get to work. You call the fire department while I go and check on the patients.'

'A fire? Where? Who should I call?'

'Emergency services. One-one-two. Tell them your name and that there's a fire, and then give them the exact address.'

'What's the address here? How am I supposed to know it? Where's the telephone?'

Siiri led the hysterical girl to the break room, hastily wrote the necessary information on a piece of paper, and went to look for Irma. She felt strangely calm, as if she knew perfectly how to behave in this situation. She turned on the torch and was glad she had it with her, because without it she wouldn't have been able to see anything. There was quite a lot of smoke in the corridor, and when she got to the end of the hall, she noticed flames coming out of the sauna room. She had to get Irma out fast. She rushed into Irma's room, where a profound silence reigned. Both old women were fast asleep and there was surprisingly little smoke. They were tied to their beds. Siiri was grateful to Anna-Liisa for her silly knife, with which she easily cut the straps away from Irma and her room-mate.

'Are you taking me to Karelia? Shall we sing?' the old war refugee asked, but Irma just slept. Siiri tried to wake her, pinched her earlobes and shook her by the shoulders. She could hear the distant shouts of other patients and wondered in horror how she would get to them all in time to help. She dashed out to see how great the emergency was in the other rooms, the knife still in her hand. Maybe she could free the rest. This was the beginning of the revolution!

In the next room two old people were awake and calling for help. Siiri tried to calm the two women with a lie, telling them that everything was all right as she tore at their straps with the knife. In the first bed they broke easily, but in the second one she had to saw at the straps, and cut a gash in her thumb. Just as she was sucking on it to stop the bleeding, two firemen sprang into the room. It felt like they'd taken hours to get there. They looked at her in astonishment.

'At last!' Siiri shouted, continuing to saw at the straps in a near frenzy, heedless of the blood that was staining the sheets.

One of the men was carrying an axe. Without saying a word they grabbed Siiri with practised hands.

'Now, now, everything's all right here . . . you must have been woken by the smoke . . . let's go now, calm down . . . how about you give me that knife . . .'

They dragged Siiri out of the room, all the while trying to

calm her, although Siiri felt almost icily calm in this catastrophe. She refused to give the knife to the firemen, and they talked over her, imagining that she didn't understand anything that was happening.

'Are there a lot of these thumbsuckers here?'

'Fourteen, somebody said.'

'We can get by with this gear, then.'

'Yeah. Let the old lady keep her knife. This is just one floor, and they seem to be light and easy to carry. Some of them can probably walk, like this one.'

Siiri didn't say anything. It seemed easier to pretend to be demented than to explain what she was doing in the Group Home with a knife in her hand at three o'clock in the morning. She asked the firemen to rescue the people at the end of the hall first – Irma and her room-mate – because the fire was right on the other side of their wall in the adjoining sauna. The men left her in the lobby and went about their business.

The atmosphere in the retirement-home common room was entirely different to what it had been half an hour before. Firemen, ambulance crew and police were running back and forth tugging hoses and shouting orders, radios crackling. The Hiukkanens were there, standing against the wall, Virpi in a see-through nightgown, Erkki next to her in dishevelled clothes and boots. The girl nurse who'd awoken to the fire was still hysterical and Virpi was focused on berating her.

'I saw someone running outside,' Siiri tried to say to the

people in uniform running past. 'Should somebody check to make sure there isn't a patient out there?'

'Siiri Kettunen! What the hell are you doing here?'

In two vigorous steps, Virpi Hiukkanen was in front of Siiri. She set off to march Siiri to her apartment, though Siiri thought Virpi should have stayed to monitor the fire situation to the end and make sure that the dementia patients were no longer in danger. Virpi wasn't the least bit interested in finding out who had been running across the lawn.

'I can get there myself, thank you,' Siiri said as Virpi shoved her towards the lift in the lobby.

'How dreadful! Your hand is covered in blood!' Virpi shouted, turning her head away in horror.

Siiri wasn't going anywhere until she saw that Irma was all right and had been taken to safety, away from the flames. Virpi dashed back and forth shouting at Siiri and at the poor nurse, who was bawling like a little child with the teddy bear under her arm.

'You don't have permission to walk around here alone at night!' Virpi yelled at Siiri.

'Do people need a special hall pass in a retirement home?' Siiri asked defiantly, and then Virpi started to yell until spit flew out of her mouth and her chewing gum fell out onto the floor.

'I don't understand you. What is wrong with you? You run around all day long causing a fuss for everyone. This fire is the last straw. I'm giving your information to the police and you'll be held responsible for all the damage you've caused at Sunset Grove. Don't imagine that just because you're old you have some kind of immunity and can do whatever pops into your head. Get out of my sight! The patients in the Group Home are not your responsibility, none of them, do you understand?'

Siiri had to sit down for a moment to catch her breath. She found her handkerchief in the bottom of her handbag and pressed it against the cut on her thumb. Unit Operations Manager Erkki Hiukkanen slumped onto the sofa beside her when the firemen shepherded him out of the way. Erkki was completely numb, unable to do anything useful. As he sat there staring into space he was quite indistinguishable from the dementia sufferers being carted into the lobby in wheelchairs and carried on stretchers to ambulances. Snow was melting off his boots and forming a large puddle on the floor.

Finally, after an excruciatingly long wait, Siiri saw Irma among the last patients taken to an ambulance. Irma was walking by herself but was very stooped and made her way forward slowly, with fumbling steps. Two firemen led her to the vehicle and kindly helped her in. When she was inside the ambulance she was made to lie down on a stretcher, then the doors were closed and the ambulance drove calmly away without any siren or lights, like a hearse on its way to the chapel.

When the ambulance had disappeared into the darkness, Siiri stood staring at the deserted car park without a single thought in her head. Gradually, the hubbub inside diminished. The police and fire fighters gathered their gear and quickly left to begin another task somewhere else. The girl nurse called a taxi in a trembling voice and went home to sleep, and Virpi Hiukkanen withdrew to her office. That left only Erkki Hiukkanen and Siiri Kettunen, side by side on the sofa. The cut on Siiri's thumb wasn't bleeding any more. She put the stained handkerchief and the knife in her handbag and stood up.

'Well, I guess I should go. Maybe I can still get some sleep,' she said, and headed for her apartment, relieved.

She wasn't interested in what kind of damage the fire had caused or how Erkki Hiukkanen would recover from the shock of the experience; the important thing was getting Irma out of the closed unit. That had been the objective of their Plan, but it hadn't quite gone the way they'd expected.

Chapter 34

There were all kinds of wild rumours going around Sunset Grove about what had happened the night of the fire. Some claimed that Siiri Kettunen lit the fire, but the Hat Lady was sure that Erkki Hiukkanen was the culprit. The Ambassador, on the other hand, thought that it was a white-collar crime. According to him, it was a Finnish custom to arrange a fire when there were irregularities in the bookkeeping.

The fire was even in the newspaper. Anna-Liisa read the article aloud to Siiri. It contained an interview with Virpi Hiukkanen, who told it all wrong and claimed she was the first person to arrive on the scene.

'I smelled smoke at two a.m.,' she lied in the paper. Then the article said how quickly and efficiently Virpi and Erkki Hiukkanen had taken rescue measures. 'All of the residents of the retirement home were rescued before any harm could come to them.'

'Balderdash. Trash media,' Anna-Liisa snorted. 'They don't even say how the fire started. Do you have an opinion about it? After all, you were there, unlike all these other people walking around explaining how it started as if they knew all the details.'

Siiri didn't know what to think, although she'd thought about it a great deal. She was just going to say something about the sauna storeroom when Virpi Hiukkanen walked into her apartment without knocking, using her own key. Siiri got a terrible fright and even Anna-Liisa looked shocked.

'How are things going in here? How are you getting along?'

Virpi was cheerful, walking busily back and forth and glancing vigilantly around her. She patted Siiri on the top of her head, didn't even look at Anna-Liisa, then noticed the newspaper, which was open to the story about the fire, passed it by, and turned to go into the kitchen.

'How did the fire start?'

Anna-Liisa tossed her question out without any warning into the middle of Virpi's bustle with a fearlessness that only an interrogator experienced in surprise quizzes on the infinitive forms of Finnish verbs can have.

Virpi stopped and answered without turning to look at them: 'It started in the sauna. The police figured it out. And that's actually not part of my job anyway; it's Sinikka Sundström's responsibility.'

'What are you looking for in my apartment?' Siiri asked, and Virpi said she'd come to see how Siiri was doing. This was probably rubbish.

'Once you've recovered a little, I'd like to have a chat with you. Before the police do – so you don't blather on about who knows what,' she called, on her way out. 'You have been taking your pills, I hope. Your pill counter is on the table, filled.'

Virpi Hiukkanen closed the door behind her with a slam. Siiri tried to shout that if she was going to drop in uninvited, she could at least ring the bell, but there was no point, Virpi was already gone.

'She's nervous about you,' Anna-Liisa said. 'You're a very dangerous person to her now.'

The idea obviously thrilled Anna-Liisa, but Siiri had an uneasy feeling. How could she explain to Virpi Hiukkanen why she had been in the Group Home in the middle of the night? And what about the police? Would they want to question her too? Would some surveillance video turn up on the Internet showing her entering the dementia ward with her own key?

She asked Anna-Liisa if they could talk about something else. The fire had taken a significant toll on her strength, and she'd spent the days since then mostly in bed. Anna-Liisa had taken care of her diligently every day, brought her food, helped her to the toilet and kept her company.

'I never thought I'd be the last oak,' Anna-Liisa said, when they'd sat a little while in silence after Virpi's inspection visit. 'I thought of myself as basically weak, thought I would die before the others. And here I am, the last one standing. It's very strange.'

Siiri was a little surprised at this. If anyone was a strong person, it was Anna-Liisa. She was so unyielding; if you were to compare her to a tree, it would be an oak.

'My last name is Petäjä. The Eastern Finnish word for a pine tree. It's a pretty name, but it doesn't suit me at all.'

Petäjä was Anna-Liisa's second husband's name. They had divorced after the war because he had proved to be a violent, unpredictable man. The war had jumbled his brain, and when Anna-Liisa didn't have any children, he started to blame her for everything bad in his life. A lawyer she knew arranged the divorce without any scandal, but in the 1950s it was difficult to be a divorced woman. People said all kinds of awful things wherever you went, and especially in a small town.

'As you must know, a divorced woman is almost the same as a whore.'

When Anna-Liisa said that horrible word she lowered her voice almost to a whisper and articulated it dramatically, as if it had three Rs on the end. She talked about going to work as a young teacher in trousers, how after that there was no end to the gossip, because a woman should only wear trousers when skiing. Finally, she'd had enough and she moved to Helsinki to escape the slander.

Siiri looked at her friend and realized for the first time how tall and thin Anna-Liisa was, simultaneously delicate and imposing. She had never thought of Anna-Liisa as fragile before; she was so vigorous and knowledgeable. Even her voice was expressive and strong, not at all like a frail old woman's. And now she'd learned that Anna-Liisa wasn't even an old maid – she'd been married at least twice!

'Did you say that Petäjä was your second husband's name?'

'Yes. My first husband was studying to be a doctor when the Winter War started. We rushed to get married before he was sent to the front – it seemed safer somehow,' she said, then smiled wryly and sighed. 'He fell right at the beginning of the war. A bullet in the knee. How's that for a cause of death? There wasn't any chance to help anyone there, because there were so many wounded and in such terrible conditions. But of course you know about that. Weren't you in the Lottas during the Continuation War?'

Anna-Liisa seemed to be quite a pacifist. When Siiri made the mistake of saying something about a heroic death, she was almost angry, her eyes smouldering as she demanded to know what was heroic about dying over some trivial offence, drowning in blood out in the woods somewhere. She thought the worst thing about heroism was that it didn't let you grieve for the fallen. Even she had walked around bravely with her head held high, as if it were some great honour to be a twenty-one-year-old widow. She hadn't cried once, not even when she was alone, although she'd felt like she had nothing left to hope for in her life.

'And then, when I was ninety, I started to have a dream about my first husband, and I realized that I was still grieving for him, and I couldn't even remember what he looked like. Does that happen to you? Far-off memories come back to you all of a sudden now you're old? So strongly that even though you don't want to think about them, you have to?'

Siiri thought about her little brother Voitto, who'd died in the last summer of the Continuation War. She couldn't grieve for him, either. Nobody talked about Voitto, but a portrait of him in his army uniform was framed and placed on the piano to remind them of their silenced grief. Siiri didn't have very many memories of her brother. She remembered how Voitto would tease her and how he had broken her beautiful doll on purpose, the only one she had; he'd kicked it in the head and broken it and looked her in the eye and laughed. He'd done it on purpose, impudently. She didn't dream about Voitto, but she had started thinking about her mother, who had been a very difficult person. Siiri had thought she was over it until, when she was ninety-four, her mother started haunting her dreams and thoughts.

'Isn't it sort of peculiar?'

'People must not be meant to live this long,' Anna-Liisa said after a thoughtful pause. 'But here we are, victims of retirement home aerobics. I've never once in my life exercised until now. It's a pastime, so we'll have something to do during these pointless years, waiting for everything finally to end. What I mean is, life hands you surprises, right up to the end, even us old ladies over ninety. Who could have guessed that you and I would end up being each other's only friends? We didn't know a thing about each other ten years ago. Or that Irma would end up in the dementia ward? Or that your heart would give out before its time?'

'Before its time? Anna-Liisa, I'm ninety-four years old. And my heart hasn't given out.'

'But you've been lying in bed for almost a week. I think we have to get to work if we're going to get Irma home from wherever she happens to be at the moment.' Anna-Liisa was right again. But for now she cut short her flood of talk, gathered up her things, and dutifully set off downstairs for the singalong, although she'd always got low marks for singing in school and considered singing a primitive behaviour.

Left alone, Siiri got out of bed and got properly dressed for the first time in a long time. She went to the kitchen to look for something to eat and found the pill counter full of tablets. She looked at it, perplexed, and turned the box over in her hands. This is what Virpi was talking about when she'd told her to take her medicine. But she'd never had a pill counter, she was sure she hadn't. She got such a frightened feeling that her hands started to shake and she dropped the pills on the work surface with a clunk. What if she were the next resident lined up for transfer to the dementia ward?

Chapter 35

Irma's doctor daughter was suddenly standing in the hallway on the top floor of A wing, looking lost. Siiri didn't recognize her at first because the last time they'd seen each other was years ago. Tuula had greyed and plumped up quite a bit. She still had a few flaming red streaks in her hair and heavy, plastic-rimmed glasses with frames the same colour as the strands in her hair.

'Siiri darling! How nice to see you! Am I in the right place?'

Tuula squeezed Siiri so hard that for a moment she thought the woman really missed her mother. But that was probably wishful thinking.

'I don't really remember where Mother's apartment is. But hey, have you heard what happened to her after that horrible fire?'

Siiri hadn't heard. She'd thought about Irma every day and had been more worried about her friend than she had ever been about anyone. All kinds of things had happened in Siiri's life, but never anything as difficult to comprehend as this.

'You have to hear about it!'

Irma's daughter stood uncomfortably close to her as she spoke. Siiri tried to move aside, but Tuula moved along with her until she had her against the wall. 'The patients from the Group Home were first taken to Haartman for treatment, and most of them were supposed to come back the next day, but since the Group Home was badly damaged and there was no other space at Sunset Grove, they had to find them work-around accommodation,' Tuula began, as if she were reading a report she'd written. 'Work-around' accommodation was what they called various short-term lodgings, dorm rooms and other places to house students or patients until their building could be repaired to a usable state.

'The problem is complicated by the fact that these severe-dementia sufferers aren't Sunset Grove's concern in the first place. They're actually the responsibility of medical services. Director Sundström was quite relieved when she realized that.'

'If you ask me, she's seemed anything but relieved lately.'

'Yes, well, she told me that she lay awake for two nights before she realized a crucial aspect of her job description — the fact that it's not hers but the city's responsibility to find a place to put these fourteen dementia patients for the next few months. Her responsibility is to take care of insurance matters, and, of course, to get the Group Home repaired as soon as possible. Has the work started yet?'

Siiri didn't know. She hadn't been downstairs for several days. She couldn't stop staring at a large mole under Tuula's right eye with a black hair growing from it.

'But what happened to the flock of dementia patients from Sunset Grove is that they were swept out of the Haartman acute care and into Suursuo Hospital, except for one woman who died at Meilahti Hospital from injuries she suffered in the fire. She was quite a young person, too. My age. They didn't mention any of that in the newspaper article. So now there are thirteen left to place.'

'She died?'

Siiri slid onto the chair next to the lift. She felt like she was in a play. Irma's daughter had surprisingly similar intonations and high notes to her mother and she waved her hands around as she spoke, too. And yet she was a very different person, a complete stranger.

'This is such an unbelievable story, you can't imagine.' Tuula paused dramatically and sat down in the chair next to Siiri's. 'Well, Suursuo Hospital is where they usually keep patients suffering from self-inflicted dementia – you know, homeless alcoholics who you can't just leave out on the street, because they have severe memory and behavioural problems. I happen to know this very well, although I've never been there, at least not for work. Being an ear specialist, I'm safe from all that, thank goodness!'

She laughed musically, like her mother, and when she slapped Siiri on the thigh, Siiri noticed that she was wearing Irma's gold bracelets. She was sure she'd seen the very same bracelets still on Irma's arm in the closed unit.

'I hope you don't take everything I say too seriously? This is so absurd! So listen, there they were, lying in Suursuo Hospital, my mother and the rest of them waiting there among the winos for the city to find them a permanent place to stay. At that point I was in shock, because I'd heard that the waits in a place like that can take years.'

'So is Irma still——?'

'No, no! The farce didn't end there. I'm just getting started. So then they noticed that all those Sunset Grove dementia patients couldn't fit in Suursuo, even with some of them in the hallways and linen cupboards and one in the body-washing room in the morgue – a real last resort – sheesh – but, anyway, I made sure that my mother got a proper room, and then they were all hauled over to rehabilitation so that they wouldn't end up in public care. You probably don't know but there's a point system and you only end up in public care if you're over a certain number, so it's all a question of money. So, naturally, when they performed the tests, eight out of thirteen of those dementia patients were pronounced fit enough to be sent to retirement homes, in four different places all over Helsinki. Can you imagine? Anything to save public health money! And one of them was sent all the way to Turku because she'd moved to Sunset Grove from a place near there, so that way they could get her out of Helsinki and make her the Turku district's responsibility!'

Tuula burst into laughter and wiped her eyes. Siiri looked at her nervously, because it seemed to her that under the hard shell she might have strong feelings after all. She didn't dare try to comfort her, since she was on a roll. People let out their anxieties in different ways.

'One old woman apparently still owned an apartment so

they sent her back there! Then I told my brother that we were smart to have sold mother's apartment, even though she didn't want us to. Otherwise, they might just have tossed her there to muddle through alone. And we saved on inheritance taxes, too, because we had her give us the money for the apartment a little bit at a time. Oh, Siiri, it's all so crazy, even for a professional like me who's used to the ins and outs of health care, let alone for you ordinary people.'

'You're right about that. But does that mean that Irma—'

'Now don't get ahead of yourself! Shush. So, at that point, there were five patients left with no place to go, Mother among them, because she had a fractured hip that needed treatment, which was a good thing because that got her a place in Töölö Hospital, in line for orthopaedics. They probably found a diagnosis for all the ones who were left so that they could be transferred out of sight to other hospitals or chronic-care centres. Clever, is it not?'

'A broken hip? When did that happen?' Siiri couldn't believe that Irma's hip could have been broken in the fire. She had seen her walk to the ambulance on her own two feet.

'Oh, that's an old story; it happens to dementia patients all the time, we doctors know all about it. The patient slides out of bed onto the floor, or the nurse's grip slips in the shower and that's all it takes, an old lady with brittle bones, so one of them breaks, osteoporosis, that sort of thing, and since you're not all there, nobody knows whether you're in pain or not. Or, if you are in pain, exactly where. But my mother had good luck because they found it in an X-ray, on the right side, right here – two fractures, actually.'

'Oh. Irma's good luck strikes again. That's what she always says whenever something happens.'

'I guess Director Sundström will be able to collect money for the Indian orphans in peace now!'

Siiri was starting to feel a little unwell. She hadn't known that Tuula was such a keen talker. Tuula looked at her with concern, took her hand, and began trying to calm her down just as Siiri was about to do the same to her.

'I hope you understand that I'm just kidding? I don't really think that the director isn't doing her job. I really don't envy the woman. Just think what it's like for her, spending all her days here with a lot of senile old people, and then somebody sets the place on fire!'

Siiri felt dizzy. Her heart was pounding so hard and fast that she could feel it all the way to her throat. She couldn't look at the black hair on Tuula's mole any more because it made her feel ill. She struggled mightily to put her thoughts onto an even track.

'And what about Irma? What will happen to her? Will she finally get to come home?'

'Home? You mean the Group Home? She can't, Siiri, dear, not until the building's repaired. Do you remember the little accident that happened there? You do, good. And it could take months for the repairs. Do you understand? Yes, you do. But Mother was transferred to Töölö Hospital and she'll have surgery as soon as a slot is available. Do you understand? As soon as a slot is available?'

Tuula's voice sounded loud and echoing. Siiri had to concentrate with all her strength to keep up with her. When

Tuula started wondering aloud whether her mother really needed to walk again, Siiri remembered Olavi Raudanheimo's miraculous recovery at the Hilton and she understood that their Plan had, in fact, progressed remarkably swiftly while she had been in bed recuperating from the fire. Because the doctors were hardly likely to operate on Irma until they'd evaluated her prescriptions and discontinued her unnecessary medications.

'Unnecessary medications? What do you mean? There was a temp doctor there from some company, a Russian, who went through all of mother's papers and made it clear that he thought I'd neglected her treatment, as if I were responsible for the whole thing. Supposedly, there were incorrect dosages and some odd prescriptions, but this sort of quibbling between colleagues is nothing new. I didn't take it personally. But of course I'm glad that this Russian fellow is not working there permanently.'

Siiri could breathe again, and her heart was beating more regularly. She was grateful to Irma's daughter for this information. She complained of tiredness, said she was going to go and rest, let Tuula give her a rather unpleasantly tight hug goodbye, and went back to her apartment. She didn't even remember why she'd gone out in the first place, but it didn't matter. She found some red wine in the cupboard, drank a glass, and lay down on the bed without taking off her shoes. And then she folded her hands and prayed. She hadn't prayed since her childhood, if then, but now was a time to use every tool at her disposal.

'Dear God, if you're there somewhere, help us, and let the Russian doctor take care of Irma Lännenleimu and make her well as soon as possible. She, at least, believes in you. Amen.'

Chapter 36

Siiri looked through her magnifying glass at the pile of pills in the porridge bowl. She thought it was odd that the tablets didn't have anything written on them – no manufacturer, amount, nothing. She didn't see any pills that looked like Amarilly pillies, the only one she was supposed to take every day. And it was interesting that the pills were so varied – round ones, small ones, longish ones, thick, thin, blue, red, pale orange, and, of course, white ones too.

She had moved the tablets from the pill counter to the porridge bowl every day so that it would look like she was popping them obediently. Once a week the pill counter replenished itself, as if a ghost were waiting in a corner to dash out and refill it. The nurses always just happened to come to refill them when she was asleep or out – that had to be it.

Someone she had never met must have prescribed tranquillizers and stimulants, pills to go to sleep and pills to wake up, although Siiri was healthy and slept well at night. There might be some medicine in there for her heart troubles, too – they had tried to press those on her. She was sure that the pill counter was part of some sort of plot by the Sunset Grove staff. If she took the pills, she would turn senile. If she returned them and reported the matter, her medical file would accrue dubious notes that proved she was senile: 'Doesn't recognize her own possessions. Forgets to take her medication. Refuses treatment. Uncooperative.'

Siiri took three pills out of that day's morning slot and three out of the midday slot, put them in the porridge bowl, then put the bowl in the cupboard behind the rice and buckwheat. She put the magnifying glass back in its place on the bookshelf – or maybe she should put it in the drawer of her bedside table, where she could get to it easily. Was she sure she would remember she'd put it there? Today was an important and slightly nerve-wracking day because she and Anna-Liisa had decided to go and visit Irma at Töölö Hospital.

They were so excited about seeing Irma that they rode to Ruoholahti and Jätkäsaari on the new number 8 route to gather strength from the novelty of seeing a new neighbourhood. Ruoholahti seemed pleasant. There were a lot of people there, a large shopping centre, massive buildings, the old cable factory renovated into an arts centre, and exciting places like a Nepalese restaurant, the Helsinki Aquarium, and an eyelash-extension salon. And, of course, the Baltic Sea.

There was a new bridge from Ruoholahti to Jätkäsaari, and Siiri and Anna-Liisa couldn't figure out why it was named after the composer Bernhard Henrik Crusell. He probably didn't get to Helsinki much, and if he did, he certainly wouldn't have come to Jätkäsaari.

'Better that than the Bell Bridge in Itä-Pasila. It sounds like Venice and looks like East Germany,' Anna-Liisa said, and admired the canal that led from under the tram bridge into the bay.

Jätkäsaari looked rather depressing, though in a different way to how Siiri had imagined it. Maybe it would become a real neighbourhood some day. Now it was just muck, piles of gravel, pieces of cable and chunks of concrete. But they had built a new tram platform there, which was a promising beginning.

'We've never been here before. What business would we have had here, even in our youth?' Anna-Liisa mused. 'Especially since we didn't have a youth.'

Youth was only invented later, when they were already in the middle of work and family chores and building a new society after the war. When the war ended, Siiri was a mother of three and wouldn't have known how to yearn after her lost youth.

'And I was a twenty-five-year-old widow and divorcee,' said Anna-Liisa. 'Every small-town wife's nightmare.'

They watched as a grey-haired man stepped onto the tram wearing a long ponytail and blue jeans, though he had to be at least sixty-five. He was one of those people who'd had such a wonderful youth that he couldn't bear to give it up. They talked about things like that, about whatever came to mind, because they were trying to calm themselves down. They hoped, of course, that Irma had undergone the same miraculous recovery as Olavi Raudanheimo had when he'd got out of the closed unit and been transferred to the hospital, but then they remembered what had become of Olavi in the end, and they felt uneasy again.

'This hasn't gone exactly according to the Plan,' Anna-Liisa said, and Siiri wasn't sure if she'd caught a reproachful tone in her voice. 'We just have to hope that you don't end up in jail. Otherwise the Lavender Ladies Detective Agency really will be doomed.'

'What are you saying?'

'You must understand that Virpi Hiukkanen wants you to be blamed for the fire. That's what the pill counter is about. If you had taken all the pills like you were told, you would quickly have gone so senile that no one would have listened to your testimony and everything could have been spun as your fault. But luckily, because of the fire, we don't have to steal Irma and take her back to her apartment. That was actually a pretty daft idea.'

Siiri tried to think what it would be like to spend the rest of her life in jail. She imagined talking about it with Irma, as they'd talked about so many difficult situations. She used to have conversations in her head with her late husband, but lately Irma had taken his place as her imaginary confidante. Irma would almost certainly say that prison might not be any worse than Sunset Grove, and the idea wouldn't seem so bad once she'd made fun of it.

They had left Jätkäsaari and Ruoholahti, ridden safely down Mechelininkatu and into Töölö, and were just passing the Reitz Foundation. It had a museum on the top floor that no one ever went to, and on the ground floor was Restaurant Elite, which was always full. When Siiri was a child, there had been a large boulder where the building stood and she used to play on it in the winter. When the building was constructed later, it had an amazing outdoor terrace with seats that stretched along the length of the park and was quite a sight.

They got off at Töölö market and Siiri stopped to admire the Sandels building, which Anna-Liisa had never paid much attention to.

'An ordinary, modern structure.'

'No, it's not. It's unusually beautiful. It has a strange way of bringing light in and out. Look at those windows!'

Anna-Liisa wasn't listening; she just hurried single-mindedly down the street.

Töölö Hospital was in an unkempt condition. From the outside it looked badly weathered, and once they were inside it was messy, dirty and unpleasant. Sedated patients and rubbish bags were wheeled up and down the hallways. The paint was peeling from the walls and the corridors were full of old computers, tables, chairs and beds, as if the place were a warehouse instead of a university hospital. One doctor had to work among the junk, so passers-by could see that she was examining a femur on her computer screen.

Anna-Liisa and Siiri found Irma on the third floor, in a room for six. She was lying in the middle bed on the left, and looked much better in her pink hospital gown than she had in the grimy, 'sexy' T-shirt they had given her at the Group Home. Her hair was washed and combed and she almost looked like her old self. Anna-Liisa stood back but Siiri sat down excitedly on the edge of the bed and took hold of Irma's hand.

'Cock-a-doodle-doo!'

Irma didn't recognize Siiri. She didn't say anything or even smile; there was none of the twinkle in her eyes that Siiri had expected to see.

'Irma! Anna-Liisa and I came to see how you're doing here while you wait in line for your new hip. Irma? It's Siiri. Don't you remember me?'

Irma didn't seem to understand where she was or what was happening. She didn't respond at all. Siiri got up, confused, and went over to Anna-Liisa. They stood for a long time in silence looking at Irma and waiting for something to happen. Irma stared back at them blankly, then a happy smile spread across her face. She reached both hands out to Siiri and said:

'Mama! You came to see me after all! Mama, I'm so thirsty!'

Siiri's eyes grew wet and she couldn't say anything, just held her handbag tight with both hands and swallowed.

'Give her some water.'

It wasn't until she felt Anna-Liisa give her a sharp dig in the ribs with an elbow that Siiri responded. 'Yes, yes, of course. Sorry.'

With trembling hands she poured some water from the pitcher into the glass on Irma's night table and sat wearily down on the bed again.

'Here, Irma. Have some water. I don't have anything better to give you right now. I'm Siiri. Remember, Irma? I'm your good friend Siiri. Would you like me to sing "Oh, My Darling Augustine"?'

Irma drank the water greedily in big, loud gulps, like she always did on the rare occasions when water was what she wanted. When she'd emptied the glass, she gave it back to Siiri and stared into her eyes with a long, searching look.

'Thank you.'

Irma closed her eyes and turned her back to Siiri. She seemed to want to be left alone. Siiri pulled the covers over her friend, rubbed her back for a moment, then got up and took a deep breath. She looked helplessly at Anna-Liisa and, to her surprise, Anna-Liisa had tears in her eyes too.

'Let's go, Siiri. We're not making anyone happy here,' Anna-Liisa said, and turned her Zimmer frame towards the door.

Chapter 37

The final straw was when Sinikka Sundström and Virpi Hiukkanen were awarded medals for the bravery they'd shown at the time of the fire. Siiri choked on her instant coffee when she heard the news from Anna-Liisa.

'Bravery! Director Sundström wasn't even there. And Virpi Hiukkanen was mostly just yelling at me.'

Siiri and Anna-Liisa went to the Sunset Grove bravery ceremony out of pure curiosity. The event was held in the downstairs common room and the cafeteria, which had been combined into a large space for the unusual occasion by opening the partitioning doors. The more disabled residents were wheeled in their chairs and beds and positioned along the outer walls. The whole scene looked like a public festival was about to begin. The Remember to Sing dementia choir from the Evening Rest retirement home performed 'Sink, Oh Sink, into the Bosom of Thy Country' and a little man from city social services gave a short speech which must have been written by Virpi Hiukkanen, because it was nothing but lies from beginning to end.

'At three o'clock, Nurse Hiukkanen was the first to notice

the fire, which started with an electrical malfunction in the sauna. She quickly alerted emergency services and courageously directed the rescue personnel, whose efficiency can be thanked for the fact that not one of the residents of Sunset Grove was injured and the property damage was minimal.'

Siiri couldn't believe Virpi's lies. She was deliberately giving incorrect information about the fire. Lying about the time it started was bad enough but covering up the fact that someone had died was unforgivable. Siiri had to stop herself from speaking out. She knew that she couldn't reveal her involvement in the incident in front of all of these people.

It remained unclear what Director Sundström's part was in the rescue operation. The city functionary spoke about the medal and said that only fifty-two brave heroes had thus far received it. With hands shaking nervously, he went to pin the medals on Director Sundström and Virpi Hiukkanen while the residents looked on in silence. Virpi Hiukkanen wasn't wearing her usual pullover; she was dolled up in a sheer, pale-blue dress that made her look rather pasty. The functionary didn't know where to put his hands in order to pin the bauble to her chest. The longer he hesitated, the tighter Virpi's mouth screwed up, but she treated him like an elderly resident who'd taken ill – which is to say, she didn't lift a finger to help him. Sinikka Sundström, on the other hand, smiled radiantly, took the medal from him, and pinned it to the collar of her bright-coloured cape with her own hands. When this task had been carried out, the functionary began the applause and the old people dutifully clapped along.

'Last I heard, the fire started at two o'clock,' Anna-Liisa whispered to Siiri. 'They've tightened up their story. But shouldn't you say something? Maybe ask where Sinikka Sundström was, since she was nowhere to be seen at the fire? Or why Virpi Hiukkanen didn't get there until after three o'clock? And where is the nurse who called the fire department? She was the one who called, not Hiukkanen, right?'

But Siiri couldn't say anything because she wasn't supposed to be in the Group Home at night. No one had yet thought to ask how she'd got into the closed unit, because it would hardly occur to them that a resident would have keys to all the doors in the retirement home. Siiri watched Virpi Hiukkanen with a stern eye but Virpi didn't notice; she just stood there smiling, with the medal on her chest and a certificate in a craft-shop frame under her arm. She hugged her husband Erkki, without whom the operation would have been an overwhelming task. Sinikka Sundström, too, looked blissfully happy, as if this were all a rare stroke of luck, this fire, because it had made a devoted government worker into a hero.

'Excuse me.' The Ambassador's voice rang out from the back of the hall. He stood up and straightened his tie before continuing. 'I'd like to ask why it is that highly flammable disposable incontinence pads were being stored in an electric sauna? The Group Home's pad storage was in the sauna, was it not? Doesn't that constitute a significant safety risk that has now been actualized? In addition, according to the information I've received, one of the patients died from injuries suffered in the fire, contrary to what you have just given us to believe.'

Total silence fell over the room. Sinikka Sundström reddened but continued to smile, and looked at Virpi Hiukkanen, who fiddled with the hem of her dress and glared commandingly at her husband Erkki, to no avail. Finally, the granter of the city social services medal stepped forward and raised his eyes to the ceiling, as he'd been taught to do in the city employee acting club.

'As I understand it,' he said. For a moment, he imagined he was in the National Theatre on a big stage, about to begin Hamlet's soliloquy, but he quickly came to his senses and continued with this bewildering pause long enough to make it seem as if he'd done it on purpose, for effect. 'As I understand it, a thorough investigation of the entire incident is being conducted, and is still underway.'

A loud murmur ensued among the old people. Everyone had something to say to his or her neighbour, the medal recipients, and the social services functionary. Sinikka Sundström clapped her hands together and demanded silence.

'My dear patien— residents! Everyone is invited to the cafeteria for free cake and coffee in honour of this honour! I would also remind you that there is still time to participate in the collection for the Indian orphans, which has got off to a good start. There are donation boxes on the tables, and if you're interested in Indian orphans, there will be a presentation on the subject in the auditorium after coffee.'

The nurses began pushing the wheelchairs over to the cafeteria and Siiri went to thank the Ambassador for his courageous words. The Ambassador was pleased by all the attention – and there were actually more people surrounding him to offer congratulations than there were Director Sundström and Virpi Hiukkanen. Anna-Liisa gave him a warm, tight, long hug.

'You deserve a medal, too,' the Hat Lady said, and someone suggested a certificate for bravery.

When the worst of the hubbub was over there were just six of them left in the common room: their whole card circle, or what was left of it. They decided as one to skip the coffee. The mood was boisterous, and eventually Anna-Liisa suggested that they go to the Fazer Cafe in Munkkivuori for proper cake and coffee.

'That we pay for ourselves!'

'It's such a long way,' Margit Partanen said, because she was stingy and didn't really like Anna-Liisa, but the Ambassador promised everyone a free trip on his taxi coupons, and so they all ended up in disabled vans on their way to Fazer. The vans came astonishingly quickly after the Ambassador paid the girl at the information desk five euros to speed things up. Margit said that sometimes you had to wait on the phone for more than half an hour to order a disabled van, and you had to pay for the call by the minute. The drivers were friendly and helped everyone in, one at a time – wheelchairs, Zimmer frames and all. There was a blue light on the ceiling of the van and holders for bottles and cups.

'All that's missing is the champagne!' the Ambassador grinned as the van pulled out of Sunset Grove onto Perustie. Anna-Liisa, sitting beside him, laughed out loud.

'I don't know how taxis work, and I don't usually go to Munkkivuori. The trams don't go there. For me, anywhere the trams don't go might as well be in Timbuktu,' Siiri said with a smile, but Margit was serious.

'You can get an ordinary taxi quickly but a disabled van is a different matter. The system just doesn't work very well. The elderly and disabled have to wait in the rain for hours, not knowing when their lift will come. If you have to be somewhere at a certain time, like a family event or a concert, you might be horribly late. And then some tiny little girl shows up who can't lift a wheelchair. Or some Negro fellow who can't speak Finnish well enough to even say hello,' Margit complained, oblivious of their driver, an African man who spoke fluent Finnish.

'Fellow of colour,' Anna-Liisa corrected her, but Margit paid no attention.

'You can get to Munkkivuori by bus, you know,' she said to Siiri.

But if Siiri took the bus even for a short trip, she started to feel sick. When her oldest son was in the Jorvi Hospital before he died, Siiri had to go all the way to Espoo to see him, and, once, she got so motion sick on the bus that she had to get off and had no idea where she was. A crazy thing like that could never happen when you took the tram, since you could always follow the tracks, and trams moved so smoothly, not gyrating around on some road out in the Espoo woods. The air was fresher than it was on a bus, too. Buses were always far too hot.

'You must have someone working for you in the travel

department, because they're planning tram routes to Munk-kivuori now,' the Ambassador laughed as they stood on the pavement waiting for Eino Partanen to descend on a sort of lift from the back of the cab. 'They'll lay down tracks by the kilometre just so that Siiri Kettunen can get to Fazer Cafe and have a pastry! Have the police questioned you yet?'

He threw the question out like it was a joke, although he was, of course, in earnest. But Siiri didn't know if the fire was even a police matter. She had for some time been uneasy about the possibility of being questioned, but nothing had happened and Virpi Hiukkanen was no longer running around her apartment interrogating her, so she had started to think that the fire would be dealt with in the same way Olavi Raudanheimo's case had been. They would just wait for the key witnesses to die, and then they would cook up a pros-ecutor's motion to dismiss it.

'But you're never going to die,' the Ambassador said, holding the cafe door open for everyone. 'Reino always said that you were the prettiest girl at Sunset Grove. You don't look a day over . . .'

'Over what?' Siiri asked laughingly, because now the Ambassador was in a tricky situation. If he wanted to flatter a ninety-four-year-old, what age should he say?

'Not a day over twenty-seven,' he said with a laugh.

'So you only need to live seventy more years,' Anna-Liisa said, sounding sour for some reason.

They ordered an assortment of pastries and a round of coffees with no regard to the price. But the girl at the counter refused to carry their order to the table.

'This is self-service.'

It took a while to carry all the trays. Anna-Liisa balanced a coffee and a slice of cake on her Zimmer frame, the Ambassador took care of his own espresso cup, and Margit Partanen first pushed her husband to a window seat and then brought their trays one at a time to the table. Siiri carried the Hat Lady's butter-eye pastry and juice carton on her own tray and forgot her cane at the counter, but a nice young man brought it over to her. The pastries were delicious and the coffee so strong that Siiri added sugar to hers from a little paper tube.

'It looks like drugs,' Margit said, and Anna-Liisa asked how Margit came to know so much about drugs.

The Ambassador returned to the subject of the fire and told them he had filed a criminal report as soon as he'd heard Sinikka Sundström's nonsense at the information session the following day. Anna-Liisa patted his arm and said she was proud of his courage and initiative. Margit Partanen gobbled down her butter bun and fed tosca cake to her husband Eino. Crumbs and almonds sprinkled all over him and he smiled contentedly.

Chapter 38

People have very different ways of ringing a doorbell, even if it is just a mechanical device, and not a musical instrument as such. You can tell a person's temperament and mood in the way they summon you to open the door. Now there was someone outside Siiri's door who was full of energy and obviously in a hurry, maybe even in a panic, so it wasn't a resident of Sunset Grove, and it couldn't be the cleaner, or, for that matter, anyone else ringing the doorbell as part of their job – not Sinikka Sundström, because she wasn't energetic and enthusiastic, and not Virpi Hiukkanen, because she never rang the doorbell, she just let herself in. So it had to be Mika Korhonen.

'Happy Spring,' Mika said, so enthused that he walked right in without taking off his shoes, though Siiri had mentioned this to him before. It hadn't occurred to Siiri that it was spring already, but it was, at least according to the calendar, the beginning of March. The streets were covered in grey slush and unmelted ice.

'Where in Finland do you suppose Josef Wecksell wrote his poem "Demanten på Marssnön"? Siiri said to Mika, who smiled uncomprehendingly. '"The Diamond on the March Snow". He couldn't have written it in Helsinki, because the only snow we have here in March is in old grey heaps. More like "The Diamond on the March Slush". It's a Sibelius song, too, one of his most beautiful, but I like "Första Kyssen" even better. That one is from a Runeberg poem, I think. It always makes me think of my first kiss. Imagine, it happened to me with my husband, right here in Munkki-niemi, on what used to be Linna Road, which is Holland Road now. I never had any other man but that man. My husband, I mean. He died twelve years ago.'

'So, about the fire,' Mika said, launching crisply but volubly into a monologue about everything connected with the fire. He was very angry about everything that had happened, and the cascade of talk was difficult to follow. He searched for words, raked the air with his big hands, and kept adjusting his stance. His voice was hoarser than usual and his blue eyes were strangely aggressive. Siiri had to interrupt him when he got to the part about the fraudulent bookkeeping and the incontinence-pad storage used for drug storage.

'Excuse me. I should ask Anna-Liisa to come over, if that's all right. Since both of us are soft-headed, we might remember more and understand something if both of us hear it.'

Luckily, Anna-Liisa was free that day. She had skipped aerobics and was in her apartment reading *Buddenbrooks* in German when Siiri called.

'I'll be there in three minutes and forty-five seconds,' Anna-Liisa announced, and she arrived in almost exactly that amount of time. She shook Mika's hand and looked disapprovingly at his muddy shoes.

'Don't you know how to undress yourself?'

'Huh?'

Siiri feared Anna-Liisa was being rude because she had all sorts of suspicions about Mika, but Anna-Liisa was actually being quite friendly, flirting like a schoolgirl as she wrung all she could out of the word 'undress'. Mika dutifully took off his shoes and carried them to the hallway. There was a large puddle on the living-room floor, which Siiri rushed to wipe up, to save him from embarrassment. Anna-Liisa sat and watched the hubbub she'd caused with satisfaction. Siiri took the rag into the bathroom, sat down on the sofa next to Anna-Liisa, and asked Mika to sit in the armchair, because that was where her husband had always sat.

'Yep. The place of honour,' Mika said, and then they listened carefully as he continued his explanation of why the fire wasn't an accident and didn't start by itself. He wasn't as forceful and angry now, but his flailing hands, darting eyes and continuously tapping foot indicated his restlessness.

'Siiri did see someone running outside!' Anna-Liisa cried.

'Good point,' Mika said, and continued his rapid-fire talk. He believed that the fire had destroyed important evidence to do with prescriptions, money and the drug market. That explained why he was angry – he was frustrated about losing some documents he was looking for.

'Why did you take those pill bottles from Irma's apartment?' Anna-Liisa suddenly asked him, just as he was getting to the part about Russian ice hockey, which apparently also had something to do with the incontinence-pad storage in the closed unit. Mika didn't bat an eye, didn't behave in the least as if he'd been caught out; he simply explained which of the drugs could be sold on the black market and how the transactions worked. Apparently, Irma's prescriptions were really hot stuff.

'Imagine that!' Siiri said, not knowing what else to say. She was mostly baffled by what she was hearing, and in a way Mika's visit just added to her fear and uneasiness. What he was saying was like a startling gust of wind from some utterly foreign world. And yet everything he was talking about had supposedly happened right here at Sunset Grove. Mika looked hungry and tired, and Siiri realized with horror that she hadn't offered anything to her guests.

'Would you two like some liver casserole? I can warm some up. It will only take a minute on the stove.'

Mika grimaced. It seemed he didn't like liver casserole, which was understandable, because he was still young — maybe forty? Siiri hadn't asked him, and it was hard to guess his age since he was purposely bald and it may have made him look older than he really was. Anna-Liisa had already eaten some mashed potatoes and gravy with the Ambassador in the cafeteria and she had no hankering for liver casserole either.

Suddenly Mika took a wad of money out of his pocket and handed it to Siiri. It was several hundred euros in wrinkled fifty-euro bills.

'From Virpi Hiukkanen to you,' he said defiantly.

'Good heavens! What's this about?' Siiri shouted in

horror. An offer of money from the head nurse had to be some kind of bribe to stop her from blabbing to the police. Was Mika in league with Virpi Hiukkanen now?

'Your relative Tuukka figured out your accounts and found a lot of blatantly fraudulent charges. I went and talked to Hiukkanen about it, which scared her so much that she forked out the money.'

Siiri didn't know that Mika Korhonen and her great-granddaughter's boyfriend Tuukka had made each other's acquaintance without telling her. She felt bad that Tuukka had been dragged into all this, because he was a good boy.

'I should have gone to talk to the accountant, but I couldn't get hold of him. Hiukkanen was in quite a hurry to pay up immediately. She probably didn't like the idea of the accounting manager finding out about these little dips into the direct-deposit accounts.'

'Is there an accounting manager? Is that the director's husband, the one who works at the fish market?'

Mika laughed for the first time since he'd arrived. She was talking about Kalasatama, the new Fish Harbour office development. But Sundström's husband was only the quality control manager. The person Mika had been hunting down was the one in charge of the money.

'That money fellow has his work cut out hiding the evidence,' he informed them.

'They certainly have enough managers,' Anna-Liisa said, 'for a place so understaffed.'

Mika thought that Siiri's case was a simple one. Since she

hadn't ordered a cleaner, she couldn't be billed for one, nor for the plumbing work she hadn't ordered.

'But how could the head nurse give the money to you?' Anna-Liisa wondered.

'I said I was Siiri's elder-care advocate. She didn't question it, she was so damned scared.'

Siiri almost screamed. First Mika had stolen the keys to Sunset Grove, then Irma's medical records, and now he'd tricked Tuukka into poking around in criminal matters and had lied about being her advocate. What kind of hot water had they got themselves into?

'Sign your name on this piece of paper,' Mika said, and handed her a pen from the pocket of his leather jacket.

Siiri's hands were shaking, she was now so frightened. Luckily, Anna-Liisa was there as a witness if she ended up in even bigger trouble because of Mika. She needed to go and fetch her glasses from her bedside table so that she could read the paper carefully. She walked nervously around the room and forgot what she was looking for until her eyes fell on her handbag sitting on the kitchen worktop. She found her reading glasses in the bottom of the bag and sat down next to Anna-Liisa on the sofa to look at the document, which said that Siiri Hildegard Kettunen had designated Mika Antero Korhonen as her elder-care advocate two weeks earlier. The margins and line spacing were beautifully done, she noticed that immediately.

'Antero is a seer's name. But why is your name Hildegard?' Anna-Liisa asked, as if to tease her. 'You're not from Fennoman stock, are you?'

To Siiri's surprise, Anna-Liisa thought the document was an excellent thing, and she didn't find any grammatical errors in it, either. Because Mika wrote Finnish so beautifully, her doubts about him seemed to be decreasing, and all her pointed questions started to fade. She no longer seemed to feel that Mika was in league with or in the pay of Virpi Hiukkanen. Siiri looked doubtfully at Anna-Liisa, who nodded very formally.

'Sign it. Irma was always telling you that you needed an advocate. And since Mika has figured so many things out, I'm sure he knows that you don't have any big legacy to leave to him, even if you died tomorrow. Would you be interested in becoming my advocate, too, Mika? I don't have any children, so you could get a couple of rugs and coffee cups from me for your trouble.'

Mika and Anna-Liisa were now getting along like old friends – or partners in crime. Mika laughed at Anna-Liisa's proposal and agreed to be her advocate, but only on the condition that he wouldn't have to find some corner to put her junk in, and Anna-Liisa wasn't the least bit offended. God help her if Siiri had referred to Anna-Liisa's treasures as junk. There would have been a tremendous row.

'Can you write an official document like this by hand?' Anna-Liisa asked him, and then they wrote up a contract on Siiri's kitchen table that stated that Mika was also her designated advocate. Siiri signed her document with some relief, and Mika joked that he was now the second man in Siiri's life.

'Don't get your hopes up,' Siiri laughed, and felt carefree

for the first time in months. What did she really have to worry about now she was ninety-four? She could always die of old age or hunger if things went really wrong. And being in prison could hardly be any more tiresome than being at Sunset Grove without Irma. It might even be rather interesting.

'I doubt that,' Mika said. He nodded towards the wad of notes he'd given her. 'Put that money in the bank, so no one steals it.'

'Right you are. My lovely silver hand mirror was stolen here, if you can believe it, right out of my apartment,' Anna-Liisa hastened to say. She grabbed her new advocate's arm and started confiding in him. 'I'm sure it's not terribly valuable, but it had sentimental worth because it was my mother's morning gift from my father on their wedding day, so it was important to me, of course, but that's the sort of thing they do here: they take things out of the residents' apartments. That mirror's probably been sold already. Russian connections you said they had? There are a lot of antiques collectors in Russia these days. These post-Soviet nouveaux riches, what else are they going to do with their money? So they buy themselves the semblance of a respectable past by purchasing other people's family heirlooms.'

'Heirlooms?' Mika smiled, but he didn't feel like hearing any more about Anna-Liisa's mirror. He got up to leave as quickly as he'd come. He grabbed his backpack, slipped on his shoes, and left a new puddle behind on the welcome mat. Siiri didn't ask when he was coming back again because he probably wouldn't tell her.

'But now we have an official relationship with him!' Anna-Liisa grinned happily, and asked Siiri to get the red wine out of the cleaning cupboard so that they could make a toast to Mika Korhonen. Sometimes it seemed to Siiri that Anna-Liisa was an awful lot like Irma.

Chapter 39

Anna-Liisa suggested that they go to the bank on their way to see Irma at the hospital. Siiri wasn't thrilled at the idea — an old woman has no business doing two things on the same day. But it was futile to resist, since Anna-Liisa was brimming with vim and vigour. She really looked almost girlish in the new red hat she was wearing.

Siiri had tried to go to the bank in Munkkiniemi the day after Mika's visit and deposit the wrinkled bills he had given her. But the door had been locked in the middle of a weekday and there was a sign that said you could only get in by appointment and that the branch no longer handled cash transactions. It was really shocking. Siiri had kept an account at the same bank since the 1930s, though the bank had changed its name several times. Originally, it had been Finland United.

'Oh, so you're an anti-Fennoman. My bank is Citizen's Cooperative, of course,' Anna-Liisa said self-righteously.

It said on the bank window that the nearest branch with staff was the one in Lassila, and Siiri couldn't understand why she should have to take a bus all the way to Espoo and get carsick just to put money in her own bank account. Anna-Liisa said that Lassila was in Helsinki, not Espoo, but since you couldn't get there by tram they decided to go to the branch in Punavuori instead. It sounded pleasant, and safer in every way.

As they rode the tram they pondered what the bank's business could be if it wasn't cash transactions. Siiri suggested stocks and bonds, but Anna-Liisa thought those had to be cash transactions, too.

'They probably do something with accounts. They don't want to serve ordinary account holders, just deal with investments and funds and other more lucrative financial matters.'

The door to the Punavuori branch was broken. It was supposed to open automatically, so there wasn't any handle to pull on. For a moment they thought that this branch was closed, too, but then a miracle happened and the doors suddenly slid apart.

'Open sesame!' Siiri shouted.

Three middle-aged men rushed in at once, talking on mobile phones, not even noticing the two old ladies pressing up against the wall to get out of their way. Siiri and Anna-Liisa let them go first since they were in such a hurry, then went inside and looked around to see where they were. The bank looked like a government office, with birch-veneer counters, a TV screen and casual furniture. There were several rows of chairs like at a health clinic, where you waited for your number to be called. There was no sign of the luxury of yesteryear, no arches, no marble, just a look of dull utility.

They went bravely up to the number dispenser, pressed all the buttons, just to be on the safe side, and got numbers 721, 13 and 221. The number on the board read 438.

'This is like the lottery!' Siiri said happily, but Anna-Liisa started squawking, although it had been her idea to stop at the bank on their way to the hospital.

'At this rate we'll never get to the hospital. There must be some mistake.'

Off to the side, in front of an advertising placard, stood an idle-looking security guard in uniform. Siiri asked him why the number board read 438 and the numbers on their tickets were 721, 13 and 221.

'Do you think these will ever be winning numbers?'

The guard said he worked for a security company and wasn't officially employed by the bank, except to stand guard and keep order. Siiri thought she might be disrupting order, so all they could do was sit down and wait their turn. Luckily, Siiri had her green cushion with her, because the seats were hard and uncomfortable. After a moment it became clear that there were four queues, each one with different numbers, and the best one had 38 customers ahead of them.

'Well, then! This should all go swimmingly! Only two more hours to wait,' Anna-Liisa said sourly and adjusted her red hat, its shiny trim gleaming in the glow of the halogen lighting.

Siiri suggested they play a word game to pass the time,

because she knew that Anna-Liisa liked those. They thought of adjectives that began with a K, verbs that began with a vowel, and nouns that ended with an S. They couldn't think of a single nice neighbourhood in Helsinki that began with an L, and to finish up, Siiri even declined some nouns into whatever grammatical case Anna-Liisa gave her. Anna-Liisa was quite impressed with Siiri. She'd had no idea that Siiri knew her case endings so well. When Siiri remembered the comitative case she gave an appreciative whistle.

'Seven two one! Bingo!' Siiri squealed when she saw one of their numbers come up, and ran to the counter in two steps with the number in her hand. She often leapt into motion like this out of habit, although she shouldn't any more. Irma had always scolded her about it, told her that one day she was going to fall down and break a bone and spend the rest of her life rotting in bed, and Irma didn't intend to come delivering gruel and liver casserole.

'I can't be your designated caregiver, even if I wanted to, because they won't pay for it if you're over ninety,' Irma had said, and told her about her cousin Tauno who took care of his senile wife to the day she died and didn't get a penny for it because he was overage. And now Irma was lying in the hospital in line for a new hip because she'd been drugged into senility and tied to a bed that she fell out of without anyone even noticing. Siiri would rather break a bone running a few steps than falling out of bed.

She greeted the young lady in the window politely, put the notes on the counter, trying to smooth them out as much as possible, and said that she wanted to deposit them into her account. She wrote her account number on a piece of paper to avoid any error, but it wouldn't do.

'You need an IBAN number.'

'But I'm sure this is my account number. Or do you want my PIN?'

'We have to have an IBAN number. An international transfer number. It's an EU rule.'

Siiri had no idea what she meant, so she dug her bank card out of her handbag. They ought to be able to figure out the right number from that.

'You mean you want to put the money in your own account? That's not possible, unfortunately.'

One of them had to be confused. It wasn't possible that a bank wouldn't let a person put money into her own account. What harm could possibly come of it?

'You see, you can put money in someone else's account – make an account transfer, in other words – but depositing cash into your own account is no longer, like . . . it's not done. You ought to keep that money, because you're gonna hafta get cash sometime anyway, right?'

Siiri explained patiently that she didn't need such a large sum of cash, and that she was living in a retirement home where all kinds of funny things happened, and that it was much too dangerous to keep large sums of money in a biscuit tin under her mattress.

'Oh, OK. Well, maybe we can sorta make an exception this time. Wait a minute.'

The young lady left and came back with an older cashier. They whispered between themselves and looked at the wrinkled notes as if Siiri were a thief. Even the security guard was standing unnecessarily close behind her, ready to settle the dispute. Siiri clutched her cane and handbag in one hand and her green cushion in the other, trying to remain calm.

'All right, so a deposit is charged for at the bank's costs, so it'll be twenty-seven euros. But you can deposit your cash; it's possible with, like, special dispensation.'

'Kekkonen was made president with a special dispensation,' Siiri said, and told her to put the money in her account, regardless of the cost.

'D'you need a receipt?'

Siiri took a receipt, thanked the cashier, then remembered to her chagrin that it was special legislation that had got Kekkonen re-elected, not special dispensation, but she couldn't bring herself to explain her mistake to the bank cashier. She found Anna-Liisa in the waiting area with the other old people, reading a Donald Duck comic. Siiri would have thought that Anna-Liisa would consider comic books rubbish, but she was completely engrossed in the happenings in Duckberg and gave a start when Siiri interrupted her artistic appreciation.

'Donald Duck comics are different,' Anna-Liisa explained. 'They help Finnish children learn to read. The Finnish language in them is exceptionally good and always current. I'm interested in it mainly in a professional sense.'

Anna-Liisa still considered herself a teacher at the age of ninety-three. It wouldn't have occurred to Siiri to look at the world from a typist's point of view, but, of course, that was because typewriters didn't exist any more, and her job had never been that important to her. It seemed that once you were a teacher, you were always a teacher.

Chapter 40

'Cock-a-doodle-doo!' Irma crowed from a long way off, and Siiri and Anna-Liisa knew that she had finally recovered from her medication. She still looked a little small and strange in the Töölö Hospital bed, but that always happened to people when they were in hospital.

'You two probably thought I was going to die.'

Siiri could have purred like a cat, she was so happy that Irma was Irma again. She sat down on the bed next to her dear friend and felt a warm glow spreading through her, all the way to her toes – although she usually had a chill in her feet. Irma was obviously at a loss as to how she'd ended up in the hospital and all that had happened. And who would have told her? Her daughter had popped off to Patagonia or Iceland and her sons and her grandchildren had no idea what was going on at Sunset Grove.

'They were pretty amazed when I was as sharp as a tack again. They all thought I would lie here like a vegetable for the next ten years. That sure would have been a dreary hundredth birthday party. Can you imagine!'

'We can, actually,' Anna-Liisa said in her grim way, and then even Irma turned serious.

They had to tell Irma what had been happening over the winter, but it was hard to know how much she would understand and how much she could take in. Anna-Liisa made things frighteningly clear, in chronological order, and Siiri watched Irma's reactions, enjoying her voice, her gestures and her joyful eyes. Everything was like it used to be.

'Well, my, my,' Irma said several times. She shook her head and muttered to herself, 'Good gracious me.' At times she didn't believe them. 'You must be kidding!' she would say. There were some very important things she had no memory of. 'Who's Mika?' And to Siiri's great pleasure, she laughed heartily again and again, or let out musical little screeches of delight. She most enjoyed hearing about her own fit of rage in the Group Home.

'Did I honestly bite the nurse's hand?' she asked, wiping tears from her eyes with her lace handkerchief. 'Oh my, oh my. I'm about to pee in my pants!' That was always the climax of a good story for Irma.

Then she started to sing 'Oh, My Darling Augustine,' and wanted to know what her growl of rage had sounded like. Siiri tried her best to perform it, and Irma started laughing again. Anna-Liisa was surprised by this tangent. She would have preferred the story to continue in a logical order. She stood up, leaned on the bed railing, and rapped her knuckles smartly on the footboard.

'May I have a turn to speak?'

Irma and Siiri looked at her in surprise, and then Irma clapped her hands together in rapture.

'You have a lovely new hat!'

Anna-Liisa just knocked on the end of the bed again.

'Listen, Irma! In January, we were at Reino's funeral and in February Olavi Raudanheimo died. He killed himself in the hospital by refusing to eat.'

'No we weren't!' For once Siiri got to correct Anna-Liisa. 'We weren't at Reino's funeral. We went to the wrong funeral. You're going to like this story, Irma.'

'Stop! There's one very important thing that has gone completely undiscussed!' Anna-Liisa almost shouted, but then quickly regained her self-control. 'I'm talking about the fire in the closed unit, which started in the incontinence-pad storage room.'

'Right. But think about it – we went to a memorial reception for some Uncle Jaakko. And we were the only guests!'

'Siiri, you're impossible. Focus!'

Anna-Liisa's brown eyes smouldered frighteningly, and Siiri had to give up the battle. Anna-Liisa sighed audibly and began an explanation in a laboured tone.

'As you may recall, the pads were stored in a former—'

'Tuula, would you say hello to Siiri Kettunen, and ask her to come and visit?'

Siiri froze. Irma's eyes looked strangely empty again, like they had in the closed unit. She thought Siiri was her daughter. Perhaps Irma really was permanently senile and this had been only a temporary window of happiness, or a last swan song before the final catastrophe. But on the way home

Anna-Liisa assured her that it was all completely normal. People with dementia had all kinds of different days and moments. Senility and alertness might alternate very quickly, and things like physical health and fatigue could influence mental states.

'Irma was tired out from babbling about all sorts of trivial matters for an hour, which is why we didn't get to tell her all the important facts.'

'But . . . does that mean that Irma really is senile? That she isn't going to be her old self again?'

'Dementia is a symptom, not a diagnosis, as I have explained many times. But I'm no doctor, either. We'll just have to take it one day at a time.'

'It'll never clear up, unless it does. *Döden, döden, döden* – oh, I'm sorry. I forgot that you don't like it when I use Irma's sayings.'

When they got home, Siiri was really tired. She had an empty ringing in her head and felt like she was becoming more useless as the days went by. She went to bed exhausted and fell asleep in the middle of an Eeva Joenpelto novel, which fell with a thud to the floor without her even noticing. She had an incredibly fun dream about Irma, young and pretty, dancing uproariously in the middle of a huge dance floor and trying to coax Siiri to join her, but Siiri wouldn't dance. She just enjoyed watching Irma's happiness.

Chapter 41

A loud clatter from Irma's apartment interrupted Siiri's meal of liver casserole. Fearless, she marched straight over to see what was going on. And Irma would have laughed so hard to see it!

A flock of Irma's darlings were dividing up Irma's possessions, just as if she were safely dead and buried. Things were packed in moving boxes, and everyone had their own bags that they were filling with any object that struck their fancy. The boxes were marked 'flea market', 'summer cabin', and 'rubbish'. The box of rubbish was by far the fullest.

'We all got together and decided to do it this way,' a funny-looking boy said, holding one of Irma's favourite pictures in his hand.

'Since it looks like Grandma's never coming back,' another one said. Siiri assumed that these two were the beloved gay grandsons Irma always talked about. And they were handsome boys, who looked her in the eye politely when they spoke to her. It was no wonder Irma was charmed by them.

The others started to defend themselves, too. A woman with a small child wrapped around her leg explained that the apartment was much too expensive for Irma's heirs and none of them could afford to pay for it to sit empty, and there were long waiting lists for retirement-home spaces and some old person in better health might need a home. The small child reminded Siiri of the inmates at the Group Home: a sparse-haired thing in nappies, of indeterminate sex, with just two teeth in its mouth. It was holding Irma's television remote in its hand, sucking on it until it was slick with saliva.

'Grandma,' the child said, pointing at Siiri with its thick, drooly finger.

'I'm not your grandma. Your grandma is in the hospital. But she's doing very well and is sure to come back home soon, and when she does, she's going to want to watch the *Moomins* and *Poirot* on television, and she won't be able to, if you suck on the remote until it won't work any more. Nowadays televisions won't work without a remote. It's so crazy, don't you think?'

Siiri was letting out a flood of words because she was so taken aback that she didn't know what to do. She babbled to the drooly child in nappies, who had started to cry, and cried harder the longer she spoke. The positive side to this ridiculous situation was that Siiri was able to tell the one-year-old what she wanted to tell the grown adults standing around it.

'Yes, you can turn on a television without a remote,' said one of Irma's grandchildren, a boy with a long beard, as he shoved an electric mixer into his bag.

'Oh, can you? So have you all decided who gets the television? It's brand new. Digital.'

Irma's darlings had strange looks on their faces. The one-year-old stopped its crying.

'We don't want it. Nobody watches TV any more,' one of the grandsons said.

'Because it's all on the net,' continued the other, as if they were Donald Duck's nephews.

'Grandma?' the one-year-old said, tugging on Siiri's trouser leg. The child was clearly the bravest and most intelligent of the bunch. Siiri told her new friend that they were going to give Grandma a new hip with a couple of screws in it and then Grandma was coming home and they could eat cake together again, and drink wine.

'Grandma shouldn't drink so much alcohol,' the woman said knowingly, prying the child off her leg while trying to fit Irma's jewellery box into her handbag. In her opinion eating sweets or drinking alcohol of any kind was dangerous for Irma's health.

That's when Siiri got angry. She got so tremendously angry that Irma would have been proud of her. She felt like the pretty, young Irma who had danced in her dream, not caring what other people thought, just sashaying around without any inhibitions, and she let this gang of young people who called themselves family know just what she thought of them and their health warnings.

'Your grandma is as healthy as a horse and will soon be back here, needing you – and her stuff! If you take one silver spoon or TV remote out of here, I'm calling the police! And if you can't afford to pay for your grandma's rent at the retirement home because you'd rather travel around the world twice a year, then I'll pay for it out of my pension. Don't think for a minute that Irma is senile, and that she's turned into a vegetable! She's coming back here and we're going to eat as much cake as we like and drink wine and maybe Irma will smoke a couple of cigarettes while she sips her evening whisky, and then we'll dance for the rest of the day in our nightgowns and do whatever takes our fancy, because you know what? I'm ninety-four years old and your grandma is ninety-two, and at our age there's not very much that's so terribly important, least of all things that might be dangerous to your health. They're just used to frighten you all, so you won't die of affluenza. For your information.'

It certainly did her good to have a proper yell. She felt strong and supple, she had a heady feeling of well-being, and her blood was flowing furiously, right down to her toes. At some point in her monologue she'd lifted up her gaze as if she were dancing, and she may even have taken a couple of light steps before performing what looked like a pirouette. The one-year-old clapped its hands in admiration and tried to dance with her.

'Old people can do whatever pops into their heads, unlike you poor working folks, who don't dare even to think, to use your own brains. Stealing old women's mixers! You can all just drag your bones right out of here and not come back until Irma sees fit to let you come back. No ifs or buts.'

'Butts!' screeched the one in a nappy, twirling around crazily, excited about the new dance and this new grandma. The child's antics piqued the interest of its older brother, who had been hiding behind the sofa.

'You're a butt!' the big brother said quietly, giving Siiri a murderous look, which caused her to burst out laughing. The adults tried to laugh a little too, but then Siiri straightened up and ordered them all to leave.

'*La commedia è finita*,' she said in a deep voice, and nobody understood that she was quoting Leoncavallo's *Pagliacci*, which ends with that line. Irma's darlings were baffled and troubled. One of them put a picture back on the bookshelf, but the jewellery box remained in the know-it-all's handbag.

'We thought Grandma was out of the game . . .'

'We were trying to be helpful.'

They looked so sad that Siiri had to explain why Irma's recent recovery was good news. She assured them that they shouldn't worry, that one, happy day, Irma would die, and her grandchildren could then divvy up all her things among them and bake a cake with her old mixer. So Irma's darlings gathered up their bags and left.

The box of things labelled 'rubbish' was left in the middle of the living room: sheaves of photographs, knick-knacks, tablecloths and silk long johns. Siiri slumped into the flowered armchair to rest for a moment. It smelled like Irma's perfume, strong and too sweet, but it was Irma's scent, and Siiri breathed it in until it went to her head and she again felt the light, floating feeling she'd had in her dream.

Chapter 42

Anna-Liisa and Siri had got into the habit of going into town together to perk themselves up. They had read all of *The Tottering House* and had started Juhani Aho's *Panu*. Anna-Liisa was a pleasant travel companion because she knew to sometimes be quiet, unlike Irma. Siri had learned all kinds of other things about Anna-Liisa over the months that Irma had been away. She'd come out of her shell and proved to be a warm, fun person, quite brave and sometimes even boisterous. It was amazing and interesting to Siri to make a new friend at the age of ninety-four.

'I think I've grown twenty years younger this winter,' Anna-Liisa said as they rode the 3B and admired the new university library. 'And it's all down to you and the Lavender Ladies Detective Agency.' The library had scads of little square-shaped windows that were rather amusing, although Siri suspected that it might not be so fun to sit inside and look out at the world through such small windows.

Siri unfortunately could not claim to have grown younger over the winter. Quite the opposite; her age had never weighed so heavily as it had this past year, with events flooding over her uncontrollably. It felt like people over ninety lived on their own deserted island, completely separate from the rest of the world. The banks wouldn't take cash, the retirement home was a nest of criminals, and they were just supposed to drag themselves from aerobics to memory games all day long. Even on the tram they looked out at real life scurrying by from a distance, as if it were a TV show with no remote. There was just one taxi driver who'd taken an interest in their affairs, and even he seemed to be doing it for partly criminal reasons.

'I don't mistrust Mika any more at all,' Anna-Liisa said, and looked more radiant than she had in ages. Siiri praised her red hat and her rosy springtime cheeks, and Anna-Liisa smiled with satisfaction. 'Not only have I got to know you, I've had other experiences to shake my life up a bit. Wasn't that place designed by Lars Sonck? I think it's always been called the Arena Building, although that's not its original name, of course. Or maybe it is? What do you think – when was that place built? Did you know that Lars Sonck's offices were on the corner of Esplanadi and Unioninkatu and he had a habit of taking a bath in the Havis Amanda fountain?'

Anna-Liisa had read about it in a book that the Ambassador had given her as a gift. The book was called *A Skin-disease Doctor Remembers*. She explained that this was a euphemism, because in the old days everybody understood that a skin-disease doctor was a venereal-disease doctor. She'd learned from the memoir that a diagnosis of syphilis could be made by examining the eyebrows of the other passengers on public transport.

'They called it omnibus diagnosis.'

'Really? So, do I have syphilis?' Siiri asked, and Anna-Liisa let out a musical laugh like a young girl and said Siiri's eyebrows were very healthy. For a moment they looked at the other passengers' eyebrows, but Anna-Liisa thought they all looked syphilis-free. Although there was one woman who had plucked her eyebrows off and drawn a black line in their place, so she might be a carrier, but the diagnosis was uncertain.

'Sparse eyebrows indicate syphilis,' Anna-Liisa explained.

'Well, then the Ambassador certainly doesn't have it,' Siiri said, and Anna-Liisa's face flashed a secret smile. Siiri wondered what the Ambassador's first name was, but Anna-Liisa was still focused on venereal diseases.

'Maybe syphilis doesn't exist any more. There's probably more AIDS nowadays, although even HIV is not as virulent as it was in the last century. Did you know that the Hat Lady died the other day? And she was supposed to live for ten more years with her stent.'

The 3B was like a rollercoaster on any day, but with Anna-Liisa with her it seemed even more thrilling than usual. Siiri hadn't yet recovered from the syphilis conversation and yet Anna-Liisa had already moved on to the Hat Lady's death. It was remarkable that Siiri didn't know any more about it than she did about the Ambassador's name. The Hat Lady had been part of their group of friends. Siiri had thought she was mostly troublesome. But now Sunset Grove's itinerant preacher had gone and died, and wouldn't come begging for sweet rolls any more, and in spite of everything it felt sad.

'She wasn't begging, she just wanted company and she used the sweet roll defence to get it,' Anna-Liisa said, 'if you know what I mean. I probably wouldn't have approved of one of my pupils using an expression like "sweet roll defence", but I can't think of a better way to put it at the moment.'

'The sweet roll con?' Siiri suggested, and Anna-Liisa laughed happily again. Lately, she laughed a lot, brightly, in a way that gave her ordinarily gloomy voice a bit of sunshine.

'She died of old age. A poor, unfortunate insomniac who finally fell asleep,' Anna-Liisa said carelessly.

Just six months ago she would have given a lengthy lecture on how in Finland you're required to die of pneumonia, a heart malfunction, or some other invented pathology. And on how much money was spent on cutting a body open just to find out how a ninety-two-year-old woman died in her own home. Finland certainly was a wealthy country, there was no way around it.

But now she just sat quietly, not even enthused about autopsies. Instead she said: 'His name is Onni.'

Siiri didn't have a chance to ask whose name was Onni. She was looking out of the window at the stop next to Brahe sports field, and there stood the Sunset Grove caretaker Erkki Hiukkanen in his overalls and cap, plain as day. He got on the tram through the centre door and Siiri hoped from the bottom of her heart that he wouldn't notice them. He glanced around and looked important somehow, as if he were on a top-secret mission. Why in the world was he wandering around Kallio in his work clothes at this time of day? Siiri tried to warn Anna-Liisa, but she was in her own happy world.

'Did you know that Onni can recite all the old Finnish market towns? Alavus, Anjalankoski, Espoo, Forssa, Grankulla, Haaga and so on.'

So Onni was the Ambassador's name. Siiri was sure that she'd never heard anyone address him by his first name. She turned warily to look at the back of the tram and saw Hiukkanen sitting far away from them in the disabled seat with a blank expression on his face. There was no danger of him noticing them, even though Anna-Liisa let her voice echo through the tram in all her happiness.

'That kind of brain aerobics is good for you – and fun, too. I've already learned quite a few myself. The end goes like this: Vantaa, Varkaus, Virrat, Ulivieska, Äänekoski,' she recited, tapping her hand on her thigh. Siiri thought the red gloves she was wearing were new. Stylish, expensive-looking leather.

'You have to recite it clearly so that you get the meaning and remember it better. Want to try?'

Siiri smiled and started learning the names of the old market towns to please Anna-Liisa. Life certainly was full of surprises.

Chapter 43

The Hat Lady's real name had been Aino Marjatta Elin Nieminen. There was a pleasantly large crowd at her funeral, some relatives and a surprising number of old workmates from public radio, where she'd had a forty-year career from errand girl to editor.

'Public radio employees have time to go to funerals. On our tax contributions,' said the Ambassador, loud enough to be heard.

'Public radio funds come from licence fees, not taxes,' Margit Partanen corrected him even more loudly.

'But didn't they just change it? Isn't it taxes now instead of licence fees? Our tax payment doubled. They've laid on so many taxes that pretty soon they'll tax you to get laid,' her husband said, and Margit silenced his babbling as efficiently as ever by hissing a threat in his ear.

Munkkiniemi Church had slippery, pale-coloured pews and the floor sloped steeply downwards. This had its good points, because you could see the coffin even from the last row but the downside was that their Zimmer frames and wheelchairs kept rolling uncontrollably downhill. The pastor spoke into a microphone. This was hard for them to understand – why weren't people able to talk without a microphone? Even in churches built in the fourteen hundreds, there were microphones and speakers now, as if no one would be able to hear without them.

'What? Hear what?' asked Margit as everyone fell silent for the prayer.

The pastor was a relative of the Hat Lady and was certainly over ninety himself, a tottering old man whose voice broke from emotion and a heart malfunction. He had to take long pauses and lean on his crutches, and when he trowelled some sand onto the coffin, '. . . from dust you came, to dust you shall return . . .' and so on, they feared he was going to topple over completely. But by some miracle he made it through alive and dragged himself with the last of his strength to sit down on a chair behind a pillar. The cantor had such a jazzy intro for the hymn that it took them a little while to realize that it was the familiar, lovely tune 'Come with Me, Lord Jesus'.

The presentation of flowers wasn't until the end of the ceremony, but they didn't dare go up to the coffin. They would have first had to slide down the hill and then find the strength to climb back up afterwards, which was a recipe for tragicomedy. The other mourners were more interesting to watch than usual anyway.

'To Aino, an editor who was a cut above,' said a stocky man with an awfully familiar voice as he put a bouquet of glowing red roses on the coffin.

'Isn't he the sports announcer who was drunk at the

Sapporo Olympics? It was a terrible scandal. What was his name?'

They tried to beat each other at recognizing the public radio personalities who were taking turns leaving flowers and saying their personal farewells to the Hat Lady.

'I'll never forget your hat,' whispered a bent, bearded man.

The Ambassador and Anna-Liisa almost had a fight about this bearded fellow when they couldn't make up their minds whether he was an anchor or a correspondent. Or, rather, a former correspondent, since all of these people were long past retirement and not likely to be wasting the Ambassador's tax money. After the presentation of the flowers the cantor improvised a cacophonous piece and eight decrepit men, most of them radio legends, carried the coffin, huffing and puffing, up the hill to the foyer, across the courtyard, and down some stairs to the hearse. It hadn't occurred to the architect to just put the stairs in front of the door.

They decided to go to the memorial service, upstairs at Restaurant Ukko-Munkki, because they hadn't yet had a chance to name all the famous public radio retirees and it was exciting to think of a memorial with such drinking companions as these.

'Public radio live,' the Ambassador said, and Anna-Liisa almost giggled, hanging on her new friend's arm.

The pastor-relative who was at death's door didn't come to the bar at all, but a scar-faced, long-haired lay preacher from the Hat Lady's Bible study group served as host. He spoke fervently, leaning on the bar, of Ms Aino's deep faith and the fulfilment of her life after her long journey, by which he meant her death, and then he took a saw out of a violin case – a perfectly ordinary saw – and started to play it. He drew the bow and bent the blade of the saw in such a way that something like a melody came out of it. The sound had a piercing, skull-penetrating quality and Margit Partanen put her hands over her ears. First he played what was probably 'Finlandia', and then several hymns, or perhaps they were modern art pieces. It was God-awful.

'Lucky they haven't used this music to cheer us up at Sunset Grove. That thing is some kind of torture,' Anna-Liisa said, loud enough to be heard, and it looked to Siiri as if the Ambassador took hold of her hand under the table as he said that they had their own ways of cheering themselves up nowadays.

'What do you mean, Onni?' Siiri asked, and the Ambassador jumped when he heard his own name.

'I mean that I don't like the musical saw, or hymns. Do you?'

Then he poured himself and Anna-Liisa more red wine. There were several bottles on each table so you could pour yourself as much as you liked. The bottles at the public radio tables were emptied immediately, but the scar-faced man diligently fetched some more. The stocky radio announcer gave a fun speech where he told a few naughty stories about the Hat Lady and their leisure activities on Fabianinkatu in the 1970s, and thanked dear Aino, almost tearfully, for all the times she'd rescued all the public radio staff and clocked them in when they were drunk or had passed out.

'In memory of studio ten!' he said in conclusion, and lifted his glass high. All the public radio people exploded into laughter and the Sunset Grove table fell into uncomfortable silence.

'There is no such studio,' a pudgy woman with teased hair whispered to them. 'We always called the Kellarikrouvi bar studio ten.'

Siiri found it hard to believe that they were at a funeral – wine was flowing, the saw was playing, and old people were furiously flirting under the table. By the time they left to go back to Sunset Grove, the Ambassador and Anna-Liisa had taught the first fifteen old market towns to Eino Partanen, although he was supposed to be senile and suffering from memory loss.

Chapter 44

Irma's hip surgery went well, and she was moved the very next day to Laakso Hospital for rehabilitation. There were no screws in her hip, the helpful Egyptian nurse told them, just one large spike at the top of her thigh bone. Irma claimed she could feel it poking her, but Siiri found it hard to believe they would drive a spike into an old lady.

'And when I smoke, I get this strange feeling that it's glowing!'

'Have you started smoking here in the hospital?' Siiri asked, though she didn't want to sound like she was nagging.

'Just a tiny bit. There's nothing else to do here.'

Irma's glowing spike was made of titanium, and she was sure that titanium was very valuable. She was even planning to tell her blessed darlings about it so that when the time came they could ask the funeral director to extract it for them as a keepsake, maybe to put over the hearth at the summer cabin. And if they hit hard times, they could sell this titanium part from their grandma, and she also had a gold filling in one tooth that shouldn't just be burnt up with her bones. They made up a saying about it – to 'throw the gold filling out with the urn ashes', so they would have an alternative to the baby and the bathwater.

Siiri had brought Irma's medical papers with her, the whole record of horrors, but she didn't dare show them to her. They had now gone over the events at Sunset Grove to some extent, the fire and the wad of money Siiri had been given, but this part was difficult, despite the fact that Irma understood that her dementia had been caused by her medication.

To avoid the unpleasant subject, Siiri told Irma about Anna-Liisa and the Ambassador. Irma practically fell out of bed, she thought it was so horribly funny, and she immediately started to tell Siiri about her cousin who'd got married for the first time at the age of eighty-seven, to the first love of her youth, after waiting sixty-five years for the man to be widowed.

'Almost like Solveig of the fjord, although my cousin's suitor wasn't a cad like Peer Gynt.'

The cousin had had a real wedding, a ceremony in the cathedral and a big reception, just as a young couple would have had. There was the first waltz, the cutting of the cake, throwing the bouquet and robbing the bride, and at the end of dinner the eighty-seven-year-old groom sang a serenade to his damsel.

'Just think, we might have a party like that at Sunset Grove! But they should have the ceremony somewhere other than Munkkiniemi Church, so the bride's Zimmer frame doesn't roll down the hill to the altar.'

Irma's attitude was infectious, though at first Siiri had

been caught short by Anna-Liisa's great love; she realized, to her surprise, that she disapproved of it. To go and get all lovey-dovey while all sorts of horrible things were going on around them seemed indecent somehow. But gradually, as they talked about it happily like this, the love between Anna-Liisa and the Ambassador seemed like good news.

'Why should we live alone, remembering the past and grieving for husbands who died a long time ago? Old people should absolutely seize the moment and fall in love and enjoy each other's company, just like everyone else should.' Irma stopped for a moment. 'Hmm. I don't know, though. Does this relationship between Anna-Liisa and Onni include . . . everything? What do you think? Do you think they've even kissed?'

They pondered this question for a while and came to the conclusion that Anna-Liisa and Onni most definitely had kissed, and that they didn't want to think any more about the subject. After a moment of uncomfortable silence, Irma remembered another cousin; he was dead but Siiri had met him several times. He had been left a widower when his much younger fourth wife got so depressed about her husband's age that she jumped off a balcony. And then the fellow had had the audacity to give Irma the nod and started popping in at Sunset Grove.

'Einar and I drank some red wine together a few times. He would always pick up another jug at the Alko when we ran out, just dash right out – he was in good shape, a regular Kekkonen, an avid volleyball player till the day he died. No, it was President Koivisto who played volleyball, not

Kekkonen. Anyway, Einar would dash out to the Alko to get another jug of wine while I gathered my strength and took a catnap. But then one time, when he'd finished fetching all the wine and was on his way out of the door, he suddenly kissed me, and I mean a manly kiss, like my Veikko used to give me. I was in quite a dither, it was so unpleasant. And a week later, the poor fellow died . . . at least a little happier, I hope.'

Siiri liked sitting on the edge of Irma's bed; she was never in a hurry to leave. Irma was starting to look more and more like her old self as the days passed and Siiri knew that soon they would be sitting at Sunset Grove together again, eating an ever-so-slightly spoiled liver casserole. This was the fourth hospital that Irma had stayed in since the fire had rescued her from the closed unit, and both of them thought it was very interesting getting to know so many of Helsinki's hospitals.

'First the Hilton, then Suursuo, after that Töölö, and now Laakso – yep, it's four hospitals. Töölö Hospital has the best food, all of them have the same awful nightgowns, and every one of them has exceedingly nice nurses. Though, of course, I don't remember anything about the Hilton or Suursuo, but I'm sure it was very pleasant there, too.'

But, of course, who wouldn't be nice and pleasant to Irma? Siiri had so missed Irma's '*Döden, döden, döden*' and her stories about her cousins and all the fun they'd had together that she was as ready to burst with happiness about Irma's recovery as she was about Anna-Liisa's Onni.

When Irma started to get tired, Siiri tiptoed out and got

on the number 4 going in the wrong direction out of sheer joy, and took it into town to say hello to the old tram halls. She didn't head home until she'd ridden once around on the number 3 through Töölö and Kamppi. As the tram was passing the nursing school, she thought she saw Erkki Hiukkanen sitting on the same tram as she was, right behind her on the other side of the aisle. She didn't dare turn to look to see if it was really him. She had an unpleasant, uneasy feeling and all her humming high spirits disappeared in a moment. Was it a coincidence that the caretaker was always on her tram route? And when had Hiukkanen started flitting around the city?

As Siiri was walking from the lift to her apartment, Virpi Hiukkanen came hurrying down the hallway towards her and brushed past her with her mouth in a tight line, hardly even greeting her. When Siiri had closed her door and taken off her coat, hat and walking shoes, she went into the kitchen. She put her handbag down on the kitchen table next to her pill counter, and froze. The pill counter stared at her from the table. She was sure she hadn't left it there. She always kept the stupid thing on the side, where it was easier to take out the day's pills and hide them in the cupboard, which is exactly what she had done that morning, she could have sworn it. But now the pill counter had been moved and it was full of so many different kinds of pills that the extra slots had pills in them now, too. Virpi Hiukkanen had been coming into her apartment and filling it, just as she had suspected.

Chapter 45

'It's you! My angel!' Siiri squealed into the telephone. She was so happy that Mika had called. She immediately started telling him about Irma, who was rapidly recovering from her hip surgery, and listing all the different hospitals, though perhaps in the wrong order, but she didn't stop to think, there was so much to tell him. 'They're trying to force pills on me, and the caretaker is following me as well. He's been running around the city after me. I know it sounds crazy, but that's the point: they're trying to drive me crazy.'

'Can I see you? I've got something to tell you,' Mika said quickly when she'd finished talking.

They met in Munkkiniemi. Mika left his taxi parked at Laajalahti Square and had to buy a ticket on the number 4 because he didn't have a pass like Siiri had. He thought two euros eighty was a steep price to go a couple of stops, but Siiri pointed out that he could use the ticket to travel for an hour if he wanted to. They went to sit in the spot where the two halves of the tram met, the spot hidden around the corner near the door. They could talk about whatever they liked there without being bothered, but Mika was so burly that it was a tight fit for him. He grunted and searched for a good position but his knees wouldn't fit comfortably no matter what he did and he had to tuck them up in a comical position.

'But don't you think the tram drives so quickly and smoothly?' Siiri asked.

'Sure does,' Mika sighed and then he relayed everything he'd learned. The goings on at Sunset Grove included falsified drug prescriptions, secret links between companies, bogus billings, and contacts with Russia. Siiri liked Mika's cryptic way of talking about it, his large hands groping the air. Mystery and clumsiness were part of his appeal, along with his blue eyes and gruff voice.

When they got to the old tram halls, Siiri felt so sorry for him sitting in the cramped tram seat that they got off. Mika wanted to go for a coffee and Siiri promised to treat him to a cardamom roll, too, since he'd got so little value out of his tram ticket. There was a cafe and museum in one of the oldest tram halls. It was a pleasant surprise to Siiri. She'd never been in the building, which was designed by Waldemar Aspelin.

The cafe was a charming spot. Part of the hall had been left unchanged, and you could look at the old trams there, while part of the building had been made into an exhibition space and restaurant. Siiri peeked into the gallery, which had large, colourful pictures on the walls, and insisted that Mika go through the exhibition with her. The pictures in the gallery were very beautiful, very bold and powerful, but Mika thought they were too expensive.

'You'd have to be crazy to pay twelve thousand euros for a painting.'

'I may be crazy, but I wasn't planning on buying one; I just like looking at them,' Siiri said, and calculated that it had been thirty-one years since she'd retired and bought herself a painting to mark the occasion. 'I haven't bought one since then. But it was a good purchase. I've looked at that painting every day, and it's always the same, happy and colourful, even though everything else has changed.'

'Yep,' Mika said, and he told her that he'd been born four years before she'd retired.

They walked around, looking at the trams from various decades. It was incredibly fun – all the wooden seats, driver's cranks, old tracks and signs! Old route 15 from Diakon to the old Töölö customs gate and her beloved number 4 from Munkkiniemi to Hietalahti – she remembered them all from some faraway place, and here they were again.

'An open-air tram,' Mika read with a chuckle. 'Transfer marked only upon payment.'

You could go into some of the trams and sit down, and Siiri told Mika about all kinds of things she remembered, even the smells – wet wool, sweaty working men, and winos who ate onions just like apples.

'It was cheap, and a lot of food for someone living on the street, but it gave off such a peculiar smell, that mixture of homelessness and alcohol and onions. That smell doesn't exist any more.'

Mika listened politely and started to look like he might just be a little bit interested in trams after all. He even tried out the driver's seat, although it probably wasn't allowed. Finally, they went to the cafe, where there were two lovely trams from the 1950s, and Siiri bought them coffee and a cardamom roll, as she had promised. The coffee was poured into soup bowls, which seemed very strange, but the girl cashier didn't react at all when Siiri marvelled at it, and didn't seem to understand what a saucer was. They settled into seats by the window. Siiri looked at the old trams and felt as though she were on some fantastical trip back in time. She told Mika about the ticket takers and about Sipoo Church, also designed by Aspelin.

'The ticket takers were always women, very busty and plump, sitting in their nests in their grey uniforms all dignified and full of themselves, so serious, hissing their S's.'

Mika grinned when Siiri showed him how they would peer at your ticket and stamp it.

'They were all Swedish speakers, from Sipoo – back then, you still had to know how to speak Swedish on the Helsinki tram – and people called their apartment block the "Sipoo Church", because it had a steeple like a church. It was a very beautiful building, right next door to this one, but it was probably torn down before you were born. Now there's just an ugly concrete box there.'

'To hell with compulsory Swedish!'

Siiri thought it was important to speak other languages, and she had always felt bad that her grandmother hadn't spoken Russian with her. Swedish was one of the funniest languages she knew, and Selma Lagerlöf really should be read in the original language. Mika looked bored and didn't seem to be listening. He wanted to tell her about Pasi. Did she remember Pasi, the social worker at Sunset Grove who'd got the sack shortly after Tero's death?

'I remember. You were very angry at him and even blamed him for Tero's death. You called him a snitch. That's an insult, isn't it – snitch?'

'Yep. He ratted to the cops – all lies. And it was that pathetic user that Tero decided to fall in love with.'

Pasi had also been there when Olavi Raudanheimo was attacked.

'And he isn't the only veteran who's had an unpleasant experience in the shower,' Mika said.

Siiri could hardly believe her ears, the thought was so repugnant. She always felt faint when Olavi Raudanheimo's terrible incident was mentioned.

Mika thought it was a stroke of luck that assaulting old people wasn't Pasi's only crime. He might never have been caught for his shower games, but his drug and money problems had provided Mika an opportunity to hand him over to the police. Pasi was just one link in a long chain, but the police had to start somewhere. It would probably be a long time before all of the activities of Virpi and Erkki Hiukkanen's various companies were combed through. But it no longer interested Mika.

'I'm just glad Pasi got caught. As far as I'm concerned, the Russian pill patrol can keep their little incontinence-pad service going as long as they like.'

Siiri would have liked to simply enjoy her time travel, and to relish the fact that Irma had recovered from her dementia symptoms while touring Helsinki's many hospitals. But she couldn't. No matter how she tried to float off on her own thoughts, she couldn't get the problems of Sunset Grove out of her mind. Assaults, drug deals, fires . . . and somehow all of it was connected.

'We should have talked about that fire.' Mika's look turned troubled and his hands raked the air. 'About the keys, the Group Home keys . . . you shouldn't have used them to go . . . well, to go anywhere, and it could, like, cause some problems, a lot of problems. For you, I mean. Serious problems, because you used the key to get in at the very moment when Erkki Hiukkanen was starting a fire in the sauna.'

Siiri was ashamed of herself. Here she was, reminiscing about the smell of her beloved old trams, when at any moment she could be charged with breaking and entering. Her head started to buzz and throb, the roll and bowl of coffee in her stomach churned. At a loss for what to do, she fished her handkerchief out of her bag, blew her nose, and dabbed her forehead. 'Do you believe . . . do you think I could go to jail for the fire?'

'I doubt it,' Mika said, and ate his roll in one large bite.

Siiri didn't consider that gesture sufficient reassurance. He certainly could have arranged matters better for her, since he seemed to be able to direct the activities of the police so skilfully when it came to Pasi. He was her advocate, after all. And he was the one who left the keys on the table, as a signal that she should do something.

'That's one way of looking at it. But I do have your medical records from Sunset Grove. They were trying to shove you into the dementia ward, or declare you incompetent, and blame you for the fire, too. There were papers there with all kinds of insinuations about points scored and the need for enhanced care.'

Mika rummaged in his cluttered backpack. A pair of binoculars, a pocket knife, a wallet, a telephone, an asthma inhaler, and a box of liquorice lozenges appeared on the table. The hum in Siiri's head softened a bit and she had to tell Mika about all the things Irma kept in her handbag.

'Whisky? That's one thing I don't have in here,' Mika laughed, finally licking the sugar from the sweet roll off his lips and slapping a large stack of papers down on the table.

Siiri looked at the pile sombrely. It was just like the heavy stack of papers from Irma's file that she'd been carrying in her handbag for more than a week now. The buzz in her head started up again. So she had been right about this, too. She wasn't paranoid. She looked warily at the documents, flipped back and forth through them and tried to remain calm.

At least her medical documents weren't as upsetting to read as Irma's had been. Although Siiri's did have some strange memos and groundless claims written in familiar, rounded handwriting. Even before the fire, but especially afterwards, the records claimed that Siiri was senile, fatigued and paranoid, just like the claims about Irma earlier that winter. Siiri was scored according to some scale and she was just 0.2 points below being classified as a patient requiring enhanced care – thank heavens, because otherwise her charges would have been even more expensive than they already were. She had been charged for a tranquillizer, a stimulant and sleeping pills, without a doctor ever seeing her.

'Par for the course,' Mika said.

'You'd make a good Sarastro,' Siiri said, shoving the papers aside. 'You have a really fine bass voice, a really rare voice.'

She had to explain to Mika who Sarastro was, and regretted having blurted it out in the middle of a serious discussion about her medical records, which Mika had stolen for her without even being asked.

'In *The Magic Flute* you don't know at first what's good and what's bad, because the Queen of the Night's evil is only revealed when they get to Sarastro's kingdom and they see everything in a new light,' she said, trying to speak quickly so that she wouldn't bore him. 'It's a story of the growth of the human spirit, and that's the way things are in real life. It's often hard for us to tell good from bad, and vice versa.'

'Especially at Sunset Grove,' Mika said gravely.

He packed up his things and offered Siiri a liquorice lozenge for digestion. It seemed like a good idea, and Siiri waxed enthusiastic, recounting long sections of *The Magic Flute* until Mika started tapping his foot on the floor to indicate that it was time to leave. He said he was satisfied now that Pasi had been caught. He'd done what he'd set out to do. He didn't intend to investigate the goings on at Sunset Grove any further.

'Pasi'll be in for a long stretch. That's enough for me.'

'And what about us?' Siiri asked, not knowing herself what exactly she meant.

'Well, we're practically married,' Mika said with a bewitching smile. 'An advocate can't just take off.'

But then he did take off, into the evening sun, without picking up his taxi from Laajalahti, saying that another driver would come to get it. And they hadn't even begun to solve the matter of the fire and Siiri's possible prison sentence, not to mention the falsified medical records. Was she supposed to figure this mess out by herself?

Chapter 46

Anna-Liisa wanted to go clothes shopping. Siiri thought it a funny whim, but then she remembered the Ambassador and understood why she wanted something new in her wardrobe. She already had her red hat and gloves.

'I got them from Onni,' Anna-Liisa revealed when they were on the tram. 'What do you think – does the hat flatter me?'

'Very becoming,' Siiri replied. It was what Irma would have said.

Siiri couldn't remember when she'd last bought clothes. She'd gone to Stockmann now and then to buy silk long johns and vests for Irma, but she didn't care for them herself. Coats, trousers, shirts – she'd worn the same ones for the entirety of this century. Shopping for shopping's sake was pointless and boring. But it was nice to go into the city, away from Sunset Grove where her thoughts trod over the same tedious paths from the fire to the pill counter to the Hiukkanens.

'You don't have to buy anything,' Anna-Liisa told her. 'It's still shopping, even if you just wander from shop to shop and look at everything. It's extremely popular. Do you remember when there used to be signs that said no begging or peddling? And yet there were always peddlers coming to the door. Sometimes that was fun. I used to always let one blind war veteran sharpen my kitchen knives and I bought lace napkins from a gypsy woman. There was no harm in it.'

They began their shopping trip at the Forum. It was bustling with people but there wasn't a single shop suitable for someone over ninety. Anna-Liisa steered them out of the Forum, past the Chapel of Silence and into Kamppi, the huge shopping centre at the old bus station, or rather on top of it, since the bus station had been forced underground. It looked to Siiri like Kamppi had all the same shops as the Forum, but Anna-Liisa was more observant.

'These are all one-brand shops. Shops have gone branded now, so each shop only sells one company's clothes. That's how you know that Kamppi has higher-quality products than the Forum.'

'So, if I want to buy some trousers, I have to look in each separate shop? That's rather complicated.'

None of the escalators started where the previous escalator ended. They had to walk a long way to the next one and got lost several times. They were surrounded by inappropriately short skirts and tops with multi-coloured lace and ruffles. One shop sold nothing but hairbands. For men, there were shops with tasteless green trousers and pink shirts. Siiri's husband never wore anything but black, brown and grey. Even the Ambassador was hardly addled enough with springtime love to put on a pair of red trousers. The idea of it made Anna-Liisa laugh wonderfully, her voice high and musical. They sat down on some cafe chairs to rest for a moment, but a man working at the ice-cream parlour shooed them away, saying that the chairs were reserved for paying customers.

'We are paying customers!' Anna-Liisa said.

They had bought coffee in paper cups from the neighbouring shop, which seemed to be a bookstore of some kind. But that didn't matter. They had to get up. So they stood next to a rubbish bin with the two empty chairs in front of them and finished their coffee. Shopping centres weren't meant for old people – there was too much noise and bustle and the businesses were confusing. People shoved and elbowed each other and some of them were just standing around, obviously not there to buy anything, but just to watch what the others were doing.

'Let's go to Stockmann,' Anna-Liisa finally groaned. This sounded sensible.

They got to Stockmann through an incredibly long underground passageway carved into the bedrock, which was handy, since large drops of sleet were falling outside in honour of spring. The passageway made them think of bomb shelters and the bombing of Helsinki. Anna-Liisa had been in Töölö and Siiri in Munkkiniemi on 30 March 1939. They remembered how some of the bombs had struck right near them and they both got an uncomfortable feeling just like they did on New Year's Eve when people went outside to light rockets.

'Fireworks always make me think of the war. I can't

understand how anyone really enjoys all those explosions and that dreadful racket,' Anna-Liisa said as they emerged into the freezing rain just a short walk from the shelter of Stockmann. The department store was full of even more people than the shopping centre, such a mass of people in the middle of the day that they were driven by the crowd onto the descending escalator.

'Tram routes and the arrangement of the departments at Stockmann are two things that should never change,' Anna-Liisa said when they noticed they were on a floor labelled with the English word 'basement'. They argued about this for a moment, because Siiri was quite pleased with all the new tram routes that had appeared in Helsinki lately. She wouldn't mind if they ran tracks to Munkkivuori, too. A little adventure was always refreshing, including here in Stockmann.

'Now look at this gadget. I'll bet you've never seen this kind of vacuum cleaner . . . yes, it's a vacuum cleaner, not a humidifier, like I thought it was. It moves by itself, goes into the corners to suck up the dust. Isn't that a fun invention? And you would never have found it, if you hadn't come looking for it.'

'We're not really looking, we're just browsing,' Anna-Liisa said and strode to the escalator to get back to the ground floor.

Siiri reminded her of the fun of shopping and sang a bit of Schubert, the song that starts with 'Das Wandern ist des Müllers Lust, das Wandern', but Anna-Liisa silenced her with a sharp elbow in the ribs.

'Don't sing,' she said, and tried on an orange scarf.

In the end she bought a white scarf and a new black hand-bag to replace her old black one. The orange scarf was unnecessarily bold in her opinion, and the white one could be worn anywhere, even at a funeral, which made it a very practical purchase.

They caught the number 3 on Aleksanterinkatu and took it past the Tennis Palace to the Opera, where they planned to change to the number 4. This had become Siiri's habitual route from the city centre to Munkkiniemi. As they sat on the number 3, they wondered where old ladies like them were supposed to buy their clothing. There were no such stores, specializing in old people's clothes, although you heard all the time that there were more things for old people every day.

'We can't walk around in flashy, bright-coloured young people's clothes, like lunatics.'

Anna-Liisa thought anything at all could be an old lady's clothes as soon as an old enough lady wore it. She looked Siiri up and down appraisingly.

'It's not as if that poplin coat you're wearing is particularly designed for ninety-four-year-olds.'

While they waited for the number 4 at the new opera house they played with the idea of fashion just for old people.

'The trendy granny this spring is wearing shades of pear and olive. A gracefully draped skirt covers varicose veins handsomely, and brings out the legs from behind a Zimmer frame. The heels on her colourful sandals are subtle but youthful, and a polka-dot chiffon scarf completes the ensemble.'

Siiri extended her ankle and pivoted like a model, just as Irma had done when they were planning what to wear to a funeral – it must have been Tero's. There certainly had been a lot of funerals since then.

Just as the number 4 pulled up to the stop, Anna-Liisa said she was going to Tallinn for Easter with the Ambassador, on a veterans' rehabilitation tour, where spouses could come along for free.

'Just think of it – a sea crossing! And I plan to leave the Zimmer frame at home completely.'

It was only then that it occurred to Siiri that Anna-Liisa hadn't brought her Zimmer frame with her on their shopping trip. She walked perfectly without it, her red spring hat balanced on her head. It seemed she didn't need her old support now that she had a real gentleman friend to lean on – a cavalier to escort her to the crematorium, Siiri thought, and missed Irma terribly.

'You know, Siiri, I feel so young and alive. It's just like you always say – life is certainly amazing.'

'Do I say that? And did you just say that veterans' spouses get to go to Tallinn for free?' Siiri was shocked and a little envious of these travel plans.

'Yes! Since there are so few veterans of the war left, they're paying all expenses for spouses, too, although back in the eighties they didn't pay for anything. And since the spas are so much cheaper in Tallinn than in Finland, they're sending us there to save money!'

'But you're not the Ambassador's spouse, Anna-Liisa. At least, not to my knowledge.'

Siiri noticed that she was getting worked up and her voice was unnecessarily sharp. She had certainly never sponged off the government like that. Anna-Liisa didn't seem to notice Siiri's annoyance; she just told her proudly how clever Onni was at arranging the visas and everything – all taken care of in a snap.

'And he said we can always buy the rings in Tallinn if they're required.'

Chapter 47

Finnish Easter week was a dreary holiday, and it was a particularly hard one now, because on Maundy Thursday Irma's apartment was emptied. Some Estonian men came early in the morning and started carrying her things out to a truck parked in the car park. None of the darlings were present, just these foreign men who knew so little Finnish that Siiri couldn't figure out what was going on. Apparently, Irma's things were being taken to some storage warehouse, because the men were talking about a container. On Good Friday, the same men carried some cherry-veneer tables and a horrible, black TV stand into the apartment.

'Why are someone else's things being put in Irma Lännenleimu's apartment?' Siiri asked Virpi Hiukkanen when she saw her in the A-wing hallway. Without blinking an eye Virpi let flow a pack of lies, all about serious dementia, long-term care, a special exception being made to provide Irma a bed in the Group Home, long waiting lists for the apartments, and these difficult times.

'You can't live your life thinking that a ninety-two-year-old chronic patient is going to experience a miraculous recovery,' Virpi said. She couldn't remember the new tenant's name.

Siiri called Irma's doctor daughter Tuula ten times before she answered from some resort in Japan where it was night-time in the middle of the day. The call didn't go well.

'Living in a retirement home isn't cheap. It's not fun and games, as I'm sure you are aware,' Tuula said, yawning audibly, and Siiri could already guess what had happened. 'Virpi Hiukkanen advised this course of action. She has kindly arranged everything – I simply don't have the time.'

'May I ask where Irma's things were taken?'

'Things? It was just a lot of junk. The young people in the family went and looked at it and none of them wanted anything. Electric mixers and other antiques, and, to top it all, some addled retirement-home resident came in yelling incoherently at them. The only valuable item was the TV, but they didn't bother with it. Did you want it? For practical reasons everything was put up for auction through a company Virpi Hiukkanen recommended, but I doubt we'll get much money for it.'

Siiri didn't want to spend Easter at Sunset Grove. The new tenants were in the craft room with feathers and toilet-paper rolls covered in yellow trimmings, and the cafeteria was serving *mämmi* – black rye Easter pudding – for the second week in a row because it was so easy on the old people's mouths and it never went bad. Siiri didn't like *mämmi*, but it was Irma's favourite. She always heaped sugar on it by the spoonful – and then poked a hollow in it so that she could fit more sugar and cream in.

On Holy Saturday, Siiri bought a tub of *mämmi*, a kilo of sugar, and a carton of cream from Low Price Market and headed for Laakso Hospital. There were little plastic chicks on the hospital windowsills.

'But no Easter *mämmi*! Just the same old fruit trifle, can you believe it? Oh, Siiri, you're a treasure, bringing me real *mämmi*. And a kilo of sugar! You're a wonder.'

'The store didn't have granulated sugar in anything smaller. You'll eat it up in no time. Why not put it on your rye crisp? It'll crunch nicely between your teeth.'

Irma got a cup and spoon from the refugee-turned nurse and ate the *mämmi* with relish, although the cup might have been some sort of specimen container. Irma offered some of the viscous black pudding to the nurse, but the woman couldn't believe her eyes when she saw what Irma was spooning into her mouth, and hurried away.

'It does look a bit like crap,' Irma said, humming and crunching the sugar between her teeth, in an impossibly good mood. Siiri couldn't bear to tell her what had been done to her apartment, although she knew she ought to. Irma said her rehabilitation was progressing rapidly. She had walked three steps yesterday without support, and had got to know two sweet therapists.

'Very gentle. One of them has a two-year-old daughter named Irina. Isn't your daughter named Irina, too? The one who graduated as a nun in France? Why don't you ever talk about her? Do you think we should become nuns, too? Why haven't we ever thought of that before!'

Irma seemed half serious. She immediately started

thinking about the upside of a nun's life. No abbess could be as mean as Virpi Hiukkanen, although Virpi wasn't a boss like an abbess was, of course, just a sort of vice-abbess, which wasn't even a real title. There would be no men there, and it would be nice not to have to worry about anyone forcing hugs upon you in the lifts or kissing you in the hallways or feeling you up while you waited at the water fountain. It would be too hard for Anna-Liisa, of course, now that she'd started her new path in life. And the main thing was that in a convent nothing would cost anything.

'We would save thousands of euros a month and we could buy enough goats and cows to fill Africa!'

'True,' Siiri said, and thought grimly that a convent might, in fact, be their only alternative. 'But I would probably have to become a believer.'

'Oh, that's easy. No one will question that you're a believer, in the last leg of life. Just say that you've come to the conclusion that there is something eternal, that this can't be all there is to life. I'll be your godmother at the christening, of course. It'll be fun. Is there an entrance exam for a convent?'

Siiri got Irma to stop her dreaming by telling her about Mika Korhonen, and since Irma was already in the mood, she practically had an experience of enlightenment when she finessed who Mika Korhonen was.

'Our archangel! The boy who drove the taxi, who wanted to be bald and took us to eat peppery food in the new plastic Restaurant Kämp. Why haven't you talked about him before?'

Death in Sunset Grove

Irma still had good moments and bad moments. Siiri decided to use this lucid moment while she had the chance and told her about Mika's latest findings. Irma was mostly interested in the fact that he was Siiri's advocate now. She started to laugh, because she thought that an advocate was the same thing as a guardian and she remembered how it used to be that every village had some mentally retarded person who had been placed under guardianship.

'There was a case like that in Rossini's *The Barber of Seville*! Dr Bartolo was Rosina's guardian, wasn't he? Is Mika your Dr Bartolo now? The doctor was a complete ninny and just wanted to marry her. Aha! Could that be what's happening here? Mika must want to marry you!'

Eventually, Irma got back to where she'd started and came to her senses. She was pleased with Siiri and Anna-Liisa's initiative and happy that the guardianship didn't apply to her, since she had a big family and lots of loved ones, unlike Siiri, whose children had died from affluenza and escaped reality to live in convents.

'So I don't at all need to start asking people I meet on the street to be my guardian.'

'But my family isn't about to start dividing up my possessions while I'm still alive,' Siiri let slip, and Irma looked very serious.

Then Siiri had to tell her about the apartment, about the Estonian moving men, the warehouse and the auction. She tried to make it sound vague and confused and repeated many times that no new tenant had moved in yet, and she didn't know whether anyone would. This was true in a way,

301

because Virpi Hiukkanen had just talked about long waiting lists and hadn't mentioned anyone by name. But Irma understood all too well, including the things Siiri wasn't telling her. She'd had time lying in various hospitals to think about all kinds of things and had come to the conclusion that maybe she wasn't all that important to her precious darlings.

'It's my own fault, of course. Maybe I'm just a nagging old lady. A bad mother and a tedious grandmother, a burden to everyone.'

She started to cry and said how she had gradually realized that she was no joy or any earthly use to her children or grandchildren. They were actually waiting for her to die and get out of the way, and it was a relief to them when she was moved to the dementia ward to be a vegetable so that they could forget about her without feeling guilty.

'They can't wait to get my electric mixer. I'm worth about as much as an old kitchen gadget. Can you believe it? I've had it for more than thirty years. It's just a piece of junk. Although it is a Philips.'

'Well, your granddaughter seemed to want your jewellery, too, and I'm sure that's valuable,' Siiri said consolingly, but Irma wouldn't laugh at anything now.

'Nobody but you and Anna-Liisa has come to see me in the hospital. It didn't occur to any of my family to come and cheer me up with some *mämmi* – they've never even noticed that *mämmi* is my favourite. They're all in Cairo and Japan and in a great hurry, even when they're on holiday, but that's probably an excuse. If they have time to go to the other side of the earth, you would think they'd have time to visit the hospital and tell me I'm homeless. Oh, I wish I knew how to die. That would be the best thing I could do for them.'

Siiri had never heard Irma talk this way. It sounded unflinchingly honest, which was why it was so awful. Siiri started to feel like her own life was actually pretty good, since she didn't have to wonder why no one remembered her. She hugged Irma, who had grown oddly small and thin. She wiped her tears away with a lace handkerchief and tried to console her. Loneliness was part of growing old, and there was nothing you could do about it. Even old people who had lots of things to do and saw people every day felt lonely. You couldn't sit by the phone growing bitter because nobody called. Your children and grandchildren had their own lives, and so they should. Everybody was focused on their own life. Old people too. And Siiri and Irma in particular, because they still had lots of things they knew how to enjoy.

'You can move in with me. We still have time to do lots of fun things together,' Siiri said, and Irma's smile returned. She said that Siiri snored, that she could hear her through the wall and no earplug was tough enough to keep the noise out. She blew her nose loudly into Siiri's handkerchief, tucked it into her sleeve as if it were her own, and explained that if you blow your nose all the time, then the stuff that comes out isn't snot, it's allergy fluid. Then she let out a deep sigh and wanted to hear more about the romance between Anna-Liisa and the Ambassador, and when Siiri told her about the trip to Tallinn for veterans and their spouses, Irma laughed so much she gave herself a stomach ache.

Chapter 48

Siiri Kettunen was summoned for questioning at the East Pasila police station. Her last contact with the police had been in the autumn of 1946 when they'd tried to pump her for information about a weapons cache, but she hadn't been as nervous then as she was now.

Luckily, Anna-Liisa was coming with her. She felt partly responsible for Siiri being questioned because the Ambassador was the one who had reported the fire to the police, which was why Siiri was in a sticky spot now. The Ambassador escorted them to the door at Sunset Grove and gave a lengthy speech.

'The police work for us. Have faith in yourself and great things could come of this. You have a tremendous responsibility in the name of justice and morality. Remember that. I demanded justice, and you are my envoys,' he said, his voice trembling, and then he kissed Anna-Liisa on the cheek and shook Siiri's hand ceremoniously, as if they were on their way to discover a new continent. He left behind a pleasant smell of aftershave.

Siiri knew that she couldn't possibly tell the police anything but the truth. It had been a different matter in 1946. Then it had been a matter of patriotism, and it had been her duty to protect her friends and relatives, even though her lie had come to nothing, of course: they were all sent to jail. Brave men.

She had gone over the night of the fire in her mind many times. She couldn't swear that the person she saw running across the courtyard was Erkki Hiukkanen. Since the fire, the caretaker hadn't been seen in Sunset Grove's hallways, the air ducts and drains had been left to clog up while Erkki concentrated on following Siiri around the city. The more she thought about it, the more confused it all became. But she wanted to believe that evil would be punished.

'Not necessarily,' Anna-Liisa said as they crossed Bell Bridge. 'Many criminals are never caught. If your statement finally made the police understand what kind of game is going on behind the scenes at Sunset Grove, it would be a monumental achievement.'

The police station was one of those depressing concrete boxes that stand shoulder to shoulder all over Pasila. There was an information desk inside the entrance just like at a bank – or at least the ones that still had customer service. Siiri took a number and sat down with Anna-Liisa among the assorted crooks. Siiri looked around nervously, but Anna-Liisa was already absorbed in a battered old copy of Donald Duck that someone had left on the waiting-room table.

'You stiff-legged old tightwad!'

'Sorry?'

'Magica de Spell just called Uncle Scrooge a stiff-legged old tightwad,' Anna-Liisa said. 'I think it's a funny thing to call an elderly duck. Look – it's the one where the police come to take the nephews away. Kind of matches the theme today. He's eloquent, that Donald. He's an example of the nuanced language of comics. Listen: "Those flatfoots are nabbing my nephews and hucking them in the hoosegow with everybody in town watching." Hopefully things don't go as badly for you today.'

When Siiri's turn came they were told they were in the wrong place. A friendly policewoman showed them to a lift that would take them to where they were supposed to be – an echoey little room on the third floor, where a very young man sat. He was dressed in everyday clothes, wearing a tie, and he introduced himself with a somewhat timid mumble.

'Senior Constable Kettunen.'

'Master of Philosophy Petäjä,' Anna-Liisa replied, and then went to sit down next to the wall.

'I'm a senior Kettunen, too!' Siiri cried happily, but when the young man held his earnest expression she apologized, since they probably weren't related. There were lots of Kettunens in Finland, and besides, it was her late husband's name. Siiri's maiden name was Närviö, but she preferred the more ordinary Kettunen, because Närviö was a made-up name, forced on her family in the 1880s by her Fennoman grandfather, who wanted to be among the first to Finnicize his name, Neovius, which itself was made up by someone named Nyman, who was going to Turku in the 1700s to study at the university and thought it sounded Latin.

'Do you have any identification?' the policeman interrupted.

He was absorbed in flipping through the papers on his desk, of which there were a lot. He read them in the same way a doctor reads a patient's files, as if he'd never seen the papers before. Siiri found her social security card in her handbag, but apparently it wasn't identification. After a moment of looking she found her driver's licence, which she hadn't needed in ages.

'What's this?' the constable asked.

It was a pink-paper driver's licence in a plastic pocket with a smudged stamp on it from 1978, the last time Siiri had renewed it. But the Senior Constable seemed to think that it had expired, in spite of the fact that she'd renewed it. He said driver's licences looked quite different nowadays, and to assure her of this he showed her his own, which was a plastic slab that looked like a bank card. In any case, a driver's licence was no longer sufficient for identification. She had to show a passport or official proof of identity, which was also a plastic slab that looked like a bank card. Siiri, in other words, had no identification.

'Not even a passport?' the boy asked, and Siiri wondered what she'd done with her passport. The last time she had travelled was in the 1950s, when she took the MS *Oihonna* to Hamburg. Unlike some people, she wasn't the lucky bride of a war veteran and couldn't go gallivanting around at the government's expense to heal from her traumas. Then

Anna-Liisa dug her passport out of her handbag. It was quite new. She'd ordered one in March, in preparation for her trip to Tallinn, without mentioning a thing to Siiri.

'Don't start bickering about it,' Anna-Liisa snapped, and then turned to the policeman. 'I can vouch for her identity. And her pedigree she has already presented.'

The Senior Constable finally gave in but then shooed Anna-Liisa into the hallway. He continued to look at his papers, and Siiri waited for such a long while that she had time to count the folders on his shelves twice before he began the questioning. He asked her about obvious things, like whether she remembered her identity, did she know what month it was and who the President of Finland was. Siiri recited all the Presidents of Finland from Ståhlberg to Niinistö, just to be on the safe side, because she had lived through each administration, and she said she even remembered her PIN by using a mnemonic: the second number was the first number cubed, the third number was the first and second numbers multiplied and then divided by three, and the fourth number was the sum of the first two minus three.

'Oh, heavens – now you know my PIN and I'm not supposed to tell it to outsiders! But of course you can be trusted because you're a policeman. Did you get that the common factor in all the rules is the number three?'

Senior Constable Kettunen put an end to this memory game and finally cut to the chase. He wanted to know what day the fire happened, where the retirement home was, and when Siiri had first noticed the fire. She told him that she had been at the door to the Group Home at 2.30 a.m. and had noticed that there was smoke coming from inside. After a moment's hesitation, she also told him that she had let herself in with a key, because her shouts weren't awakening the nurse.

'As I understand it, the nurse then called for help, on your instruction.'

The policeman didn't seem to wonder why Siiri was prowling the Sunset Grove hallways at night or where she'd got a key to the Group Home. But how could the poor boy have known what kind of place a retirement-home dementia ward was and what kind of rules it had? Then he asked Siiri if she had seen anyone outside.

'I thought there was someone running outside . . . a man,' Siiri said, no longer chattering aimlessly.

The Ambassador would have been greatly disappointed in her because she didn't use the opportunity to report Erkki Hiukkanen for starting the fire. The constable had nothing more to ask her, and an unpleasant silence fell over the room. All that could be heard was the hum of the ventilation system. When nothing seemed to rouse the constable, Siiri tried to lighten the mood by telling him about the artist Sigrid Schauman, who, when she was being questioned by the police following a car accident, was asked whether she'd had any dealings with the police before, and she'd answered, 'Yes, when my brother shot Governor-General Bobrikov.'

The very young Senior Constable looked at Siiri with empty, pale-blue eyes, almost like Irma's eyes on her worst days in the Group Home. Maybe he didn't know who Sigrid

Schauman was. Or Bobrikov! Siiri thought about the Ambassador and about Anna-Liisa sitting out in the hallway. Then, Mika Korhonen appeared in her thoughts with his backpack, followed by Irma roaring, in a wheelchair and a sexy T-shirt, and she could no longer contain herself. She burst into a flood of words. It was a long outpouring. At first the policeman looked at her in bewilderment, then with close attention. He was left-handed, and was taking notes with his hand at an awkward angle and listening to her as if he were extremely interested in what she was saying.

'You must have something in those hundred and thirty-eight binders about the rape of Olavi Raudanheimo. And this fellow Pasi must be well-known to you. Mika said so. But I don't remember Pasi's last name. From what I understand, Pasi was questioned several times and he's going to end up in jail.'

When she'd finished her barrage of talk, Siiri's heart was pounding and her hands were shaking.

'You said that the head nurse left you lying on the floor in her office. When did this happen? And how big was the package that you found on your postbox without any information about the sender or recipient?'

Siiri didn't remember mentioning the package. She couldn't say when the package appeared, but the occurrence in Virpi Hiukkanen's office had definitely happened the same day. What day was that? Siiri felt faint. She asked the boy for a glass of water. But before he could get up from his chair, her eyes went dim.

The police station devolved into chaos because a ninety-four-year-old woman had fainted. Senior Constable Kettunen thought at first that his client had died on his office floor. He bent uncertainly over her to look for signs of life, and when he could see that she was breathing, however weakly, he called the department assistant, who berated him for not immediately calling the emergency services. An eternity was spent waiting for the emergency services to answer, and after that Constable Kettunen was asked a slew of questions that he couldn't answer. He got testy, at which point emergency services got testy because Constable Kettunen was the seventy-seventh caller in a row who'd had the nerve to get annoyed, even though the emergency-services worker was just doing her job as well as she could, based on what she'd learned at training camp.

Constable Kettunen finally lost his temper and started bellowing into the phone in such a loud voice that Anna-Liisa appeared at the door to witness the scene, looking angry. She grabbed the phone from him and started shouting orders at the emergency service centre in no uncertain terms, and the call ended quickly.

'An ambulance is on the way,' she said grimly and ordered Constable Kettunen to fetch some water.

The old lady lying on the floor revived, drank a little water, and was then able to sit up with her friend's help. Constable Kettunen stood helplessly beside them, glancing nervously at the clock, not knowing what to do in a situation such as this, other than complain afterwards that it took too long for an ambulance to get to the police station. The department assistant came to the door to scold him, and soon half the department was there watching as the ambulance crew carried a half-dead woman out of his office on a stretcher.

'Well done, Siiri,' Anna-Liisa said in the ambulance, squeezing her hand tightly. Her red hat was askew, her hair dishevelled, her aspect agitated. Siiri's other hand had an IV connected to it and the ambulance man was bustling about efficiently in the tiny space.

'She's conscious,' he said, but Siiri didn't bother to introduce herself because she'd learned by now that ambulance crews didn't waste their time with polite niceties. 'Take her to the retirement home!'

The ambulance drove down Mannerheimintie at high speed with the siren blaring, as if Siiri was in mortal danger and they were rushing to save her life before it was too late.

'Why do you have the siren on?' Siiri asked.

'For amusement. It's more fun this way.'

Siiri thought it was scandalous, disrupting traffic like that. She was ashamed, embarrassed and upset. No doubt she would be getting a bill for this joyride. What a waste of money.

Chapter 49

After May Day, a tremendously fat seventy-two-year-old woman who got around in a wheelchair and never even said hello moved into Irma's apartment. The name on the door was Vuorinen, but no one was sure what the woman's first name was. Nurses were running to the apartment day and night to turn Mrs Vuorinen, a task which always required at least two girls, so with all her care needs she was a significantly more lucrative placement for the Loving Care Foundation and Virpi Hiukkanen's agency than Irma had been.

Irma's affairs had, in the meantime, grown more complicated. She was gradually recovering from the installation of her titanium hip but had now been transferred to the Kivelä Hospital Trauma Therapy Unit. There wasn't much to recommend the hospital except that it was on Sibeliuksenkatu, which was a street with a lovely name.

'It's part of the homecoming process,' Anna-Liisa said. 'But it doesn't seem to be a simple matter.'

'It certainly isn't,' Siiri said. 'Irma doesn't even have a home!'

Anna-Liisa had been to visit Kivelä Hospital to quiz the staff and had refused to leave until they'd given her a pile of brochures on the care recommendations of Irma's multi-professional team, including questions for loved ones, monitored exercise, and a home-evaluation system based on a scale of designated performance measurements.

Anna-Liisa read it aloud in her formal style: 'An elderly person's physical abilities can be weakened by even a short stay in the hospital. Older people have a small homeostatic reserve and often have other accompanying illnesses as well.'

'I'm sorry, a small what?'

'Don't interrupt. Those responsible for the care and treatment of these illnesses can exacerbate the atrophy of a patient's physical capacities. The hospital environment and prolonged bedrest can also contribute to complications.'

'Good Lord. And I thought that you went to the hospital to get better!'

'I'm not done yet.'

They felt sorry for poor Irma, being put through the mill like this. Who would have guessed that coming home from the hospital could be a life-threatening procedure associated with loneliness, insecurity and fear? According to the brochure, going home from the hospital was a traumatic event because the hospital was a protective environment – a claim no doubt connected with the fact that the person who wrote the brochure worked at the hospital.

'There certainly seem to be plenty of traumas and risks involved. And to think that at the end of the war they just tossed the men from the front out to rebuild society and pay back all the war reparations. The only assistance they got was from the state-owned alcohol store,' said Anna-Liisa when she got to the end of the brochure. She was so angry she couldn't speak for a moment and just slapped the flyer down on the edge of the table.

'Isn't this the fifth hospital Irma's been to for one broken hip?' Siiri asked, to make the tapping stop. 'Did you read that article in the paper about hospital tourists?'

'The term is medical tourist. They use it to refer to sick people from other countries who come here to get treatment, not patients like Irma, who go from hospital to hospital. But listen to this!'

Anna-Liisa plunged into another brochure, as if they were tremendously entertaining.

'The patient should be seen as a results-oriented agent in his or her own rehabilitation process.' She was silent for a moment, shook her head, and looked hopeless. 'Just think. Even I, a veteran language and literature teacher, find it harder and harder nowadays to understand the language.'

For an elderly patient to be allowed to go home, she had to pass certain tests that sounded so nonsensical that it made them laugh. The patient had to undergo such things as naming the parts of the body, and self-esteem reinforcement through touch. Perhaps this was a positive development. Siiri had once had a friend in hospital who'd been anaesthetized and prepped for surgery before they discovered that she was the wrong patient for the surgery being performed, and she'd simply been whisked out onto the street to wonder where she was.

'That method of sending a patient home is altogether too swift,' Siiri said. 'What they're doing with Irma is thorough, at least.'

'We have to intervene somehow,' Anna-Liisa said, turning serious. 'What dignity is there in quizzing an old person about parts of her own body? And what good will all these silly procedures do you if, in the meantime, your home is being taken away from under your nose? Is this just a matter of providing employment for young people? Do they need so many professionals deciding every little thing? Common sense has been lost from the world, it seems to me.'

All this foolishness started to make Siiri so angry that she got up off the bed and warmed some blood pancakes on the stove. They were perhaps no longer quite fresh, but when you put lots of melted butter and lingonberry jam on them they still tasted good. While they ate, they chatted about how people used to scrape the mould off bread, or even jam, a thick green layer of it, and just throw it in the slop bucket and eat the rest with a good appetite, and no one ever got sick.

'What doesn't kill you makes you stronger,' Anna-Liisa said, and she would have liked a glass of red wine, but Siiri didn't have any.

'In that case I'll go over to Onni's. He has an alcohol cabinet,' Anna-Liisa announced as she wiped up the last of the jam from her plate and dashed out of the door in her spring hat. She'd taken to wearing it even indoors these days, which, of course, was perfectly acceptable for a woman of refinement.

Chapter 50

Siiri's great-granddaughter's boyfriend Tuukka had noticed on his computer that a private ambulance company had billed Siiri eighty-seven euros thirty cents for urgent transport. He sounded very worried on the phone, which wasn't like him. He was usually so businesslike.

'I just had a fainting spell while I was out,' Siiri said, not daring to tell him about being questioned by the police, or about her crime. 'The silly ambulance men kept the siren on for no reason at all and, of course, with the siren on it costs more. The whole thing was unnecessary, for heaven's sake.'

Tuukka had some experience with ambulance charges and explained that the more unnecessary the trip, the more it cost.

'The patient pays. If you don't need treatment, as apparently happened in this case, it costs more than taking a taxi. It's big business nowadays, transporting the sick.'

Siiri was astonished, but she believed him, because he was a very conscientious boy and always got to the bottom of things. It seemed that city ambulances took care of the most urgent cases and the rest were left for private firms who could charge whatever they liked.

'But I didn't order the ambulance! I was lying unconscious and somebody else called emergency services. Why should I be punished for that? Is somebody trying to get rich off picking up sick people?'

'Of course they are,' Tuukka said calmly. But there was another reason he had called. He had found out that Mika Korhonen was now Siiri's advocate.

'Do you understand what that means?' he asked, as if Siiri were a child, or slow-witted. Tuukka thought that appointing an advocate was practically the same thing as putting yourself under guardianship, like voluntarily signing yourself up for the poorhouse.

'You said it. This retirement home is a poorhouse.'

'No, that's not what I meant. If you have an advocate, it means you're not capable of handling your own affairs.'

'I'm not capable of it. That's why you're taking care of my bank account and making sure Virpi Hiukkanen doesn't bleed it dry.'

'Right, and now you want Mika Korhonen to take care of all your affairs. I know his type, and if I were you, I wouldn't trust him. But it's your decision, of course. And I also called to ask if you want me to transfer your Internet banking rights to him. You seem to be getting along without my help now that you've found your own Hell's Angel.'

This hadn't occurred to Siiri. The whole advocate issue had come as a sort of surprise to her and she herself hadn't been that thrilled with the idea. She should have told Tuukka about it and asked his advice. He was almost a relative, after all, and a university man, and he had good reason to be hurt by Siiri thoughtlessly acting behind his back. She didn't really know Mika at all. What did she know about him? That he was a cook and a taxi driver and was born a couple of years before she retired. But did he have a family? Where was he born, who were his relatives, where did he live? He never talked about himself or his own life.

Tuukka said that Mika had filed a report at the magistrate's office, and now Siiri was so frightened that she almost felt faint. She couldn't bear any more dealings with the police. What was she being dragged into?

'Don't worry. He's just filed as your advocate. Otherwise it wouldn't be official. There's a guardianship office there where they keep track of these things.'

'A guardianship office? That sounded like exactly what Tuukka was talking about, as though Siiri had been declared fit for the poorhouse. A guardianship used to be a horribly shameful thing, like being a halfwit. That's what Irma had said, too – the village idiot. But nowadays they positively recommended that old people appoint an advocate. They'd had even had a presentation on it at Sunset Grove. There were so many old people in Finland whose relatives had forgotten them, people who needed a trusted person to make decisions in case they fell down and hit their head and had a cerebral haemorrhage and couldn't remember their blood type. If you didn't appoint an advocate yourself, you might end up having some unknown city official as your advocate. Virpi Hiukkanen had made an announcement, volunteering to be the advocate for residents at Sunset Grove. Siiri hadn't gone to that lecture, but Anna-Liisa had sat through the whole thing and taken notes so it was one more thing she knew all about. And Mika was, after all, Anna-Liisa's advocate, too.

'So should I give Mika your bank information?' Tuukka asked again. There was a sound of clicking computer keys in the background. He was, it seemed, beginning to worry about Siiri, an old woman who didn't understand her own affairs and had to have everything explained to her twice.

'I'm sorry, Tuukka. I didn't mean to offend you,' Siiri said, and asked if he would continue to be her personal bank-business person as long as she was still alive. Tuukka agreed, the wonderful boy, no longer sounding annoyed, and ended the call by wishing her well.

Chapter 51

Irma was enjoying her four-person room at the Kivelä Hospital Trauma Therapy Unit for Geriatric Assessment and Rehabilitation tremendously. She had started to develop a routine for adjusting to a new hospital and she had quickly got to know her room-mates. Kivelä was the fifth hospital where she was the oldest patient in the room, sort of like the *oltermanni*, the old village alderman.

'Or is that only men? And Oltermanni cheese?'

The hospital was built in the 1930s, but it had been re-modelled several times since then. The ground-floor lobby looked like it had been designed by some Alvar Aalto worshipper, with a broad staircase and terracotta floor tiles.

'Do you know, I found a sign downstairs that had a twenty-six-letter word on it,' Siiri said.

'No! What was it?'

'It was ... hmm. I can't remember now. It was a very complicated medical term.'

Irma could move on her own now, and was able to get around quite well with a Zimmer frame, although her progress was still slow and unsteady. She was eager to go on her first circuit of the hospital and look for Siiri's word.

'We can get some coffee while we're out. There's a cafeteria next to the stairs.'

Siiri helped her to her feet, which wasn't much trouble because Irma was so thin and had more energy than before. She took firm hold of the Zimmer frame and started pushing herself forward.

'It's peculiar when your head and your feet aren't going at the same tempo. But singing helps. I sing with my physical therapist – my father was a soldier, young and handsome, too . . . and voilà, my feet get marching. The main thing is not to end up in a wheelchair. That would be horrible.'

It was a long way from Irma's room to the lift and another complicated trip from the lift to the cafeteria. But they weren't in any hurry. They found a bronze plaque on the wall that said that President Ryti had spent his last years at Kivelä Hospital.

'In other words, he died here. I don't see how that's such a great honour for a hospital,' Irma snorted. She started to turn her Zimmer frame, with some difficulty. Once she'd got herself facing the right direction she lifted her gaze to the door across the hall.

'*Omahoitotarvikejakelupiste!*' she said, overjoyed. Self-care supply distribution point! 'There's your word! Wait, let me count.'

Irma's soprano singing voice echoed gloriously as she counted the letters, crowing and laughing. She noticed that next to the *Omahoitotarvikejakelupiste* there was an *apuvälinelainaamo*, assistive-device loan centre, but to her disappointment the word had only seventeen letters.

They admired the lobby and thought Kivelä was a very nice hospital, the most pleasant one in Helsinki, so far. Irma thought the physical therapists at Kivelä were better than the ones at Laakso, but the food was worse, and the beds were awful. The other patients in her trauma therapy unit were a very colourful bunch; among them were a few recovering from serious brain infarctions and their behaviour was unpredictable. One man slunk around the ward at night and came into women's rooms and stood next to their beds. A lot of the patients were afraid of him, because it was unpleasant to wake up in the middle of the night and find a complete stranger standing there staring at you. There was a woman in Irma's ward who was very confused and had a filthy mouth and thought Irma was a madame at a bordello.

'Was I that confused in the Group Home?'

'Well, you thought I was the nurse and you came out with all kinds of crazy things. You ordered me to pack a meal in a backpack and make sure I brought the alphabet book along, too.'

'Like I did back when Kekkonen was president! Oh, how funny! But how could you stand me like that?'

'Of course I could,' Siiri said, carrying their coffee cups to a free table by the wall. 'After all, I knew that you weren't really dotty. It was all because of the medication.'

'And that thought never occurred to my darlings.'

They sat down to enjoy their coffees and Irma started to talk about her dreams for going home. They actually called it the 'homecoming process', and Irma was supposed to meet several times with a group of people called the multi-professional team, as threatened in Anna-Liisa's brochure. The group included a social worker, a physical therapist, a nurse and an occupational therapist, all of them cute young interns soon to graduate. The occupational therapist seemed to be like the activities directors at the retirement home. Irma had asked if she had to make an Easter chick before she could go home, but the girl had said that it would all become clear over time and that an activities director was a very different thing from an occupational therapist.

After a good beginning, however, Irma's homecoming process had come to a halt because they couldn't get hold of her family.

'None of my darlings are answering the phone! They should be ashamed of themselves. I told the social worker that it was because all that appears on the little screen is an unknown number when you call from the hospital. My children have told me that you shouldn't answer calls like that because they could be from anyone – a cold-caller or some other annoyance. Although sometimes they do have good things on offer. I once got a free Japanese kitchen knife and some Swiss wrinkle cream when I ordered a set of books, which I gave to my darlings as Christmas gifts. The nurse didn't believe me. But let's talk about something more fun. Tell me about Anna-Liisa's spring fling!'

Anna-Liisa and the Ambassador, now known as Onni, were going around everywhere holding hands and there was no sign of the Zimmer frame at all. Onni told impossibly long stories about his diplomatic adventures and Anna-Liisa listened with her cheeks glowing, believing everything he said, though half the Ambassador's stories were pure hogwash.

'Heaven protect us! And Anna-Liisa has always been so critical!' Irma squealed and laughed so hard that her coffee went down the wrong way. Siiri pounded on her back, and Irma coughed and crowed.

But that wasn't all. The craziest thing about the blossoming love at Sunset Grove was that Anna-Liisa and Onni quizzed each other about interrogative case endings, pronouns that demand the dative, and Finnish bodies of water while they played doubles solitaire. Last weekend they had both memorized the price list for the Sunset Grove cafeteria, in loud voices, and had thought it great fun. When they were in Tallinn, they had danced the foxtrot and the waltz and spent time with a lot of complete strangers, other veterans, in a 'jacuzzi', which was a tub filled with hot, bubbly water. They brought back a linen tablecloth with pink hearts and white angels on it as a souvenir for Siiri.

'The tablecloth of love, so you'll remember the wonderful veterans' holiday!'

Irma was sure that Anna-Liisa and Onni would end up getting married, and she made Siiri swear to ask if they could be bridesmaids. They could wear lacy dresses and purple silk bows in their hair, which Irma promised to make for them in the craft sessions for her homecoming test. Irma laughed so hard that she peed in her pants but it didn't matter because everybody at the hospital wore incontinence pads.

'They make you. It's horribly uncomfortable and humili-
ating. But the nurses don't have time to help the patients to
the bathroom, and no matter how hard I swear I can walk
there myself, they won't believe me.'

The pads were changed three times a day, which was
apparently a great luxury because at the Malmi Hospital they
only changed them twice, or that's what someone had told
her.

'One poor woman was positively in agony yesterday at
lunch because her pad was so full, but the nurses just said
that she could have a clean one at four o'clock. As if it were
pre-programmed that you have to wait all day!'

When they'd finished their coffee, Siiri accompanied Irma
back to the first floor. The staff had been looking all over the
ward for Irma, but the nurses didn't get too upset, as long as
the patient was capable of finding her way back to her own
bed. Siiri was frightened, though. She had lured Irma into
breaking the rules. She knew that patients were supposed to
just lie there and wait to be rehabilitated. After their little
escapade Irma was happy and fell asleep as soon as she got
into bed.

On the way home, Siiri was vigilant, and justifiably so,
because she saw a man who looked like Erkki Hiukkanen
standing around on Ruusulankatu with his back to her. He
had the same dishevelled hair and sloping shoulders. Siiri
quickened her step and saw to her horror, from a reflection
in a restaurant window, that the man was following her. She
managed to cross Mannerheimintie before he did and the

number 4 came just as the pedestrian light turned red. Relieved, she climbed aboard the tram and left her pursuer staring into a bridal-shop window.

Chapter 52

Late in the spring, Siiri received a letter from the Judicial Registry in Hämeenlinna. She looked at the letter in dread, not daring to open it at first. She had no idea what a judicial registry was, but she remembered that there was a women's prison in Hämeenlinna. She was just getting ready to go with Anna-Liisa on a post-book-club tram ride and then to Kivelä Hospital to look in on Irma when she found the letter in her postbox. They had finally finished reading Aleksandr Solzhenitsyn's *Gulag Archipelago* and Siiri thought a trip to the hospital might lighten her mood. No doubt Anna-Liisa was waiting for her in the lobby, because Anna-Liisa was never late, but the stupid letter froze Siiri in her tracks at her own apartment door. She decided to open it and pulled her index finger across the folded top of the envelope. It hurt her finger and made an ugly tear. She tried to read the letter quickly but she couldn't understand it at all. She glanced at the clock, panicked when she saw how late it was, tossed the letter and envelope in her handbag, and dashed to catch the lift.

By the time they were on the tram, she had already forgotten the letter and instead was telling Anna-Liisa that she feared Erkki Hiukkanen was spying on her. Anna-Liisa didn't take it seriously. She was in high spirits, full of excited fantasies about all kinds of silly things.

'He probably thinks you're part of Mika's ring of criminals and has decided to find out what's what. Either that or he intends to do you in, maybe even rob you. Or maybe he found out that you're a wealthy heiress and he's after your money. After all, you might have some rich, childless cousin in America, right?'

It wasn't until they were sitting with Irma in the shade of the broad staircase at the Kivelä Hospital cafeteria that Siiri remembered the letter from the Judicial Registry and took it out of her handbag.

'Hämeenlinna? Are they summoning you to prison?' Irma said excitedly, but Anna-Liisa informed her that the Hämeenlinna Prison was a museum now.

'It's two words, you know. Hämeen, the genitive form of Häme, and linna, which can be a castle, a fort, or a prison.'

'What are you babbling about? What difference does it make? Is this some kind of language reform where compound words are declared separate words? What next, Cata Lonia? Are we just putting spaces into words now?'

'You really are crazy, Irma. But it is a fact that people's ability to recognize compound words has diminished dramatically.'

While Irma and Anna-Liisa went off at on this tangent, Siiri read through the letter twice and felt quite dizzy –

sabotage, vandalism, criminal liability, compensation for damages, taking into account the felon's age.

'That means your age!' Irma said. 'Are you a felon now?'

The police and emergency personnel had determined the Sunset Grove fire to be sabotage and vandalism, and the Ambassador's reporting Erkki Hiukkanen hadn't led anywhere, except perhaps to Siiri being accused. Apparently, Siiri's outpouring in Senior Constable Kettunen's office had made matters worse. Instead of investigating Virpi and Erkki Hiukkanen's activities, the police had straightened the whole thing out by making Siiri out to be a criminal. It had been foolish of her to prove her sanity by reciting the Finnish presidents and explaining her PIN system. Now she had no mitigating factors except her age.

'Finally, you'll get some use out of being over the hill,' Irma said.

Irma had other reasons to rejoice. She had been freed from the hospital's incontinence-pad requirement because she'd established such good relations with several of the nurses, and that reminded her of several rambling stories about the nurses' children, until Siiri requested that she please concentrate for a moment on the letter from the Judicial Registry because its contents still weren't clear to her.

The prosecutor had confirmed the summary judgement of the police, which was forty daily equivalence fines for common vandalism. The courts were behaving just like the health system, writing up punishments and prescriptions without the judge or the doctor ever laying eyes on her.

Where did this prosecutor come in? The only person Siiri had talked to was Senior Constable Kettunen, and she didn't see his name anywhere in the letter. But she did see the name of the advocate for the accused, Mika Korhonen.

'Why would they call lighting a fire in a dementia ward common vandalism? What's common about it?' Irma wondered, and she looked at the letter carefully.

'It's a juridical term. Common vandalism,' Anna-Liisa explained. 'Vandalism can be categorized as nominal, common, or gross. Siiri should probably be glad the stunt was judged common rather than gross. And vandalism is a lesser charge than sabotage, which is a frequent charge in the case of fires.'

'How do you know all this?' Irma asked in astonishment.

But Anna-Liisa pretended not to have heard the question. She was poring over the commentary enclosed with the letter that explained the commutation of the prison term to an equivalent daily fine. Three daily fines were equal to one day in prison. She calculated quickly in her head that Siiri's forty daily fines would be thirteen and one third days in prison.

'That doesn't sound bad. It might even be interesting!' Irma said, and offered to serve the sentence on Siiri's behalf, since she was homeless anyway, but Siiri couldn't join in her merriment. She felt very weak and wished she could stay on at Kivelä Hospital as a patient.

'How much is it going to cost me?' she asked Anna-Liisa wearily, as she seemed to be the most informed about her case.

'That depends on your net worth. There's an explanation of it here,' Anna-Liisa said. Calculating the daily fine was very complicated, because first you had to have a net worth above a certain amount and then they divided that net worth by something. Rather like Siiri's PIN.

'Is there someone there for me to call?' Siiri asked helplessly.

But all the letter had was a web address and Mika Korhonen's name. Now was certainly a time when she could have used an advocate, but they hadn't heard a peep out of Mika since he'd brought the social worker Pasi to the attention of the authorities. Irma tried to brighten the mood by talking about her homecoming process. She had been invited by her team of female professionals to a care-counselling session that was held in spite of the fact that none of her relatives showed up. The nurses and physical therapists had diligently put together a test for her, which she thought she would pass easily.

'My self-image is getting so strong that my head is buzzing. I can recognize my toes, fingers, even my kidneys, without the intern girls having to touch or pet me. And believe it or not, my occupational therapist has her own little playhouse here at the hospital.'

Irma was going to have to prepare a breakfast in the test kitchen before they would let her out of the hospital, because that was what was demanded of a housewife and mother of six. They decided that she should surprise the occupational therapist with poached eggs and a cheese soufflé.

'And then you can take a shower with your inspectors watching! Is your fitness inspector a man, by any chance?' Anna-Liisa asked.

Chapter 53

'Mika, you have to save me. I'm a convicted criminal and an arsonist and I'm going to prison!'

Mika was calm and brief on the other end of the line. He told Siiri to relax and promised to meet her in an hour at the Tram Museum Cafe where they served coffee in soup bowls.

'Bring the letter with you.'

Siiri left for her date well ahead of time. As she walked towards the number 4 stop enjoying the spring sunshine, she once again had the feeling that someone was watching her. This was really becoming a nuisance. She was behaving like a complete lunatic, couldn't even take a step without having paranoid thoughts. Erkki Hiukkanen was everywhere, pestering her, a bloodhound – with a pistol in his coat pocket, naturally – and now she'd ruined her light-footedness by imagining dogs wearing coats with pockets. She took a deep breath, stopped for a moment to lean on her cane, and tried to ignore her own thoughts.

She continued on her way, and as she quickened her steps she had the distinct impression that someone really was at her heels, matching their footsteps to hers. She stopped in front of the bank, pretending to look at some window flyers for apartments for sale, which actually did always interest her a bit, although she was never going to buy a new apartment again.

As she stood there she saw who it was that was following her: Erkki Hiukkanen, of course. This time she was sure it was him. She could see his gawking face and messy, thinning hair, which was unmistakable, although Anna-Liisa had been right when she'd said that Finland was full of men who looked like Erkki Hiukkanen. Hiukkanen was wearing blue overalls and a dirty poplin coat and rubber boots, on a warm, spring day so dry that the dust was swirling in the streets.

Siiri stood in front of the bank window for a long time and listened to the uneven, frantic beating of her heart. Why was Erkki Hiukkanen after her? Was he trying to find out where she was going, who she was meeting? How had he known that she had arranged to meet someone in town?

'They listen to all our telephone calls, you know,' Anna-Liisa had said. Anna-Liisa and Onni thought that they should disconnect their landlines and get mobile phones because they were harder to tap.

Siiri turned her back on Erkki Hiukkanen, who had stopped to stand in the shadow of a florist's kiosk. Just then she noticed the number 4 coming down the street. She went to the window of the hardware store to look at the frying pans and ladders, waiting for the tram to leave the stop at Low Price Market. It was taking an excruciatingly long time. Finally, the tram started into motion. When it got near Siiri's stop, she dashed intrepidly across the street at the very last minute. Erkki Hiukkanen crossed too, at the crossing like a law-abiding citizen, and ran in front of the tram towards the stop, but Siiri waited on the tracks behind the tram, hidden from sight. Not until the very last person was boarding did she approach the back entrance. There were two schoolboys dawdling in front of the tram door, apparently unable to decide whether or not to get on.

'Excuse me,' Siiri said politely, pushing her way forward and shoving them onto the tram as she did so. 'No point in you loitering at the tram stop.'

The boys smiled beautifully, bewildered. They were her rescuers. Erkki Hiukkanen couldn't see what was happening at the back of the car and was left standing at the stop wondering how a ninety-four-year old woman had disappeared into thin air.

'My heroes! Here's ten for each of you!' Siiri said to the boys, digging two notes out of her purse. The boys didn't quite understand why the scruffy man left standing at the tram stop was following her just because he was a caretaker at a retirement home where she rented a one-bedroom apartment in the A wing and had lived there for ten years.

'Didja escape?' one boy asked. He seemed to think that you're not allowed to leave a retirement home and go outside.

'He's spying on me,' Siiri said, still breathless, trying to look mysterious. She told them that she was a dangerous criminal who started fires and poked her nose into all sorts of things. She told them to take care that they became law-abiding citizens.

'Use this money wisely. You don't smoke, do you, you silly boys?'

The two boys looked abashed. One of them still had a burning cigarette in his hand, and it was only then that Siiri understood why they had hesitated at the door of the tram.

'So you do smoke. But what business is it of mine? It's good to die in time anyway, so you don't have to live to be old.'

'How old are you? Over eighty?' asked the bolder of the two boys. Siiri laughed gaily, like a divorcée falling in love.

'I'm ninety-four.'

'No way. Respect.'

'You gonna stay standing?'

Siiri asked them to sit down with her so that they could chat. They told her about their grandparents who were really old, maybe seventy, and always travelling, mostly in France, where they'd bought a vineyard. They didn't have girlfriends, and they were both christened, but they didn't believe in God and didn't know what happens after you die. Siiri told them she was going on a date with a thirty-five-year-old cook, and they laughed easily because they didn't believe a word she said.

'Fucking tough dudette,' the bolder one said when he thought she couldn't hear him.

Chapter 54

Mika Korhonen was waiting for Siiri at the Tram Museum Cafe. He looked different somehow and it took a moment before Siiri realized that he had grown an unusual-looking beard, very small, but long, and tied in a funny little plait.

'Well, you certainly look cute. I mean, it's fun – your . . . plait. Your beard, I mean.'

Mika smiled happily and tugged on his chin plait. He had bought her a bowl of hot drink.

'Lactose-free latte,' he said, as if he had to explain or apologize.

It was coffee mixed with hot skimmed milk, but Siiri said it was good so as not to hurt Mika's feelings. She remembered Margit Partanen talking about her sister who ended up drinking tomato soup out of a coffee mug when she couldn't tell which buttons were for food and which were for drinks. That was what happened when you had to get everything at a cafe out of a lot of machines, pressing buttons while the staff stood behind the counter and watched to see if you'd survive the ordeal.

'Yep,' said Mika, who wanted to talk about the most

important things first. He was very curious to hear what the letter from the Judicial Registry said. Siiri took the letter out of her handbag, apologized that the envelope was torn, and let him read it. To her surprise, Mika wasn't shocked to see his own name in the letter.

'Speak of the devil. I'm representing you in this thing, since I'm your advocate.'

So Mika had known more than Siiri had about this police matter the whole time, and he hadn't bothered to call her! This made her angry, but Mika defended himself, saying he had wanted to protect her, because of her heart and everything.

'Everybody has a heart. Don't be ridiculous,' Siiri said hotly, but she relented when he took her hand sweetly, looked at her with those blue eyes, and said that Siiri's heart was bigger than most, so it was more important that some person who'd been hardened by life such as himself should handle her police matters and criminal cases.

'But I did go and talk to a boy at the police station,' Siiri said proudly, and Mika knew that, too, of course. He'd read the report on Siiri's outpouring, a very long and detailed report, and thought it a very creditable one. But Siiri shouldn't be surprised that the wild stories of a ninety-four-year-old with fainting spells didn't lead to charges being brought.

'You didn't file a criminal report,' Mika said reproachfully.

Siiri had thought that all she had to do was tell the police about everything. But it seemed she was supposed to have itemized the horrors of Sunset Grove according to the type of criminal charges that could be brought, such as harassment, abandonment, neglect, endangerment, defamation of character, and who knows what else. The police would only investigate things that were presented in the form of a crime, and even then only lazily, if the victim was a nearly dead old woman lying on the police-station floor.

'Most criminal reports don't lead anywhere,' Mika said.

'Then why make them, if they're not investigated?'

'Well . . . often it's a gamble,' Mika said, and fiddled with his plait again. He didn't rake the air with his hands as much now that he had a beard to hold on to while he searched for words.

'Then there're the Hiukkanens,' Siiri began bravely, although she feared Mika would think she was batty. 'I don't know what to do about them. Virpi's trying to use medication to make me senile, and when I was on my way here, Erkki was following me again, actually spying on me. But I gave him the slip! That's the sort of thing nobody would believe, not even you. Can you tell me what possible reason he could have?'

'Be careful,' Mika said simply. He seemed to believe Siiri and happened to know that numerous criminal reports had been filed about the Loving Care Foundation. The Ambassador wasn't the only one. According to Mika, the police had only been investigating them for tax evasion and other financial goings on, maybe a few falsified prescriptions, but after the fire there had been a motion to dismiss even those charges.

'There's that expression again!' Siiri said, spooning up the rest of her coffee. It was unpleasantly cold by now and there was no getting around the fact that it was half milk.

Mika said that Siiri ought to be glad that all she got was a daily equivalence fine of forty days. It could have been worse, if Mika hadn't fought for her. Originally, they had prosecuted her for sabotage, and she would have had to pay a large amount for the costs of repairs. At worst, she might have been sentenced to several months' parole.

'Parole? You mean a prison term?'

Siiri started to feel faint. Wasn't there an upper age limit for prison sentences, like there was for caregivers? Could they just throw anybody they wanted into prison in Finland?

'No, and no. It was your age that made them decide to fine you instead,' Mika said, as if Siiri's undeserved sentence was a sign of great clemency, proof of society's benevolent attitude towards the generation that fought the war.

'You just have to pay it. Kind of like the war reparations,' Mika said.

'Darn it! I won't pay it! Let them come and drag me out of the retirement home, if they dare!'

Siiri pounded on her handbag in her fervour and laid into Mika about all the awful things that had happened to her and finished up by talking about the unfair treatment of the Lottas, although none of her catalogue of injustices was Mika's fault.

'I was a Lotta on the Front, and I never got a penny for school or rehabilitation or any other help from society, not even maternity leave, and certainly no sabbatical. They make a fuss over the men as if they were the only ones in the war! The Ambassador has been on resort holidays twenty times at the government's expense, and now they're letting him take his girlfriend with him, too, sent them on a free trip to Tallinn to splash around in a whirlpool bath.'

Mika started smiling, and laughed out loud when Siiri told him who the Ambassador's girlfriend was, and how Anna-Liisa was walking around with her hat on even indoors. Gradually, Siiri calmed down. She felt tired and wanted to go home to her apartment to lie down. Mika walked with her to the tram stop, escorting her beautifully, patiently walking at a slow pace and asking all about Irma and Anna-Liisa's Onni, but he didn't get on the number 8, even though Siiri prodded him to with tales of the new canal and bridge and the entire new neighbourhood being built at Ruoholahti.

Chapter 55

On Saturday morning, Siiri's telephone rang but she didn't answer it because she was sitting in her armchair watching *Une Famille Formidable*. It always put her in a good mood, the way the French characters loved each other, ate long meals with gusto, and forgave everything, even when their spouses were unfaithful and their children bizarre. She liked the French language and was watching the show with such concentration that she nearly died with fright when Virpi Hiukkanen was suddenly standing beside her. Siiri hadn't heard her come in.

'So this is where you're loitering,' Virpi said, her eyes darting around as they always did. She had new black-rimmed eyeglasses just like the ones Siiri's husband had worn in the 1960s.

'Where else would I be? Why are you coming into my home like this?'

Siiri didn't bother to get up, she just turned up the volume on the television. Virpi grabbed the remote out of her hand and turned the TV off with an angry punch of a button.

'I came when you didn't answer your telephone, even though I knew you were home.'

Then Virpi softened, spoke in a gentle murmur and looked like she might start petting and caressing Siiri at any moment, like Director Sundström. She said she was very worried about Siiri, since she was alone and having these constant problems with her heart and sometimes even seemed to have lost her zest for life.

'You refused a pacemaker. We here at Sunset Grove want to do everything we can to ensure that our residents are safe and feel happy. You might participate in the Sunset Alert mental-health group sometimes, so you wouldn't be alone with your problems.'

Siiri looked at Virpi's thin hair and wondered why she dyed it that mango-melon colour. Having your hair dyed was terribly expensive, and Virpi must go for a touch-up nearly every month. Then it occurred to her that Virpi was afraid of getting old. The idea of grey hair was probably dreadful to her, and she was reminded of it day after day by the retirement-home residents. Siiri got up and walked to the front door.

'Can you please leave? I'm quite all right.'

'I wanted to talk to you about your elder-care advocate,' Virpi said, and aimed the remote at her as if it were a map pointer. 'You may not know what sort of criminal Mika Korhonen is. If I were you, I would dissolve that advocacy agreement immediately.'

The falser Virpi's words were, the tenser and higher-pitched her voice grew. Soon she was marching quickly back and forth across the small room, like she had when Siiri had passed out on the floor of her office. She said that Mika Korhonen was a well-known player in organized crime and was mixed up in all sorts of shady goings-on, which Virpi seemed to know about in remarkable detail for someone whose life's work was championing the well-being of the elderly. She was spouting the same stuff about falsification of prescriptions and drug dealing that Mika kept talking about.

'You're being taken advantage of in a perilous way. Of course, there's no way you could have known about Mika Korhonen's friend Pasi Peltola, who's just been given a long prison sentence for the crimes these two gentlemen have committed. It's just a matter of time until your advocate is brought to justice for what he's done. I, at least, had the good sense to act quickly when our poor cook, Tero, killed himself while he was under arrest. I insisted that Pasi Peltola be given the sack right then and there, because the Loving Care Foundation cannot condone any kind of illegal activity among the staff.'

Virpi was trying to turn everything upside down. How could Mika be involved in the business, if he was the one who had turned Pasi in? Siiri had to walk back to her armchair and sit down to collect her thoughts. How could she tell who was right, Virpi or Mika? She looked at Virpi, who was standing in the hallway waving her arms around and shouting profanities until she was hoarse. Siiri compared her to the always imperturbable Mika with his angelic blue eyes. She couldn't help it, but as Virpi Hiukkanen zipped around the room, she reminded Siiri of some sort of swift-moving reptile.

'An iguana,' she said, when she'd thought of it. Virpi stopped yelling and stood still for a moment.

'What?'

'Could you please give me my remote back and leave my home?' Siiri answered with a sweet smile. 'You have no right to interfere with my advocate or listen to my telephone calls. You won't get anywhere, sending your husband to follow me around and spy on me when I go out. I don't know how, but my advocate and I are going to find a way get to the bottom of the fire in the Group Home so that the real culprit can be caught, and it isn't going be me. I just have to hope that I don't die before we're done, like Olavi Raudanheimo did. He was treated abysmally in this retirement home and in the end he killed himself. He stopped eating in the hospital.'

Virpi Hiukkanen looked bewildered and downright afraid and, for a second, it looked like she might dry up completely, like Olavi Raudanheimo's gravy lying on a hospital plate. She trembled, then jerked, then burst into tears. She sobbed out loud and great big tears fell on her brown shirt, leaving dark spots on the fabric. She threw the remote on the floor, tore at her mango-melon hair, dashed frantically back and forth, and generally behaved like a maniac.

'You are going to drive me crazy! You're all crazy! I'll lock the lot of you up in the Group Home! Are you sure you're taking all of your pills? What do I have to do to you? What is wrong with you?'

Siiri walked calmly to the door, picked up the telephone

receiver, and laid it on the table, although she was sure that Virpi Hiukkanen's hysterical breakdown could be heard downstairs with or without the phone. And lo and behold, for the first time ever, the Sunset Grove security system worked as it was supposed to and help arrived quickly. Director Sundström was standing in front of Siiri's door with a strong-box in her hand, her hair askew, staring dumbfounded at the deranged head nurse.

'Virpi ... good gracious, Virpi, dear ... What's happened? What have you done to Virpi now?'

Sinikka Sundström cast a shocked look at Siiri and took Virpi in her arms like a small child. They stood there for a good while, leaning against each other, and then Sundström led the sniffling head nurse away.

'Not Erkki too. My poor Erkki. What is happening to my Erkki ...' Virpi sputtered as they went down the corridor.

'Stop crying now, sweetheart. Everything's all right,' Sundström soothed, and gradually their voices disappeared into the lift.

Siiri closed her door, put the phone receiver back in its cradle, and picked the TV remote up off the floor. Then she got herself a glass of wine and started reading Isaac Bashevis Singer's *Enemies, a Love Story*. It was about Jews who survived the holocaust.

Chapter 56

In June, Mika and Siiri went together to file a complaint about Siiri's fine at the Pasila police station. Everyone was very polite, which was no doubt due to the fact that Mika was with her. He had left his ever-present leather jacket at home and looked quite dapper, in spite of his chin plait. The police explained that the prosecutor would have another hearing on the case if there was new information. It was also possible that it could be brought up in district court.

'How exciting. Will I have to come and testify?'

Luckily, they didn't need to decide that now. Mika could represent Siiri because she was so terribly old, and he was her advocate. But it would be a long time before the hearing. The official at the police station told them all this as if he was afraid Siiri might drop dead before the case made it to court.

'Is that what you're afraid of? That I'll die? But I'm never going to die. They said so in the newspaper.'

'In that case, there's nothing to worry about,' said the official. 'But I thought it would be best if you knew our normal schedule for hearings.'

Siiri had no interest in discussing the matter further, and

the official promised to discuss the case with Mika. Getting Irma home from the hospital was the important thing. Anna-Liisa spent every day with the Ambassador, flitting around who knew where. They didn't feel like playing cards any more, which was odd, since it had once been the Ambassador's one and only passion. The last time she'd seen the two lovebirds had been in passing, in the lobby at Sunset Grove, on their way to the antiques fair.

'And in June we're going to Stockholm to see the Passion exhibit at the national museum. Won't that be fun?'

Siiri had asked a bit too sourly whether their trip to Stockholm was also a war veteran's affair, although she didn't actually want to cross a sea to look at erotic pictures herself, whether the government paid for it or not. She had read a lot of books, listened to music, and played solitaire, and all of it was pleasant, but sometimes she needed someone to talk to and someone with whom she could do all the fun things that Irma always used to think up. She'd lost weight, too, because she didn't feel like warming up a liver casserole or blood pancakes just for herself, so she just had a sandwich, or a banana, and not much else.

She wasn't interested in getting to know the new residents at Sunset Grove. They mostly kept to themselves, like her new neighbour, Mrs Vuorinen, who must have been in severe pain because she yelled loudly every night, louder even than Margit Partanen on a good night. Eino Partanen was in such bad shape that Margit was exhausted with taking care of him and prayed every night for him to die. She had even calculated what it would cost to move to Switzerland and give him a euthanasia pill, but apparently it was so expensive that they couldn't afford it.

This late spring had been the loneliest in Siiri's life; in fact, the first one in which she'd ever suffered from feeling lonely. To be alone wasn't a bad thing in itself, but this was something else, a desolate, oppressive feeling, and it made her feel so weak sometimes that she had to force herself to get out of bed in the morning. Sometimes it took her two hours before she was dressed and on her feet, she'd got so stiff and sluggish.

On the way home from the police station, Siiri thought of a fun game. She suggested that they only get off the tram at stops shared by at least two routes.

'And then we always have to take the first tram that comes along. It will make the trip an adventure!'

Mika was a little doubtful of the idea. They might end up going around and around without ever getting anywhere. But Siiri informed him very authoritatively that there was no tram that didn't cross paths with another.

'We can get to Mannerheimintie, you can be sure of that. Let's get off here!'

They switched from the number 7 to the number 9 at the Bell Bridge stop, then to the number 6 in Sörnäinen, and the number 1 at Hakaniemi market. Siiri thought her new game was brilliant.

'You may not know it, but every tram route has its own feeling. The seven is unpredictable, the eight is melancholy.

The number four is safe, so it's kind of boring. The number three is my favourite: it's quick and cheery. But, hmm, this number one is one I'm a bit unfamiliar with. Don't you think it's a little antique-looking?'

'You're brave,' Mika said abruptly. Siiri didn't understand. Was he talking about the tram adventure? But then he started talking about the fire and her sentence. He wouldn't have thought Siiri had it in her to fight for her rights, because her position wasn't a terribly strong one. And there was always the possibility that her sentence could be changed to an even more severe punishment.

'But I have nothing to lose,' Siiri said airily. She wanted to know something about Mika, too, for once. 'You don't talk much about yourself.'

Mika sat silent and looked out of the window.

'I really don't know anything about you.'

Mika squirmed in his seat and Siiri saw the outpatient laboratory orator get on the tram through the middle door.

'I've been thinking that—' Mika began, but then the lab assistant started her presentation on styrofoam boxes, livers and kidneys, Kai Korte and Paavo Lipponen, and finished up with the itching feet. Mika laughed when she said everything just as Siiri had predicted, but Siiri was tired of this tram artist. They switched from the number 1 to the number 3 at Senate Square.

'Were you going to say something?' Siiri asked as the tram turned onto Urho Kekkonen. The driver took curves at such high speed that Siiri had to hold on to Mika's arm.

'This is like the rollercoaster at Linnanmäki!' she shouted, and Mika smiled. 'Are you starting to like the tram?'

'Yep.'

Nothing would make Mika say what he had been about to say. Siiri lightened the mood by telling him about the composer Ilmari Krohn, who went out every day in the winter for a ski on the rocks at Temppeliaukio, where the church was now, and Yrjö Kilpinen, who walked across the school playground at the Girls' Normal School every day in his dressing gown for a morning swim at Hietaniemi, always when the girls from the school were on their break, of course.

'He swam naked, you see. You probably don't know who Yrjö Kilpinen is, do you? Or Ilmari Krohn? The Normal School doesn't exist any more, but the building is still there; it was designed by Onni Tarjanne, the same architect who designed the National Theatre. You must know the National Theatre? If you ask me, it's an ugly building, but the old girls' school is beautiful and well-proportioned.'

Siiri looked at Mika, her big, handsome angel, who didn't quite fit in a tram seat.

'Hey, at the Tram Museum Cafe you said that I have a big heart and that you've been hardened by life. What did you mean by that? You're still a young man!'

And then, finally, Mika started talking. He told her how he'd messed up in school, drank and got into fights, got put in observation class and learned to be tough. Mika's father was some big executive who'd cheated on his mother and then taken off, and his mother hadn't really been able to look after him. The first thing he ever got really interested in was motorcycles. That was what actually gave him a real grip on life, getting into the motorcycle club and going to cooking school. But he'd always found it hard to trust people, except for Tero, who'd been almost like a little brother to him.

He said all this very matter-of-factly, almost harshly, and didn't paw at the air with his hands at all.

'So it's cool when someone comes along who doesn't ask any questions. Just takes you as you are.'

'Like me?'

'Yep.'

Mika said he'd been wondering why Siiri trusted him, when no one else ever had. She'd even made him her advocate, although he was, in fact, a criminal. Siiri thought about what Virpi Hiukkanen had been croaking about in her apartment, looking like an iguana, but she didn't say anything about it, as she didn't want to hurt Mika's feelings.

'I just trust my instincts. That's what I've always done with people,' Siiri said. 'And I mean real instincts, not those odd instincts that Irma talks about. I don't think life has hardened you, even though life has treated you unfairly. You're the only person who's offered to help me and Irma. We both would have been in the dementia ward if it hadn't been for you, except that I would have been in prison. Do they have a dementia ward there, too?'

'If you go to jail, I'll tell my mates. They'll take care of you there.'

They both laughed and got off the tram at the ice arena. Mika said he was leaving now; he had somewhere to go.

'But before you go, can I ask you one more thing?'

The sun shone in Mika's eyes, which glowed with blueness, although he was forced to squint in the dazzle. 'Ask away.'

'I was wondering . . . do you have a cat?'

Mika burst out laughing, a joyful belly laugh. Siiri thought he was more of a cat person than a dog person, and she wanted to know if she was right. If she could still trust her instincts.

'I don't have a cat or a dog.'

'But would you think you'd be more likely to get a cat or a dog?'

'A cat, of course,' Mika answered, and smiled.

He waved to her and strode off towards the ice arena, his backpack on his back. Siiri watched him as he walked away, until she realised she must look stupid standing there smiling to herself in the middle of town, and headed for the stop on Mannerheimintie. The number 4 arrived quickly, as always, and Siiri got on, calm and contented, until she got to the Aura building and remembered Irma. A homeless hip-replacement patient in a trauma therapy ward, abandoned by her darlings, still waiting to learn if she'd passed her homecoming test.

Chapter 57

A sign was taped to the wall of the A-wing lift at Sunset Grove announcing that Head Nurse Virpi Hiukkanen was temporarily on sick leave. This provoked endless chatter at the cafeteria, card table and memory group. Everyone had their own theory about Virpi's illness. Many believed that her altruistic self-sacrifice to improve the lives of the elderly had finally taken its toll, but there were others who said she was suffering from an aggressively malignant form of breast cancer. Only Siiri Kettunen knew that Virpi Hiukkanen had had a nervous breakdown.

'Because of you,' Irma said happily as they talked at Kivelä Hospital.

Anna-Liisa had come to visit, too, since the Ambassador was out on some secret errand in town, and she gave a full report of the rumour mill that Virpi's sick leave had set in motion.

'But I didn't tell anyone about your part in events, Siiri.'

Irma was once again in excellent spirits. The task of boiling water in the therapeutic test kitchen had gone well, and an odd instinct had even reminded her to turn off the stove afterwards. Siiri's and Irma's husbands would never have passed such a test, even at the height of their powers, and they wondered whether the test was the same for men and women. After all, you couldn't expect too much in the kitchen from men their age.

'My darlings think that I can't get along on my own any more. Or that, even if I can now, I won't be able to for long, so it would be best to get me into storage in some institution ahead of time, preferably a proper nursing home so that this waiting for the crematorium won't be so expensive. They haven't made it here for a meeting because they're busy at work, so they had to fill out a close-family distance question-naire.'

'You made that name up,' Anna-Liisa said.

But it really was called a close-family distance question-naire. It was an online questionnaire given to close relatives of a patient when they had to take care of their horses and couldn't come to the hospital.

'Ah. I see. The term suits your family remarkably well.'

The report from Irma's homecoming team was crucial to the apartment question. If Irma had got a bad score – in other words, the highest possible number of points – she would have been thrown into an institution for memory-loss patients, which was what her children wanted, because then the city would pay for it. But since she'd got a clean bill of health, her problem was that she had no place to live.

'So which is worse?' Irma asked. She didn't want to go to a nursing home or a dementia ward, and surely Finland wasn't a country where a ninety-two-year-old veteran of the Lottas was thrown onto the street to beg.

'Watch out – you might very well find me in front of Low Price Market in my Lotta uniform next to that handsome gypsy accordionist singing "Oh, My Darling Augustine" with a coffee cup at my feet. I still have my old uniform in the wardrobe, and maybe I can fit into it again after my hospital tour. Oh, that's right. I don't have it. No doubt my darlings took it to the flea market. Would anybody buy such a thing, when they probably don't even know what it is?'

'I've been thinking,' Anna-Liisa began dramatically, interrupting Irma's train of thought.

'What about?' Irma asked.

'I've been thinking that if I moved into Onni's apartment – he has three rooms and a kitchen in C wing, after all – then you could have my apartment.'

It was a stupendous idea. They had to let it sink in for a moment before they fully appreciated what a wonderful idea it was.

'Does the Ambassador – I mean does your Onni – know about this scheme?' Siiri asked.

Anna-Liisa said with great satisfaction that it had been Onni's idea, but there were still some kinks to iron out. Then she changed the subject to the weather, because she was sweltering in the heat, just as they all were. It was well into summer and the hot weather was difficult for old people. It was even hotter inside than outside, and they couldn't find anything suitable to wear, because a ninety-four-year-old woman can't walk around in a sun dress with her arms bare.

A lot of old people died of the heat, and Siiri'd had to remind herself to drink enough water. It would be embarrassing to dry up and die of dehydration in this land of thousands of lakes.

'What would be the best way to die?' Irma asked.

'From a heart attack, of course,' Anna-Liisa said, and Irma told them about her cousin who had had a heart attack right after she had taken a shower, rubbed herself down with lotion, and settled into bed to read Finland Illustrated magazine and listen to Bach's Goldberg Variations. That's how her children found her – freshly washed.

'But it's too late for us to think about it,' she continued. 'We should have died before everybody else wished we had. Before they started emptying out our homes and distributing our belongings to the poor.'

Irma showed them an envelope that had all of the many papers and reports that made up her homecoming-test results. She had been declared a very viable individual, but, even so, her homecoming evaluation ordered a nurse to visit her three times a week in her home, though she didn't have one.

'Some poor nurse has to come and give me food and medicine. If she has time, she can wipe my bum, too, and on holidays I might get to go with her to take a shower.'

Irma had been put on the waiting list for the city nursing homes, but the social worker said her chances were low because she was too healthy and capable. She would be placed temporarily in the Suursuo Hospital chronic ward unless some miracle happened fast.

'I was already there once! Am I going to start the hospital merry-go-round all over again?'

Siiri admired Irma's ability to be so cheerful even in this situation. She didn't dwell on her difficulties, she just wanted Siiri and Anna-Liisa to read her the death notices and obituaries. Then she wanted to know who had died while she'd been on her adventure in the Group Home and getting to know the hospitals of Helsinki. Siiri listed them for her again: Olavi Raudanheimo, Reino, the Hat Lady, and a few others whose funerals they hadn't gone to. The details of the Hat Lady's memorial reception at Ukko-Munkki put her in a particularly good mood. Then some odd instinct made her remember something she'd forgotten.

'Anna-Liisa, were you serious when you said that you might move in with the Ambassador and give me your apartment?'

Anna-Liisa nodded but looked serious. Unbeknownst to them, she had given the matter considerable thought.

'There are certain problems that have come up,' she said, fiddling with the corner of the blanket on the hospital bed, which wouldn't fold the way she wanted it to. 'Namely, that Sunset Grove doesn't allow cohabitation.'

Anna-Liisa and the Ambassador had to be married, if they wanted to live in the same apartment.

'Why is that a problem? Just get married!' Irma suggested.

'Yes, that's what we thought,' Anna-Liisa said, still very serious, though Irma and Siiri were positively elated. 'But it's complicated, because of Onni's past.'

'Oooh! How exciting! Is he a criminal, too, like me?' Siiri

said, and she and Irma laughed so that it seemed they would never stop, just like teenagers on a tram. Anna-Liisa was annoyed at their hilarity, so they tried to calm down and listen to her revelations about Onni's past.

The Ambassador was not a criminal, but an official who'd had a considerable diplomatic career and had lived in many different countries that no longer existed, such as Yugoslavia. The mother of his children had died long ago. But after that he had remarried and divorced at least twice while abroad, and now he had found out that in Finland they only recognized Finnish divorces.

'So he's a ninety-year-old widower with two wives and a girlfriend? Actually, that's quite an accomplishment!' Irma said, and told them about her cousin who had three brothers and twelve sisters-in-law. Then she started to wonder whether registered lesbian partnerships were allowed at Sunset Grove.

'In that case, Siiri and I could move into the Ambassador's big apartment.'

The Ambassador had been so enthusiastic about Anna-Liisa's bold plan, however, that he had started to get his papers in order. As a diplomat and a Freemason, he was used to taking care of things with two phone calls and a bank transfer, but clearing up his divorces had proved unusually labour-intensive. Anna-Liisa was afraid that once her Onni's affairs were delved into, more scandals might turn up.

'More scandals? What nonsense are you talking about?' Irma asked.

By scandals, Anna-Liisa meant children, especially any born out of wedlock, but Irma and Siiri didn't understand what the Ambassador's flock of children had to do with Anna-Liisa's life.

'Children want an inheritance,' Anna-Liisa explained patiently. 'And if they're very greedy, the way children are, they'll prevent our union because they'll be afraid that I'm after Onni's fortune. You see, he's very wealthy.'

She said this very secretively, leaning so close to Siiri and Irma that their heads almost bumped together. Anna-Liisa imagined that everyone at Sunset Grove, and probably everyone in Kivelä Hospital as well, envied her and the Ambassador their love and their money. Irma suggested that they write a prenuptial agreement. That way, the Ambassador's hypothetical children wouldn't have any reason to fear her intentions.

'That's what I suggested, but Onni refuses to do it.' Anna-Liisa sighed. 'He wants to treat all his wives equally. And he's never had a prenuptial agreement with any of his other wives, so he refuses to have one with me. He's certain that the other wives will die first, but as far as I know, all but the first one are still alive.'

'How fun! You can invite them all to the wedding!' Irma crowed, and started laughing again. 'Do you promise to make us your bridesmaids?'

Anna-Liisa burst into a young bride's laughter and never answered Irma's question. Only after they had left Irma to rest in her bed and walked down Sibeliuksenkatu to the tram stop did she suddenly say:

'There isn't going to be a big wedding. We're going to a magistrate.'

Chapter 58

Irma's ninety-third birthday arrived. Suursuo Hospital was full, so she was still being stored at Kivelä. This had caused a chain reaction: Laakso Hospital had collected several rehabilitated hip-replacement patients who were waiting to go to Kivelä for the homecoming process, which meant that Töölö Hospital had people who had just had their hip surgery and were lining up to get into Laakso for rehabilitation, and another crowd of patients was at the Hilton waiting to get into surgery at Töölö.

'Is there a queue for the crematorium, too, do you think?' Irma wondered as they drank sparkling wine in the hospital garden in honour of her birthday. Siiri and Anna-Liisa had smuggled in the bottle and glasses, but they hadn't been able to bring a cake because it would have been too much to carry. The hospital canteen had strawberries for sale, though, and that made for an excellent ninety-third-birthday celebration. The sun was shining, the birds were singing, and the traffic was roaring. Irma even smoked a cigarette, and claimed she could feel the titanium spike glowing in her hip.

The situation at Sunset Grove was an odd one. Virpi

Hiukkanen's sick leave just kept on going, and there was no one to replace her. Director Sundström was completely worn out from work, walking around nervously and lamenting that she had no time for children in developing countries. But the strangest thing was what had happened to Erkki Hiukkanen. Anna-Liisa had heard about it from Margit Partanen, who had finally got her husband into the closed Group Home and herself out of being his personal caregiver.

'And who should she see there but our caretaker, dozing in a nightshirt with the other patients,' Anna-Liisa said.

Erkki Hiukkanen had been diagnosed with early onset dementia, the kind that happens to sixty-year-olds. He was quite demented and, according to Margit, downright sweet. He told the same three dirty jokes morning to night and liked doing arts and crafts. He had probably been senile already when he was following Siiri around the city.

'And when he stole my silver hand mirror and Onni's *ryijy* rug,' Anna-Liisa said.

Siiri thought that Anna-Liisa was just speculating about her hand mirror and the *ryijy* rug, but it turned out that Margit Partanen had seen the silver hand mirror in Erkki's handbag in the closed unit.

'He has a handbag?' Irma said excitedly.

The handbag was stolen, too, but no one knew whose handbag it was. It probably belonged to a resident who had died a long time ago. But Anna-Liisa was very happy to get her mirror back, her mother's morning gift, at long last.

'What should we buy you for a wedding gift, then? I had been thinking a silver hand mirror was a good idea,' Irma said. 'Maybe something more practical. Sheets? No – I've finessed it: matching nightshirts! Yes?'

'Or maybe a frying pan from the Munkkiniemi super-market? Egg cups? Or a year's subscription to Donald Duck comics?' Siiri suggested.

'I know: the *Kama Sutra*!' Irma crowed, and she laughed until she had tears in her eyes.

Anna-Liisa let them babble, but finally demanded a chance to speak with a pound of her fist on the bench. It seemed that the Ambassador had used his diplomatic connections to get his divorce papers from abroad with remarkable swiftness, even the ones from non-existent countries. Every paper had to be dragged to one magistrate or another and only then could they beg for a certificate of non-impediment and get married.

'I thought non-impediment was when they have to let you get from one place to another in your wheelchair,' Irma mused, serious once more. 'Half the apartments have to have bathrooms where an invalid can take a shower.'

'Onni has been very energetic and it looks like we're going to get married in August, and you can move into my apart-ment even before then, Irma. But under no circumstances will we accept any wedding gifts.'

'It's a lucky thing that Virpi Hiukkanen is out of the pic-ture,' Irma said, and she was right. 'I'm sure she would have prevented us from trading apartments.'

Anna-Liisa said that she'd sent forms and documents to this place and that and had arranged things very cleverly, so that the Loving Care Foundation couldn't help but approve the plan.

'Onni bought my apartment and now he's going to be Irma's landlord!'

'I didn't know anybody could buy an apartment there,' Irma said in wonder.

'They probably can't, normally,' Anna-Liisa said. 'But Onni has connections, and if you buy the place, you don't have to wait. Otherwise, you couldn't have just moved in. There are dozens of seventy-year-olds in poor health waiting in line. And apparently retirement-home apartments are an incredibly good investment, because there are more and more old people all the time and the rents are going up every week.'

'Lord, help me! I'll go bankrupt!' Irma cried.

She had good reason to worry. Even if her rent was reasonable, her life was getting more expensive in other ways. The hospital homecoming team had ordered so much home care for her that it was going to cost hundreds of euros a month, if not more.

'But do I have to follow their treatment plan?' Irma asked with a sly smile after they'd drunk quite a few glasses of wine. A couple of nurses had come to sit with them, and one of them said that Irma didn't have to follow their orders. Because she would be living in her own apartment she could decide herself whether she needed care or not.

'You mean you did all that work for nothing?' Irma lamented, and they made a toast to all the craziness in the world.

Chapter 59

Mika Korhonen came with a friend to help with the move. It was fantastic, because they couldn't have managed it without these big, strong men. Anna-Liisa had a tremendous number of things, and since half of her belongings were books, there was a lot of carrying to do. The poor fellows were drenched with sweat. Siiri told them to take off their leather jackets so they wouldn't be so hot, but they refused. Their motorcycles gleamed beautifully in the Sunset Grove car park, and attracted deserved attention.

Anna-Liisa was an efficient supervisor, accustomed to command, and she had a detailed plan prepared ahead of time. She stood in the middle of the apartment with drawings in her hand and issued clear and audible instructions. Quite a large load of the Ambassador's possessions went to the dump, because otherwise Anna-Liisa's treasures wouldn't have fit. Two walls had to be cleared for bookshelves, and Mika kindly spent an entire day assembling them. Anna-Liisa wanted the books arranged in alphabetical order according to language area.

'The German novels on my right, the Russian ones on my

left. The Finnish fiction here in the middle at my eye level, and the Finnish non-fiction in the same spot on the other wall.'

The boys were rattled. They didn't know which books were fiction and which weren't. Anna-Liisa was admirably patient with them, and didn't get upset, even when one of them thought that Joel Lehtonen's *Wild Chervil* was a book about plants and the other one asked what language group Thomas Mann should be in.

'I'm a language and literature teacher. I've seen it all.'

The Ambassador was nowhere to be found on moving day. He had gone to his summer house to meet his offspring and former wives from abroad and tell them about the new turn his life had taken – the marriage, in other words, which was to take effect the following week. The announcements had been made, the non-impediments taken care of, and Irma and Siiri were almost going to be bridesmaids, or at least go to the Pasila courthouse to serve as witnesses.

'Should we put ribbons in our hair?' Irma asked, but Anna-Liisa just snorted and continued issuing orders to her leather-jacketed army.

Irma's apartment, Anna-Liisa's old apartment, was quite empty, of course, because her relatives had sold all her possessions. They didn't hear anything from the darlings, which Siiri thought was shameless behaviour, but Irma was terribly understanding about it and said that of course they were embarrassed and that was why they didn't dare show their faces. And they were so busy, too, because of the summer holidays. Irma seemed unfazed. In fact, she seemed positively thrilled at the chance to decorate her new apartment.

'Is thrilled the opposite of unfazed? What do you think?' she asked as she thumbed through the IKEA catalogue.

Siiri couldn't quite believe what she was seeing. Irma had always lived among her ancestors' antique furniture, cherished them like relatives, told stories about them, how her uncle had spilled liqueur on the card table and left a stain that would never fade, how the bust of Runeberg had made the rounds of the summer cabins, frightening innocent victims, and how they'd found a wad of currency from the time of the tzars that was of no use to anyone now, in a hidden drawer in the chiffonier. And here she was, blissful at discovering IKEA. She thought the veneer furniture that you put together yourself was awfully cute. But there didn't seem to be any rose-print upholstery at all.

'They have such funny names, too! Klumpen, Stumpan, Buller and Bang!'

Those were names she'd made up out of her head, but what did it matter? Mika Korhonen had promised to come over to carry and assemble her new furniture, and Siiri was glowing with more happiness than even Anna-Liisa, because Irma was herself again, and making Siiri's days happy ones.

Siiri had ridden the tram every day to visit Irma in the hospital, on several different routes, and sometimes the trip from Munkkiniemi to Töölö had taken almost two hours, if she was feeling particularly adventurous. Helsinki was so beautiful in the summer. It felt as if the whole place were designed just for summer – the plazas and market squares and all the new construction that had gone up in the past few years. Helsinki in July was like a big amusement park, and the tram was the rollercoaster.

Irma made her apartment very personalized. She combined traditional white Swedish furniture that looked like something out of an old Carl Larsson illustration with bright-coloured modern furniture designed for children. IKEA was an amazing place. You could get cheese-cutters and flowers for your balcony and finish up by eating some meatballs and chocolate. Mika came with them on their IKEA adventure and acted like an experienced tour guide.

'This is the real amusement park,' Irma said as they lay on the test mattresses in the bed department.

A young sales clerk wanted to know Irma's weight and all kinds of other information, such as what position she slept in, and Irma started to flirt with him until Siiri was embarrassed, but he just laughed and sold Irma an enormous bed with mattress, pillows and bedclothes.

'It's called the Sultan. Can you believe it?' Irma enthused.

'What, no harem?' Siiri laughed.

Mika had his work cut out for him, painting the walls white and putting the furniture together, but they were in no hurry, because Irma had been told she could stay at Kivelä Hospital until the end of August.

In the meantime, there was Anna-Liisa and Onni's marriage ceremony to attend, and Siiri and Irma served as their witnesses. Both members of the wedding party were wearing formal attire.

'Why get married in black?' said Irma in wonder, as they waited in the hallway for the ceremony.

'For practical reasons,' Anna-Liisa said. 'We can wear the same clothes to funerals.'

'Clever!' Irma said. 'So that's what you'll look like standing next to my coffin.'

The magistrate's wedding chamber was small and drab, and the judge behaved about as enthusiastically as he would withdrawing cash from his own account. Anna-Liisa was very touched, in spite of the ordinariness of the setting, and said 'I do' much louder than she needed to. The Ambassador behaved in his accustomed manner, positively shouting his 'I do'.

Irma and Siiri didn't have any real role in the ceremony; they just sat in the drab office chairs and wrote their names on a piece of paper when it was over. A problem arose, of course, when they didn't have anything but their old driver's licences as identification, but Anna-Liisa handled the matter with her own passport like an old pro. She wouldn't need to request a new passport, because she wasn't changing her name.

'Onni's last name is Rinta-Paakku,' she explained.

Anna-Liisa and Onni left Pasila in a taxi to go to Restaurant Lehtovaara, and then somewhere for their honeymoon. It was quite absurd, but Anna-Liisa was very secretive about it and said that Onni had arranged everything and even she didn't know where he was taking her.

'To Tallinn with a veterans' tour group,' Irma whispered to Siiri, and they hopped happily onto a tram home – yes, home, because now that Irma was at Sunset Grove again, and Virpi and Erkki Hiukkanen were nowhere to be seen, it was finally starting to feel like a real home.

Chapter 60

When they got to Munkkiniemi, Irma wanted to treat Siiri to lunch at a French restaurant on Laajalahdentie. Siiri didn't know that before her hospital adventure Irma had been to the restaurant so often that she knew all of the staff. A dazzlingly handsome young man rushed over to give her a hug and another man with a beard took her coat. They spoke at length in French and then the men hugged Irma again.

'Did you notice how I haven't forgotten my French, even though I'm soft in the head?' Irma said proudly, when finally the men had gone back to their work. The short one was the chef, the taller one the waiter.

'He's from Martinique,' Irma began, and she told Siiri the man's life story, which was teeming with siblings and surprising twists. 'So it will be a loss to our nation when he leaves us.'

'What do you mean, leaves us?'

'Don't you understand any French at all, after taking the beginners' course at the community centre seven times over? He just said that he'll only be here for two more weeks, *deux semaines*. That's why he gave me such a warm embrace. First, because he thought I had died, and second, because he's going to be leaving us.'

'You actually could have died,' Siiri said, to get Irma to say what she'd been waiting for her to say for a long time. But Irma paid no attention.

'It's a pity they don't sell red wine here. We can get wine at IKEA, but not in a French restaurant at lunchtime.'

Siiri agreed. After all, they were celebrating the fact that Anna-Liisa was married for the third and last time, and Irma had come home. That Irma wasn't demented at all, and her hip, with its glowing titanium spike, was healing up and her new home was coming together nicely and quite quickly. She was still using a Zimmer frame, but Siiri felt sure that she would be done with it before the snow fell, and then she could go back to her beloved Carl the Cane.

'Maybe. And in September, we'll celebrate your ninety-fifth birthday,' Irma said contentedly, planning her life out like she used to do.

A very small baby at the next table started to whimper. Irma went quite gaga over it – she had always had a weak spot for babies. The smaller they were, the weaker she became, and this one was perhaps only a few weeks old. Irma learned that the baby's name was Rudolf and he kept his mother up quite a bit at night. Then the baby's mother whipped out her breast and started nursing Rudolf right there in front of them, even though they were eating lunch. Even Irma had trouble smiling at her new friend and searched feverishly for a new topic of conversation.

'How is your criminal case going?' she asked carelessly, as

if they were discussing window cleaning. Which was another thing you had to do yourself at Sunset Grove – no one had come to wash the windows, although summer was almost over and the windows had got so dirty over the winter that the sun couldn't get in. There they sat in the dark, all those miserable oldies who couldn't get out to a restaurant in the way Siiri and Irma could. They didn't even know if it was summer or winter.

'Don't change the subject. Are you going to jail for arson?'

Siiri told her what she knew. Mika Korhonen had kept her up to date, no longer evading the subject or avoiding her. Siiri's complaint had been shoved somewhere and it was working its way through the requisite cogs of justice so she didn't have a ghost of a worry. She knew what had really happened, and, more importantly, what hadn't happened. Even if she did use the key to the closed unit without permission, they couldn't put her in jail for that. She hadn't started the fire, and if there were any criminals at Sunset Grove, they were on the board of directors of the Loving Care Foundation. She knew that evil would be punished eventually. And besides, their detective work had kept them busy. She had felt useful, as though her life had a purpose again, and she was sure that this wasn't to be the end of it.

'It'll either never be solved, or it will someday,' Irma said, and sprinkled some sugar on her baguette.

'At any rate, it'll take a long time for the case to run its course, and anything could happen to me in the meantime.'

'It certainly could. You might die, for instance. Ah! I love how the sugar crunches between my teeth!'

'True. And that's really a relief, you know. And, it's so wonderful that you're alive again!' Siiri said, and she meant it from the bottom of her raggedy heart. Irma understood and said that they had to have a big party in honour of her resurrection, before Siiri's birthday.

'Since we didn't get a wedding party. Let's have the kind of party where you serve champagne. Even though it puts knots in your stomach and makes you belch. Maybe we should just make some punch.'

'Punch or champagne, anything will do,' Siiri said, worn out with happiness. 'What else have you got planned?'

'We're going to start playing four-handed piano. I've already been to the West Helsinki music school to talk to them about it.'

Siiri suspected that the music school was just for children, but Irma had asked about that, too. The rector had enquired if they'd ever taken piano lessons before, and when Irma told her that they had got off to a good beginning but were interrupted by the start of the Winter War seventy-three years ago, the rector didn't ask any more questions.

'But before we start piano lessons we're going to take an Internet class.'

'What?'

'You heard me. They have them at the Munkkiniemi senior centre, next door to the health clinic. They take you by the hand and teach you what the Internet is and how to get on it. I'm sure you realize that you can't carry on without the net.'

'Do we have to buy a computer?'

'Of course! And it's not a computer any more, it's a tablet, and you brush it and stroke it and it politely obeys you. That's the kind we're going to buy. I want a green one. I've seen them in the Stockmann preferred-customer flyer.'

'For heaven's sake, Irma!' Siiri cried. 'With you around I don't know where in the world I'll end up!'

'Dead,' Irma laughed, and finally said what Siiri had been waiting for her to say: '*Döden, döden, döden.*'

extracts reading groups
competitions books new
discounts extracts
competitions
books
new
events books
extracts
new reading groups
interviews
events extracts
discounts
new books events
events new

www.panmacmillan.com

discounts extracts discounts
extracts events reading groups
competitions books extracts new